I0565053

YOUR LAND

IS

OUR LAND

H. Edward Schmidt

Upper Falls Books
PO Box 114
Upper Falls, Maryland 21156

First Edition 2016

Dedication

Dedicated to everyone,
Jews, Arabs and the rest of us who believe
that peace and harmony in the Holy Land is possible

Foreword

Where does one begin when searching for peace? Very simply, begin within the hearts of those who struggle for a place in this small piece of land. Let each person acknowledge the rights of others as equal to his own, no greater, no less, and there can be peace

Professor Charles Malcom

Syrian Protestant College

Beirut

April, 1947

Prologue

"Compared to what lay southeast, it is the land of milk and honey, indeed."

October, 2014

John still felt the warm glow from the half Guinness as he stood on the beach. Guinness was not a favorite of his, but who could resist slaking their thirst at Molly Bloom's green lacquered Irish Pub, just steps away from the roaring sea below. Only the top of the red sun was visible now, slowly sinking into the dark green Mediterranean. The October breeze was warm and gentle on his face; the beach still crowded; the rising and falling sea moving onto the beach then receding, drowning every sound but its own. As he turned to walk down the beach, he could see the lights of Jaffa and the blinking lighthouse beacon. Over a hundred years ago! It was there that the Poletsky family came ashore, there that they viewed the land of their dreams*!*

To his left, Tel Aviv had turned on its lights, their glow replacing the light of the sun. What must have it been like then, when his great grandfather Captain John Nevers had soldiered here and he and his great grandmother Sarah had fallen in love? After the shameful murder of her husband, the British community expected her to return to England. She did not but stayed to devote her life to the young Palestinian children she loved so dearly.

John Nevers V knew Palestine well. His grandfather had grown up in Jerusalem, the city that Jews, Christians and Muslims all considered their spiritual home. As a child of the British community, many of his friends were British, or members of the other European and

North American enclaves. Yet his grandfather often reminded him that Great Grandmother Sarah had a different and wider circle of friends that included Muslims and Jews. His grandfather told him he could often sense the discomfort that existed with Sarah's American and European friends in her presence. Sarah was born a Jew, became a Christian like John, and dedicated her life to teaching Palestinian Muslim children and all those clever things the foreign community might want to say about Jews and Arabs couldn't be said in her presence.

The beautiful beach and the Mediterranean before him, and recalling his visits as an engineer to other parts of the Middle East, it was easy to see why this land always was fought over, and religion was but one part of the reason, perhaps not a reason at all, but a justification. Compared to what lay southeast, it is the land of milk and honey, indeed.

Shoes in hand, he stood for a long time and watched the white caps form, felt the water rush over his feet, and basked in the warm breeze. How peaceful the land seemed and how blessed! It made him think again of Grandmother and how she is remembered throughout the world as one of gallant few who caused the miracle of 1939.

Part I

... and now the entire village was out of their houses, beginning to move closer together as the sound grew louder.

October, 1935

To Yusef, the thin layer of windblown clouds made the moon appear to race across the sky, lighting the pampas to the horizon. From the west, storm clouds that seemed to rise out of the ground behind the hills. The wind had increased from the southwest, flattening the tall grass, making the herd restless; held together only by the dogs that seemed to know which of the massive bulls might cause the herd to bolt. Yusef smiled as he watched the dance of the prancing, snorting bulls and the silent dogs which would dart in to confront the bulls then rush to the next that might panic the herd. He was one of the first to use herding dogs on the pampas, importing them from Australia, crosses between English herding dogs and dingoes.

Five gauchos circled the herd, singing softly to quiet the restless cattle, nervously watching the lightning bolts flash across the sky to the west. The thunder claps louder, the lightning bolts coming closer and more frequent. Yusef has chosen a spot in a draw to make it easier to control the herd when the storm struck. When the Indian gauchos spoke of the tall man with the piercing black eyes, they spoke of his riding and roping skills and of their loyalty to him, and they called him the Turco. They knew to many it was a derisive name of those who came from the Middle East, to the gauchos when they spoke of Senor Yusef, it was a title of respect.

1

Yusef al-Dajani had collected his cattle over the past week and should reach the railhead the next day. Since his arrival fifteen years ago, he had worked to become the estancia owner he was today. Persuading the Bissett's to loan him the money almost ten years ago, he had purchased the 4000 hectare ranch when beef prices were depressed and Alfonso Diaz wanted to sell and live out his life with his family in Cordoba. There had been times when Yusef could barely meet the payments on his loan, but the last years had been good ones. The drought in the United States had reduced the number of cattle for market and raised the price of Argentine beef. Getting the herd to the railhead and settling with the buyer should make him the free and clear owner of the Diaz estancia. He had not changed the name; he knew that his Arabic name still made him an outsider with the other ranchers. Like other Arab immigrants, he was a Turco. Although the Turks had been defeated and swept from Palestine almost two decades ago, the immigrants were still called Turcos. He smiled when he the thought of the time twenty years before when the Turks were his bitter enemy. He knew he was different, too, because he chose to live on his estancia. Most ranchers with large estancias like his lived in Cordoba and Buenos Aires, some in Spain and England and had never been to Argentina.

The moon slid behind the storm clouds; darkness enveloping the pampas. Only vague outlines, the roaring wind, the bellowing cattle, the excited voices of the gauchos as they struggled with the dogs to keep the cattle huddled together. Yusef heard it before it struck. Hail! Stinging the men and animals, ice pellets quickly coated the earth with a layer of fast melting ice. Behind the hale came the rain, so heavy that the men could not see the heads of their horses.

Men and animals no longer could be heard above the roar of pelting ice and torrential rain. Yusef spurred his mount to move among the gauchos, shouting to them.

"Move the herd to the top of the hill! Get them out of the draw!" He could not hear the running water but sensed it, knowing what could happen if the herd is caught in the torrent that was sure to come. Quickly, the gauchos circled behind the herd and with the dogs that seemed to know what had to be done, joined in moving the cattle. Within minutes, the herd began to move like a single beast. Water began to rush past the short legs of the Herefords that quickened their pace, sensing death if they were swept away. As the gauchos cleared the draw, the hail stopped and the rain slackened to a steady downpour.

The storm ended with the same suddenness as it began. To the west, the sky turned indigo blue and the moon lit the edges of the racing clouds. Soon, the moon appeared, brightening the pampas. The terror gone, and the animals slowly began to herd up and settle down. Many quickly lay down, once again becoming the gentle animals before the storm.

The mestizo gauchos were smiling now, talking rapidly among themselves as they passed each other. The drive would be over and they could see their families again. Yusef sat by the fire, gazing at the flame. In such moments he often thought of home and his homeland, Ahmed, family and Sarah.

February 1936

At first, when the word was spread through the small valley, there was disbelief. The land they had farmed for generations no longer belonged to the owner in Beirut but had been sold to the Jewish National Fund. The holdings took in the entire valley, over 20,000 dunams. Over five hundred families were living on the land, able to feed themselves and earn a small surplus each year. Part of that surplus had to be paid to the owner of the land Georgios Pakapolous who had acquired the land in the nineteenth century during the time of the Ottoman Empire land reform. Although there were often grumbling among the tenant farmers, the arrangement allowed life to go on in their village. They paid little attention to the news that land nearby had been purchased from absentee landlords and taken over by the Jewish settlers. They became more concerned when relatives among those evicted from their land came to the small valley asking for help for their families. More mouths to feed families and to have homes just made each a little poorer.

3

It was then that the villagers who farmed the valley came to the Mukhtar, expressing their fears of what might happen to them. The Mukhtar promised he would contact British officials in Nazareth and relay their concerns. Within days of the meeting, officials from Nazareth arrived in a motorcar to meet with the Mukhtar. When news reached the farmers in the fields, they quickly assembled in the village to hear what the visitors had to say about their land. The Mukhtar, Yusef Batat, felt better that the officials were all Arabs who had lived among them for years. Surely, they would understand the desperate situation of the farmers and would offer some hope for staying on the land and working for the new owners.

Wasif Khaleh was the spokesman for the visitors. He was accompanied by two armed men. Abd Hamdan, one of the leaders among the farmers, watched Khaleh begin to squirm as he spoke. The two men with him seemed to be expecting trouble. Abd felt his heart sink before a word was spoken.

Khaleh read from a paper from a case he carried. "The land in this valley has been purchased by the Jewish National Fund in Jerusalem from Georgios Pakapolous of Beirut. The size of the purchase is 20,000 dunams and the transfer is complete. The Jewish National Fund is the new owner. A representative of the fund asked me to inform all the tenant farmers on this land that they must vacate the houses in the villages and that they will no longer be able to farm the land. Although the Fund has the right to demand that the tenants vacate immediately, they will allow 30 days to find other accommodations and work. The Fund will also provide transportation for all your families within 100 kilometers of village."

The crowd that stood in front of Khaleh was silent—stunned by what they heard; trying to sort out what was just said. Abd Hamdan spoke. "We cannot leave the land. Our fathers and their fathers have farmed this land. We want the new owners to come talk to us. Until that time, we will stay in our village and farm our land."

Khaleh looked at the men in front of him. Fear raced through him like an electrical shock. What he did next would determine whether he left the village alive or not. The two armed guards, nervously touching their handguns could not protect him. The position he held in the property records office paid well. His family lived well, better than most other families he knew who did not work for the British. Yet there was a price to be paid, a very high one. He was branded a pariah by all who knew him. Looking around at the angry faces, he packed away his papers and spoke quickly: "I will ask that someone from the Fund get in touch with you" glancing quickly at Batat. He nodded toward his two bodyguards, who followed him quickly to the motorcar. The stunned men of the village dispersed and the square was soon empty. Left only the sound the motorcar and that, too, was soon gone.

Weeks had passed. The farmers met often, and when they did, their words were angry and driving their anger the fear of a future they could not accept as real. Surely, Allah will not let them lose their land. The British will not desert 500 families, over three thousand souls. The Jews will allow them to stay on the land. Abd Hamdan was almost alone in trying to lift the spirits of the others, of trying to rally them to resist.

***

A lone rooster crowed defiantly as the sky began to lighten over the hills east of the valley. The farmers in the village who had wakened first heard the low rumble coming on the road from Haifa. Darkness still covered the valley floor and all but the crowns of the hills. The sound grew louder and now the entire village was out of their houses, beginning to move closer together as the sound grew louder.

Now the outline of motorcars and lorries could be seen. The motorcars were open and the men inside were visible. The lorries that followed were full of men, packed together. The motor car and the lorries were sand brown, the color of the British army! Abd

5

Hamdan had seen such convoys many times heading toward Haifa or west toward Tiberius. Perhaps they will simply pass us by, he thought. But the fear and excitement that filled him told they would not pass by.

The main road to Tiberius was a half kilometer from the village. The convoy was approaching the turnoff. Soon, he would be sure. The lead motorcar slowed then turned toward the village. A woman began to wail, then others and men were shouting and running in all directions. The village chief Batat walked toward the approaching convoy hoping his boldness would calm the villagers. He fought the weakness in his knees as the commander of the convoy approached him. The convoy halted at the edge of the village and the soldiers moved quickly to form into squads. At command, the soldiers moved toward the villagers, who stepped away, stunned at what was before them.

A tall thin officer led the way. Walking beside and slightly behind the British officer was Wasif Khaleh. Batat thought bitterly of Khaled's last remark, that he would have the Jews get in touch with him. No, the British would do the contacting. It was Khaleh who translated the British officer's remarks.

The officer approached Batat. "Chief, I am Captain Jenkins of the Royal Engineers. My orders are to evacuate everyone in the village by sunset today. Your people will be given twenty-four hours to be completely off the land. Any men remaining in the village after sunset will be shot. Any members of your village in the valley by mid-morning tomorrow forcibly removed to the nearest town." After each sentence, Khaleh interpreted. He could hear the murmurs in the crowd as the orders were translated. Jenkins raised his hand, and the soldiers began to move. Two lorries turned to face the main road, then backed to the edge of the village. Mounted in the bed of both trucks were Bren machine guns each manned by two men. As if for effect, or to check their weapons both fired two quick bursts into the side of one of tallest buildings, showering chips of granite onto the square below.

A squad of engineers moved to an open area in a pasture nearby and began erecting a makeshift enclosure. Khaled knew this was where men thought to be dangerous would be held until the move was complete. Other squads moved to positions around the village.

Abd Hamdan could see what was happening. Anyone attempting to leave the village other than by the main road would be shot. Men thought dangerous would be detained in the temporary enclosure and either released when the evacuation was complete or moved to a more permanent camp.

Captain Jenkins spoke using a megaphone "British soldiers will move through the village seeing to it that you are preparing to leave. Every able bodied person, man or woman, is expected to do their share. You will be allowed to take what you can carry or any animal can carry and you can take your animals. Whatever you leave behind will be confiscated or destroyed." He handed the megaphone to Khaleh. Khaled's, his voice quivering, repeated the Captain's orders. The translation caused further murmuring then shouts of protest. Women began confronting the soldiers and then it happened. One of the women struck a soldier on the arm. He responded with the butt of his rifle, striking the woman on the side of the head, who collapsed at his feet, blood seeping into the sand below her head. An elderly man raised a large stick he was carrying to strike the soldier. Two shots rang out from a nearby soldier hitting the man in the chest, who dropped to the ground, writhing and screaming in pain; then lay still.

A second villager, the blacksmith stepped forward, whether to help the old man or attack the soldiers would never be known, because he was riddled with rifle bullets and died instantly. The smell of blood and cordite and fear filled the air as the men of the village retreated from the two dying men. Facing the rifles leveled at them, they turned away and began pack their belongings. Corporal Evans, who had served in Northern Ireland during the Troubles shook his head. "Poor bastards. Yeah, life is unfair, ain't it. Sticks against Enfield's. Well, that the jist of it, right mate." Private Holmes, had seen it all too, just nodded. "Right".

7

Throughout the day, the villagers struggled to get as much as they could carry together. Hamdan worked with the rest, doing more than most while walking among the younger men like him talking about what they could do to fight back. Qassam was somewhere in the north. He had been fighting the British and the Jews for three years. He would find a way to join him, bringing others with him. Three randomly selected men were forced into the makeshift enclosure. It seemed unnecessary but the British seemed to want to strike fear in the men, to keep them in line until they were out of the valley. Hamdan caught Corporal Evan's eye. He walked up to him then beckoned Khaleh over. "Wasif, old boy, tell this gentleman they are looking for strong guys like him in Haifa, working on the docks. Pays not too bad and you can find a place to live if you have any relatives there."

Hamdan looked at the friendly face. Why, he wondered would this ajnabi want to help him. Then he felt himself relax. Why not accept what the Englishman was telling him as an act of kindness in a cruel world. He smiled and Evans smiled back. "Thank you."

"OK, mate. Good luck to you. Maybe it won't be too long before you're back home and I'm back home."

Abd watched the stiff backed soldier walk away. Maybe he would have to kill him someday. "Pray to Allah that day will not come, my friend."

By sunset the village was empty. The dead man and woman had been buried. Among the animals, only a few stray cats and a rooster remained. As Hamdan made his way west, he heard the explosions. The Royal Engineers were destroying his village. He could not know that the General Officer in Command, Wavell had passed along this Order from the Agency. He could not know that by next morning settlers would be arriving to erase the old village and replace it with their own.

Captain Jenkins was pleased with himself. He loved his job but Wasif Khaleh did not. He could not make his hands stop shaking as he made out his report. He felt it. His death was very close. He needed to get away. What was the name of the friendly man he met in Nazareth? He said he was from the Statistics Office and needed some figures on the new settlements. Halevi? Yes, Uri Halevi. Halevi had an important job in Jerusalem and he had thanked him personally for all the work he had done for the Fund. Perhaps he could help find a place where he would be safe.

March, 1936

The Saturday morning parade was over, the officers and men were returning to their quarters. It was a beautiful spring day in Jerusalem. The sky above the British flag a constant whited blue, no clouds in sight; at the base of the flag pole, daffodils and tulips in full bloom. From where they stood, they could see the soft gray walls of the Old City glistened by the high noon sun.

High Commissioner Arthur Grenfell Wauchope and GOC General John Dill stood together overlooking the parade grounds. "The Higher Arab Commission is challenging the Empire, asking for an end of Jewish immigration, an end to the Mandate and the creation of a democratic state of Palestine." Dil could not help but notice distaste with which Wauchope uttered the word democratic.

Wauchope had turned to the General as he spoke. The General noticed there was no anger in his voice, no indignation that Husayni had the effrontery to make such demands. Curious, he thought. Was he questioning our policy of a Jewish homeland? An end to Jewish immigration?

Was this some sort of test? What did he think personally? Well, it was not the sort of trap a good military politician would fall in to.

"The policy is clear enough, Commissioner. We continue to allow immigration and see that the Arabs behave themselves. We are bound to keep order." He paused, then added: "and be fair about it."

They were the words of a good yet ambitious soldier. No matter he resented having to enforce a policy which made the British Army the handmaiden of the Jewish Agency. No matter, he and his men had to endure the smirks of Jewish leaders when he sought to be even-handed in meting out punishment, when those leaders knew that the military orders could be easily countermanded in London. Not the kind of situation that made you feel good about yourself or the Empire. Being duty bound just made it easier to endure.

General Wauchope suppressed a smile, remembering his days as a soldier. He believed in a Jewish homeland in Palestine. That was why he was the High Commissioner. A spare, non-descript man, child of the upper class and rich, he knew a great deal about rebels and how to deal with them. His last post had been Northern Ireland and the time of the Troubles. And he knew about the anti-Semitism in the British military and police, part of it coming from the prevailing attitudes of the lower classes and part from their experience in Palestine. They little appreciated the Bible calling the Jews home or the superior culture of the Jews when compared to the Arabs.

He smiled at Dill: "Very well said, John. The policy is clear and it will be followed." The General did not miss the fixed stare of the High Commissioner as he spoke nor the smile that ended abruptly. Was it a challenge? No matter, he was due for a change in post soon and to speak his mind served him not at all.

February, 1938

Ahmed was the first in his village to hear them, the sound of men running. They had moved into the village, surrounding it to prevent escape. Ahmed knew they would come in darkness, but not so soon after the ambush of the convoy yesterday morning. Most of the Arab fighters had fled to the mountains to the north. Ahmed had returned to the village because his son was very ill. Only the old men and he, with the women and children were still in the village. The crazy Englishmen would be leading them. He began to pray. A loud crash, the door bursting open. A soldier, a member of Purdom's raiders, pointed his bayonet ready rifle at him. "Out, you

10

blasted wog!'" Then pointing his weapon at the two women, his grandfather Hassan and his own children. "Everybody out!"

The British soldiers and Jewish militia forced everyone into the square. The tall commanding officer must be Purdom, the mad one, Ahmed decided. It was he who led the night attacks. It was he who created the raiders, using mainly Jewish militia under his command. All the Arabs knew about Purdom and his hatred of Arabs. He stood now before the hushed villagers. He began to speak in perfect Arabic. "All of you know what happened on the road to Tulkharem yesterday morning. Filthy Arabs attacked a settler convoy and killed two settlers. The British Government and the Yishuv will find those killers and they will be shot or they will be hanged. When one of you attacks the settlers or any British citizen, you who harbor them are also responsible and will be punished. My men intend to question each of you and remind you what will happen if you don't tell us who in your village is responsible. We will not leave here until we know who is responsible and where we can find them."

Ahmed was surprised that they had not first questioned him. Purdom did not even look his way, making him uneasy. Was there an informant?

The interrogations had gone on for two hours, the shouting of the raiders and the cries of pain heard by everyone. Those who were interrogated were segregated from those waiting. He was proud of the men in the village, stoic as they waited and as they were led away. Then he was alone. He was the last. In the darkness, he could feel the accusing eyes of the men, women and children. It was because of him. Silence and then a clear voice:

"I do not blame you for this Ahmed. It is not you who takes our land and jobs. It is not you who destroys our crops and kills our animals. It is not you, Ahmed."

Then Purdom himself entered the square and pointed at him. Two militiamen approached him. He knew about the militia. Purdom

11

made it known to his superiors that most of his men would be sabras and settlers. As they approached, Ahmed tried to make them look at him, to read what was in their eyes. They were both young, he guessed in their late teens. They did not look at him but moved behind him'

Pain brought him to his knees. The rifle butt struck him below the ribs in the soft tissue covering his kidney. He rose to his feet when the bayonet pierced his skin. They yelled at him as they drove him inside the house of the Mukhtar. The large room had been cleared but for one wooden chair. The smell of urine and feces stung his nostrils. Two raiders stood behind the chair, their eyes fixed on him as he entered the room.

Purdom entered the room. "Strip him!." The voice was soft, reminding one of the missionary doctors from Beirut. "Undress, please". He stood before his interrogator naked. He felt the tears welling in his eyes and began to shiver, although the night was warm. "Sit down." And he did so. "Look straight ahead." He did so. The pain exploded in his head, as the whip descended on his back. Again. And again. He began to pray to Allah for strength.

They removed his fingernails, demanding information before each was ripped away. He told them nothing. They burned his feet with lighted cigarettes. He told them nothing. There was nothing left but to die. His swollen face made his tormenters seem but shadows. He asked Allah for the mercy of death.

Perhaps their commander, whom the Jewish commandos called Shammah and who imagined himself like one of David's Mighty Men, sensed Ahmed's wish. "We're not going to kill you, Ahmed. We want you to live so others may see what we do with murderers and thieves."

A bucket of oil appeared. Purdom nodded as two of the largest raiders held the writhing Arab and the third pushed his head into the bucket, holding it until Ahmed thought his lungs would burst.

12

Then they released him to stand naked among the others in the village.

The raiders forced the old men and Ahmed to form a line. A young English corporal looked at the people of the village, who stood erect looking at no one. What he saw was hatred in their eyes. He had listened to the Major's speeches, calling on the troops to make the Yishuv safe. He wondered whose side Major Purdom was on.

On command, the raiders formed up before the village men. The major approached the Arabs. Without warning, he pulled his revolver and shot Hassan in the head, the oldest man in the village fell at his feet, his body twitching, then lay still. The women began to wail and the children to cry. The village men were silent. They had seen it all before.

One last act. In a house at the edge of the village, the raiders moved quickly, setting their explosives. Moving away from the village, it was Purdom who set the timer. The explosion was heard in all the surrounding villages. Sooner or later, he knew, they will learn.

March, 1938

Classes had ended and the children were on their way to their homes. Sarah looked to the west, watching the clouds roll in from the sea. There might be rain this evening. It was quiet, but for the chatter of shopkeepers and shoppers and their endless haggling. For weeks, things had been peaceful in Jerusalem and throughout Palestine. Shops were open and the streets were still crowded with people shopping or heading home from work. If only it would last, she thought.

As she walked down the narrow street to the small house in the British enclave, she heard it! The too familiar stomping of boots -- now coming from an alley way to her right. Then they appeared-- British soldiers moving quickly in tight formation toward the Arab quarter. They passed, the officer taking no notice of her. So what will it be, she thought-a mission after a rebel or rebels or merely

13

just another show of force. Was it Emma Forsythe who told her that her husband, the commercial attaché', told her this was the largest number of British troops policing another country since the Great War. She was not surprised. British troops, along with Jewish militia and the largely Jewish police force were everywhere.

She missed young John, now at Eton preparing for university. Like the Nevers before him, he would attend Cambridge. So much like his father, she worried how well he would get along with his classmates, how he would be accepted. She smiled at the thought of the British sabra, as she liked to call him. Raised in the Anglican faith, yet aware of his Jewish heritage, and fiercely attached to a Palestine for all faiths, how would the others see him? She was comforted by the thought that the Nevers family had a long history of diplomacy on behalf of the British Empire and who more diplomatic than her own father. She had often wished young John could have known Arach Poletsky. Her father, who came to Palestine so hopeful for his fellow Jews, so saddened with what he saw that he left Palestine. With Rivka gone, there was no reason to stay. Sarah and Yitzhak were old enough then to make their own decisions and both decided to stay in Palestine. It was still painful to think about Yitzhak, so filled with the dream of a greater Israel and caught in a deadly web that destroyed him. Yet, she was consoled by the memory of the greatest sacrifice, giving his life to save Ismael. Such bittersweet memories of the three of them growing up together, forming a bond that never broke. Yitzhak gone almost twenty years; Ismael the same. Yes, John was jealous! The thought made her smile.

"I did love him, John. I still do. Like Yitzhak. Like a brother, I love him. I know it is wrong to think this way, but I am grateful that he killed the British officer who murdered you".

She had all of his letters. The first had arrived almost a year after the British had confirmed his death in Ramleh. The British never pursued the disappearance of Yitzhak Poletsky, but the Yishuv did. And the Yishuv and the Jewish Agency kept a file on Ismael Latif. What they were not able to discover was what happened to him. They had lost his trail in Marseille. Latif was listed among the many enemies of the Yishuv along with the Bissett family that had helped Latif escape the British.

The letter was short, written in Arabic but with an outside address in Roman letters. The postmark was from Marseille.

My dear Sarah,

I hope you and young John are well. Please let my family know that all is well and I miss them. I shall pray for you and John and my beloved Palestine. Until I am able to return, I am your faithful servant

Ismael

All of the letters for his family and to her and John were sent to her. It was not until 10 years had passed that he revealed his new identity that he was now a rancher, owner of a 4000 hectare estancia! Forty thousand dunams! Still the letters talked of home and the sadness and anger of what was happening.

As she turned onto her street, she heard them. It was the same sound heard daily, the sound of aero planes. They were flying high, so high they were hidden by the darkening clouds. Within minutes they were gone. Then she heard the explosions, five in all. They were bombing another village. Then silence, as the people on the street who had stopped when the planes flew over began to move about their business of staying alive.

April 1938

Abdul al Rahim al Hajj Mohammad could count on less than a hundred men now. More British soldiers arriving in Haifa every day. Most of the roads were watched by the British, Jews and Peace Bands. He smiled at the name. Mercenaries, Arabs like his men, paid by the Jews to kill other Arabs. Informants were everywhere. The sky seemed to be always filled with British planes; they could

15

only move at night or for short distances during the day. Caught in the open in daytime, British planes, with their bombs and machine killed the men and their horses. His men were tired and hungry. Soon horses, many starving, their ribs protruding and eyes listless, would have to be killed for their meat. Food from the villages was seldom available now. Villagers throughout the north had embraced the revolt at first, aiding the rebels with food and shelter, even their young men. They soon learned the bitter price they must pay, as British troops and Jewish militia killed, tortured and imprisoned the able bodied, destroyed the village food stores, their crops, even their houses.

Al Hajj Mohammad was born to be a warrior. To those who followed him and saw him as their savior, he was Abu Kamal. His grandfather had fought the Egyptians; his father joined the revolt against the Ottomans. He was a soldier in the Ottoman Army, conscripted to the Great War against the British and their Hashemite allies. When the war ended, he entered his father's business as a grain trader. He had been successful, dealing with the important merchants in Palestine. But success did not last. The British and the Zionists allowed cheaper wheat from abroad to be imported into Palestine. He petitioned the High Commissioner on behalf of grain traders and the farmers in Palestine who stood to lose their farms because of cheaper wheat from Syria and beyond. He soon learned that neither the British nor the Jews cared about the welfare of Palestinian farmers or grain traders in domestic wheat like Abu Kamal. He was ruined along with the thousands of farmers who lost everything and were forced into overcrowded cities and hopeless lives. Like many others, he decided not to live a life of despair, but to fight for a free Palestine.

Although the loss of his fortune made him bitter, the threat of losing Palestine to the Jewish invaders was a far more bitter pill to swallow. He had heard all the words about Jews and Arabs living side by side, but each new boatload of settlers, each step to impoverish the Arabs and enrich the settlers, each new British action to aid in the invasion made such proclamations by the British and the

Zionists empty words. He remembered being challenged by one of the Nashashibi's about the word invasion. They were not invaders, he would protest, they were settlers. And Abu Kamal had replied, if anyone enters your land without your permission to occupy your land and is protected by rifles, machine guns, tanks and aero planes, is that person an invader or a settler?! If that person settles on your land, and protects that land with a rifle, is he a settler or an invader.

Sitting next to a small fire under a rock overhang at the foot of the mountain, his commanders around the fire with him, he knew the revolt was dying yet he would continue to fight because it was the honorable thing to do. Things were not always this way, there was a time when hope and optimism warmed him like sun in early spring.

***

It was the spring of 1919. Abu Kamal had come home. He had been spotted by a small boy tending a goat herd as he descended from the rocky hills into the village. When he entered the street where the great house stood, a large crowd had gathered in front of the family home.

A very tall lady burst out of the crowd, and ran toward him. His mother had not changed at all; then as she came closer, he could see the worry wrinkles around her eyes, the face not so firm as before. As she was almost upon him, she stopped. She looked at his boots worn through, his filthy and ragged uniform hanging loosely from his emaciated body, a great wide grin on his face. Quickly, she moved toward him, placed both hands on his ears, and kissed his face again and again.

"My son, my son, you are home. Praise be to Allah." It was a bittersweet cry. One of her sons, and two of her brothers would not return.

By now, everyone had surrounded him as he walked, reaching out to touch him, shouting his name and their own, trying to touch him

17

with their words. He was home. Away from a war that he did not choose to fight but to the end fought well. All the dreams of what he would do when he would return, to work beside his father, to rebuild the grain trading business.

The Turks were gone. All that was good and all that was bad about them would be memories. It was an old land but a new nation. He had fought against the British and the Hashemite's, now he was thankful for what they have given him and his family.

The first days in the village were pleasant ones, recent memories forgotten, old ones rekindled. Alone with his father, there was time to talk of the family business, what had happened to it during the war, and of a hopeful future. Before the war, business under the Ottomans had been good. As the war drew on, things worsened. Grain was confiscated for the war, the export market disappeared and the Ottoman lira trusted less and less. Gold had disappeared. At the end, they survived by barter alone.

Talk soon turned to what things would be like under the British. Would they be like the Turks? Or would the Arabs have their own nation? What would the nation look like? Would it include the Levant from Turkey to Egypt, or would Palestine by a separate nation, like Lebanon, Syria, and Egypt? No matter, the land would not be governed by people from Europe or Asia, but by Arabs. And what of the Jews? There was talk among the men from the village and from Tulkharem and Nablus about the number of Jews coming to Palestine as soon as the Ottoman's left. All the merchants knew about the Balfour Declaration of 1917, but no matter, Jewish immigration would be managed by the new nation, and that new nation would decide how many Jews would be allowed to enter Palestine. The war was over and all such agreements were a thing of the past.

As a merchant, Baba understood that the Jews coming to Palestine were rich and they paid good money for grain. "Perhaps, my son, the Jews will be good for us. The Arab merchants are as poor as we and plain to see, the new Jews are rich." Abu Kamal nodded yet he wondered. Absentee landlord had been selling huge tracts of land. He had heard the stories of tenant farmers being forced to leave land they had farmed for generations, replaced by Jewish settlers. But this will change soon, he decided.

Spring, 1938

Otto Lutz hoped that in this troubled land, the people of Waldheim would be left alone. They had been through so much in the last thirty years. Filled with hope and blessed by God with courage and vision, the Templers had built the community from meager beginnings. The brethren had started Waldheim living in mud huts but with hard work, resources from their brethren in Haifa, and funds from Germany, they had planted 5000 square meters of grapes, 500 olive trees and imported dairy cattle which allowed Waldheim to create a cooperative dairy and supply fresh milk to Haifa. And then all was lost when the Ottoman's were defeated and the British deported all of Waldheim's residents but for a few who were not German citizens. The British took possession of the property and collected rents, all the while allowing what the Templers had built in a decade to be sold off, what remained to go to ruin.

God answered their prayers when the British allowed the Templers to return. With help of a Templer Society bank, formed in 1925, Waldheim had been restored to the Templers and vineyards, olive orchard and dairy were thriving again.

Yes, Otto thought, Waldheim and all the other Templer communities were doing well. In Haifa, the Templers were instrumental in building the city, their roads and buildings examples which the rest of the community followed. The Templers had excelled in marketing their products in Europe, and Jaffa oranges, produced by the Templers became so popular in Europe that all oranges from Palestine were labeled Jaffa oranges.

The Bank of the Temple Society, formed in 1925 with its head office in Jaffa and branches in Haifa and Jerusalem, became one of the leading credit institutions in Palestine. Small businesses, many owned by Christians of all faiths, were being extended credit. God demands we be humble, but he could not help but feel pride in what had been done in a few short years.

But all around them, there was trouble. The Arabs had revolted against the British, determined to prevent the Jews from returning to their home. The Templers struggled with the rights and wrongs of the struggle, and there was disagreement among its members. The wanted desperately to be left alone, to live in peace, and pray for the Jews to be restored to their homeland and for the Arabs who had lived on the land for centuries to be treated fairly. Amidst it all, they prayed for peace in a troubled land.

And now this. Adolph Hitler had come to power in Germany. Yesterday, Mayor Klein had been visited by a member of the Nationalist Socialist Party, the NAZI Party. Gerhard Steiner had arrived by automobile from Haifa. He carried with him the Nazi flag, symbol of the new Germany. From this moment, the mayor of Waldheim had been told, the Templer settlements must display the flag. All of the teachers in their school must be members of the Nazi Party. It had taken years for Waldheim to be accepted by the Jews and the Yishuv had been a growing market and now this. It had taken years for other Christians and the Muslims and Jews to accept them. Now the actions of misguided men threatened to destroy it all. There was rising tension within Waldheim. The young spoke proudly of the new Germany; the old prayed that what had happened two decades ago would not happen to again.

April 1938

Uri and Rachel had laughed when he opened the invitation from the High Commissioner to attend the annual spring garden party at the Government House. The residence of the High Commissioner, it stood on the Hill of Evil Counsel south of Jerusalem. The view was magnificent, and the residence befitting a High Commissioner in the British Empire. Uri supposed Rabbi Halevi, his father now dead the last ten years would have enjoyed the irony of it all. A graduate of the University in Hamburg, his life had been uneventful as a clerk in the vital statistics office in Hamburg. He had emigrated from Germany amidst the growing condemnation of Jews there. Unemployed with no definite prospects, he, his wife and their two children found a way to Jerusalem. Among the responsibilities of the newly formed Jewish Agency was to find places for promising young men where their skills might be needed. It was his good fortune to find a position as the Deputy Director of Vital Statistics with the Mandate. He found the job fit his training, and the job of tracking the population of Jewish settlers very rewarding. His skill quickly came to the attention of the High Commissioner, and the invitation to him and Rachel to attend the annual spring garden party.

To Uri Halevi, the worst was over. Two years before, the Zionist plan to create Israel, a homeland and a nation was in serious peril. The Arab leaders like Husayni and Khalidi were demanding independence and a stop to immigration. There was, at first disbelief, then alarm as the revolt grew. Something unbelievable might actually happen! As much as he resented their arrogance, he knew it was the British who granted them a homeland and in the time of peril saved them. In Whitehall, 10 Downing Street, and Parliament friends and those who feared them made failure unthinkable. Within the British army they had friends at the top. Some, he knew were reluctant friends, who had been cowed by men like Wauchope and Churchill, but they would do what they were told. Many of the British military leaders saw the revolt as an opportunity to sharpen their anti-guerilla skills, to test new weapons and tactics useful to the Empire in Asia and Africa and to prepare for the war with Germany.

Uri had listened to the heated talk in the coffee houses and taverns about the British. Jews did not trust them. Sure, their politicians supported the Jews but there was more than the protection of the Jews on the minds of the British. The oil pipeline from Mosul to Haifa was essential to the British, and the Arab gangs were sabotaging the pipeline. That brought the British soldiers in force, along with their navy and air force to snuff the revolt.

For whatever reason, the revolt had served the Yishuv! The British were arming their allies, the Jews, he thought wryly. For Ben-Gurion and Jabotinsky, the revolt was seen as an opportunity to create an army too strong for the Arabs to prevent immigration. Men like Purdom and Tegart and now Montgomery were teaching them how to defeat guerrillas and to fight against large armies. Soon they would not need the British. Privately he and his friends welcomed the day when the British would leave Eretz Israel. Always, he thought, dependence created resentment. When the Arabs are defeated, which will be soon, it will be time to ask the British to leave.

Conditioned to denigrate bourgeois behavior such as that before him, Uri was nevertheless impressed at what he saw as he entered through the garden gates of the High Commissioner's residence. The garden party was lively on this lovely spring evening. The fragrance of spring flowers drifted among the guests, the string quartet from Tel Aviv lifting the spirits of everyone. Halevi, Shurtok, Ben-Gurion, the Habibi's, General Wavell and Commissioner MacMichael all having a good time, all conversing with familiar faces and no doubt subtly mixing in matters of state and business. He noted important Arab notables were missing.

Tariq Nashashibi deeply regretted the anger of other notables in Jerusalem, Nablus, Haifa and throughout Palestine toward his family. Was it anger or was it envy because his family was prospering and the other families not? He had made it clear to all of them that he would continue to deal with the British and the Jews, that a revolt would only destroy them. To the Husayni's and the Tougan's, deal with the world as it is, you cannot change it. Yes, he had been awarded contracts well beyond their true value from the Jewish Agency, but no matter. Yes, he was supporting the peace movement, even though he knew it was made up of gangs of criminals paid by the British and Jews to split the Arabs and crush the rebellion. Beyond all the corruption, there was something that he did believe.

We can only share in the wealth of a new Palestine if we cooperated, if we accepted things as they are and will be. Otherwise, we will have nothing. He truly believed that Ben-Gurion and Weizmann were reasonable men, practical men like himself and something could be worked that would benefit the Arabs as well as the Jews. He truly believed? Or did he? No matter, he decided. He thought of his appointment with George Haddad in Beirut. Best he find ways to transfer his money out of Palestine to a safer place. Beirut with its connections with European banks has always been that place.

Moving among the guests, he spied George Antonius, the trouble making government clerk who was very open in his criticism of the heavy handed manner in which Montgomery was stamping out rebel resistance. He had protested to High Commissioner McMichael that only earned him a harsh rebuke. Nashashibi knew that directing protests to McMichael was of no consequence in any event since the word had come from Whitehall that henceforth policies and actions would come from Wavell. It was now a military action, out of the hands of the High Commissioner.

"Good evening, George." Shaking hands and nodding, his eyes turned to the tall angular Englishmen talking to Antonius. Gracious as ever, Antonius introduced Nashashibi to Leslie Smythe. "Mr. Nashashibi, may I introduce Mr. Leslie Smythe, who has been in our Commercial Section since March. Leslie Smythe, may I introduce Tariq Nashashibi who for many years has numerous business dealings with the Mandate. His family has lived in Palestine for generations."

"I am sorry to say, we have never met, Mr. Nashashibi, but I am aware of your many ventures with us. It is a genuine pleasure to meet you."

"Although we have never met, Mr. Smythe, I think I have seen you before at some gathering or other. You are a friend of Sarah Nevers, are you not?"

"Yes, I met Mrs. Nevers over a month ago. I visited her school. Two of my boys are enrolled in her school."

"I am surprised that your children do not go to the English School as most of the English children do."

"When I met Sarah and she told me about her school, that there were students from Palestine and from the Continent, Emma and I decided we would ask Sarah if she had room for John and William." He smiled at Nashashibi, looking for a reaction of some kind, then added. "We couldn't be more pleased. Where else can you find a headmaster fluent in English, French, Arabic and Hebrew."

Antonius looked at the two men. He found it easy to like the young Englishmen. Katy found him the same. They had been guests at a dinner party held by Sarah and after a great deal of testing of the other's views, finally became comfortable with each other when they talked about events and conditions in Palestine. Antonius was aware of what happened to Sarah's husband John, that the British had killed him to silence him regarding the connection between the High Commissioner and the assassin band known as the Circle. He knew about Sarah's father who had left Palestine to go to the United States because he disagreed with the British policies so tilted to the Jewish settlers and their treatment of the Palestinian natives. There were many like him in the British Foreign Service, who knew the history of Britain's relations with the Arabs and the understanding the Arabs had about independence in return for warring against the Turks.

Although many in the Foreign Service were sympathetic with the Jewish settler movement, they saw the heavy-handed and brutal actions of Montgomery against the Arab rebels as a betrayal. They also saw the matter as bound to turn out badly when Whitehall had instructed the British army to arm the Jews and hang any Arab found with a gun.

Smythe had heard about the Nashashibi's before, perhaps they had been mentioned by Antonius at some earlier gathering. The family seemed taken with the idea that they could work with the settlers and the British to end the rebellion. They had even gone so far as arming what were called ironically "Peace Bands", who, as far as he could tell, were no more than armed thugs hired to kill Arabs fighting the British and the Jewish settlers. Nashashibi had grown wealthy during the Mandate while most Arabs were hurt by British endorsed policies which allowed the Jews to discriminate against the Arabs in hiring, and gave the important contracts to Jewish firms. The Nashashibi's were among the families who were given contracts and favored in other ways for their support of Britain's pro-Jewish policies.

In Smythe's brief experience with the Foreign Service, and his conversations with other Foreign Service officers, the decisions they made had to meet one essential test, were they in the best interests of the Empire. While many British actions were insensitive to the colonized citizenry, they found the best decisions were those which were sensitive to the needs of the natives, because they turned out to be in the best interests of the Empire.

But Palestine introduced something into the process that was unique, with small exceptions. In Palestine, Foreign Service officers must contend with the power of an important British constituency, the Jews. There was little disagreement among Foreign Service officers that the best decision would be to grant nationhood to the people already in Palestine, to give them power over their own affairs, and lead them toward self-government. That was what the Mandate System was set up to do. The formal objective of the League of Nations Mandate system was to administer parts of the defunct Ottoman Empire, which had been in control of the Middle East since the 16th century, "until such time as they are able to stand alone".

And that is where the politics in Britain, and the influence of important Jews, he thought, created a monster. To allow continuous immigration of Jewish settlers meant there would never be a sovereign nation "able to stand alone" unless the distasteful, immoral "stand alone" point in time will be when the

Jewish settlers will be the masters of Palestine. Thinking about the future, it was becoming clear to Leslie Smythe and many other career Foreign Service officers that the real starting date for nationhood was not creation of the Palestine Mandate but the Balfour Declaration in 1917. For it was the Declaration that guaranteed a homeland for the Jews with an immigration policy for settlers which Britain no longer can control. To make the situation even more difficult, the Roosevelt Administration, on which Britain must depend in the upcoming battle against Germany, is applying pressure to allow even greater numbers of Jewish immigrants from Germany to come to Palestine.

Smythe found that Tariq Nashashibi was looking at him with a puzzled look on his face. "Is there something wrong, Mr. Smythe? You seem distracted."

"Sorry, Mr. Nashashibi, I'm afraid I have terribly bad manners. I was thinking how much the boys were enjoying school and how much they adored their headmaster." He tried his best to ingratiate this Arab Notable with his best smile. "If you will excuse me, I need to find my wife. We like to get to our apartment before the boys are in bed. It was a pleasure meeting you, Mr. Nashashibi and I am sure we will meet again soon." Smiling at George, he moved among the guests to find his wife who most likely was in an animated conversation with some of the wives. He really did enjoy the minutes together with Emma and the boys at the end of the day. Still, he was not very comfortable chatting with Nashashibi—loyalty to one's own was clearly lacking in the man.

***

Haj Amin al Husayni was a bitter man. For too long he had deceived himself by believing that the British would protect the interests of the Arabs in Palestine. He thought of the wording of the Balfour Declaration, of establishing a homeland for Jews but protecting the rights of the people who lived in Palestine. He now knew that he had been deceived He now saw things as they really were, that the

Jews would continue to come to Palestine until they overwhelmed the Arabs and yes, to throw the Arabs off their own land, to expel them from Palestine. Throughout Palestine, the Arabs were in revolt. They expected him to lead them. He smiled wryly to himself. Yes he would lead them by following them.

July 1938

Avi paid no attention to the azure blue sky and the shades of blue of the harbor, the sea's color deepening to indigo on the horizon. Nor the towering headland of the Mount Carmel range which separated the coast from the rich Jezreel Valley. Nor did he note the ships docked in the harbor now low in the water with oil piped from Mosul. Instead, he watched the crowds in the market, now increasing at mid-morning. He checked his watch and nodded to the two men standing in front of the coffee shop. He watched the first man head quickly away from the harbor, taking the road to Mount Carmel. One minute later, the second man turned and moved away, not hurrying but following the first. To a bystander, there seemed no connection between the three. Avi watched the two British policemen who had come into the square where the vendors had set up their shops. He smiled. "Two birds with one stone." He checked his watch again. Two minutes. He turned, careful to slow his movements and followed the other two.

As he moved past the glistening white buildings with their red tile roofs on each side of the boulevard leading to Mount Carmel, he quickened his step. The ticking in his head grew louder and his heart raced and pounded in his chest.

The explosion could be heard in Acre and to the south for twenty kilometers. He wheeled to watch as the debris and body parts began to fly through the air, the wind blowing the black smoke toward him, the screams and shouts growing dimmer as he moved away. The motor car would be waiting; he would be back in the settlement in an hour. Within hours, he thought, the news would reach Europe and America. Within hours, the world would hear of the great carnage caused by Arabs fighting Arabs, settling old feuds or exacting revenge for the earlier atrocities in Jerusalem. There would be the skeptics, of course, who would claim that the Irgun exploded the bomb in the marketplace. Their voices, he knew, would be viewed as shrill and hysterical, blaming the Zionists once again for their own bloody murders. The British police were another matter. The code of honor among so many of them would cause them to examine what happened very carefully. No doubt, fingers would be pointed at the Irgun. No matter, the days of the British were numbered. He would do his part to see that they would be few.

***

Sergeant Hamish Murray took charge of the scene, his men and the Haifa police moving quickly to disperse the angry crowd that had gathered around the carnage. Amidst the blaring sirens of ambulances and police vehicles he could hear the screams and cries of pain. Brits and the Arab police formed a cordon to hold back stricken relatives, mothers, fathers, son and daughters who fought to get to their loved ones. Attendants moved quickly among the victims, sorting out those still alive and shouting to stretcher bearers or attending them on the spot. Tough men who had seen it all in Palestine and elsewhere quickly collected body parts and covered them before transport. Murray saw the rage in the eyes of the Haifa police, some with tears streaking their dusky faces. "What a god awful mess." He muttered to himself. "A beautiful place turned to shite. What in bloody hell are we doing."

He knew the shouts of anger were directed at him and his men. And he understood why. The British spent little time protecting the Arabs. They were the wogs whether Africans or Arabs, they all seemed the same to the British. What we did do, he thought bitterly, was protect the Jews, even arming them while shooting and hanging any Arab found with a weapon. And what do the Jews do? They curse us for not doing enough! They need us now. But soon, he thought. Soon, there would be trouble.

He stood apart from obscenity before him, the awful smell of burnt flesh, blood and excrement, the cries of the wounded and dying. Who did this thing, the killing of women and children in so pitiless a manner? This was not an act of rage, of revenge for who could hold such anger for women and children, but a cold and calculated act to instill fear. But why? Why instill fear? Was it to cause the Arabs to rebel against their own fighters, those who are trying to drive us and the Jews out of Palestine? Surely that has not worked. Or is it something even more unthinkable—to force the Arabs to leave. No, he decided. The Irgun could not possibly believe they can force all the Arabs to leave Palestine, to create a state just for Jews. "Perhaps I am building a straw man. Perhaps there is no reason at all behind this terror. Perhaps it is just madness."

Murray was a family man. His wife and two children lived in Edinburgh while he served his tour in the police constabulary in Palestine. The pay was good, and he had been able to save a good deal of his pay living like a bachelor in Haifa. Their dream, he and Glenda, was to purchase a small sheep farm in the highlands after he retired. He thought of home, and counted the days when his tour in this very unpleasant place ended.

He was a tough man, tough in spirit and quick of mind. His job in Haifa was to try his best to stop violence, too often between Arabs and Jews, but too often, too, between British soldiers and sailors and the locals.

In the two years of his tour, he had noticed a change in the attitude of the Jews toward the British. Always hostile to the Arabs, of late they had openly expressed their hostility toward the British, and it was commonplace to show their disrespect for the British uniform, whatever the service.

Before he came to Palestine, he was briefed on the job he was expected to do. The British were to protect the settlers, the Jews who had come to Palestine after the Great War. Perhaps he was unrealistic in what he expected when he arrived in Palestine, but he had not expected the open disrespect of the Jewish settlers toward his uniform. He had expected gratitude and had received either disrespect or indifference. From the Arabs, he had expected hostility, and that existed. But in his contacts with Arabs, he, more often than not, was treated with respect and appreciation when something was done to protect them.

What he found, as well, was differences of feelings toward Arabs and Jews among the British uniforms. Many seemed to dislike the Arabs simply because of who they were, while others treated them as they were treated. If the Arabs showed respect, they would return it. For the Arab Christians and Muslims, it must have been puzzling in deciding how to deal with the British. They knew why the British leaders sent them to Palestine, yet their encounters with the British uniforms often sent a different message. The British uniforms were often respectful and generally fair.

In such a world, Sergeant Hamish Murray carried out his duties. Whatever his superiors had told him, he had taken the time to read the Balfour Declaration, when all of this started, at least as he saw things. It said clearly that both Arabs and Jews were to be treated the same, as the job he had to do in many ways was little different than the one he was asked to do on the streets of Edinburgh.

The explosions in Haifa that occurred during the year tested his sense of duty. The headlines in the English speaking papers invariably stated or hinted at Arab gangsters committing these atrocities. In some cases, suspects taken from lists provided by the Jewish Agency had resulted in killings, hangings after military trials and imprisonment. In many of those cases, the Sergeant's investigations suggested that the terrorists might be Jewish.

The bombing in the marketplace had killed 47 people, men, women and children. Two were policemen. Forty four of those victims were Arabs. Fifty three more were in Haifa hospitals, many of those would not survive. Murray had been given the lead to investigate the killings. If the past was to be his guide, he could expect little from the High Commissioner beyond the platitudes he was so fond of. He would do his best because that was who he was.

Hamish had one lead. Two men were seen watching on the hill leading to Mr. Carmel in the Templer community.

There was a witness, Hans Klein, who operated a bakery on the wide avenue leading up the mountain.

Klein called the police. Murray went to the bakery to personally question Klein.

"There were two young men standing across from the bakery looking down to the harbor. I noticed them because I hadn't seen them before."

"What made you call us, Mr. Klein?"

"I went back to baking when I heard the explosion."

"I understand but what was it about these two young men that made you call us?"

"When the explosion happened the two young men began walk quickly up the hill."

"You thought that unusual?"

"Wouldn't you, officer? Why were they there and why did they start to walk away so fast?"

"Could you describe them?"

"One was skinny, the other was thick but not fat. The skinny one was taller."

"Were they Arabs?"

"I don't think so but I don't want to say."

"Why is that?"

"Well, your next question would be do you think they were Jews and I don't want to say that, either?

"Could you tell me why?"

"I don't want to say."

"Do you think they saw you?" Klein was scared. He understood, surprised he had told him this much.

"I don't think so. The light shining on the bakery window makes it impossible to see inside the bakery. At night yes, during the day, no."

"What time was it when you noticed the two men?"

"It was mid-morning. Maybe around 10."

The explosion had occurred at ten twenty.

"Thank you, Mr. Klein. Someone will come around to take your statement. I have my notes; you just have to repeat what you told me, unless you think of something else."

Hans Klein watched the Sergeant leave. He did what he felt he must do. He hoped nothing would happen to him or the others because of it. A day seldom passed when there was something hateful about the Germans in the papers and many times it included the Templers in Palestine

***

The professor's mind was wandering as it often did after classes were out and he was alone in his study. He sometimes thought that in such moments he was like a supply clerk, taking inventory, not of tangible things but all he had witnessed since arriving in Beirut twenty years ago. As he gazed out the window at the harbor, royal blue in the bright spring sunlight, his mind settled on a time almost twenty years ago.

By a simple stroke of luck, he had attended a talk given by a visiting professor from the Syrian Protestant College. Back then, he had recently received an appointment as an assistant professor at Oberlin in the new field of political science. He had attended the lecture out of curiosity and because young professors were expected to fill the room when guests spoke. What was his name? Jamal Haddad, that was it. But when he heard the man speak, he knew what he wanted to do. Then by a stroke of luck, family contacts-mother and father had been missionaries in Africa- and a vacancy, he became a professor of political thought at the Syrian Protestant College. That was two decades ago. Now the small college had mushroomed into a full-fledged university and even took on a new name-American University of Beirut.

It had been an exciting time, where new nations were spawned, and the entire Arab region was fired by the Wilsonian manifesto of self-determination for the people no longer part of the Ottoman Empire. All about him, men, even women were brimming with new thoughts and dreams, thoughts about the possibilities of a changing world and their place in it. The College and now the University had been part of it all. It was here that students had their minds stimulated by political thought of Plato, Ibn Rushd and Locke and others and such documents as the Magna Carta, the Declaration of Independence, the Bill of Rights and the remainder of America's Constitution. Important families sent their children to the University. It was here that contacts were made with other future leaders. Many were now leaders in the Levant and beyond.

"Professor Malcolm, you have visitors." The voice of his young assistant startled him from his revelry. He quickly regained his composure. "Thank you, Antoine. Show them in." Standing in the doorway, a serene and expectant smile on his face, the little man was leaning on his cane, a young priest to his side but slightly behind.

Charles Malcolm own smile widened as he looked at his visitor. How long had it been? "Father Michael, what a wonderful surprise. How long has it been? Nineteen thirty four! You look well. And who is your companion? I don't think we have ever met." He smiled then. Realizing what he was doing he smiled. "I'm sorry, I haven't let you say a word. Both of you, please come in and sit down. "

"My good friend, I am sorry so much time has passed since our last visit. I think last time I was once again asking a favor, to find a place at the University for a young student of mine." Father Michael leaned forward at the same time, placing his hand on the shoulder of the young priest beside him "Let me introduce Father Yusef Alawi to you. He has been kind enough to escort me to your beautiful city."

The Professor remembered their first meeting in the hospital in Damascus almost twenty years before. He had come to visit one of his former students, Amin al-Dajani who had been wounded by an assassin who murdered Yusef Shukri. The good Father had been blinded by the assassin's bullet. Despite his blindness, he had continued as the pastor of St. Michael's in Nazareth and headmaster of the school St. Michaels operated. He wondered why Father Michael had come to see him.

"I came to see my sister's grandson. He has taken a position at the University hospital. He is a surgeon like his father and grandfather before him. I suggested to Father Alawi that we might drop by to see my good friend." The Professor remembered the Dr. Nuri Boutin who had saved the life of Amin and treated Father with such care and compassion. "They have taken most of the older boys--- put them in those terrible camps." The sadness in his voice as he spoke filled Malcolm with pity. "There are few older boys left now. They have either left to join al Hajj Mohammad or the British have taken them away. The masses for the dead are so many these days."

What could he say? He was touched that Father Michael came to see him and decided that the visit was no more than the release of talking to someone about the terrible times in Palestine. The Professor was not surprised by what the Father told him; Beirut was filled with news and a large number of Palestinians who had either been deported or came to the city to escape the British and the Jewish militias.

Beyond the Levant, the hounds of war were baying loudly across the sea. The Germans had turned on the Jews and many were seeking refuge in Palestine. Hitler stirring the peoples in lands lost in the Great War. Chamberlain had lost the British people and Churchill was threatening war. Sadly, between the two demagogic charismatics, there was no place for reason or sanity. The cost in life and misery is unthinkable, but no matter to such men where personal glory trumps the tragedy it portends.

Old times, the bitter and the sweet, took up most of the afternoon. Both the professor and the priest apologized several times to the young priest for excluding him, but then continued to do so. Sarah and Amin, of course Ismael came up often, the conversation often melancholy, as if they could never believe or accept that such a time of hope had turned out so badly.

Evening approached when the professor walked them to the door, shaking the young priest's hand first, then allowing him to move away while the two old men stood together looking down on the city. The shadows grew long as the sun descended into the sea and the breeze coming through the windows grew cooler.

"You must know, Michael, that whenever I see you, or hear about you, I feel hopeful. I am reminded that there is much that is good about the world, and there are many, many good souls that shine their light on the rest of us. Good doesn't always triumph over evil, but it is heartening to know that the light has never gone out and never will."

He looked at the priest who was looking at him with the tiniest of smiles and the slightest shake of his head.

"I'm afraid I have made you uncomfortable, Michael. I should know that such praise is not welcomed. Sentimentality sometimes overcomes me."

"There is goodness in us all, Charles. And like me, you would prefer that others not point it out to you. I think that comes with a little humility but also a little vanity, as well."

"Have you heard any news about Ismael. Amin tells me he is a very successful rancher in Argentina."

The priest looked up at his friend. "There are rumors, Charles." As if to discourage any further conversation, Father Michael cupped his hands over the extended hand of the Professor. "Goodbye, Charles. You must come to Nazareth soon."

Markham watched the sprightly old priest moving quickly toward the waiting Father Yusef. They both waved.

Rumors. He had heard them, too.

***

He was always pleased with his dinners, held weekly and attended by the important people in Britain. Always the perfect host, careful to avoid asking favors of his guests, making each feel the center of the event. Careful, too, to dampen the wont of egotistical men to be combative at the dinner table or in the drawing room where he took care to provide the latest best cigars and perfectly aged brandy and to lighten the discussion away from the business which was always foremost in his mind.

Chaim Weizmann took care of the important British politicians and they took care of his dream. He always understood that behind the platitudes of public service was the drive for personal gain. At first he had been surprised how politicians and bureaucrats who had such power could be so easily purchased. But getting politicians and bureaucrats to do your bidding was not simply about money. He knew that such men guarded a self-image of public service and was careful never to challenge that image, but to nurture it. His craft was a fine mix of persuasion and coercion, the first foremost.

He enjoyed bringing important people together to engage in ventures that benefitted both. He saw to it that money never passed from his hand to theirs, but that financial benefits were found in ventures he arranged. He assured them coverage in the London press, sometimes even in New York and Paris. Yet there were occasions where money under the table seemed to be the only course open, and that came easy to him. And he was always sure to see that those who helped the Yishuv without urging were rewarded.

He was a cultured man who admired much of what was British, and in his mind, he was a loyal subject of the Kingdom. But his actions as a British subject must always pass through the Zionist filter. It was never troubling to him that such actions by any objective standard were not in the best interests of the Kingdom but made to appear so, nor was he bothered that the not so powerful and the easily marginalized railed against actions by his good friends Balfour and Churchill, shouting shrilly they were harmful to the Empire.

Churchill and Balfour always behaved toward the Jews in a way that served the national interest, he decided. How well he remembered the Churchill tirade at one of his dinner parties against those who questioned the heartless treatment of Arabs and favoring the Jews. He was pleased at himself for getting the word abroad that Winston was in his cups when he told his guests, "We will do whatever he tells us," referring to him.

To allow Winston's outburst to get abroad without explaining "Well, that's just Winston in one of his moments" could have made things very difficult. The press had been good about it all, leaving his remarks on the cutting table. Feeding the press, often sympathetic regardless, was part of Weizmann's great value to the cause of Eretz Israel.

He was troubled now because there was a great deal of infighting among the Jews in Palestine. He feared what he had patiently built over thirty years was being threatened by aggressive and demagogic leaders in Palestine. It was ironic that such men as Jabotinsky and Ben-Gurion wanted the same thing, but they were no longer willing to go after Palestine with patience. At least they understood they still needed the British.

Even now, there are firebrands who want to challenge both the British and the Arabs and blatantly shout about hastening the departure of the British. Little did they appreciate how it was his reputation and influence that stiffened the backs of the British and convinced them that our loss would be theirs, as well. Did they not understand it was he who persuaded the British to bring in Tegart, Harris, Wavell and Montgomery, and to bring the full force of the empire to crush the revolt?!

Part II

"Turning their backs to the rain, the two men stood silently in the darkness and listened to the launch move out to sea."

September 1938

At first, Andre Monet was disappointed in his assignment, to go to the Levant and report on the rebellion in Palestine. At least, Le Figaro had allowed him to establish an office in Beirut, where the Parisian atmosphere surprised him. His first dispatch was received in late September on the activities of rebels in Beirut, who were openly trying to raise money to purchase arms and to rally support among the Arabs. He wrote of the influence of a cabal of professors at American University who were openly supportive of independence for Palestine, as part of Greater Syria or as the state of Palestine. Among those often quoted was Professor Charles Malcolm who had been with the University when it was known as the Syrian Protestant College and Palestine was part of the Ottoman Empire. When the first dispatch was received in Paris, the information was so rich that the editors asked for more about the views of Charles Malcolm. It was Le Figaro, using Monet as a byline that provided the historic context for the rebellion in Palestine and in Iraq, Syria and Egypt. It was Malcolm, in his understated manner, who informed French readers and much of the world what Zionism might mean for the rest of the Middle East. The Balfour Declaration, the McMahon-Hussein correspondence, and the Sykes-Picot Agreement taken together provided readers with conversation grist like never before. One reader offered a letter to the editors entitled Monet Turns on the Lights.

Dispatches were daily and soon became part of the conversation wherever people gathered in to Paris and in days the Editors of Le Figaro found themselves in the center of a firestorm. Criticism grew stronger daily and threats of withdrawing advertising became real. Other Paris papers like Liberation chimed in and anti-Semitism and the Dreyfuss affair became part of the debate. Criticism went across the Channel and the Atlantic with even greater force. Quickly and dramatically, Le Figaro, once owned by Francois Coty, an openly anti-Semitic business magnate, bowed to the pressure and a cable went out to Beirut recalling Monet. A wag in a letter to the editor offered the rejoinder Baron de Rothschild Turns Out the Lights.

Monet received the recall cable in his office at the Lebanese newspaper Le Jour. A brilliant intellect, prone to depression by nature, Monet retreated to his hotel room with several bottles of Bekaa Valley merlot. The sun had dropped below the Mediterranean horizon and the room dark when there was a knock on his door. Monet prided himself in his capacity to drink and remain lucid, although those around him wondered about his lucidity when on a binge. He rose, and willing himself to walk steadily to the door and open it, he found a tall young man smiling at him. He stood at the door, appraising the visitor, wondering why the great grin.

"Good evening, Monsieur Monet. My name is Henri Bissett, may I come in?"

Monet bowed slightly at the waist and with a sweeping movement of his hand slurred a reply, "Please".

Bissett looked around. It was clear the hotel did not have maid service and Monet cared little for order. Clothes were thrown where he had taken them off. The unexpected visitor caused him to quickly move about the room, clearing a chair and tossing clothes into the small closet.

"Please, sit down. I won't pretend that the condition of my room is unusual for me, because it isn't." He looked at Bissett, trying to guess the purpose of the visit. As if suddenly aware of the darkness he clicked on the lone electric lamp in the room. Taking a seat on the unmade bed, "May I ask the purpose of the visit?" He tried to speak as amiably as possible, but his head was beginning to swell from the wine and the question came out like one from a lawyer questioning a hostile witness.

Since that was not his intention, he needed to rid the room of the tension he had created. He looked at Henri Bissett, still standing and the smile, albeit smaller and more guarded remained.

"Please accept my apology for my bad manners". Pointing to the now clean chair, he gestured to Bissett. "Please sit."

"You asked the reason for my visit. I will get to the most important one last but first, I would like to congratulate you on the dispatches you sent to Paris these past weeks. Seldom does Europe and America get a chance to read what you wrote. I congratulate you for discovering early on the rich sources within American University, and for using the greatest source of them all, Charles Malcolm. For those in the Hejaz, in Egypt and the Levant, everywhere in the Middle East, it gave us hope."

Bissett removed a cigarette case from the breast pocket of his coat, opened it and offered one to Monet. He noticed that the correspondent's hand shook ever so slightly as he carefully removed a cigarette. Bissett quickly struck a match and lit both cigarettes, pulling the pungent Turkish tobacco into his lungs, then slowly releasing the smoke. The process was like a ritual, observed by both men and brought a stillness to the room.

Silence was broken by Bissett leaning forward to speak stayed by a small gesture by Monet. "I'm afraid your hope, and the hope of others, was ambushed today. Monsieur Bissett. I am being recalled."

"I know." Bissett watched the expression on Monet's face, surprise and wonder at how quickly the information had become known in Beirut. "Although we were hopeful, we were not surprised by the owners of Le Figaro. As you may know, they are new owners, trying

41

to shed the image branded on the paper because of its previous owner. Francois Coty was accused of being an anti-Semite. Because there is such a huge price to be paid because of the image, El Figaro has behaved as most western institutions and enterprises behave, to assiduously work to shed the image. What they soon discover is that such an image will be lifted only when the Jewish leadership in the country lifts it. Like other individuals, institutions and enterprises, they simply shed objectivity and do and say what is acceptable to the Jewish leadership. Truth is a casualty, of course, but that, in truth, is the way of the world."

Monet was silent and Bissett could see he thought him confused and irrational. Scapegoats are always easy to find.

Bissett, a young man educated in France, and a traveler throughout Europe and America smiled as he saw the skepticism and displeasure on the correspondent's face.

"Francois Coty did hate Jews; perhaps it is more accurate he hated what he thought the Jews were doing to France. His error is a very common one, he lumped the few that were hurting France with the many who were not, in fact were doing the opposite, and the few made sure that he paid the price. Although Henry Ford was too powerful to be brought down as Coty was, he was guilty of making the same error."

"You seem obsessed, Monsieur Bissett. You seem to want to lay all the blame on the Jews for what is happening in Palestine."

"Monsieur Monet, if you do return to France, I want you to remember the words I have spoken. For what you will find is that you have been branded, and your freedom of expression and action will be sharply curtailed. You may be able to accept such restrictions and continue to have a newspaper man's career, or you may not, and you will no longer have a career."

"That sounds wildly exaggerated."

"There is another avenue for you, Monsieur Monet, you can embrace all the dreams and aspirations of the Zionist movement and with your obvious talent, and you will be a great success."

Monet's head still ached but the conversation had sharpened his thinking.

"You said you came here for and important reason you would discuss last. What is it you want to talk about?"

"We want you to continue to report from here." He looked closely at Monet. "We want you to sever your ties with Le Figaro and become a freelance reporter."

"You are asking a lot." He focused his gaze on Bissett. "By the way, you used we several times this evening. Who are we?"

"The 'we' starts with the Bissett family. George Bissett was my uncle. Uncle George was educated in England and France before becoming the owner and editor of the Jaffa Times. The year 1920 was a stormy time and he fiercely defended the Palestinians who were being hurt by Jewish immigration. He spoke out against policies of the Yishuv hiring only Jewish workers and denying work to Palestinians. He fought against displacement of tenant farmers when land was purchased by the Jews. He became a thorn in the side of the Yishuv and he was assassinated, run down and then stabbed in front of his home.

But the' we' is more than that. It is the thousands of persons like me, educated and aware of the world around them, that want freedom and justice everywhere in the world but more importantly in the Middle East. We want it for our families and our neighbors. In Palestine, we want it for all who live there."

Monet was a reporter. He had heard a lot of speeches like the one delivered by Bissett but none more eloquent. Perhaps before the French Assembly, the British Parliament, or the American Congress those words would make a difference. But in this tiny room in a cheap hotel in Beirut it means nothing. What if he; Andre Monet could find a way to share his reports with the rest of the world? He looked at Henri Bissett, studying him for a moment but said nothing.

It was growing late. Bissett rose. "I will stop by in the morning" Should he try to tempt Monet? Appeal to his mercenary side, that his name recognition and access to the rebels might mean handsome fees for his work? Something told him no. Andre Monet must decide on his terms

October 15, 1938

Only twelve men remained under Hassan Latif's command. They had escaped from Jerusalem when the Old City was retaken by the British twelve hours before. Moving past the British by night, they had commandeered a passenger bus beyond the Damascus Gate headed toward Jaba and the highlands to the north. If they could reach Tulkarem, they would join al Hajj Mohammad's fighters. Hassan's men were among the last to leave Jerusalem and now they were fleeing for their lives.

Twenty miles north of Jaba the autobus ran out of petrol. They had to find cover quickly; news of the stolen autobus would send British patrols and aero planes to search for them. Hassan cursed at their luck, now stranded beside a road where there were no trees or other cover. It was early in the morning; thanks be to Allah there was still coolness in the air. He looked at his men, worn out by the constant firefights with the British. None had more than a few hours of sleep the last three days. On both sides of the road, only an occasional cedar dotted the countryside. To his left, farther up the hill, was a cluster of houses surrounding by corrals holding goats. Two hundred yards beyond the houses was an olive grove and a small stone church behind the grove. "Quickly, men, head for the olive grove. I will see if the priest will help us."

As he entered the olive grove, he could see the church more clearly. Small. The stone walls clearly not the work of a stone mason, the cross on its peak tilting slightly, the windows without glass save one at the front of the church. Yet it was a church and Hassan hoped that the British would respect the sanctity of a church and the priest give them shelter, water and food.

+++

John McDermott could see the autobus parked beside the road. He wondered what it could be doing there. Although his small church was hidden from the road as you passed it by, from where the vehicle was parked, his church could be seen from the road. Where were the passengers and driver? Daily service was over, always attended by the same elderly ladies from nearby villages who would walk several miles each day to attend. He thought he saw movement in the olive grove.

John came from a family of Presbyterian missionaries possessing rock hard convictions about heaven and hell but like so many sons and daughters in such families, John strayed. When his family came home from China, it was to their house in Montreat, North Carolina which had been in the family for four generations. The McDermott's never really asked whether John wanted to be a missionary, but his father, the Reverend Rafer McDermott made the decision for him. He would study at the College in Montreat, then leave for a mission, most likely somewhere in the Far East. John was seventeen. The family was surprised when they woke one August morning in 1917 to find a note on the kitchen table. The note was one sentence or two. "Goodbye. I am off to see the world. John."

And John McDermott did just that. Hitchhiking to Asheville, some young men he met told him they were going to join the Army to fight the Huns. So John did, too. When he went through training before going overseas, John's upbringing and genes betrayed him, since his own betrayal would mean carrying a rifle and killing Huns. Tall, thin and blond, his gentle demeanor led him to the medical corps, where he was trained to treat the wounded and drive an ambulance. When he arrived in France, he was immediately sent

45

to the front where he quickly found himself in the line of fire when bringing the wounded back to the trenches and the infirmaries and hospitals behind the lines. Wounded twice, decorated for bravery, he finished the war, uncertain what he would do next. Eighteen and alone, he read and re-read the letters from home, always they urged him to come home. But the resolve that had him leave the McDermott household was still with him. He would see the world.

So here he stood beside a window which gave him a view of the autobus, still wondering about the occupants. These were troubled times. In his travels to Jerusalem and Bethlehem, he often met British and the newly arrived immigrants from Eastern Europe. The British soldiers were like those he met in France and conversation was easy. With the Jews, it was different. Few spoke English and very little Arabic, and, of course, he spoke only English although his Arabic improved every day. One would have to be blind not to see the smoldering resentment of the Arabs toward the new immigrants, who seemed to have disdain for the Arabs. The Arab's anger at the growing presence of Jews reached a boiling point two years before and the violence escalated. Beginning with early childhood, he was reminded of the Jews passion to return to the Holy Land and he was aware that the British had assured the Jews of a homeland in Palestine. But living among the Arabs, both Christian and Muslim, he understood their attachment to the land could go back to the time of Jesus and perhaps beyond.

Standing before the window, his musing brought him to his arrival in Palestine almost ten years ago. In the course of his travels, his roots were never lost, and the desire to serve God in some small way brought him to this humble church. Word had reached him through a friend that an elderly minister with a small church north of Jerusalem was seeking someone to carry the ministry to his flock. Reverend Smithers turned out to be a recent widower longing to return to the green fields of north England. John was prepared for a modest flock but surprised it consisted of twelve families that could offer little to support the Church. There was often little enough money for the simplest things he needed, but no matter. What he was doing for the last ten years brought him peace and happiness, greater than anything before. And with the help of the mother Church in Leeds where Reverend Smythe now lived he had been able to get along nicely. He was pleasantly surprised just a few years earlier when his oldest parishioner deeded the olive grove just to the south of Christ Church. The olive grove gave him a source of income and the opportunity to attract more souls to his small flock. It was there that he saw men who must have been on the bus. They had placed themselves behind large boulders at the edge of the field where they could not be seen from the road.

He watched one of the men, armed with crossed bandoliers and rifle approach the Church. He went to meet him just as he heard a knock on the side door. He noted the look of concern on the face of his cook as he opened the door. The man who stood before was not quite as tall as he.

"Welcome to Christ Church my friend. What can I do for you?" It was not the first time the Reverend was confronted by an armed man. He had long ago decided to trust in God and grant such men the courtesy of assuming they intended no harm to him or his flock.

Quickly, Hassan presented his petition, honestly telling the Reverend the danger they were in and the need for shelter, rest, water and food and a place to hide from the British who would soon discover the autobus and be in hot pursuit. He was hopeful as he made his plea because he saw concern in the eyes of the man who stood in the door of his Church.

"Bring the men to the basement, Hassan. There is room enough there. I'm afraid we can't offer you much but I'm sure Christina can find you something to eat and there is plenty of fresh water." He smiled at his cook, who stood beside him shaking her head. A Muslim who lived in a village nearby, she had simply appeared one day, offering her help to the Reverend whose charity and love made no distinction by religion. She had served his Church almost the entire time he had been in Palestine, still a Muslim. She worried that the Reverend was once again putting himself and his Church in

47

jeopardy. She turned and walked away, thinking all the while what she could find to feed thirteen hungry men.

In the distance, the whine of motorized vehicles could be heard and in the far distance, Hassan could hear the steady drone of aero planes. The Reverend saw the expression of concern on the rebel leader's face. "Bring the men in quickly. We will lock the basement door. Pray to Allah and I shall pray to God that the British do not insist on searching the Church."

Again, John McDermott took his place at the window that faced the road. An armored car and two lorries filled with soldiers began the climb up the hill to where the stranded autobus rested. Spotting the autobus, the convoy stopped and an officer stepped from the armored car, binoculars in hand. For several minutes he scanned the area around the autobus, stopping to focus on the olive grove and then the church. He remounted the armored car and the convoy continued then stopped within fifty yards of the autobus. The officer pointed at the machine gunner in the armored car, who commenced to fire rapidly into the autobus until the officer signaled him to stop.

On command, both lorries emptied and the men formed a skirmish line and began to move toward the hovels clustered 100 yards to the front. Two men waving a white flag came running toward them. They know what the British could do to their village, he thought.

The men turned toward the village and gestured to the soldiers to follow them into the village. For a time, the two men repeated their dance until two soldiers followed them. It took no more than thirty minutes for the soldiers to return and report to the officer who had held the binoculars in his hand earlier. It seemed to Pastor McDermott that the soldiers were persuaded not to attack the village.

The officer returned to the armored car which then moved off the road to higher ground above the village and the olive grove, the gunner checking his Vickers, sighting it above the moving troops and into the olive grove. The village must have reported that the men from the autobus had escaped into the grove.

The basement of the Church was without windows and completely dark. Hassan spoke. "Complete silence until the Reverend opens the door." He thought of the two men with painful gunshot wounds. Gradually, the men grew accustomed to the dark and could make out the outlines of their comrades. All wondering whether the Christian priest would betray them, knowing what could happen to them, their families and their villages if they were discovered.

Leftenant Cartwright watched the men advancing toward the olive grove. Within 100 yards of the grove, he signaled for the men to stop and take up firing positions. He turned to Corporal Ready manning the Vickers. "Traverse left to right, Corporal. Commence firing." Cartwright watched the first effects of the .303 caliber rounds and they ripped through the grove, tearing off limbs, ripping huge chunks out of the trunks. He then signaled for the men below to commence firing into the grove. He had been sharply rebuked by the colonel for losing three men in the last firefight. He would not risk losing any more.

The Reverend could not believe what he was seeing. Surely, the soldiers did not have to destroy the precious olive grove. They could have simply knocked on the door and asked if there was anyone hiding in the grove. I would have gladly walked through the grove with their commander. Why!? In heaven's name, why? McDermott had always been a man slow to anger, slower to judge but this outrage, he thought, tested him mightily. The soldiers began to advance quickly, still firing but the Vickers was silent. Within minutes the men were in the grove, the firing stopped. Slowly, the men came out of the grove yet maintained their distance from each other. He could see their commander leave the armored car and walk down to join the other men just outside the grove.

It was then that he saw the commander turn and look toward the Church. The thoughts of what he would do were never carefully formed in his mind but instead nagged around its edges. He knew why although he hadn't thought that through either. The commander began to walk toward the church, accompanied by several heavily armed men.

The why was simple enough. The consequences of what he would do would decide the future of the men in the basement. The stories were common enough. Men caught with arms were hanged. Their families and their villages were punished. From his flock he heard the stories of random killings by the British soldiers and Jewish militias. He looked once again at his ruined olive grove, opened the door and walked to meet the men walking toward him.

Cartwright spoke first. "Good morning, Reverend. I am Leftenant Cartwright. Sorry about the olive trees. Lost three men last week in an ambush; can't be too careful, you know. A gang of Arabs slipped past us in the Old City and commandeered the bus you see out on the road. We suspect they are nearby."

"I am John McDermott, I am the pastor here. I am sorry about the loss of your men, Leftenant. Loss of life among the young is always tragic. I pray things will be better soon." Taking a step forward, McDermott fixed his eyes upon those of the young man in front of him. "It must have occurred to you that there was a connection between our Church and the olive grove. Would it have been asking too much if you had consulted me firing into the grove!? I would gladly have escorted you or another of your men into the grove to assure you that there was no one hiding there." He tried to keep the anger out of his voice, understanding his first duty was to keep it out of his heart.

The back of the young officer stiffened. "My job first and foremost is to protect my men, to keep them out of harm's way whenever possible. That is what I did. As to the trees, I suggest you contact the High Commissioner if you want to be paid for the damage."

McDermott noticed that the young man spoke with concern in his voice but he suspected that this was just another performance to let the man in front of him know there was nothing personal in all this.

Looking at the young man who was in such a powerful position on this morning, he decided there was no use in antagonizing him. In fact, it was important that he do his best not to for the lives of the men in the church basement depended on it. He had thought of all the questions and how he would answer each.

"Did you see the men in the autobus, Reverend?"

"No, I did not. There was a service here this morning. When we finished the service, one of the congregation saw the bus. It was empty." McDermott smiled to himself at the word congregation. There were twenty families and at most a hundred members who came to church during the course of the year.

"No one saw them?"

"I don't think so. No one told me they saw them." McDermott saw a sergeant, much older than the leftenant, shaking his head. Cartwright ignored him.

"Would you object to our searching the Church?"

"Yes. The Presbyterian Mission is very clear on the subject. Soldiers are not permitted to enter our church for other than peaceful purposes or when invited by the minister. There are, of course some situations where soldiers might enter, for example, if fired up from the church or its grounds." He had bent the truth already and another twist or two would do no further harm to his soul.

McDermott could see the old sergeant was anxious to speak, but conditioned never to speak to an officer without being requested to do so, he remained silent.

Cartwright stood for a moment weighing the choices he had. Forcing a smile and with a casual salute: "Thank you Reverend" turned and walked down the hill toward the armored car. The men assembled and marched smartly back to the lorries.

The armored car worked its way slowly down the rock strewn hill and onto the highway. Troops filled the lorries and the convoy moved north toward Nablus. Hassan Latif could feel the sweat on his body grow cold as he and his men listened for any sounds that would mean discovery. He trusted the priest knowing immediately that he would try to protect them. But what could he do if the British decided to search the building. They were in a refuge but it could be a tomb. Pray to Allah and ask the Prophet Jesus to protect them. They had lost track of time, but knew it was hours since they were led in the basement. Hassan jumped when he heard the knock on the door.

The door opened and light from the floor above flowed into the room. McDermott and a young boy entered; the boy carrying a jug of water and a cup. Behind them came the cook, who carried a large basket with bread, beans, a jar of olives and grape jelly.

"I'm afraid we eat very little meat here, my friends. After you have eaten, try to get some rest. You have almost eight hours before dark. You need to be far away by tomorrow morning"

Hassan looked at the tall blond man who stood in the doorway. A kind man used to being obeyed. Again he thanked Allah for their good fortune in finding such a man at such a time. "You remind me, Father, of a man my family knew a long time ago. He was an Englishman but a true friend."

McDermott was curious. "What was his name?"

"His name was also John. John Nevers."

"The husband of Sarah Nevers?"

"Do you know Sarah?"

"We see each other often. I try to send at least one of our young people to her boarding school each year." John Nevers; like a spirit who resided forever in Sarah's heart. John McDermott remembered the first time he met Sarah Nevers. He had never married and loving a woman was never part of his life. That was until he met the school marm from Jerusalem. Since then she was always on his mind. He began to find reasons to come to Jerusalem, to visit the school and to see the headmistress. As much as he tried to capture her heart, there were the other John's. One was her son, the other her husband dead almost twenty years. As gently as she could, she let him know there was no room for another John. Stubborn by birth, he decided he would not give up.

Hassan Latif looked closely at the man in front of him. "Perhaps she spoke of my brother?"

Of course, the name of Latif. Hassan was his brother! He had heard the story of Ismael Latif. When he by chance had mentioned his name to Sarah, he was startled by the change in her. It was a mixture of joy and sadness when she spoke. She spoke only one sentence. "Yes, I knew Ismael."

He had not pursued the matter further with Sarah but by chance a visitor, who was English and had lived in Palestine since the end of the War, told him the story of Sarah, Ismael and her brother Yitzhak. He smiled at the mention of her name by Hassan. "Yes, she did,"

Hassan glanced at his men, letting them know they would be leaving soon. It was easy for the other men in the room to see the bond that had formed between the Palestine patriot and the priest.

"I will leave you now, Hassan. Godspeed. Pray for peace"...he hesitated for a moment: "and justice. If I see Sarah, I will give her your regards and if you see her, please do the same for me." He rested his hand gently on the arm of his new friend. "Goodbye."

"Goodbye, my friend."

It was two hours after the sun set when the rebels slipped out of the church and into the ravine at the edge of the olive orchard. Early that evening, contact was made by Mustafa, a young man sent by Al

Hajj Mohammed to guide them to his camp. They were to make their way to a hideout five miles south of Sanur. There they would be provided with horses for their journey north.

October 11, 1938

The rain squalls that swept the beach reduced their visibility to only a few yards. Turning their backs to the rain, the two men stood silently in the darkness and listened to the launch move out to sea; anxious about its discovery by the British boats which patrolled the Palestine shore. Ismael and George Bissett had traveled almost 8000 miles to return. They knew what would happen if they were discovered. Ismael because he was still a wanted man, still considered the most dangerous of all the Palestinians, George because he was the nephew of George Bissett, the editor of the Jaffa times murdered by the Circle because he threatened the Yishuv.

None of the Bissett's remained in Palestine. Some had moved to France, others to Argentina, others to Lebanon. Yet George was drawn to the uprising, to the chance to create a democratic nation in Palestine, one where those who lived on the land would govern it; one which would honor his uncle's memory.

He understood the enormous challenge of forging such a nation in the face of forces which seemed beyond compromise and reconciliation. Both were controlled by forces outside of Palestine, the Jews by Zionism, the Arabs by a cultural coherence. Palestine was the battlefield. To George, a lawyer by training, several things were clear. One, peace would never be possible without the English. They could clear the path for a viable state. Two, the power of the extremists on both sides must be diminished by more moderate men, those which saw the necessity of creating a democratic nation. More importantly, men and parties supported by the British to build a nation.

The two men had not spoken since they came ashore. They knew that silence was essential, that the British soldiers and Jewish

54

militia were everywhere, that the beaches were being patrolled, and hanging awaited them if they were caught. Certainly, this was true for Ismael. His own influential family might save him, George thought, but that was unlikely. If caught, he would simply disappear. Perhaps that would be true of the tall man beside him, as well. His feet in the sand of Palestine, wet and cold and afraid, he prayed.

They had many conversations in Cordoba about Palestine, what was happening, what its future could be, what the chances for a new nation. George was struck by the similarities of views they had about Palestine. Perhaps influenced by his many talks with Lawrence during the Great War, Ismael, too, wanted a nation free from outside control, not the part of anyone's empire. But why was he here? Unlike Ismael, he had never been in battle, had never fired a weapon, had never killed or even attempted to hurt anyone. No, he was not a warrior with a rifle but there was something he would do. Words were a weapon he knew something about. He would use his contacts in Lebanon and Paris to tell the world what was happening, how the cause of freedom and liberty for Palestine was important. That he could do.

Both had intended to leave the past behind them, to make their future in Argentina, yet both were drawn to Palestine.

Ismael felt it. War. Was it still the same? They had spent three weeks in Marseille where they were contacted by rebels who had been part of the fighting and others who supported the rebellion. There, he had tried to prepare himself for what it would be like, to recall what it had been like two decades ago. He had viewed each contact with suspicion, aware of the army of informants recruited by the British and the Jewish Agency.

As the waves rushed ashore and receded, Ismael felt the sand shifting under his feet and moved to solid ground beyond the reach of the waves. The enemy was out there in the darkness, perhaps very near. The rain had stopped. He listened, only the sounds of the waves rushing ashore and the wind in the trees beyond the beach.

Beckoning to Bissett, he moved quickly to the trees fifty yards from shore.

They were told the village was no more than a mile from where they now stood. There they would make contact with Al Hajj Muhammad's men; horses and weapons for their journey awaited them.

The rain had stopped. The moon was below the horizon, the stars blurred by the fog that blanketed the land. Ismael watched for movement looking away from the areas he searched, hoping peripheral vision would aid in detecting movement. With Bissett close enough to touch, the moved in the direction of the village. Two hours before daylight, they must hurry to reach the village as the first faint rays of light appeared on the rims of the hills far to the east.

Bissett watched the man in front of him, seeing the change as they touched the beach. No longer Yusef al-Dajani, the estancia owner but Ismael Latif, the feda'ee. Falling in behind, he felt the unexpected thrill, his pulse racing-his fear gone. He found himself wanting to shout, to tell his companion what he was feeling. He knew he could not.

Out of the darkness, two men appeared. One moved within three feet of Ismael and spoke quietly.

"Purdom is in the village with his raiders." They could not see the village from where they stood, but they could tell the location by the lights which reflected off the low clouds near shore.

Ismael waited for the speaker to continue. "We found out they knew you were coming yesterday morning. They are looking for you up and down the coast. So far your good fortune holds. Allah must be pleased with you." The speaker was smiling. "The mad one will be angry. The villagers will pay with their blood, I'm afraid." There was sadness in his voice. "Come. The horses are two kilometers from here. We must hurry."

Bissett found it hard to keep up with the swiftly moving men, who seem to drift across the land, moving easily among the trees, then scanning the open ground, and moving quickly across it to the next clump of trees. No more than thirty minutes later, they had mounted and headed east. When offered a rifle and bandoliers, Bissett had refused. Their guides looked at Ismael, who nodded. The leader shrugged then prodded his horse into a canter.

October 12, 1938

The four traveled by night, always on the lookout for British patrols, squads of the Hagenah, or even Arab peace bands out to kill rebels for the bounty paid by the British and the Yishuv. Those they met, and there were few, were questioned and warned what would happened if they betrayed the rebels. This surprised Ismael. The taller one, Kalima, spoke. "We're not all Arabs united against the British and Jews? The British and the Jews pay handsomely for information"

Noting the look of surprise on Ismael's face, he continued. "You have been away too long, Ismael. Some have thrown in with the British, willing to sell out their countrymen for a few measly coins. They grow fat while the peasants starve. They pretend that they care about their fellow Arabs, yet they betray us every day. Yes, they are few, but the British and Jews tell the world that the rebels are few. They do not even call us rebels. They call us gangsters and terrorists. Yes, they call the people whose families have lived in Palestine for centuries and fight for the right to their land—they call us gangsters."

Kalima turned in his saddle, keeping his voice low, he continued. "My father fought with the Turks. He was in the artillery. By good fortune, he never fought against Faisal's army so he would not have known of you or the men who fought with you. When he returned to our village, it was then that we heard of you, of Ismael."

Kalima and his companion pulled up their horses at a place that could not be seen from the trail and dismounted. Ismael and

George did the same. An evening shower had left pools of water in the rocks and they were able to water their horses and fill their water bags. To the east, the sky began to glow along the rims of the hills and the soft grey of morning began to change to the colors of day. The horses, relieved to be free of their riders and saddles noisily ate the tough grasses that grew on the hillside.

From where they stood, they could see the great valley spread out before them. Kalima broke the silence.

"My father and his brothers were welcomed in their village. The Turkish officials were gone and whether one fought for Faisal and the British or the Pasha and the Turks did not matter. They were home and rumors were that the Arabs would have their own country, free from the Turks, the British and the French."

The three rebels had found a large rock which served as a bench. To the east, the sky on the horizon was now orange, white and blue, the same sky Ismael remembered from 18 years before. He listened to Kalima as the young man continued.

"Father heard all the rumors about the Jews, and there were many who lived on the coast and in Jerusalem. There were settlements in the Galilee. And then he learned that the Jews had been promised a homeland in Palestine. But he was assured by the British that his rights as an Arab would be protected. It was a bitter pill to swallow but there was still reason to hope that the British would keep their word."

Ismael was silent as Kalima spoke. All the memories returned. The murder of his father, the murder of George Bissett by the Circle and the killing by the British of his dear friend John Nevers; then the giant manhunt by the British that forced him to leave Palestine 18 years ago. During all those years he was away, Palestine was always in his thoughts. Now he was back.

Kalima continued: "My father became a foreman at one of the largest orange groves and then a company representative selling the oranges abroad. We were happy and father lost interest in the move to stop Jewish immigration and force the British to leave. But he came to understand that not to fight for independence was a mistake when he was replaced by a Jewish foreman from the Ukraine when the company was purchased by the Jews. What he came to discover too late is that what was happening to him was happening to Palestinians everywhere"

Ismael nodded. He had kept abreast of what was happening. Jews were hired to replace Arabs, Arabs were forced from their land when Arab landowners, some living in Beirut and Cairo sold their land to the Jews. Jewish settlers replaced the Arabs who were left with nowhere to go but to large cities living in hovels and searching for work that paid next to nothing.

The British destroyed the Arab farmers that were left by flooding Palestine with cheap grain from abroad. Some of it, he knew, came from Argentina. While the Jews were enriched from abroad, with capital pouring into their banks for Jewish businesses and farmers, the Arabs had no such source of capital, and what the British provided was far too little. All the while Arabs were being dispossessed and impoverished, the immigration of Jews continued, and became a flood by 1930.

The sun had risen above the hills to the east and the plain to west was in full daylight. The sound caused the four men to leap to their feet. Aero planes, more than one coming from the south! The two men with Ismael had chosen their resting place well, hidden from the trail they had taken and from the searching eyes of the pilots who manned the bombers and search planes. Flying low, they passed over them, heading north. In the distance, Ismael could see a village in their path.

Abd, who had been silent most of the trip spoke. "They are heading to Suffariya. " He looked at Kalima, speaking in a monotone. "That is my village." Kalima watched his companion stiffen, his eyes grow wide. "Perhaps they will pass over, God willing, Abd."

They watched as the planes began to dive above the village, the pitch of their engines rising. They saw them first, the mushrooms of smoke rising above the village, then quickly following by the sounds of the explosions upon impact. As the planes climbed above the village they turned sharply and the staccato sound of the machine guns over the village and the fields where cattle and sheep grazed.

Tears filled Abd's eyes and the anguish he felt made him choke on the words. "They are killing the cattle and sheep. They are killing everything. They are destroying everything." The other two watched helpless to salve his pain, feeling their own and the hatred that welled up inside. It was Abd, the most devout of the three, who spoke: "Allah will never forgive them."

They could see the fires in the village, helpless for the British soldiers and Jewish militia were waiting for such men to come to the aid of the villagers. They would wait until dark then move to join the others.

Bissett tried to hide the fear he felt. It seemed unreal that he was there and what was happening in front of him. He recalled watching picture shows, where all the violence was projected onto a screen and he was sitting in a comfortable seat watching. But this was real. His heart pounded in his chest and he fought the nausea that rose in his chest. There was fear but fear was quickly replaced by anger at what was happening and pity for the stricken Arab who could do nothing to stop what he knew was happening to his family.

The four men rested in a thick grove of pines at the base of the mountain and watched the endless flight of planes that they knew were searching for them.

Ismael looked at the valley floor to the south. The movement of British military vehicles moving quickly in both the direction of the Sea of Galilee and the Mediterranean made him wonder what he could possibly do for the people of Palestine.

His life as a soldier in the Hejaz, the search for his father's killers almost twenty years ago then ranching in Argentina made dealing with uncertainty a way of living. But still Ismael was shaken by what he found. The vehemence with which the British dealt with the Palestinians, the methods they were using to put down the revolt, the arming of the settlers were all part of a betrayal he never thought possible.

Somewhere out there he knew Hassan was fighting for Palestine. Others were dying for freedom. He knew that he must fight for them. The first step would be to fully understand what was happening around him, and he looked to the two young men with him to begin. Abd and Kalima were inseparable, never far from each other since he first saw them on the beach.

Ismael found Abd to be a surprisingly keen observer. Still in his teens, his father had made a good living in his leather shop in Suffariya. After witnessing the attack on his village, he had accepted the likelihood that the shop was gone, and all his family had built destroyed. His sole wish was that the lives of his family had been spared.

Ismael looked at the dejected young man who continued to speak.

"I joined my brothers against the British and the settlers because I believed in the power of justice, that Allah could not deny the Palestinian people that which was rightly theirs. In some of the early battles with the British and Jews, there had been victories. We destroyed parts of the oil pipeline from Mosul to Haifa, ambushed British and settler patrols and cut rail lines."

"Do you think you can defeat the British and the Jews?" Ismael needed to know how men like Abd and Kalima saw the rebellion.

"We know we cannot throw the British or the settlers into the sea. We can only hope that by fighting we can make them understand that giving us our freedom would be best for them, too. With all Arabs against a Jewish state in Palestine, surely they would say to the Jews, enough, we have done enough. We must give the Arabs what they want, we must be fair.

"We soon learned that the British were not interested in talking to rebel leaders, only killing them, putting them in camps and even deporting them. Whenever we struck the response was even more soldiers, more armored cars, more aero planes."

Kalima joined the conversation "We could no longer consider large numbers of fighters against theirs. Whenever we struck, the unit we struck would use the wireless to contact their command post and within hours, sometimes even minutes aero planes would appear overhead to strafe and bomb us. Reinforcement would arrive in armored vehicles armed with light machine guns and squads of soldiers.

"Whenever the British or Jews lost men, the nearby villages would be bombed or attacked, killing livestock, destroying our fields and even executing men in the village.

"Still we fight and hope." Kalima looked at Ismael. "We need you, Ismael."

Ismael said nothing but walked away from the three, and stood staring across the valley. Had he made a fool's journey? No matter, he decided. He would fight for what Abd and Kalima believed, that their cause was just.

When it was dark, they followed a trail that took them through the forest heading east then turned sharply to the north toward the foothills. George could make out the outline of a hogback in front of them. They had traveled an hour in silence. Kalima raised his hand, signaling the riders behind him to stop. He moved quickly out of sight of the three. Ismael glanced at Abd, who seemed relaxed for the first time since the trip began. Ismael heard the rider before he saw him; it was Kalima who now beckoned them forward. Ismael could sense the presence of men around him but saw no one.

Riding in single file they passed over the hogback and dropped into an open area on the other side. Throughout the open area, fires could be seen and the outline of men moving about. By the light of the fires, Ismael guessed there were less than a hundred men scattered over perhaps two hectares. The camp was surrounded by hills. He guessed there was more than one exit and entrance to the camp.

They dismounted and led their horses toward the campfire at the center of the clearing. A lone man stood facing the four men, his featured hidden by the back light of the fire. He appeared wary, Ismael thought. It was the high price paid by the hunted, never sure of who and where your enemies were. He stepped forward and extended his hand. Ismael offered his.

"Welcome, my friend." As Abu Kamal spoke, he pulled the taller man to him and kissed him on both cheeks.

He then turned to Bissett, shaking his hand. "Welcome." He gazed into the face of Bissett and then smiled. "My father knew your uncle, George like you. A brave man. And I have had the good fortune of meeting your cousin who surprised us with a visit only two days ago." He smiled when he spoke as if hiding a pleasant surprise.

By this time, everyone in the camp had gathered around their leader and the two visitors. It was barely past midnight, but Ismael suddenly felt overcome by fatigue. Abu Kamal spoke sharply to the men behind him who moved quickly moved away, leaving him alone with the three arrivals.

"There is a tent ready for you. I know you are tired. I will see to it that your horses are watered and fed and we can talk in the morning."

As he and George were led to the tent set up for them, Ismael tried to imagine what Abu Kamal and his men were thinking. Surely, their leader understood he could not work miracles but he wondered. They will know soon enough.

Barely asleep, Ismael leaped from the sheepskin bed as he heard the flap of the tent moving. Beside him, Bissett had opened his eyes and sat up in his bed, then leaned back on his elbows. Easy to see the man in front of them was not an Arab, possibly a Circassian but likely a European.

"Greetings and welcome to Palestine."

The grin was contagious and both men returned the smile. "My name is Andre Monet and you owe my company to your cousin, Henri. " Looking at George, "And you are George, yes?"

He turned to Ismael, who like George, was enjoying the banter of the tall, spare young man.

"My introduction to you, Ismael occurred at the University in Beirut. One of your admirers is a man you have never met, Charles Malcom, Professor. Another, I am told is Father Michael, a priest in Nazareth who I hope to meet." Realizing his bad manners, Monet paused.

"You seem to know a great deal about us, Andre, but what brings you to Palestine and to a rebel camp."

"We have something in common, George. We both want to tell the world what is really happening in Palestine."

"Are you a reporter?"

"A journalist, actually.

"Which paper do you work for?" Ismael was intrigued.

"Well, until a week ago, I was a correspondent with Le Figaro. They sent me to the Middle East to report on what was happening in Palestine. After the first two dispatches from Beirut, where I relied heavily on people at the University and particularly Charles

Malcom, the Editor decided I was doing my job too well and they recalled me to Paris."

George was puzzled. "But you are here and not in Paris."

"It is still somewhat of a mystery to me, my friend. When I received news about the first responses to my dispatches with my name on them, I was elated. When Le Figaro advised me that controversy regarding what I wrote required me to return to Paris, I was angry and depressed. Although my bravado made me think of becoming a freelancer, that soon faded and I was ready to return."

George was smiling, then catching the meaning Ismael began smiling. "It was Henri, yes?"

"Yes, he is a very persuasive man. And he is clever. He told me he would not attempt to influence me leaving it for me to decide. The following morning I did, and now I am here."

"So what will you do, and how can I help?"

"Since you do not look like a warrior, perhaps we can do the job together. And Abu Kamal's help will be critical. Henri provided a camera and we have contacts in three cities where they will see that the dispatches and the film reaches Beirut and Henri will see to it after that."

Ismael was impressed. The propaganda war had always been won by the Jews and the British and the Arabs had always been painted as the villains. He remembered a time when newspaperman Lowell Thomas made his friend an international hero and the Arabs brave and able fighters. He looked at Andre Monet. Perhaps.

October 17, 1938

Avi and Shlomo were best friends. Avi came to Palestine as a young boy in 1930. He made his living as a house painter which allowed him to determine his own work schedule. Avi read a great deal, and was a follower of Ze'ev Jabotinsky but sometimes he felt Ze'ev was too cautious. That is why he joined the Irgun, because they believed as he did. Both the Arabs and the British must go.

Shlomo met Avi at one of the Irgun training sessions. Shlomo worked as a motorcar and lorry mechanic. He was very good mechanic which made him a very valuable member of Irgun. He was fascinated with explosives, their power and their deadly effects. Avi was drawn to Shlomo because Shlomo could help him build bombs, bombs controlled by wire detonators, bombs detonated by pressure, bombs that could be set with timers, and the really complicated bombs which could be exploded by radio signals. There were other reasons the two were drawn together, both lived in the same building, both liked to walk to the top of Mount Carmel and gaze at the Haifa panorama. On a clear day like today they could see Acre, the ancient city where the Crusaders were swept out to sea by the Muslims. Avi liked to read about history, and while the two of them sat on the mountain, they would talk about things like the Diaspora and the Crusades.

"It's ironic, you know, Shlomo."

"What's ironic?"

"Back during the Crusades, the Muslims and the Jews fought against the Christians. Saladin was a good guy."

"What happened?"

"From what I read, Muslims and Jews got along until the Ottomans lost."

"Now it's switched around. The Muslims and the Christians hate the Jews."

"Pretty soon, Shlomo, we won't have to worry about the Muslims or Christians. We'll have our own country."

"So what happens to the Muslims and Christians here now?"

"Ben-Gurion thinks we should find a new home for them somewhere."

Beneath them, they could see long rows of troops leaving a large ship that had arrived this morning. The troops quickly formed up and marched toward them..

"The British sure know how to put on a show." The both could hear the military band playing Rule Britannia as the troop ship began to empty.

"How many thousand do you think have come ashore, Avi?"

"Hard to say."

"Well, guess!" It came from Avi like a command. Shlomo irritated him when he wouldn't commit. He was like that with everything. How much gelignite should we use? Shlomo would shrug. How long should the detonator wire be? Where should we place it? What time should we set the timer for? Always the shrug until Avi would decide.

Out in the harbor, the HMS Malaya and the HMS Repulse rested at anchor, standing guard over the troop landing. Avi remembered the awesome power of His Majesty's ships when they bombarded a concentration of Arabs beyond Mount Carmel. And the Royal Marines coming ashore after our last bomb went off in the marketplace and the Arabs rioted. They were impressive.

Yet, like his Irgun brothers, he hated the British, but they did know how to run a war and kill Arabs. They had to go as soon as they took care of the Arab rebels.

"Look at that, Avi!" Lifted off the ships by crane, armored cars like great iron boxes, came ashore and immediately were started and moved away from the harbor. "They look like prehistoric monsters."

Passing in the opposite direction, lorries pulled onto the pier and began loading troops. Other troops formed up and began marching toward the city.

"They say all these troops are to protect us. I think they're here to protect the oil pipeline from Mosul."

"Maybe so, but they sure helped us out of a mess."

Why do I like this guy?! Everything I say he disagrees with. Avi liked Shlomo to agree with everything he said.

They had been watching since early morning and it was now close to noon. "We need to be in Nablus by nightfall. Our ride is waiting down by the German school."

"Do you know what Zelesney wants?"

"I think it's the railroad station. Always busy. He wants us to make it look like the work of Abu Kamal."

October, 1938

Arach Poletsky no longer went to his Wall Street office and had sold his share of the partnership with John Williams and Jacob Kurtz. He had found his work as an investment banker rewarding and had done well, but like all of the bankers, been hurt by the Crash but had more than enough to satisfy his moderate needs. He had his books, could walk to the library, enjoyed the pocket park by his lower Manhattan apartment and the small group of friends that he spent much of his days with. They often talked about home; most were from Russia and Eastern Europe and envied Arach because he had been to Palestine.

At first, he had tried to keep such conversations as short as possible. Parting with Yitzhak and Sarah had been difficult and he had his regrets. Thinking about the children, memories were always bittersweet. Grief over the loss of his son had been less and less painful as years passed, and he found a place in his heart for pride that his son Yitzhak had given his life to save Ismael's. He felt solace when he thought of Ismael, such a fine young man. Sarah had written and said she had heard from him. He was living in Argentina! A hacendado, an owner of a 40,000 dunam estancia! He smiled at the thought of the young man. He was not surprised at his success. He was a remarkable young man and after the murder of his father like another son.

It was a beautiful fall day, the sun casting long, deep shadows under the elms and oaks. People seemed caught by the mood the day caused, moving briskly, often smiling at those they passed. The melancholy he felt this morning was gone. It was good to be alive.

"Why don't you join us, Arach. You've been looking out over the East River like you're trying to see Jerusalem. It's your move." Morty slid the chess board closer to Arach, sensing that maybe, just for once, he might have him trapped.

"Sorry, Marty. I was thinking about the movie show we watched last night. Ginger Rogers is really something. You know what I wish. That I could dance like Fred Astaire."

"You watch a Ginger Rogers movie and you think of Fred Astaire." He let out a deep breath. "Your move, Arach."

"OK. I think you have me this time, Morty."

"I don't like you should talk like that. It always means I'm in trouble." He pushed the board closer. "There's always a first time, and this is it." Two of their friends, Marty and Conrad were sitting on the same bench. Morty turned to them, still speaking to Arach. "Why should you learn to dance. You pay no attention to the widows in the neighborhood. I know at least two who would like nothing better than to teach you to dance."

69

Short burst of laughter from the three who looked expectantly at Arach, wanting him to respond.

"I was blessed with my Rivka and I never wanted to dance" there was a twinkle in his eye as he looked at each of his dear friends—"with anyone else."

For a moment, there was respectful silence for someone they felt they all knew.

Conrad, the quiet one looked at his friend. "How are Sarah and John?"

"John is away at school in England and Sarah is still the headmistress at her school. She is concerned about what is happening there."

Marty had gone to the picture show with Arach the night before. Something they did each week to watch the make believe world that Hollywood had made. The newsreel had a short piece about the bombing in Nablus. Something about the short piece troubled Arach. It was likely, he thought, that the rushing ambulances and harried stretcher bearers were reenactments of what had happened. Sinister faces of Arabs appeared on screen and a British officer spoke into the camera decrying the perfidy of the Arabs and Abu Kamal, who appeared on horseback leading rebels across the screen.

Arach was sorry he gave his friends an opening. All the while he had been with his friends, he tried to paint a different picture of Palestine and of Arabs who were much like the Jews in their thirst for learning, their ambitions for themselves and their families, but he found there was little change in their attitudes.

The three knew how Arach felt and seldom brought the subject up in his presence. But what was happening in Germany had fired them up about Zionism, and for the Jews to have their own home, where they would be safe. Most of his friends were educated Jews who showed great concern for others and were ardent supporters of President Roosevelt and his New Deal. But when they spoke of Palestine, and the Arabs, tribal bonds controlled their emotions and their concerns for people like Negroes never carried over to the Arabs.

It was Marty who spoke. "There will only be peace when all the Arabs are cleaned out, wiped out or thrown out, it makes no difference." The vehemence shocked even Morty and Conrad, who looked at their good friend Arach, who once again was steeped in silence, staring across the River to Jerusalem.

November 1917

Menachem Abramson had worked with Arach Poletsky for the last five years. Together, they had assessed land, searched titles, bargained with sellers, registered deeds, and did the myriad of others things associated with buying land by the Jewish National Fund. This day, the two of them were looking at property near the Dead Sea and had decided that a trip to Masada was in order. Both interested in the revolt, they had talked often of visiting the ruins if they had the opportunity. As they stood among the ruins, looking down on the Dead Sea they talked about the meaning of Masada to the Jews.

Arach spoke to his friend. "Eighteen hundred years ago, Menachem."

"Closer to eighteen hundred fifty years, Arach."

"You are right, my friend. Eighteen hundred and fifty years". He looked around him. "This is where their dreams ended, my friend."

"Their dreams did not end, only their lives."

"True, the dream is still alive." Arach nodded to Menachem, as if conceding the second point.

"Have you read today's paper, Arach, It talks about our dream."

71

"Yes, I have. I read the letter from Lord Balfour to Lord Rothschild."

Menachem read aloud:

"His Majesty's Government views with favor the establishment in Palestine of a National Home for the Jewish people, and will use such endeavors to facilitate the achievement of this object..."

Thanks to the Rothschild's and Chaim Weizmann, we have a homeland guaranteed by the British Government. After all these years, we have won."

Arach looked at his friend. Menachem's last sentence. "After all these years, we have won."

"Are we speaking of the time of the Diaspora until today or are we talking about the date the World Zionist Organization was created twenty years before? Or does it refer to some other time of awakening during the last century when groups talked about nations and self-determination? For connected to the time is the meaning of "we". Certainly the Jews in America, where they have more freedom than at any time in the last two thousand years, don't think of Palestine as their homeland. To visit and pray, yes, but would they leave America? Yet even among American Jews there is exhilaration at the thought of the nation of Israel. One of the most powerful men in America, Jew or non-Jew, Lewis is pushing for nationhood in Palestine."

He remembered that the thought of what it might mean unsettled him then; now what worried him then had come true. It seemed only yesterday when he spoke to his friend.

"You know, Menachem, whenever the Declaration is discussed among Jews and among Christian Zionists, we seem to stop reading at that point. We do not want to discuss the remainder of the Declaration which says:

'It be clearly understood that nothing shall be done which will prejudice the civil and religious rights of the existing non-Jewish communities in Palestine....'

Before Menachem could respond, I continued; "Let me correct myself, we have no trouble discussing what follows that troubling clause..."or the political status enjoyed by Jews in any other country."

That clause, as you know, is troubling to many non-Jews since it appears to mean that Jews, alone among peoples in the world, can enjoy political rights in at least two countries.

Menachem quickly interjected:" I have no problem with the clause regarding the non-Jewish Palestinians, do you?"

I knew my friend was being disingenuous but responded in a calm voice. "The issue, my good friend, is what we mean by homeland. I think we will interpret it as it fits our needs. I am afraid that we and the British have colluded in a monstrous sham.

Menachem looked at me, his friend for the last five years as if he were seeing me for the first time. His voice showed his anger. "What you are saying is that this document hides something sinister that was agreed to by the British and the Jews. You refer to what sham. You accuse us of what."

I looked at my friend and chided myself for voicing my concerns— they will only make me enemies and unlikely to make my friend look through the same glass as me.

Menachem, wanting to avoid any further conflict decided there was a way to change the subject. "You know, the British and their allies haven't won the war yet."

"We agreed that once Britain had convinced America to come into the war, it was all but over. The Declaration is real and we must live with it."

"We must not only live with it, we should celebrate it.!"

"If the Balfour Declaration can keep faith with all of its language, it is a good thing. What worries me is that the internal inconsistency of a Jewish homeland and Arab civil and religious rights can only harm the Arabs because it allows the Jews to create a nation by crushing the Arabs. Two clauses in conflict with each other and only one will be honored. I hope I am wrong."

I remember wishing then I had just nodded when Menachem read the Declaration. Now, he must finish for his friend and for himself.

Menachem looked at me genuinely puzzled. "I don't understand."

"Let me put it this way. If this letter had been a letter to the Emir Hussein or one of his sons, and the clauses were reversed and Jewish civil and religious rights would be protected, I would have the same suspicion in the opposite direction, particularly if it were the British Empire acting as the guarantor, as is the case of the Declaration."

"I think you are overreaching," Menachem protested. I knew it was his way of saying he understood.

***

Was it really so long ago when he decided he no longer could be part of an inevitable travesty, of an amoral enterprise cloaked in sanctimony? Was it cowardice that drove him out, that caused him to leave his two wonderful children? Perhaps if his dear Rivka had not died. Of course, Rivka would never have left Palestine. It meant too much to her. But it was done. He remembered the faces of Sarah and Yitzhak. Sarah so beautiful and wise and Yitzhak filled with the pride that goes with belonging.

He awoke from his reverie, seeing the concern on the faces of his three friends. Morty still hovering over the chess board; waiting for his good friend. He smiled at Marty. "Cleaned out, wiped out or thrown out", mimicking his words. "You are a good man, Marty when you are a Jew. But you cannot always be a Jew and a Zionist at the same time."

He looked into Marty's angry face and thought of Menachem twenty years ago. "Forgive me, Marty. I shouldn't have said that. You are all my friends, please forgive me."

Marty was still practicing law. "So your sorry for saying what you did to your friends, but not sorry for what you said."

"Yes." It was not so fine a point.

The breeze was blowing off the river moving the leaves on the trees overhead. The sun's rays were disappearing, glistening off the tall buildings on the river's far side. The four men sat in uncomfortable silence for a while, then each rose from the bench and went their separate ways.

Arach walked slowly, regrets, new and old, aching inside him.

"Rivka, if you had stayed with me I would never have left."

"Pardon?" The little black lady walking alongside was looking at him.

"Sorry". I guess it's the day for saying I'm sorry, he thought to himself.

He smiled at the lady. "I talk to myself. My daughter takes after me. Just like you did to me, people will ask who she is speaking to." She has a nice smile, he thought. "My name is Arach. I live close by."

"So where does your daughter live?"

"Palestine."

"Palestine? You mean where Jesus was born?"

"Yes."

"Well, Mr. Arach, you take care of yourself." She smiled. "Maybe you should go visit your daughter. When was the last time you saw your daughter."

"Sarah", her name is "Sarah. About five years ago. What's your name?"

"Well, it seems to me you should be visiting her again soon." She looked at Arach. She was pleased she made him smile. "My name is Josephine. I got to go to work."

Part III

"…..my god, they are killing the prisoners"

October 20, 1938

Abraham Meyersohn has bylines in the London, New York and Paris papers. Not a young man, he got into the news business as a Trotskyite in Kiev. When he is asked to renew his contacts to get the news back to Moscow and Leningrad, he finds it easy to do so. He views himself, rightly, as a journalist and that is validated by his wide readership among Jews in America, England and France. He is looked upon as the source of what was happening in Palestine and the Arab uprising. Editors, already sympathetic with his journalistic views, seldom questioned the viewpoint expressed and suggested in his reports.

He is a Jew, he believed like Ben-Gurion, Jabotinsky, Shurtok and others in Palestine in a Jewish state. He remembers a time in his life when he would never accept views from only one side, and he would take risks to find the "other side." Older and a believer, what there was of the other side would have to come from the side he relied on. Sometimes the British offered a challenge to his reporting by reporting events objectively, sometimes even favoring the Arab version, but that could easily be dealt with by reports of others who tended to refute what the British source told him.

It could also be dealt with by knowing your sources. Once, he remembered asking the schoolmistress Sarah Nevers about her views on a bombing. He knew beforehand that she was once Jewish and decided getting another opinion from someone in Palestine would make his byline stronger. He remembered the steady gaze of this woman as she raised questions about his past reporting and the slant she accused him of seeking from her. She was no longer on the list of sources.

Abe was still a member of the Communist Party and a Trotskyite. But he found himself drifting away from the once bedrock beliefs of the Party. He did not believe, as the Party did, in trade unions of Arabs and Jews. He knew he had to break his ties with the communists but he found he couldn't do it. He could not forget what the Party had once done for Jews in Russia and that he had been part of it all. He knew they were fighting for Jews in Germany before they were crushed by the National Socialists.

He looked around him, his small two room apartment served as his office. On his desk, two wonder machines, the telephone and the miracle machine he could never stop admiring—his teletype machine. What he tapped out on teletype would be news around the world in hours. The words he fed into the machine were the words people around the world converted into reality-at least his version. Some journalists he talked to were awed by the power and soul searched about it. Abe didn't see it that way. It made him a celebrity—the whole world knew who he was and life couldn't be better.

The news reached him this morning about the explosion in the train station in Nablus. The call was from a source he often used. He called himself Avi. It was the second call from him, the first the night before when he told Abe a gang of Arabs were planning to place a bomb somewhere in Nablus. In his call this morning he said that Abu Kamal had been spotted by a station guard the night before who had failed to report it until this morning. By then, the bomb had exploded in the busy waiting area of the train station. He counted twenty dead and at least thirty treated at the scene or taken to St. Luke's Hospital. It was four o'clock in the morning in New York, midmorning in Paris and London. With luck the story would appear in the evening papers in New York and London. It would take him at least two hours to corroborate Avi's report, fill in the details and get comments from the British and the Agency.

October 20

The explosion occurred shortly after nine. By ten British soldiers were assigned sections of Nablus with orders to pick up all Arab men of a fighting age. Each of the sectors were assigned lorries used to carry the men to the internment camp. Lorries with squads armed with Enfield's and accompanied by armored cars mounted with Bren guns surrounded blocks of houses, forcing everyone into the streets. Suspects, meaning young men who could fight, were loaded into lorries. The loadings were quick and brutal, forcing the men to climb into the lorries, pressing them against each other until the tailgates had to be pushed into place by a half dozen soldiers.

Loaded, the drivers moved full throttle to their destination, the playing fields for the local Lutheran Mission School, now fully surrounded by razor wire. Hearing the whine of the engines before the lorries appeared, guards opened the crudely fashioned gates and the lorries sped to the center of the playing field, forcing captors to leap for safety. The process was brutally efficient, as British police accompanied by Agency police used batons to prod the Arab suspects to leap quickly from the lorries, where they were corralled by men on horseback away from the loading area.

At the west end of the camp, tents had been set up. The captured men were kept at a distance from the tents, where uniformed men, coming through a guarded entrance to the camp moved in an out.

Groups of prisoners began to move toward the tents, their angry shouts attracting the attention of others in the camp. Additional police poured through the west entrance behind the tents and formed a wall between the prisoners and the tents. The shouts born of anger and fear burst from the crowds because they knew what was about to happen in those tents, that one by one man would be beaten and tortured for information, then marked with paint so that they were only interrogated once and no one was missed. The process was known throughout Palestine. First the gentle approach, where the suspects, sometimes as young as ten years of age, would be asked for information and offered some sort of reward. For particularly promising ones, the rewards might be money and the promise for more if they would betray the others, others it would be the assurance that nothing would happen to their families or their property.

For most, the cool men sitting at the table facing the Palestinians would read the intense loyalty and defiance in their faces and know there was only the ways of pain, the fear of pain, humiliation, and threats against them and those they loved. In time those Tegart trained men knew that most men would break, that there is a point beyond which no man can resist, but they did not have the time needed.

The lists these cool men had at the table had no immediate connection to the bombing but had been kept since the uprising began two years ago. The list was updated weekly, subtracting those already in camps, those who had been killed and those whose names were removed because they could not be found after being missing for six months or more. Most of the names had been provided by the Political Department of Jewish Agency that assiduously noted every Arab deemed dangerous or potentially dangerous.

It was the list that became central to what would happen in the internment camp in the weeks to come to the thousands of men milling angrily about this hastily built prison. The British are very good at what was to happen within the camp. It had been tested throughout the Empire wherever restless men struggled to get out from under its yoke. And this was where the informers and the Peace Bands were most valuable. Before any interrogation would begin, a screening would be done, where each man and child, for some were no more than children, would pass through to be viewed by hooded informants. Those identified as being on the list were then segregated, awaiting the kind of interrogation that would not be possible for all of the thousands in the camp.

+++

Monet had crossed the border from Syria, crossing the Sea of Galilee by boat provided by Henri Bissett and escorted from Tiberius to Abu Kamal's camp. Once in camp, he had explained his plans to act as a freelance journalist and reporting on the revolt from the rebel side of the conflict. There he had met George and Ismael and it was agreed that Monet and George Bissett would decide which stories to dispatch from Palestine.

News that the Nablus Train Station had been bombed presented the first opportunity.

Two French speaking men among Arabs from Palestine on a mission fraught with uncertainty. Andre was sitting on a fallen log, watching the activity in the camp.

"George, I am surprised at something I did not expect."

"What is that?"

"They are like us. They think like us. Except for their religion, they believe in things just like we do. They talk of their families just as we do. They laugh at the same things, and grow angry at the same things."

"What did you expect?"

"I don't know but it makes me feel better about what we can do. I want them to have what every man has a right to, and I want to help them get it."

"Sounds awfully idealistic, Andre."

He smiled at the irony. "You're right, journalists should report what they see, not what they feel."

"Many of the rebels were educated in England and France, you know. My uncle studied at the Sorbonne. He could have remained as a professor if he chose to do so. That's why what you are doing is so important, to tell the world about Palestinians, to make it understand that here are people who not only deserve to have their freedom and independence, but that they are fully capable of running their own affairs."

Andre changed the subject. "How will we get to Nablus? Maybe we can start by asking our friends where it is."

They had worked their way into Nablus by late afternoon with Kalima as their guide. The trepidation Monet felt when they started their journey had vanished as he watched the Arab from Suffariya move about the city, confident in his contacts and quickly finding a small room where they would be safe.

Now, Bissett persuaded Monet that they needed to find a way to get the camera close to the internment camp to report on what was happening.

Reflecting on his earlier burst of enthusiasm for the Arab cause, Monet now thought of his companion as naïve, an idealistic lawyer fired by his uncle's bravery. That bravery, he thought, caused his uncle's death and Monet smiled wryly to himself: *I have other plans for my future.*

Yet he could not erase the feeling in his heart when he thought what he was doing. Yes, he was a journalist, and yes he dreamed of being famous, but what he was doing had meaning. It was the kind of against all odds quest that made him feel good about himself.

***

They had come to Nablus to get a story, to tell the world. Abu Kamal had told them his men had nothing to do with the bombing, that most likely it was the work of the Irgun, sanctioned by the Hagenah and the Jewish Agency. Blaming Arabs was part of the propaganda war to convince the British, who were wavering in their support of the Yishuv, and those that mattered in Paris and Washington. In

Palestine, it was to goad the British army to ramp up their already intensive eradication of Arab resistance.

What had started as a search for the persons who planted the bomb became something bigger when word reached them about the British response and the internment camp. Monet argued against Bissett's plan. It was too risky, even foolish. Bissett's plan unfolded in his mind when he heard that the internment camp was being set up at the Lutheran Mission School. Was it possible to place his camera nearby in a well-hidden place on the school grounds to photograph the internment of thousands of Arabs? Monet, when he first informed George Bissett that he would go to Palestine to write about the revolt, had not counted on anything so dangerous as this. Now he was caught in the web that had been woven by the cousin Henri Bissett in Beirut and there was no way out.

"You worry too much, my good friend." Bissett worried about his young companion. Would he panic and put himself at the mercy of the British. He looked into the eyes of Monet. "I hope you will not do anything foolish."

"What do you mean?"

"Turning yourself into the British figuring they will simply deport you back to France."

"It occurred to me, George. But no, I would not betray any of you. I understand the risks, far better than I did when your cousin first talked to me. What we began together we will finish together."

The British officer who appeared at the Lutheran Mission School on the morning of the explosion made plans not only possible but likely. When Captain Burton presented himself to the headmaster, he was courteous but firm that the playing field would be commandeered to intern persons suspected of aiding in the bombing at the train station. The headmaster was given no choice but to make arrangements for boarding students to find quarters elsewhere and for the school to be closed until further notice.

Kalima was able to secure a key to the main building and a room which had a view of the camp. That evening, the three had been able to set up the camera and await events the following day. George looked at his new friend from Paris. Together they would make the world stand up and take notice. He was part of something that would hold him all his life. Forgotten were the warm summer evenings in Cordoba and the comfortable life as a successful lawyer. Whatever the outcome, he would have something to say to the world about it. He prayed that God would grant him that chance.

It was hard to sleep. Through the night they were wakened by shouts, cries of anger and pain, and twice there were volleys of shots. They must trust Kalima to keep them safe, to get them back safely. Monet thought of the plan to get the dispatches and photos out of Palestine and to the newspapers. What if the papers didn't publish what they gathered? The what if's flowed into the minds of each as they rested fitfully, waiting for daylight.

Bissett managed to understand and speak to Kalima in Arabic which he had learned when his parents had decided he should go to American University in Beirut, his father had gone to the University when it was called the Syrian Protestant College. Knowing Monet was nervous, he dutifully translated each utterance by Kalima and his response. As the Frenchman's fears subsided, Bissett would translate only when asked.

"Have you thought what we would do, if something happens to Kalima?"

"You worry too much."

"I know." The sky had begun to lighten. "If Kalima is lost, do you think you can find the other one? What if the other contact is lost?"

Bissett was growing impatient with his companion but tried to keep it from his voice. "See that Church steeple. We will head for that."

"Sanctuary?"

Bissett looked at his companion, who was now smiling. Absurdity in the face of danger. He, too, broke into a smile. "I suppose the hunchback of Notre Dame might be there to sweep us up before the British could get their hands on us."

Monet heard it first. "Listen."

The muezzin's call to prayer seemed to echo against the buildings around them.

Allah is most great
Allah is most great
Allah is most great
Allah is most great

I testify there is no God but Allah
I testify there is no God but Allah

I testify that Mohammed is the Messenger of Allah
I testify that Mohammed is the Messenger of Allah

Bissett translated for Monet.

Come to Prayer

Come to Prayer

Come to Success
Come to Success

Allah is most Great
Allah is most Great

There is no God but Allah

"Look!" Monet pointed to the field in front of them. All but a few hundred among the thousands of prisoners were bowing to the east. Prayers could be heard.

Each looked at the other as if to speak but was silent. Monet broke the silence.

"I must talk to Kalima about what we see. I think it is a big part of the story."

"I was raised with Muslims, Andre. Their faith is very strong and deep. The strength and depth of our faith is far less. In some ways, I think we resent them for it, and often mask our resentment as contempt. Others envy them for something we have lost."

Almost light now, Bissett checked the camera which Monet had patiently taught him how to use. They both had seated themselves below the sills of the two windows in the class room. During the night they had debated whether to open the window where Bissett was seated to avoid the distortion that might be caused by the glass. They decided it was too risky.

They had devised a plan if the British decided to search the school building. On the same floor, there was a large storage room. Kalima had the key and it could be locked from the inside. If the building was being searched, they could quickly move into the storage room and hide among the desks. If the searchers found the door locked, it was likely they would not break the door down, instead deciding to search elsewhere.

Daylight colors began to return. By good fortune, the sun shone across the field in front of them until the entire playing field in brightly lit. With the light, new sound could be heard. The whine of truck engines that had ceased during the night now filled the air. Already, two trucks full of Arab prisoners were waiting at the gate, their motors idling as the guards moved to open the gates.

"Two trucks at a time, they empty, leave and two more."

Then the sounds of the unloading were overwhelmed by the shouting of the prisoners. Some were surging toward the gates. At first, they hesitated when the guards formed to block their path. The officer who stood with the guards had taken out his revolver. Bissett and Monet could hear his shouts. Bissett, collected himself to begin taking pictures. Monet spoke softly: "Wait, let us see what will happen." A journalist, he sensed something worthy of print was about to happen.

The officer fired two shots in the air and the mob stopped and fell back and then began to surge forward again. Lorries began to pull up to the gate, this time filled with British soldiers. The gates were quickly opened and the lorries sped to the center of the field, crushing those unable to get out of the way. Screeching brakes, then soldiers quickly jumping to the ground and forming up smartly.

"What is that sound." Bissett put his hand up as if to ask for silence. "A horn. A Bugle. Horses, hear them. They are bringing in mounted men!"

"Have your camera ready." It was Monet whose voice was calm building the story in his mind as it unfolded.

"Look behind the tents." The gate had opened and police mounted on thick chested horses poured through two at a time.

"They are going to charge the crowd in front of the gate. Get ready."

When the mounted police were all inside the gate, they formed a line and headed for the Arab men. As they entered the crowd, the policemen began swinging their batons, skilled to strike then pull them out of reach of the brave souls who tried to dismount the riders.

"My god, they are trying to kill the prisoners." Monet turned to Bissett, his voice higher. "Now, George. Get pictures of the bastards."

While the policemen were striking at anyone in reach, whether resisting or running away, the crowd was being corralled toward the soldiers who had formed into firing position. Some in the crowd, sensing the danger, began to turn toward the attacking mounted police, grabbing at the brides of the horses, grabbing at the feet of the policemen, trying to unseat them. Two horses with empty saddles could be seen galloping frantically, their riders fallen in the crowd.

The crushing of heads and the futile resistance by the prisoners lasted only minutes when the mounted police suddenly broke off their attack and headed toward the gate behind the tent. In tight formation, with bayonets fixed, the soldiers moved toward the two policemen on the ground who were not moving. The prisoners retreated to the edges of the camp. When the area where the melee occurred was cleared, men lay scattered in the field, some trying to rise, others laying still.

Both men were silent. Both had never witnessed what they saw today. Both had been baptized.

Then they saw something that escaped them when the trouble started. Many of the men were naked! They had taken their clothes and they were left in the compound naked. Grown men stripped of their clothes, their honor and their dignity.

It was Bissett who spoke. "So this is how the mighty Empire keeps its subjects under control. Rob them of their dignity, parade them in the streets naked for all to see. Well God willing" he tapped the camera "the world will see." He sidled away from the window, no longer able to just sit. "Perhaps Andre that is the point. Shock the world but remind it of where the power lies and what the consequences are if you don't kowtow to their power. He leaned against the wall, head down, as if he saw the world and it filled him with despair.

Bissett turned to look at Monet and the Frenchman was staring at him. "So, my dear friend, we just rip up our words and destroy our pictures because what is the point of it all?"

"What we have seen Andre does make that a possibility, doesn't it? It suggests a world that makes justice and injustice the tools of power. Power can choose to be just or not but the power itself has no rules, no limits except its own."

"I will not accept that world. I hope I will die not accepting it."

I, too, my friend."

"Is there any reason to stay beyond today?"

"The day is not over." Monet stared at something beyond the window and the fenced in Arabs." "It would be a mistake to stay here. If we are caught, all we have would be destroyed."

"And the two of us, as well."   -

They watched as British medics moved among the men on the ground. Some were put on stretchers, others covered to await removal.

"They are letting some of the men go. Kalima will bring some of them to us." That was the arrangement, that the best way to find out what was happening in the camp was eyewitnesses.

It was Monet who spoke. "Kalima will do the job for us."

October 21

The briefing was scheduled for the afternoon of the day after the bombing. Three reporters, one with a trailing cameraman stood in the cobble stoned square waiting near the British command post for the latest news from the British information officer. Le Figaro correspondent Andre' Monet stood apart from the other two newsmen as a British officer made his way to the podium. He was afraid, wishing George was with him. He moved to be near the other journalists, to hide in the crowd.

Captain Hennessy waited for the cameramen to set up in front of him, then began to speak:

"Yesterday morning, a bomb exploded inside the west entrance of the Nablus Railway Station. We now know there are twenty five dead, ten in critical condition and fifteen have been treated and released from St. Mark's Hospital. Our bomb experts have determined that a single explosive device was detonated using a crude fuse and timing mechanism commonly used by Arab rebels in the Nablus area.

"While we cannot say with certainty which rebel group is likely to be responsible for this cruel and cowardly act, the evidence points to the gang led by Abdul Al Haj Mohammad also known to some as Abu Kamal. Since yesterday morning, British troops have been rounding up suspects who are now being questioned by interrogation experts from Jerusalem. Tegart himself has taken charge of the interrogation operations. A special camp for this operation has been set up north of the city."

When he finished reading the release, he stepped down behind the podium and entered into conversation with a British officer and two civilians that lasted only a few moments before Hennessey returned to face the reporters.

"We have allotted ten minutes for questions and then the briefing will end. A copy of the statement from Colonel Burston which I have just read to you can be obtained from the Sergeant sitting to my right."

The first question came from Abe Meyersohn who identified himself as a reporter for Ha'aretz. Hennessy was aware that Meyersohn was also the voice that spoke to the world through the major newspapers in London, Paris and New York.

"Can you tell us something about those who died?"

"We can tell you that four of the dead were children, and eight were women. Of the ten in critical condition, two were children and three women.""

"How many settlers and how many were British civilians?"

Hennessy looked at the slim middle aged man who always looked as if he slept in his clothes. He could see the headlines of his story and the sub-heading. Arab Gangsters Kill 25 and then the numbers of Jews, British soldiers and British civilians. To Meyersohn, Arabs simply weren't worth counting except when they are killed by settlers or the Army.

"At this time, Abe, we think eight were settlers and members of their families, five soldiers and four British civilians."

"And the others?" It was the French correspondent who spoke.

Both Meyersohn and the others beside him turned to look at the tall dark man whose credentials showed him to be with Le Figaro.

Hennessy surprised by the question, but then thought why should he be. "There were Arabs, two children, two women and four men. Does that answer your question, Mr. Monet."

Before Meyersohn could ask his question, Monet, his voice now steady, spoke. "There are reports that thousands of Arabs have been rounded up, if that is a fair phrase, and are now in a barbed enclosure north of the city. Is this true?"

"Yes, you will see that in the release I just read."

"You mentioned suspects in your release? Are there thousands of suspects?"

Hennessy felt his face turning hot. "Many are, but many simply are being held for questioning?" He thought he saw a smile on the face of the Frenchman and felt his face grow hotter. He knew when that happened, his face became very red. Someone shouted at Monet. "They are all guilty. All of them would have lit the fuse if they had a chance."

Monet watched those around him. Meyersohn was staring at him. He tried to remain calm feeling the danger all around him. He did not want to bring all the attention to himself. But the next question that he must ask was critical to what he must do.

"How did the British decide that Arabs had detonated the bomb?" From the briefings he received before arriving in Palestine, he knew that the Irgun had planted several explosives with deadly effect and the rebels were blamed. He had to know. The world had to know. He could feel the sweat running down his back as he raised his hand again. The British officer was red faced as he leaned over to speak to one of the officers sitting next to him.

But it was Meyersohn who asked the question for him. "What evidence led you to the conclusion that the bomb was detonated by Arabs?"

"Two men were seen running from the Station minutes before the explosion. Witnesses said they were Arabs."

Meyersohn grimaced as he looked at Hennessy as if to say, you need more than that.

Hennessy added, "We have a reliable source that these two men belonged to the Abu Kamal gang and that they were bragging about committing this horrific act."

The third reporter, a small man dressed in a pressed white suit and wearing a tarbush then stepped forward to be heard by Hennessey. "Isn't it true that many of these bombs have been planted by the Irgun and made to appear that the rebels planted them?" The little man's voice trembled as he spoke whether in fear or anger. He was a stringer working for Filastin and a clerk at the Lutheran Hospital.

Glancing at the little man, then addressing his answer to Meyersohn, Hennessey spoke: "We often hear of such rumors, Mr. Darwadi, but we don't think there is any substance to them."

Mr. Darwadi started to speak but the Captain cut him off. "The briefing is over, gentlemen. Good day."

Monet looked at the little man, now muttering to himself. Those around him pointedly moved away until he was alone in the square but for Monet, who had thought of approaching him, but thought better of it and moved away. The British would no doubt check the credentials of Andre' Monet because he had pulled the tail of the British lion. Quickly, he moved to one of the narrow streets leading from the square, checking at intervals to see if he was being followed.

Part IV

"It seems we have a free-lancer in our midst. Monet no longer has Le Figaro credentials."

Shurtok had a busy morning. Using all the channels available to him he had spread the word of the bombing in Nablus by the Al Hajj Mohammad gang, and to implicate the Arab Higher Committee and Husseini. He was interrupted by his personal secretary: "You have a call."

"Who is it?" It had better be important. He had no time for most of the callers and his secretary guarded his time ferociously.

"Abe Meyersohn."

Shurtok sighed. He muttered to himself but loud enough for Chaim Levy to hear. "That man is a pest." Then yelling, "Put him through!"

"Hello, Abe."

"Hello, Moshe."

"You should sound happy. I have something for you."

Shurtok started to fidget. *That is the way Meyersohn always starts the conversation. When he wants something, he offers something first.*

"Well, Abe."

"I'm in Nablus getting some details on the bombing story. Nothing new you should know except there is a correspondent from Le Figaro here."

"Well, that's good. The more reporters from America and Europe the better."

"Maybe so, but this one asks funny questions."

"For instance."

"When I asked how many of our own and British were killed, he spoke up and asked how many Arabs, men, women, and children were killed. He then asked why, if there were two suspects, they had rounded up thousands of Arab men."

Shurtok was silent, then he spoke: "Do you have a name?"

"Andre' Monet, works for Le Figaro."

Shurtok wrote down the name. "I'll check it out. Anything else?"

"Yes, by the end of the week, the Arabs are going to wish they were on the other side of the Jordan."

"Good if they were. Goodbye, Abe. Keep in touch on this guy Monet. If I hear anything, you'll be the first to know."

Theinquiryregarding Andre' Monetbythe Agencywasdonesecretly, a friend of a friend contacted in Paris, the answer obtained over a late dinner in Montmartre. Monet did indeed work for Le Figaro as a correspondent. At his request, he was sent to Beirut. From there he was to proceed to Damascus and there make contact with the rebels. When he made contact, he was to send back dispatches on the fighting in Palestine. Two weeks ago he was recalled to Paris.

***

Meyersohn visited Shurtok, wanting to know what he found out about Monet. He already knew the answer to his question, but with barely hidden glee asked it anyway. "So what did you find out?"

"It seems we have a free-lancer in our midst. Monet no longer has Le Figaro credentials. We don't know his connections yet but journalists who become searchers for the truth are nothing new."

"The British have been notified?"

"Yes, they are looking for him now. They suspect he is still in Nablus."

"You think he was able to get near the camp?"

"We don't know." Shurtok glanced around, then lowered his voice. "Sometimes the British want to show us who is in charge by withholding information. We'll get the information anyway, just through channels they don't know we have."

Shurtok pushed his coffee cup away, signaling he was about to leave. "We'll find him if he's still in Palestine. Now, we have to wait to see where the story surfaces. We'll deal with it and him then."

"Photographs. Did he have a photographer with him? Someone with a camera?"

"I don't think so. The Brits had a cameraman, but I don't think there was another. Why do you ask? You don't think anyone would care about pictures of a British officer briefing correspondents?"

"No, but they would of what was happening in the camp at the Lutheran Mission School. We don't want those pictures to be shown around the world. Wavell and Montgomery should be able to keep that from happening." Meyersohn sensed the worry in Shurtok's voice.

"The British don't know, do they?"

The question jolted Shurtok, surprise showing on his face. Then the mask returned. Then the smirk that seemed always to be on his face returned. "Yes."

Meyersohn was surprised. "How could that be?" Looking into the face of the man across from him, he knew. "You told them." And then "Why?"

"Sometimes the Irgun is out of control." Shurtok fixed his gaze on Meyersohn. "The British are looking for Nelkin and Yellen."

"Raziel will not give them up."

"We'll see."

"Then why are the British rounding up Arabs."

"Montgomery sees this as an opportunity to weaken the rebels."

"And the Irgun."

"Yes."

October 25

Monet had arranged to send his dispatches and Bissett's photographs through Beirut. Although the border was closely guarded, by concealing the dispatches and photos inside bars of olive oil soap from Nablus, they arrived in Beirut five days after the Train Station bombing. Henri Bissett was able to convince Reuters to make their teletype and wire photo lines available. Within twenty four hours, all the major newspapers had copies of Monet's dispatch and Bissett's photos.

What transpired made a mockery of the claim that newspapers were only interested in printing the truth. In Paris, London and New York, it was ignored or made part of editorials which ignored the mass arrest and killings at the Lutheran Mission School and reported on the bombing and the deaths of British citizens and Jewish settlers. Abu Kamal was blamed. In Rome and Berlin, it was front page news, both the Monet byline and the Bissett photos.

Meyersohn dropped the Berlin newspaper on Shurtok's desk. Pictures of naked men being clubbed by mounted British soldiers and the Andre Monet byline were on the front page.

Meyersohn was looking at Shurtok like the Agency had failed the Yishuv.

"You know how things are when something like this happens. Total chaos. Still, how did the British let this happen? The pictures were taken from the school building."

"You read what Monet had to say?"

"Yes. I know he questions the British charge."

"He made the connection with the Haifa bombings."

"It might be a good time to get those two shmoks out of Palestine."

"Sadeh and Zelesney think they are doing a great job." Meyersohn was looking at Shurtok, knowing he couldn't control any of the Irgun fighters and wondering if Shurtok didn't feel the same way.

Both were looking at the photographs of the outdoor prison at the school. The photographer had been lucky or good, because the photo's showed British brutality at its worst.

"Such stupidity."

"You think there is a better way of dealing with Arabs."

"I mean letting a photographer get close enough to take those pictures."

"Do you think Monet took those pictures?"

"We think the photographer is George Bissett. Our sources say he came to Palestine with Latif. Crusaders. They were a problem nine hundred years ago and they are still a problem." Shurtok pulled out a pack of Turkish cigarettes and reached across his desk to offer one to the journalist. "Only now they are missionaries, government officials, politicians, journalists and whoever else wants to protect those poor Arabs." He waved his cigarette in the air, enjoying his moment on the stage, no matter an audience of one. "What Monet and Bissett have done can't be undone but they have to be stopped. And we need to close their pipelines."

"What do we know about the two?"

"We know who they are. We know Monet is from France and Bissett is from Argentina. Monet is new to the Arab side, if he is on any side at all, but Bissett is not. You know about Bissett's uncle. We are checking with our contacts in Beirut and by tomorrow we should have what we need. I will get in touch with you when we have enough. We need to respond quickly. Your byline will be helpful. We have contacted Le Figaro."

"Coty has been useful to us even after we ruined him. The new owner has been trying hard to stay on our good side." Meyersohn thought it clever to state the obvious.

Shurtok did not respond to the reporter except to say, "They will be sending us Monet's picture and anything that they think might be of use to us."

"Anything else?"

"Well, we will be spending a good deal of time with the British to find these two. I expect you can be helpful by getting the word out." Shurtok's tone, when he needed help from Meyersohn, turned respectful. He knew the value of journalism and Abe Meyersohn.

Shurtok stood signaling that the meeting was over. "I will have someone contact you tomorrow when we have anything new on these two. When you do prepare your byline, write that the British have announced that Monet and Bissett are wanted for aiding the rebels in committing the murder of innocents in the Nablus Train Station and will be hunted down."

Shurtok watched Meyersohn as he walked across the courtyard in front of the building. The man is useful but he wondered if beneath his compliant surface there was someone who yearns to be a journalist, one you could not trust.

***

The call came from Sergeant Morrison in Nablus.

"Hamish?"

"Speaking."

"Morrison. How are you, my good man? Hope the family is doing well. How is Glenda.... and the children?

"They're doing well. Just got a letter from Glenda. Little Hamish has the chickenpox."

"I'm sure he will be fine." Two seconds and then, "Sergeant, you heard about what happened at the train station the other day?"

"That I did, Harry. Sorry mess, huh?"

"The reason I called Hamish is that I read the statement you took from one of the Templers. His name is Hans Klein. Talks about two suspicious persons who might to be connected with the bombing in the marketplace in Haifa."

"That's correct, Harry." Hamish could feel his heart start to beat faster.

"Well, then there was the type of explosives used? Seems the type of explosives is the same in the bombing at the train station."

"So you think there might be a connection and the two people that Hans Klein saw might be the same ones involved in both explosions."

"We have reason to believe that the two bombers might live in your section of the country. I'm going to send you some photos and you can ask Hans Klein if he recognizes one or both."

"When and where did you get photos?"

"Avi Nelkin and Shlomo Yellen were picked up in the vicinity of an explosion in Nablus. They were questioned and released. The Sergeant there had his suspicions and sent their pictures to me."

"Good show, Harry. Look forward to getting them. Regards to the Misses."

"I'm not married, Hamish."

"Right. Goodbye, Harry."

Hanging up, Hamish thought what Hans Klein said about the two men.

"Could you describe them?"

"One was skinny, the other was thick but not fat. The skinny one was taller."

"Were they Arabs?"

"I don't think so but I don't want to say."

"Well, your next question would be do you think they were Jews and I don't want to say that, either?

"Could you tell me why?"

"I don't want to say."

To Hamish, it was clear enough that Klein thought they were Jews but was afraid, whether for himself or all the Templers. He knew they were having a hard time both with the British and the Jews since Hitler came to power.

He shook his head. Why is it the good and decent people like the Templers become victims of the madness around them? He knew about their bank that helps small businesses and farmers, about their farms which were models for the Jews and Arabs to copy, and their beautiful buildings and wide streets. And they are afraid and have good reason to be.

So now he would wait for the photographs and hope Hans Klein would tell him the truth when he showed them to him. He needed to know why they were picked up. Curious.

October 1938

The sky was clear and the weather cool as evening approached. Sarah walked in shade; above her the sun brightened the tops of the buildings on her narrow street. She listened to the familiar shouts of the shop keepers' next street over. Perhaps she should stop and to buy some fruit. Pears and apples from Syria had arrived this week. As she turned down the side street that led to the market, she noticed a shop she had never seen before, a stack of newspapers in front.

Sarah always read Ha'aretz. She knew some of the reporters who worked on the paper and liked the way they sought out the truth and printed it. She relied on it to keep up with what was happening in Jerusalem, but also in England, France and America

The third column on the first page was a familiar story. Another bomb, this time the train station in Nablus. The heading: Fifteen Dead In explosion. Al Hajj Mohammad Gang Suspected. The story was written by Abraham Meyersohn. She read the story as she walked. An eyewitness reported that Abu Kamal had been seen inside the train station the night before the explosion. British intelligence found evidence of pieces of the explosive device which fit the type of explosives being used by Arab gangs. At least fifteen reported dead and thirty were hospitalized at St. Marks Hospital.

Sarah read the article and shook her head. She found herself wishing she had The Filastin or Mir'at al-Sharq to read their account of what happened. Her many friends among the British, Jews and Arabs, both Christian and Muslim, would share accounts among themselves of what was really happening in Palestine that readers of Ha'aretz never would hear. Especially if they got their information from reading Meyersohn. With this reporter, there was a pattern. Most atrocities reported were by Arabs, and those committed by the British and Jews were invariably in retaliation for something more heinous committed by the Arabs. She knew, as well, that the news that went to London, Paris and New York would come from Meyersohn or someone like him.

She had often thought how important it was to tell the Arab story in London, New York, Paris and the rest of the world. If the rest of the world knew, then the story itself would change. She thought of George Bissett, the fearless editor of the Jaffa Times who was run down in front of his own home almost twenty years ago. There were no George Bissett's around today.

She hoped she would find a letter waiting for her at her apartment from Arach. Funny how she had taken to calling him Arach, not Papa. Mother would have thought that outrageous. It had been a long day. She eyed the small basket of fruit, savoring the sweet fragrance, and thinking how good it will be to curl up with a good book and enjoy one of those juicy apples.

+++

The British understood how to suppress revolts. Punishing villages, clans and tribes for the acts of one of more members was common practice throughout the Empire. Torture, random killings, putting suspected rebels meaning young men of a certain age behind barbed wire, all worked in keeping their colonies under control.

Paid informants were everywhere, weakening the rebellion. Creating an army of informants was an enormous undertaking, vetting and recruiting, spending hundreds of thousand pounds by paying handsomely for information, yet considered money well spent for the army was the eyes and ears of the Agency and the Mandate.

Finding the important people to corrupt in other ways was another, for greed was like a powerful magnet to such people, who cared little about those outside their extended families.

Powerful Arab nobles were paid to form Peace Bands. The Peace Bands were the brainchild of British Intelligence but were financed in large part by funds provided by the Jewish Agency. Uri Halevi, who had been present when the Peace Bands were formed smiled to himself: create bands of thugs, arm them, and turn them against the rebels and call them Peace Bands.

But money alone did not explain why every notable agreed to form Peace Bands. Some notables formed them to settle scores with other notables. Ersheid had agreed to lead a Peace Band for one reason only: to kill the man who killed his brother. That man was the leader of the rebellion- Al Hajj Muhammad.

Mustafa worked in the busy packing and shipping department at the soap factory, where traffic of factory workers, drivers, and buyers was a steady flow in and out of the factory. Everyone knew Mustafa and the young man always went out of his way to greet passersby, often to the chagrin of his boss. They also knew that he was related to Al Hajj. There was little question that he was a true patriot, one who was willing to fight for the cause of freedom.

It was Mustafa who was chosen to make contact with Hassan Latif and lead him north. Now he moved in front of the small band, returning often to talk with Hassan, to let him know what lay ahead. Hassan followed the young man as they moved deeper into the Sumerian hills. First light, the young guide led them under a rock overhang which shielded them from search planes, their sounds as they passed overhead sometimes echoing against the sheer rock faces of the hills. They would stay here until it was dark, safe from the searching eyes of the pilots and the foot patrols that passed silently on the trail.

By good fortune and the generosity of Allah, Hassan thought, a spring nearby allowed the men to quench their thirst, water the horses, and fill their canteens. It had been almost a year since he had seen his family for he knew their home would be watched. And he had long known the brutality of the British. The visible scars of the beating almost twenty years ago when they tried to find Ismael never let him forget. But joining the rebels for revenge had never been the reason for joining the battle against the British and their charges, the Jews. It was his acceptance, after years of denial that the aim of the Jews was to force every Arab and non-Jew to leave Palestine either by persuasion, death or banishment.

For years, his dear friend Sarah had persuaded him that living peacefully together was possible, and for years Jewish, Arab and British leaders had preached the same sermon, that yes we can all live together. And while there were Arabs who claimed that the Jews intended to drive the Arabs out, he could never accept such an eventuality was even being considered. Surely, the British were sincere when they issued the Balfour Declaration, surely the Jews just wanted to live in peace with their neighbors.

It was not any single act that brought him to the conviction that held him so strongly now. Instead it was labor programs which hired Jews only for farms and businesses, banks offering credit only to Jewish enterprises, trade policies that destroyed Arab farmers by flooding the market with cheap grain, creating educational institutions which only benefitted the settlers and now the creation of a Jewish army within Palestine. Only the blind could fail to see. When the fellaheen rose up two years before, he knew he must join them. He would fight for all the families who had lived in Palestine for generations whose dignity and livelihoods are being destroyed.

They were still in the shadows of the overhang though the sun lighted the cliffs above them. The men had been quiet throughout the day, speaking in hushed tones. Only the excitable young Mustafa had to be silenced by the steady stares of the rebels.

Hassan beckoned for the young man to sit beside him. Mustafa moved quickly, crouching down in front of him.

"Yes, sir?"

"I wanted you to tell me again where we will be by morning." He looked at the young man, noting he seemed nervous. I suspect I would be as well, he decided.

"It is an abandoned grain mill three miles north of Suffariya, sir. There is water there, and food, as well. There is a trail west of the village. Horses will be waiting for us."

Hassan smiled at the young man before him. Standing up and gesturing to Mustafa to do the same: "Then we will depend on you to get us there safely." As the young man started to walk away, Hassan called to him." When will we reach Abu Kamal's camp?"."

"I do not know where our commander's camp is. The guide who will lead you to the camp will be at the mill."

"Will you accompany us to the camp?"

"No, I must return to Tulkharem."

Shadows now covered the ravine where they waited. Checking their campsite to see that nothing was left behind, the men, led by their point man Abdullah and beyond him the boy Mustafa, began the long night journey. Tomorrow night, Hassan thought, the horses can do the walking.

October 1938

Joshua Purdom felt the adrenalin rush when he heard the news. Ismael Latif was in Palestine! The man who died a fiery death almost twenty years ago had come back to life. The man who fought against the Jews and British twenty years ago was somewhere in Palestine. Eighteen years ago the British told the world they had killed Ismael, trapping him in Ramleh and burning him alive when he barricaded himself and refused to surrender.

But among the Palestinians, Ismael had never died, he had escaped and would return. Among the British community, Ismael was always spoken of as the terrorist killed by British soldiers, a reminder that resistance to British rule was futile. Not until a year into the revolt, was it revealed by Jewish intelligence that Ismael was alive and Jewish leaders had always known what had happened in Ramleh, when a Jew, Yitzhak Poletsky sacrificed his life for his friend.

During interrogations, Purdom had often been confronted with taunts when his prisoners compared him to Ismael and he had thrown the taunts back" Where is your great hero now?! Let him show his face! We will do to him what we have done to the rest of your sorry race!" But the taunts had made him lose control and the anger he felt over his weakness and the thoughts of this Arab hero made the treatment of the man before him all the more brutal.

He would find him and he would kill him. Not his men, not the Jewish militiamen, but he personally would kill this man. He was pleased to know that the Jewish militiamen called him Shammah, David's Mighty Man, he would pursue his enemy and kill him in hand to hand combat. Then the taunts inside him would end.

Patrols had covered the coastline when word came that Latif had slipped out of Marseille. There were reports that there was another

107

with him, but that was unimportant. No one was found on the beaches or inland on the night he was to return. It was a fortuitous night for the Arab, for the coastline north of Tel Aviv was blanketed by rain squalls and a heavy mist drifted across the sea and miles inland. Somehow, he had slipped past the British ships patrolling the coast and British and Hagenah patrols which were so numerous that patrols could hear others close by.

Reports from Marseille, usually reliable, noted that Ismael and another unidentified man had boarded a ship and the information the informants had was that the ship was heading for Beirut. It was assumed that somewhere between Marseille and Beirut, a power boat would be launched from the ship to a destination on the Palestine coastline. Purdom did not doubt the man was here in Palestine; he had slipped past the patrols and was heading for a rendezvous with one of the rebel leaders. .

It was very clear from the speed at which the information on Ismael Latif came down the chain of command that Latif was a very dangerous man. Montgomery had made it clear that he must be found and quickly. His orders were also clear, Ismael was not to be taken prisoner. No one with him was to be taken prisoner.

Others had received the same orders as he. Others would see killing Ismael as assurance of a bright future in the military or outside it. He would find him. He had a weapon none of the other British or Jewish units had. His raiders, tough, smart, cunning and without scruples which governed ordinary men, they were hunters of men. That he used members of the Hagenah in his units gave him another advantage. Most British units of Montgomery Eighth Infantry Division did not include Jewish militia. Not only were they denied the services of militia with their high morale, they were denied the immediate access to the intelligence of Sherut Yediot and the hundreds of informants paid by the Agency. It was from Sherut Yediot and its director Sadeh that he learned Ismael's brother was among the rebels.

He thought of the young Leftenant Cartwright chasing Hassan and was thankful he had not caught him. The circumstance of Hassan's escape from the Old City and Ismael's arrival in Palestine within days of each other was almost too good to be true. For Hassan was heading north and most likely to make contact with Al Hajj Mohammad. Some would say with luck he would find Hassan and Hassan would lead him to Ismael Latif. Not entirely, he thought, for he now knew who would lead him to Hassan.

***

Wavell considered the cable from London speaking of the urgency of ending the revolt, of crushing the rebels quickly. Mussolini was in Ethiopia, threatening Red Sea passage through the Suez Canal. Continued resistance increases the risk of Arab alliances with Germany and Italy. A month ago, Montgomery had informed Wavell that it was only a matter of weeks before the end. Tegart's fence and torture chambers had done the job well. Harris's recons and fighter bombers gave the rebels no place to hide. Anyone deemed a threat was either hanged, shot, deported or put in holding camps. Montgomery, with overwhelming force, had broken the back of the revolt. Wavell thought about his general. He had all the attributes of a colonial soldier, brutal, efficient and pitiless.

Any assessment of conditions would lead to the conclusion that one rebel, whatever his abilities, would mean little in determining the outcome. But he recalled the stories of Latif and he wondered. Ismael Latif must be found and eliminated. His orders were to do it quickly

October

Only the stars lit their way as the men moved silently toward the mill. Hassan moved close to Mustafa. A lesson learned long ago, to trust few and never strangers. In the darkness he tried to read the face and body movements of the young man as they moved closer to Suffariya. "How far to Suffariya?"

"Less than one mile. The trail comes very close to -the village."

Hassan turned to the man behind him. "Less than a mile to the village. Pass the word. Complete silence."

They had entered into a valley after a slow descent for the last hour. Flames could be seen rising above Suffariya. Soon the smell of smoke drifted through the column. Some of the men had never been away from Jerusalem and the surrounding villages and had no firsthand experience of the destruction by the British and Jewish militia of the villages to the north.

Hassan turned again. "Tell them they may be nearby." The "they" were many, the British, Jews and Nashashibi "Peace Bands". Hassan had been north and saw first- hand what happened to villages, killings and destruction, young men driven from their homes into concentration camps, goats and cattle slaughtered, grain fields burned. He knew some of the men would want to go into the village to help and for revenge. He knew as well that was what the British wanted and they would be waiting.

"We will not stop." The men understood and the column moved past, blocking from the minds what they knew was happening in Suffariya. Looking back they could still see the fires burning and smell the smoke, now mixed with the morning mist. The mill lay ahead. There they would be a second guide who would lead them to the camp of Abu Kamal.

+++

Reverend John McDermott was a newcomer to Palestine and he thought of himself that way. As a newcomer and an outsider, he thought perhaps he might see things differently than others and perhaps, just perhaps, that would make his service useful to others. At this moment, pondering the meaning of his recent encounters with the rebels and the British soldiers, he once again encountered that nagging feeling that he must do more. The stories he heard from the village and his friends in Bethlehem and Jerusalem were about death, suffering, brutality and destruction. Some spoke of the rightness of their cause, to rise up against the tyranny of the British and their Jewish clients, but most spoke of the consequences of the uprising, of the brother, father, son or cousin hanged for having a weapon, killed in battles with British soldiers and Jewish militia, placed in concentration camps or in hiding like wild animals.

By nature and nurture, he identified with the underdogs, the poor and the downtrodden. But how could he help? He was struck by the thought that for three great religions, Palestine and Jerusalem are the center of their earthly universe. The land called Palestine has been coveted for thousands of years. There were thriving civilizations thousands of years before the Jewish tribes came out of the desert and conquered it. In the Old Testament it is the land promised to them by Yahweh.

Then they lost the land to people from the east, reclaimed it and lost it to the Roman Empire. Like the Jews, the Mohammedans came out of the desert but from the Hejaz and claimed the land for Allah. It was on the site of the great Jewish Temple that they built the Dome of the Rock and the Al Aqsa Mosques. It is here that Mohammed was carried to heaven. And it was here in Jerusalem that Christ died and rose from the dead and here that Christianity began. For three faiths, holy ground yet ground where there is no peace.

How can the sacred places of the three major religions be protected, and how can Palestine be restored as a place where all the religious can move about in safety? The British, for all their faults, were wise enough to control the administration of the holy places as it was when the Ottoman's ruled. He smiled when he thought the most difficult questions arose among the Christian faiths as they battled for their places in the Holy Land. Somehow, whatever the strains, the Catholics and Protestants, the Eastern and Western Churches managed keep their frictions out of sight of the pilgrims. He smiled to himself. "Most of the time."

Somehow, a way must be found to bring the people who live on this land to feel jointly responsible for all the holy places, to hold the land in trust for the hundreds of millions of believers of the three faiths all over the world. They must be made to understand that the land belongs to no one yet everyone throughout the world.

He began putting together a list of persons who might be receptive to the ideas bouncing around in his head. Of course, Sarah was at the top of the list and he made no pretense as to why. Tomorrow he would put his plan to develop a plan in action.

October

The grain mill was built on the south side of a steep hill; a stream that ran down the side of the hill turned the large wooden wheel that ground the grain. The only sound was the creaking of the large wheel as it turned, the lone watchmen lay hidden from the entrance, the blood from the gaping neck wound thickening until it no longer flowed but formed a pool that framed the dead man's head. Above the mill, light from the stars turned men into gray specters.

The raiders entered the mill two hours after dark, observing it from a nearby hill, moving in when only the night watchman remained. An old man with an ancient Turkish Mauser rifle moved slowly about the mill, until bored, he placed his rifle against a wall, and lay down to take a short nap. He woke, startled, his cries muted by his slashed throat. Quickly, the men moved into the positions directed by their commander, Purdom. They would wait, patient and ready. Trained ruthlessly by Purdom, they grew ever more deadly, their skills honed by the dozens of raids much like this one. In the dark, with the small amount of light of the moon, black uniforms, black boots, and blackface on their face and hands, they waited.

It was Shiskin who spotted the man moving silently toward the mill, coming from the north. He whispered to Purdom, "The guide from Muhammad's camp?" Purdom nodded.

"Take him alive." He would tell them where to find Muhammad's camp.

They watched as the intruder entered the mill. He seemed oblivious to any danger, looking about for a resting place to wait for the men coming from the south. He was to lead them to the place where the horses were waiting for the trip north. As he walked past the center post, he was grabbed, bound and gagged. Now they would wait.

***

Mustafa walked beside Hassan, not speaking but guiding by hand gesture .The trail had narrowed once past Suffariya, thick bushes on each side. They were climbing now; the incline lessening as they moved. As they reached the crest of the hillock, the grain mill appeared, its gray stones reflecting the starlight.

Hassan raised his hand and moved among his men. He put his hand on the shoulder of one of them that had been with him the longest.

"Ra'eed, we need to be careful. This could be a trap." He looked quickly at Mustafa, who seemed to tense then force himself to relax.

"If you wish, I will go with Ra'eed. I am not afraid."

"Stay beside me, Mustafa."

***

The rebels watched the agile fighter move quickly down the slope, moving from cover to cover until he was at one of the openings, then disappearing inside.

Purdom watched the man enter the building. He could not help but admire how quietly the man moved. They were being tested and it made his blood rush. If his men did not panic, if they controlled their breathing and did not move, they could be passed within feet and still not be discovered.

In the moonlight, they saw the figure emerge from the mill and continue up the path heading south. He motioned to Shiskin? Did he see the body? He cursed himself for not dealing with that detail. If the intruder had discovered the body, the ambush would fail. He wanted Hassan and he wanted him alive.

He thought of the informant, Mustafa. Purdom hated informants but relied on them. Throughout Galilee, those who accepted pay to inform knew with Purdom they were as apt to be punished as rewarded, yet all knew they had no choice if he approached them. Some had the courage to say no and they or their families suffered the consequences.

***

"Did you see the night watchman? The building would never be unguarded. You saw no one, Ra'eed?"

"There was the smell of death."

The men had moved close enough to hear what the two men were saying. They began to move around, sensing something was not right.

Hassan turned to Mustafa who had started to move away from Hassan. "Your instructions were to lead us here and a second guide would meet us. Do you know when that person was to arrive?"

"No, sir."

Hassan could feel his heart pumping. Before an attack, it was the same. The mill was no more than a hundred yards to their front. He followed the trail with his eyes. It was possible to move around the mill but could it be done without being seen?

Beckoning the men toward him, it was time for council, to decide what they should do. Hassan spoke softly: "I think they are waiting for us inside the mill." Most of the men nodded their heads in assent.

"We do not know how many men are inside. We must move around the mill and find another hide out before light."

Ahmed, one of the youngest among them, spoke: "They may have a radio with them. If they find we are not headed for the mill, they will contact other units ahead of us."

One of the men pointed toward the mill. "Mustafa was running toward the mill."

"No!" Hassan ordered one of the men who had raised his rifle to shoot the fleeing traitor. They watched as he reached the entrance to the mill, now shouting and then disappearing inside.

Hassan pointed to the west, the small band moved toward the hills outlined against the night sky. There was little cover until they reached the hills, more than a mile away.

They were no more than 100 yards from the trail when the firing started. Knowing they had been discovered, the raiders raced toward the trail to catch sight of the fleeing Arabs. The ground before the hills was flat; the British and Jewish fighters had clear fields of fire almost to the foot of the hills.

All around him, Hassan could hear cries of pain as men are hit. One's that were hit struggled to keep moving, knowing what would happen if they were caught alive. He begins to have hope when the .303 bullet rips through his back, then falling face down in the open field.

+++

The ground was covered with a predawn mist as the raiders moved from body to body..

"How many are alive, Corporal? Corporal Mathers was the medic assigned to the unit. "All of them, some are in worse shape than others." Purdom looked at the Corporal. "When I address you, say sir, Corporal."

A step behind Purdom, Mustafa followed. Without turning, Purdom spoke to him. "Is Hassan Latif among them?"

"Yes, sir." He pointed to Hassan who was lying on his back. Purdom called to Mathers. "Over here, Corporal." As the Corporal presented himself with a smart salute, Purdom glared at him. "You are new to our squad, Corporal Mathers or you would know better. Never salute me or any officer on the battlefield. Is that clear, Corporal."

"Yes, sir."

"There may be a sniper nearby looking for field commanders and your salute is like my death warrant."

"Yes, sir." Gritting his teeth, the young soldier played with the thought of using that to get rid of the bastard.

"Corporal, do your best for this man. I want him alive."

Moans came from three of the men, sometimes a sharp cry of pain. One lay still and Mathers guessed he was dead.

"What should we do with these men, Corporal?

"I think we can save some of them, Sir."

"They are of no use to the Yishuv or the Empire." Mustafa walked behind him. "Which one is Hassan Latif, Mustafa?"

When Mustafa pointed a trembling finger at Hassan, Purdom nodded. Pulling his Webley .455 from his holster, Purdom moved from man to man, shooting each point blank in the head. Some were looking right at him as he placed the barrel within inches of their forehead and fired. When he came to Hassan, he smiled. "We have other plans for you. You can help us find your brother."

The bullet had struck Hassan in the left shoulder, shattering bone and ripping through the shoulder muscles. He was conscious now as he looked into the cruel face. "In another time, a man as cruel as you was after the same thing. I still bare the marks of that encounter on my body and here." He pointed to his head. "Do with me as you wish, I will not help you find him."

Purdom looked at the man who lay on the ground in front of him. He thought of the others who had said almost precisely those words. Few could endure the mental and physical torture of the interrogators. "We shall see, Mr. Latif. We shall see."

Mathers instinctively moved to collect the bodies for removal. He learned another lesson from the strangers he thought he knew. One of Jewish militia shouted at Mathers. "Leave them. Let the vultures have them!" Mathers looked at Purdom who nodded and walked away. Mathers watched his stiff backed leader. What kind of man is this? Fond of quoting the Bible, declaring he was doing the work of God, retelling the stories of Shammah and his victories, Mathers wondered, as he had many times, if this peacock had ever read the New Testament. His own ego, when offered a spot with Purdom's raiders, had trapped him. He had to find a way out, but he had to be careful. Burton, who was often berated by Purdom for "not being respectful enough" had been killed during a recent firefight outside Haifa. He was shot in the back. When examining Burton, Mathers asked one of the men nearby what happened. "Best leave it alone, mate." The Brit who made the statement had not even turned to look at Mather as he spoke, and continued on his way. He would have to be careful but he had to find a way.

117

Mustafa could not control his trembling hands nor hide his fear when he spoke. After identifying Hassan Latif, he was ignored by Purdom. He had heard terrible stories about the man some called Shammah and now he knew them to be true. He had been told by eyewitnesses of the hatred for all Arabs by this Arab speaking man. Now, he must appeal to him to help him escape, for he could not return home. He could feel the eyes of Hassan's men who escaped and were in the hills watching. If he returned home, he would be killed.

After agonizing moments following Purdom, he called out: "Please sir, can I go with you. If I return to my home, I will be killed."

"You were paid, were you not?!"

"Yes, sir."

"Then we are finished with you. You have betrayed your brothers and we have paid for your services."

Mustafa could hear the laughter of the other men. He glanced at the hills then back to Purdom. "But they will kill me."

"That is your problem, Mustafa."

"What can I do?"

Purdom glanced at the hills where he, too, suspected men were watching. "Run." The officer moved closer. "Do not follow us."

Mustafa looked toward the hills, tuned away from them and began to run. Perhaps the pastor will protect him. He would not know what he had done.

A sergeant pulling a pack mule carrying a radio approached Purdom. "Sergeant, get Sector Command on the radio. We need a prisoner taken to hospital. Let them know we have a wounded high priority Arab, the brother of Ismael Latif."

118

The men formed up in front of their commander. As with all the battles in the countryside, vultures appeared high above, circling as they glided ever closer to their prey. The rim of the hills to the east turned rainbow colors as the sun rose and the landscape brightened. The shadows that hovered over the dead men were moving east, and soon they would be immersed in the bright sunlight. Silently, the raiders began moving, heading north. Two stretcher bearers carried the wounded Arab. Their commander had considered leaving some men to wait for Hassan's men to recover the bodies but his new mission was more urgent.

The captured guide was on his feet, a rope around his neck and held by a squad member. Purdom looked into the man's eyes. Defiance? Fear? Courage? No matter. The questions could wait. They must get Hassan to a hospital.

Part V

"Well we're only talking about part of the deal, Poletsky had a lot more to say."

October 25

Sam Watkins pondered the dispatch and photos that crossed his desk this morning. As Editor of the Cleveland Herald, he pretty much decided on everything that went into the paper. When he first saw them, Lowell Thomas came to mind. Thomas had become famous for his dispatches about Lawrence of Arabia. He tried to recall Lawrence's real name but couldn't. Now this from someone named Andre Monet with accompanying pictures taken by George Bissett. The story and photos had been offered to him by Reuters and he had to give some thought to buying them given the tight fisted owners he had to contend with. The article was good writing and the photos caught his eye. What made him hesitate was the subject matter—Palestine and what was happening in an Arab revolt. Wasn't that what Thomas was writing about twenty years ago—an Arab revolt? Is Palestine and what the English are doing to the Arabs worth printing?

Watkins thought of his old friend for many years Henry King. Henry was the President of Oberlin College for years and has been gone these last four years. I miss the old gentlemen, always putting in a plug for the College when they saw each other. Henry was passionate about Palestine, and often talked about how badly the English had treated the Arabs in Palestine. He had been appointed by President Wilson, along with a rich guy and big Wilson supporter named Crane to go to the Middle East and then come back to advise the

120

President on what we should be doing there. Henry sent me a copy of the King-Crane Commission report shortly after we met.

I remember he told me something else that didn't mean much at the time. He told me that we had printed the report right after the War, right at the time when the British, Americans and French were deciding how the world should be run. Henry grew angry when he talked about the report because he claimed it was buried and not released to the public until 1922, after all the big decisions about the Middle East and Palestine had been made. He said how disappointed he was because Henry's and Crane's recommend-dations were based on what the people in Palestine wanted, which was a free and independent state for the Arabs, Christian and Muslim, and including the Jews that lived there.

He remembered asking why Wilson who was always preaching to the world about democracy would ignore the report. Henry got pretty excited then and said it was all back room politics and Zionists like Lewis and some of the important bankers in New York convinced Wilson to support the English plan to let the Jews colonize Palestine, to create a state there. He told me that the people who lived in Palestine had no objection to allowing Jews to immigrate to Palestine, but the people there should be allowed to govern themselves and decide who should be allowed in their country, Jews or others. It was our policy, he said, and the people there should have the same rights as us.

Watkins made a point of knowing what the other papers in America were printing. He recalled articles in the New York papers which were almost exclusively about the Jews making the desert bloom in Palestine and remembers vividly the Hebron massacre of Jews almost ten years ago. He had been surprised with the extensive reporting in some papers because many of the Jews he had talked to who were big advertisers in the Herald were not enthusiastic about a separate Jewish state. They were doing very well in America so why did they among all the groups in America need a separate country. Still he wondered if his friends had been completely honest with him since some might worry that they would be perceived as disloyal to America.

Should he give the go ahead to print Monet's dispatch and Bissett's pictures? The world was full of stories fit to print. Europe was in a mess and anti-German sentiment was riding high among those who mattered in this country and some were crying for us to stop Hitler and changing their tune on Russia. He knew the country overwhelmingly wanted us to stay out of a war in Europe but he was old enough that he remembered people thought the same about the war in Europe before 1917 but we went over there flags flying.

Should he send the dispatch and the photos to be printed? Old editors feel things in their bones. If the President could bury the story, why not the editor of the Cleveland Herald? Still, he had always been a champion of lost causes. Sam Watkins was a shrewd man, the editor of an important Midwestern paper for twenty years. There are lost causes and there are lost causes. Most made him a hero among the devoted readers of the Herald. There were no Arabs in Ohio to cheer him on, to hold him erect when the winds of criticism swept through the Herald building. No big Arab advertisers. The photos and dispatch sat of the corner of his desk, the round file immediately below. Watkins stood and leaned forward. With a deft flick of his wrist, both slid to the edge of the desk, teetered for a split second, then disappeared. He wondered how many other editors did the same and knew he was not alone.

November, 1938

Senators Phillip Hollister and Robert Bruce were at opposite ends of their Senate careers. They had met at one of the briefings arranged for them at the beginning of the new term. Senator Hollister had served his state of Ohio for four terms and Senator Bruce was fresh from the Governor's office in Missouri. As the Senators moved around the room, the newly elected ones working hard to be remembered by the colleagues when the time for committee assignments came, and the old ones graciously shaking their hands, looking intently into their eyes and telling them their doors would always be open, sometimes connections were made which held promise to last. When the senior senator from Missouri introduced the younger Bruce to Phil Hollister, both recognized something special about the other.

By virtue of his seniority and his interest in foreign affairs, Hollister was the Chairman in waiting if his party ever succeeded in controlling the Senate. Freshman Senator Bruce on the other hand, was at the bottom his class and in the same losers party as Hollister. They had something in common. Both found their interests in what was going on beyond America's borders. A few minutes together and Hollister decided the younger man would be an able partner on the Committee.

Now, with only a year to serve and no particular interest in maintaining bridges between his present position as Senator and his future in the law office which would add him as a partner and give him a prominent position on the letterhead, the Senator was beginning to be referred to as a loose and dangerous cannon.

Bruce, who had developed a loyalty to his new older friend, approached his new job with a recklessness that labeled him as a one termer. Although Bruce had come to enjoy the culture to which he was introduced, his unwillingness to be patient and his estimate of his own abilities made his actions remarkably like his older new friend. Often seen together, they were seen as two loose and dangerous cannons. The significance of that to those who viewed them as troublesome was that two such men acting together were far more dangerous than two such men acting separately.

The danger they posed became apparent in Hollister's last year and Bruce's second.

The painful aftermath of an already tragic world war was evident everywhere in the world. Untied from the alliance with British, the Japanese had crossed the Sea of Japan and invaded China, Mussolini was expanding Italy's empire in Africa, and Hitler had risen to claim the German speaking lands lost in the World War.

Both Senators agreed that America could not isolate itself from what was happening around them but both were wary of those who wanted America to take the side of England in Europe whatever the British decided to do. They were convinced that America would be best served if there was some knocking of heads on both sides of the brewing conflicts and we did not embolden England to be reckless in its foreign policies. They agreed that the Treaty of Versailles needed some revision and at the same time Germany needed to understand it could not be allowed to threaten its neighbors and risk a war. They were Midwesterners who did not have the attachments that the Eastern Establishment had to Britain and were wary of the bankers on Wall Street, as America should have been before it entered the War In 1917.

Keeping America out of another European war was not going to be easy, as difficult; even more difficult than the unsuccessful effort to keep us out of the last one. The major newspapers were already at work stoking the fires. Hollywood, with its immigrant ties to Russia and the Jews in Germany was already unleashing a barrage of anti-German and pro-Russia propaganda.

As often happened, the junior senator and the senior one would meet at Ebbit's grill. The ritual had already been established that two clean glasses and a bottle of bourbon would precede any talk. Patrick, who had been behind the counter for as long as Hollister remembered, kept the bottle under the counter. Waiting for a nod from the Senator the bottle and the two glasses appeared. As Hollister poured, he spoke to his new friend.

"There's going to be a war in Europe unless they put some of the people in charge over there in the nut house and find some sane ones to take their place."

"Lots of very important people want us to get in on Britain's side and Churchill is a little crazy even when he's not three sheets to the wind. I think he wants a war and he's pretty sure of Roosevelt if it happens."

"America doesn't want to go to war."

"Money and power versus the people." Bruce was not smiling when he added "And we know which one wins in that contest."

"That damn tag they put on people who don't want a war pisses me off. We're isolationists. We don't support getting our young men slaughtered and we're isolationists."

"Face it Phil, we are not going to beat them with slogans. That's what they do." Bruce hesitated. "They being the big city papers, Wall Street bankers and that crowd out there in California...and the camp followers scattered here and yon."

Hollister looked at the younger man, full of piss and vinegar. "I had a thought. What do the war hawks want the most?"

"I have to think about that."

"I know that's a hard question to answer. Put it another way, what could Congress do to diffuse a lot of the pressure to go to war."

"We could be here all night. Patrick will have to throw us out." They were sitting in a back booth at the Ebbitt Grill, which belonged to Hollister for over twenty years.

Hollister reached into his breast pocket and dropped a letter onto the table. He tapped the letter with one of his thick fingers. "Read it."

The junior senator from Missouri picked it up and immediately looked at the signature. "Arach Poletsky?"

"He was in Washington last week. Dropped in, talked to Jake Roberts, who thought I should talk to him. He had a lot to say about

125

the Jews in Germany. He said we should negotiate with Hitler to let the Jews emigrate. Since Hitler has been ranting about Jews, and has the German people riled up, the Jews are in real danger."

"How many Jews is he talking about?"

"Hundreds of thousands."

"So how do we benefit. What would we tell the people who elected us."

"Number one, it might keep us out of a war and save millions of lives."

"Is this you talking, or Mr. Poletsky? And who is Mr. Poletsky?

"Well we're only talking about part of the deal, Poletsky had a lot more to say." Hollister stopped to sip his bourbon then continued. "Poletsky is a fascinating guy. Really fascinating. When he was a young man, he emigrated from Russia to Palestine and headed up the Jewish National Fund, that had lots of money, much of it from America, to buy land for Jewish immigrants."

"So why is he in America?"

"Hey Patrick, we need a pot of coffee. He's in America because....he didn't say why, but I think I figured it out."

Bruce looked at his friend. He is really enjoying himself.

"Arach was a very successful investment banker in New York. He made a lot of money in the 20's and came out in pretty good shape when the markets collapsed. He didn't tell me that. I found out from other sources. Turns out he lives in a modest apartment and spends his time kibitzing with his friends in Lower Manhattan. They play a lot of chess."

"Two hours to closing time and my wife thinks I'm meeting with constituents. So what was your friend proposing?"

"One other thing I noticed about Arach. His eyes were sad, there was a sadness in his eyes and the way he talked and moved. My sources told me why. What they told me I'll tell you another time.

"What he proposed might sound fanciful but I think it makes sense. He proposed a bunch of quid pro quos where all the countries involved had to agree to allow the Jews to immigrate, so no one country would have to absorb them all."

"And what do these countries get out of it."

"There's a whole list. You get doctors, scientists, professors, engineers and a population better educated then the majorities in the countries that would take them."

"Then there is the money. We would offer some quid pro quos to the Germans to allow those leaving Germany to take their liquid assets with them and that these liquid assets would go to the country taking in the immigrants."

"The Germans, of course, would be rid of their Jewish problem and they would be promised a return to the trading terms that existed before we, Britain and France began squeezing them."

"Sounds like he's given this a great deal of thought."

"You don't run into Arach Poletsky's every day."

"Anything else on the list?"

"If the Jews buy into this proposal, it lessens the likelihood of war and muzzles Churchill, who is beating his war drum everywhere he goes."

"Are you done?"

"One more thing, well, two more."

"Arach wanted us to lean on the British to stop immigration to Palestine?"

"Are you serious? Why would Arach Poletsky, who immigrated to Palestine want to do that."

"There's a lot more to the story, but Arach Poletsky could no longer support Jewish immigration which was forcing the Arabs off their land. He saw what was coming, which is the violence in Palestine today, and didn't want to be part of it."

"I don't think my Jewish constituents and supporters, what few a Republican has, are going to be happy about that."

Hollister looked at Bruce over the bourbon he was holding. "There's another reason we should get some movement on this, Bob. It's the right thing to do. How many times do we have a chance to get behind something simply because it is the right thing to do. Millions of people could be saved. It would make the countries who take in the immigrants stronger. The only country that will be hurt is Germany and they may be the most enthusiastic of all the countries involved."

"Sounds like Arach Poletsky made an impression. Why did he want to see you?"

"No one else was interested in his ideas. I guess I was his last resort." Hollister started to rise and then sat down again, his eyes holding Bruce in his seat. "Something else I think you should know. Arach's son was a Zionist assassin, trapped in an organization called The Circle. They told him the only way he could leave is in a pine box. He died in a shootout with the British police—and get this-saving his best friend who was an Arab. His daughter married a British officer who was also assassinated; the story going around it was the British who killed him."

Bruce looked at his watch. He thought which would be the most believable when he got home, that he was with constituents or what the good Senator spent over an hour telling him. She probably would buy neither but telling her he was with Phillip Hollister was the last thing he would tell her. He thought about what Hollister had said. He muttered to himself: "Unbelievable."

November 1938

Abu Kamal walked among his men. A dozen campfires lighted their faces. Voices were hushed and often there was complete silence. As he approached each fire, the men rose quickly and straightened their backs, waiting to hear what their commander had to say to them. Tonight, he seldom spoke but nodded then continued moving about the camp. When he talked, it was about personal things, asking how the arm of a wounded man was healing, how the father of another might be feeling; all the time reading the faces of his men, assessing whether they were ready to go into battle once again to fight for Palestine.

He spotted Ismael Latif among the horses, checking the hooves, looking into their eyes to read their condition, and patting them gently on their withers and running his hands across the ribs that protruded more each day.

"They need grain."

Ismael turned to see his commander standing behind him.

"Yes. The mills around us have been emptied or destroyed."

"And all the settlements are heavily guarded. We might be able to get into their store houses, but the risk is too great."

"The Templers at Waldheim have grain."

"Will they sell grain to us?" Abu Kamal knew Otto Lutz was not their enemy, but knew the colony could not sell anything to the rebels. He continued: "We need grain for the horses, but we need food and supplies for the men, too." Taking from those who had never harmed them, had always been good neighbors is harsh but necessary. The British did not trust the Templers since most were German, and even robbing them would make the British and Jews suspicious.

"Ismael, take Abd with you. Find out what you can about security at Waldheim and where the settlers and the British soldiers are. We will go in tomorrow night."

In the weeks since Ismael arrived, the rebels had moved frequently, fearing discovery if they stayed too long in one place. The increase in patrols and aero planes overhead made attacks on British patrols or Jewish settlers too risky. Al Hajj Mohammad was concerned about the reaction of Ismael to his tactics yet Ismael had never given him any reason to think the man from Argentina questioned his leadership. Still, he saw the tall Arab getting restless, and wondered how long he would be among them.

Ismael Latif had watched and listened and deflected questions and suggestions about what he would be doing to fight the British and the Jews. No clear path appeared during his stay but it was clear that the rebels could not withstand the overwhelming superiority of the British and Jews; that the course they were on could not end with a victory for the rebels. What was left was simply to fight on, to hope that somehow the freedom they sought would be delivered to them.

Abu Kamal was a brave and honorable man and a resourceful fighter. It was hard to know what he thought the outcome of the struggle would be, but what was clear is that he would never desert the men who followed him, nor they him.

+++

The steady rain and the moonless night limited visibility to less than twenty yards. The band of twenty men had tethered their horses in a grove of eucalyptus two hundred yards from the gates. When the men appeared out of the darkness, the Waldheim guards were quickly disarmed and placed under guard by the rebels. It was Ismael who led the men into the compound, and he and Abd entered the residence of Otto Lutz.

"Herr Lutz, we will need the keys to your storehouses and two of your lorries. We will see that you are told where to find the lorries since we have no use for them. No one will be hurt if you cooperate."

Lutz nodded. He knew resistance to the demands of these desperate men would only result in more deaths. At the last colony meeting, there had been long discussions about what they must do if they were attacked. It was the oldest member of the colony, a man who witnessed firsthand attacks on the Templers twenty years before who spoke. Franz Steiner was a big and powerful man who stood and waited for silence:

> "The path we have taken as members of our Society leaves us with only one course to take, to trust in God and our fellow man. We have been good neighbors and what our neighbors do is in the hands of God." He looked around, seeing the skepticism on the faces of the young, yet they all understood rules of the Society. He also knew their faith would be sorely tested, and he prayed that he and they would prove worthy when the time came."

Otto Lutzturnedto Abd. Hehadworkedat Waldheimasacarpenter's apprentice before joining the rebels. He forced himself to appear calm as he smiled at the young Arab. "I heard what happened to your village, Abd. I am sorry." Lutz had heard of the many villagers killed by the bombing and the many killed by the soldiers. He thought it best not to ask about Abd's family.

In less than an hour, the lorries had been loaded. Lutz watched as they disappeared into the darkness, then, with the other members, stared into the darkness until the whine of the engines could no longer be heard. Shortly after midnight, the lorries had been unloaded and returned to the grove where horses waited for their riders.

At the sound of the lorries, the rebels watching Lutz and the others to prevent them from escaping to sound the alarm quickly left the compound and headed for the grove. The rain had stopped. He thought of the ragged and dirty uniforms of the men. Perhaps he should be angry at what they had done yet Lutz worried that the tracks made by the lorry in the soft ground would be easy to follow. In the morning, he would tally the losses and call Haifa. Thank God no one was hurt.

He thought about what he must tell the British. Always distant, the soldiers and the Jewish settlers had grown increasingly hostile because of Hitler's foolish and vengeful behavior. Most of Palestine was aware of Kristallnacht. The British, of course, did not need a Hitler to dislike the Germans. They would ask a lot of questions and make clear they doubted his version of what happened. By good fortune, if such could exist given what happened, the evidence of what happened was clear enough.

Wiser heads had prevailed when the Nazi representative had given them the swastika to fly over the compound. It still remained in its box in the storehouse, unless the rebels had decided to take it. He had heard someone repeat the old saw in their last meeting that the enemy of my enemy is my friend. Following such advice in desperate conditions was always tempting. In this case, it could just lead to even greater tragedy for the Arabs.

+++

The Rosh Pinna settlement was only three miles from Waldheim. Despite the proximity, there had been little contact between members of the settlements. While Waldheim members had visited the settlement and extended invitations to visit Waldheim, no one had ever visited the Templer community. Two days after the Arab raid, a man who identified himself as Avram Katz asked to see Otto Lutz.

Lutz heard the knock and opened the door. "Good morning, Herr Lutz. My name is Avram Katz."

The visitor did not smile. His manner made Lutz uneasy. "Please come in, Herr Katz. Welcome to Waldheim."

Katz entered and stood just inside the door. Not getting a response to his invitation, Lutz added: "Would you like to sit down."

"No, thank you." Again, Katz grew silent and Lutz began to see that Katz was playing a kind of game. He wanted to make his host uncomfortable and wondered why. He could play a similar game, he thought, but decided instead to break the silence and not to judge the behavior of his visitor.

"Now, what can I do for you?"

Katz looked at him, trying to create the impression that he was somehow reading the thoughts of his host. This time, Otto Lutz decided he could only remain silent and wait for his visitor to speak.

"You had visitors two nights ago, I understand?"

"We had intruders, yes. I informed the British and I assume they informed you."

Katz looked at Lutz as if he wanted to question his assumption then added "And they took two of your lorries loaded with supplies."

"Yes." Finally at the end of his patience, Lutz added: "Mr. Katz, you are asking questions I think you already know the answer to." Waiting for a moment then continuing "So what is it you want to know?"

"Our settlement wanted this information first hand. You know we have been attacked by the rebels from time to time and what happens near us is of great concern." As Lutz did not respond, he continued. "We were also interested to find out that no one was injured during their so-called raid."

"Mr. Katz, I assure you that we were raided and our food and supplies taken from us by force."

"Why did you not resist, you are not helpless."

"Do you know anything about the Templers, Mr. Katz? We do not believe in violence and would never harm another human being unless our own lives are threatened."

"I am not interested in your religious beliefs. I do know that some of your colonies have flown a Nazi flag until they were told to take it down and the Nazi's are very violent."

"You do not see the Nazi flag here, do you?"

"I will report our conversation to our council; they will decide what must be done."

Otto Lutz could leave things as they seemed at this moment. "Mr. Katz, you give me no choice but to get in touch with the British authorities and tell them you have threatened us."

Katz stood on the landing, looking over the grain fields ready for harvest and the sleek Holstein cattle grazing in a field nearby. "Very impressive. I'm sure you would not want to lose all of this." He turned to Lutz and met his eyes. "I wouldn't rely on the British to protect you, Herr Lutz. I think they share our feelings about the Germans."

Katz turned and walked toward the gate. It's happening again, Lutz thought. "Please God, have mercy on us all. Help them refrain from anger and revenge. Grant us the most wonderful gift of all, peace, peace among us and peace within us."

In the distance, he could see Avram Katz riding west toward Rosh Pinna. There would be a council meeting. Otto Lutz feared for the worst.

***

When Otto Lutz reached British Army sector headquarters by telephone, he asked to speak to Leftenant Gordon, whom he had spoken to about the raid. During the first conversation, the Leftenant seemed uninterested in what was lost but questioned Lutz about the men who were in the raiding party and the direction they headed when they left Waldheim.

Now he was reporting to Gordon again, reporting the threats made by Katz.

"He asked you why you didn't try to stop the rebels and you think he was suggesting the colony actually gave the grain and other supplies to the rebels. That doesn't sound like a threat to me. Mr. Katz, I'm sorry, I meant Mr. Lutz."

"He told us, Leftenant, that he would take the matter up with the council. By that I think he meant the council of Rosh Pinna. For what purpose would he say that but as a threat."

"Mr. Lutz, we have a revolt on our hands. The settlers have been beaten, murdered, their cattle stolen or poisoned and they are angry when something like this happens. You have to do a better job of keeping food and supplies from the Arabs."

"You make it sound as if we have done something wrong."

"You need to keep food and supplies out of the Arab rebels' hands. Frankly, you didn't do a good job of it." With that, the British officer cut the connection. Lutz was stunned. He could imagine such a man encouraging the settlers to punish us.

***

The councils of elders of Waldheim and of Rosh Pinna met that evening to decide what must be done.

The sun was clear of the hills when five riders approached Waldheim from the west. Moving to the edge of the grain fields and within shouting distance of the cattle grazing in the field, they dismounted. Pulling their Enfield's from the scabbards tied to the horses' saddles, they began firing. Five animals dropped where they grazed. One of the men pulled an incendiary grenade from this pack and hurled it into the grain field, and the fire began to spread immediately. In no hurry, the men mounted and turned to the west.

The Templers, men and women, rushed to the grain field to save it while others looked to the cattle, moving those still standing back into the barns. Tears rolled down the faces of many of the men, tears of sorrow for the great animals who lay dead or dying, and tears of rage they sinfully shed.

+++

When Reverend McDermott first arrived at the small church he had inherited, he thought immediately of a school for the children from the nearby villages. While the Jewish and British children had excellent facilities and teachers, support for the education of Arab children was woefully poor. It took some time and effort to develop a plan for a school and someone to help him with the teaching. It was the Templer's Bank that came to his aid a year ago, accepting his upcoming olive harvest as collateral, and with the modest sum he borrowed and several small gifts from his siblings, the building was finished. Small, but adequate, the challenge now was to find a teacher, hopefully a graduate of one of the many mission schools.

Sarah Nevers, of course, was the first person he thought of. Over the last several years, he had told Sarah of his plans, then his progress, and now his search for a teacher for the twenty students at Christ Church School. Sarah had agreed to meet him after school at the small outdoor café near the Government House. The sky was cloudless, the air cool in the late afternoon.

Sarah often seemed sad to John and she always dismissed his concerns, saying she took after her father who always seemed to have the weight of the world on his shoulders. Beneath the surface, she assured him, there was always and eagerness to laugh and feel joy at seeing something beautiful. It always made her smile inside, but sometimes it was hidden from others. She was pleased when he expressed such concern for her. Since they first met, she was aware that she attracted the Pastor, and decided very early that she would not encourage him though she admitted to herself that she liked his company and always looked forward to his visits.

Since her husband John died, there had been many who wanted to court her, and she had always discouraged them. The school and young John had always been enough for her and someone else in her life seemed a burden.

The activity around them made her regret not suggesting another place to have tea. The traffic was heavy in and out of Government House, most men in uniform. Singly and in formations, stiff backed soldiers seemed everywhere. It has grown worse since the rebels had taken over the Old City and locked the gates, trying once again to commit some symbolic act which would rally the Arabs and cause the British seek a peaceful settlement of the outbreak.

She recalled when it happened.

The British were expert in stifling resistance among its subjects; it was determined to deny any victory for the Arabs, no matter how small. Within hours, the Army, using units within the Cold Stream Guards, the Royal Fusiliers and the Black Watch has mounted a counter-attack and quickly cleared the Old City of rebels. Many were killed, some captured and there was a small number that managed to escape. When the rebels occupied the Old City, near hysteria occurred within the Jewish community, remembering what happened almost ten years before in Hebron. Surprised by the rebel attack, Sarah had been warned to get off the street and stay in her house.

She was one of the first to discover what was happening when she answered her door and Hassan appeared in the doorway. He was smiling, not the winsome smile she had once known, but small and yet warm. Outside of the door was a group of men and Sarah could quickly see that Ismael's brother was their commander. The gentle face she remembered was no longer there. Tall like his brother, the soft body she remembered was gone. Only the scars of his ordeal twenty years ago marred his handsome features. He looked very much like she imagined Ismael would look today. She had kept track of the Latif's who had suffered at the hands of the British and the Agency, and knew Hassan had left Jerusalem and was fighting as a guerrilla in the hills to the north.

"Sarah, do not leave the house."

"What about my children?"

"They are safe. The word is everywhere about what is happening and the families will see to it that the children are not harmed."

"Can I not go to them?"

"It is not safe. We have locked the gates."

"Hassan, you will all be killed. The British will not let you hold the Old City."

"We must fight, Sarah."

Hassan started to turn away. Sarah called after him. "Is there news of Ismael?"

A picture appeared before his eyes, three children playing together, riding together and he felt the pang of jealousy he had always felt. He had never been part of the gang, just the three of them, Yitzhak, Ismael and the tomboy Sarah.

"My brother is somewhere up north. There are rumors that he joined Abu Kamal."

Sarah looked at Hassan, remembering how he had been brutally beaten to force him to tell Major Hornsby where Ismael was. She knew he had not.

"Allah will protect you, Hassan."

"And you, Sarah."

She watched them move smartly down the narrow street to take their positions, waiting for the British to attack.

The British attack came quickly with the blowing of the gates. As the gates burst open, Lewis guns began spraying the area inside the gates. Suddenly they stopped and the Royal Northumberland Fusiliers poured into the Old City and the house by house battle began.

By morning, the Old City was again in British hands. The Latif family got word to her that Hassan was not among the dead, wounded or captured.

She looked across the small table at John. John appeared excited, unlike the person she knew. The words seem to burst from her friend.

"I want to talk to you about Palestine. Sounds presumptuous for a pastor with one hundred twenty members, doesn't it. But I have thought about what is happening a great deal and realize I haven't lifted a finger to help. Yesterday, I read in Ha'aretz that more troops were landing in Haifa. On top of that, someone told me that more money is flowing to Nashashibi for his Peace Bands and spies. The British are giving even more arms to the Jews and disarming the Arabs. Anyone caught with a weapon, if he is an Arab, can be hanged and they are hanging them every week up in the Acre Prison. Anyone considered sympathetic with the rebels is made to suffer. They call it collective punishment and even passed a law, which in the British mind makes it 'legal'. Odd thinking, you pass a law which allows illegal acts and magically they become legal."

Sarah was surprised at the anger in the Pastor's voice, which she had never seen before. Surely, she decided, a pastor does have the right to be concerned about injustice. Yet she found herself annoyed. Was it because he was a newcomer? Because he was John McDermott, and neither an Arab or Jew and was meddling in some sort of bizarre family squabble? And then she knew, her pique was not about John McDermott, it was about Sarah Nevers who could never reconcile who she was and who she had been.

Without being aware of her action, she put her hand on his and when she saw his face redden, she quickly withdrew it. He smiled then. "I didn't really mind, Sarah. Truth be known, it felt very good." Then she returned his smile, aware she was blushing, too.

For the first time she told him about Arach. He decided not to tell her he knew much of the story, instead listening until she had finished.

"Arach believed in the Balfour Declaration but he never saw it as a grant by the British to drive the Arabs from their land but would be a land that would welcome Jews as citizens but also a land governed by the people who lived there, whether they be Jew, Christian or Muslim."

Sarah continued. "My father came to understand that the Zionists, which in 1917 were not a majority of Jews, had no intention to accept half a loaf. They wanted all of Palestine. Yes, they would accept less, but always in the back of their minds was a totally Jewish land." In 1917, the British were complicit, they didn't care what the Arabs thought nor had a right to. Balfour and George said as much at that time. But as the reality of what they had loosed became more and more apparent, and the Middle Eastern Arabs could not be ignored, the British began to look for a solution which did take into account the rights of the Arabs in Palestine.

The British never grasped what had occurred in 1917. Yes, the understood what the Balfour Declaration was all about, but they did not know that world power had shifted to your land across the Atlantic. But the Zionists did and when they saw Britain begin to waver to correct their earlier duplicity and complicity, they turned to America where the real power was and where the British attitude of 1917 toward Palestine is the attitude of the Americans today."

"Has your father abandoned hope for the Arabs, Christian and Muslim, in Palestine?"

"Arach would never do that."

"What can we do?"

Sarah looked at John McDermott. In many ways he was a gentle man. He was not a man who would commit or condone violence. But she knew he was not a weak man, and in any enterprise he freely entered into, he could be counted upon.

"I have a letter from Arach. It describes a plan to save Palestine and the Jews in Europe."

"What can we do?"

"Arach thinks the British may be receptive to the plan. He warns that some of the Zionists are so fanatical that they will scuttle any plans which destroy their dream for Palestine."

"Even if it saves the millions of Jews in Europe!?"

"Yes. Although they would not see it that way."

"Where do we begin? I would like to help."

"We can begin by getting the British High Commissioner's attention."

"How would we do that?"

"By getting the Arabs to offer to turn in their weapons if certain concessions were made by the British."

"Judging British behavior to date, they won't agree to anything but unconditional surrender."

"Perhaps not. But the key is to establish channels which bypass the gates set by the Zionists to stop proposals like the one my father is proposing."

McDermott smiled at his own inspiration, what he was so eager to tell Sarah. "The Missions and the Churches." He hesitated. "And the Imams."

"I don't follow you."

McDermott grasped the table with both hands, leaning forward as if to rise. "Sarah, let me think about what I'm thinking about." He wanted to see Sarah smile and she did.

"I think you're telling me in your own way that we need to slow down. I think you are right."

"I am invited to dinner at the Smythe's on Thursday. There will only be five of us. If I get you an invitation, can you come?"

"I can be there." A bachelor fond of good food and getting little of it, an invitation to dinner for whatever reason was welcome.

"Then plan on Thursday."

His mouth began to water thinking about Thursday evening, for Emma Smythe was Italian, known to prepare the food herself for small dinner parties and she was a great cook.

November 1938

To know who your enemy is, where he is and what he is doing makes killing him far easier. Tegart was the master at finding ways to get such information from persons who fiercely resisted revealing it. Torture, of course, was not invented by the British Empire and those who represented it were fond of claiming that only its enemies tortured to extract information, that it, being civilized, did not engage in torture. Their aura of rectitude was protected by the kind of enemies they engaged in maintaining their claims. The British could tell their story through the vast communication networks by voice and print and their enemies had few ways of telling their version of events. Thus it was possible to characterize the Palestinians as cruel and treacherous, capable of horrible torture and the British and Jews faithfully following the rules of war.

In Palestine, the British under Charles Tegart tortured extensively to gather information and prisoners of any value could expect to be tortured. It was the quiet boast of Tegart's apprentices who actually did the torturing for the great man that no one could resist telling what he knew if they were tortured brutally and long enough. Hassan Latif, sufficiently recovered to be questioned, was about to be tested as he had been by Major Hornsby, when, like today, they were searching for Ismael Latif.

Major Fortson was in charge of the interrogation and it was his task to get Hassan Latif to reveal the location of his brother. Hassan had been prepared for his encounter with the Major by being stripped naked for two days and two nights in an unheated cell.

The cell where Latif was kept was without windows or light of any kind. His wound had been dressed when they first brought him to the hospital but had not been checked since that time. He had neither food nor water since they placed him in his cell. Because the cell was completely dark, he had no way of knowing whether it was night or day. He did not know how long he had been in the cell before he felt the bandage covering his wound fall to the ground. Soon after, he felt wetness below the wound and knew it was festering.

The sound of the key in the lock to his cell door startled him. Then the light blinded him until he slowly adjusted to it. Standing in the doorway, a tall figure faced him. The backlight made it impossible at first to see what the person looked like. As his eyes adjusted, he could see the man had a sharp angular face, long and thin. The eyebrows were thick and the eyes deeply set. Hassan thought they were gray. Like so many British officers, his mustache was neatly trimmed.

"Hassan Latif, is it not?" the Major looked into Hassan's eyes as if expecting an answer. "I expect you to answer each time I ask you a question, is that understood?" When Latif did not answer, Fortson turned and nodded to someone that Hassan could not see.

Two very large men appeared, and grabbing Hassan by both arms, dragged the struggling man to another cell which was brightly lit and contained a single chair near its center. Forcing Hassan into the chair, they held him fast with straps on arms, legs and across his chest. In the course of the Mandate, word had spread about the methods used by the British to extract information. He knew what was about to happen. Somehow he must resist. Closing his eyes, he tried to remove himself from the room, not to think of more pleasant things but not to think at all. Quickly, the two men attached the wires to all parts of his body.

The Major appeared. "I am going to ask you some questions, Latif. If we are satisfied with the answers, you will feel no pain. One of the men approached Hassan and placed a glass of water on Hassan's lips. He drank deeply and for a brief moment a feeling of euphoria overwhelmed him.

"Things can go easily for you, Latif if you answer my questions. If you answer them all, you will be allowed to return to the hospital and we will see that you are treated well until your gangs lay down their arms."

"Where is your brother now, Hassan?"

The other prisoners could hear the screams, then the shouting, and then the screams over and over through the morning.

Near noon, Fortson appeared in the hall outside the chamber. "Move him back to his cell." He thought of Purdom. The raider commander had demanded that Latif be placed in his custody, claiming that he had ways to get the information they needed. He could see the patronizing smile on his arrogant face. He had heard all the stories about this mad man and as time passed and other stories travelled among the officers and men, they were undoubtedly true. Purdom, he decided killed and tortured for pleasure. He, however, interrogated prisoners and used the least painful way of getting information. In his mind, that was the difference between the madman Purdom and himself.

He would begin again in the afternoon. Everyone has his breaking point. He stood in front of the door where the water treatment was to be administered. He had discovered in his work in India and now Palestine that prisoners who resisted electric shocks panicked when they were exposed to the water treatment.

Hassan was not able to stand and had to be dragged to the water treatment room. Though his vision was blurred and his head spinning, he recognized Fortson. Ironic, he thought. It seemed never to have occurred to his inquisitors that he may not know where his brother was. When they had shot the current through his testicles there was a moment when he wanted to cry out "But I don't know where my brother is!" Seeing his tormentor standing

145

before the door to another room, he started to laugh. The Major stared at him, wondering if Latif had lost his mind as had happened to others. Then Hassan spoke, his speech slurred. "You will not find my brother, Major, but he will find you."

The water treatment lasted only an hour. As they poured water down the throat of their prisoner until he appeared close to drowning, then stopped to renew the questioning by the Major, the heart of Hassan, weak by birth, stopped. They worked feverishly to revive Hassan Latif and stopped only when the doctor who was standing by declared him dead.

Major Fortson was angry at his failure and angry at the man who lay lifeless on the water board. He thought of what he should say in the report which would include no mention of the methods used to question the prisoner. He would not include the words spoken to him by Hassan Latif, "You will not find my brother, he will find you." He tried to forget the face and the words. He could not.

December 1938

The raid on Tel Hai eighteen years ago had never been forgotten by the older men and women who had been there then nor did they fail to drill into the minds of the new members the need to always be vigilant. The memory of what happened at Tel Hai had not been lost when the settlement became part of Kfar Giladi. In the years following the attack, the mission of the settlement had changed from defending it to attacking nearby villages. Armed with automatic weapons and explosives including grenades and land mines, raids of the surrounding Arab villages had been frequent, always in the name of self-defense.

The raid on Waldheim had provided Abu Kamal's men with warm clothing for the winter and sufficient grain for bread and for the horses. But the men were in need of ammunition for their captured Enfield's and Sten sub machine guns and replacements were needed.

146

It was the last deadly foray by the militia from Kfar Giladi that had convinced Ismael and Abu Kamal that there was a way to obtain the weapons and ammunition needed to continue the struggle. The last settler raid on Jaba had been unusually deadly, with men and women shot for only one reason, a settler had been attacked by someone from the village.. The attack by Kfar Giladi men was quick on the heels of the discovery of the attacker's village. In the report of the Jaba raid in Ha'aretz, the reporter had stressed the legal justification for such attacks was the law of 1925 providing for collective punishment. It was widely understood that the laws were only to be employed against Arabs, and that the Jewish militias were allowed to use such tactics along with the British.

***

Among the one hundred men still loyal to Abu Kamal, ten formed a war council, deciding on future actions. Ismael was one of the ten. He spoke to the rest. His words acknowledged the flickering candle of rebellion; that it was in danger of going out altogether. Risking rejection by al hajj Mohammad and those who would die for him, he spoke.

"Our ammunition is low. We need automatic weapons that we can carry on horseback and we need grenades and gelignite and we need fresh horses and mules. The British have stretched barbed wire across our borders and what we need we can no longer get from Damascus or Beirut. But there is a way we can get the weapons, ammunition and explosive we need."

Abu Kamal was interested. *Perhaps this man can do miracles.* "How, my friend?"

"Kfar Giladi."

"Each time Kfar Giladi had been attacked, there had been a violent response The response was often quick, within days and hours.

147

When such attacks came, most of the able bodied men participated in the attacks, and few men were left to guard the settlement.

In his mind Ismael reconstructed the raid on Jaba. Advancing from house to house, grenades were tossed through windows followed by the militia bursting into the houses and forcing everyone still alive into the street. When they had rounded up the villagers, the militia leader told them why the village was attacked, and what would happen if the villagers harbored rebels or provided them with food. The Mukhtar was brought in front of the villages and made to kneel in front of the militia leader. He was forced to swear by Allah that the village would never aid the rebels in any way. When he refused, he was shot. Twelve men and two women were killed in the attack.

The following morning, Ismael, with George Bissett and Andre Monet had visited the village. For Bissett and Monet, it was to chronicle what had happened in words and pictures and tell the rest of the world. For Ismael, it was to see with his own eyes what had happened, and to question the villagers on every detail of the raid they could remember. As he listened, it became clear what Abu Kamal next target must be Kfar Giladi. The attack must use the enemies own tactics against them.

Ismael had volunteered to scout the settlement alone. His plan was to approach the settlement by night, to select a position close enough to observe activity using his binoculars. He found the ideal spot, a cluster of pines that had been planted at the turn of the century by the Jewish National Fund. By the end of the second day, he counted 36 men and 16 women. There were children. Barbed wire ringed the area where the buildings were, a second perimeter with fenced in fields where their animals were kept and the grain fields, orchards and space for vegetables were located. Watching men go in and out of a stone building near the center of the compound, some bringing weapons out and others leaving the building without weapons revealed the location of the armory. Located nearby was the machinery shed where lorries were kept. Observing them closely, Ismael could see that two of the lorries were covered with armor plating. These were the lorries that had been used in the attacks on surrounding villages. In earlier attacks these lorries drove into the villages and militia with light machine guns and rifles would leap from the backs of the lorries and begin their killing. With few exceptions, these attacks were carried out at night and the militia had fired flares throughout the villages to make their targets visible. The militia was well trained and heavily armed. From the villagers in Jaba, at least twenty five were in the attack force. Locating the wireless antennae, one in the building that housed the settlers, the second in the armory, he had seen enough. He waited until dark, the moved to where his horse was tied.

The raid on Kfar Giladi depended on Jilya, twenty miles away. The success of the plan required provoking the leaders of Kfar Giladi to attack Jilya at night and on a particular night. It required coordinating the defense of Jilya with an attack on Kfar Giladi, and it required the delivery of false information to Kfar Giladi that would provoke an attack. Both Abu Kamal and Ismael were aware of the risks, that things could go wrong; terribly wrong. But both knew a victory could buoy the flagging spirits of the rebels and make the world take notice.

The planting of false information became possible when a captured Peace Band fighter, when questioned revealed the informant's name in Jilya. The informant was a prominent merchant in Jilya named Ibrahim al-Sa'idi who filled olive soap and olive oil orders to the settlement weekly. It was the Peace Band member under the threat of death by the rebels who agreed to pass information to the merchant that five men responsible for ambushing and murdering a Kfar Giladi settler two years before were in Jilya. Anticipation of success heightened when the merchant asked the Peace Band member where they could be found. The information was passed to the merchant the day before his regular trips to the settlement.

Communications were critical to the success of the operation. One year before, Abu Kamal's men ambushed a single vehicle, killing the men in the small armored car. The car was carrying a wireless transmitter and receiver, a device that had played havoc when the rebels attacked convoys. The convoys all had wireless communications on one of the vehicles, and within hours, even minutes, aero planes would appear overhead and nearby British units come to the aid of the besieged units. Several of the men who fought with Al Hajj Mohammad were familiar with the wireless equipment and learned to use it to coordinate attacks and other troop movements. The range of the wireless would enable rebels near Kfar Giladi to communicate the settler movements to rebels in Jilya.

The plan was simple. Forty men with Abu Kamal's most experienced lieutenant Abu Hamdan; deploying inside Jilya with orders to allow Kfar Giladi raiders to enter the village. Once inside, Hamdan would move quickly to the attack, disabling the armored vehicles. Mujahidin were to concentrate their fire on the backs of the lorries to prevent the raiders from leaving the lorries alive and on any survivors from the cabs of the lorries.

To avoid any possible breakdown in the wireless, lookouts were posted at intervals beginning a kilometer from the village on high ground equipped with battery operated torches. They were to signal when the raiders were spotted.

Orders were issued by Abu Kamal. If any of the raiders choose to surrender, they are to be given that opportunity. They will be useful as hostages.

At Kfar Giladi, Ismael commanded a smaller unit of 20 men. The plan was to cut through the barbed wire to the east and west, kill the guards as silently as possible, then storm the living quarters where those not on the raid slept. Two large buildings housed the settlers.

Settlers were to be disarmed and held until the operation was over. Fifteen men were to converge on the machine shed and the armory. Men who had been mechanics, there were three, were to start and drive the lorries and motor cars to be loaded with weapons, ammunitions, explosives, food and other supplies that could be found. The actions must take no more than one hour in the event communications had not been destroyed.

Abu Kamal himself remained in a camp near Jilya with twenty men if reinforcements were needed. On the roads leading to Kfar Giladi and Jilya, groups of five were dug in near the main roads to delay reinforcements and to allow the main bodies of his small army to escape.

Ismael stood beside Abd, hidden by the thick cluster of trees, and watched the lights go on all over the Kfar Giladi compound. His heart raced with the sounds of engines, their pitch rising and falling as the drivers checked their vehicles. Pressing the transmitter button, he spoke: "There is activity in the compound. Vehicles are moving. It looks like three vehicles are lining up in front of the gate. Over." The silence at the other end alarmed Ismael. "Do you read me!?" He cursed himself. He had not pushed the receiver button. "This is Hamdan. I read you. Over." Ismael was smiling. Abu Hamdan was better at this than him. "This is the last transmission. Out." It had been confirmed that the British were capable of intercepting their transmissions. If they did read the transmission, they would know something was happening but not where.

December 1938

Shurtok did not trust Zelesney. The man who was the go between with the British on intelligence matters always seemed to enjoy reminding him that he knew things that others in the Agency did not. But his arrogance was not limited to his fellow Jews, he carried it with him when he dealt with the British. He was fond of telling Shurtok that he knew most of what was happening in the High Commissioners office and the British Commanding General staff before most of the high ranking British did and any plans they had that affected the Yishuv were in his hands well before they were carried out.

151

Zelesney was the keeper of the list. The list contained thousands of Palestinians compiled since the end of the Great War. At opportune times, when the benefits were the greatest, he would share these names with the British. He could proudly point to those exiled, imprisoned or hanged that were on the list. He could also boast that the list contained those who could be persuaded to work for the Agency. British intelligence had tried to get the Agency list but was rebuffed. They suspected that Zelesney's list contained hundreds of British names. Zelesney had shared the list with Shurtok but the Agency Director could not help but wonder if Zelesney had another list and he was on it.

Shurtok was in his office now and despite the tragedy at Kfar Giladi, he felt a twisted satisfaction that Ibrahim Zelesney was caught with his pants down. Zelesney was subdued; Shurtok could see a face wiped clean of self-assurance for once. He had planned to berate his intelligence chief and decided the matter was too important for personal attacks.

"Now that we have confirmed that Ismael Latif has returned, what can we do to find him?" He thought of the loss of the entire raiding party from Kfar Giladi, the destruction of its armory and equipment, and the first-hand accounts of what happened, even when it was happening, that were being sent around the world. He could not hide the sarcasm and the man sitting in front of him seemed to wince.

Shurtok did not know much about Ismael Latif, but what he did know was a man who was smart. He had turned Palestine upside down twenty years ago and badly hurt the Yishuv and now Kfar Giladi. Twenty years ago, he thought, we turned Tel Hai into a rallying cry. This was not the case today.

He found himself unable to become too angry about Latif. Latif was a dangerous man but he was fighting against odds where he could not win. We would find him or the British would. He was certain of that and he was not a threat to the Israel the Zionists wanted. But Monet and Bissett were different. Shurtok knew the power of words, voices and pictures bombarding a public which could turn on the Zionist program, which could see the Arabs as people entitled to live in Palestine under a democratic government. That was the nightmare, that Zionist would have their own words about freedom and self-government turned against them. And it was people like Monet and Bissett with their words and pictures that were the real danger.

"Ibrahim, find Andre Monet and George Bissett and see that they disappear. They are not to be taken alive where they can have a forum for their propaganda. Set the rewards as high as you think is needed and turn every assassin in your pay loose. Find them and kill them."

Throwing the two renegade correspondents in his face was like pouring salt into a wound. *Why does this man have to throw them in my face.* He understood as much as Shurtok what these men meant. Nashashibi was worthless. The information coming in from spies was worthless. Shurtok's offer could help. Someone greedy enough would come forward. It always happens. He often heard his people tell him that every Arab had his price. He wished that were true but knew it was not. His latest lead was the article by Monet and the Bissett pictures on the front page of the Filastin. For as long as he had his position, British and Agency officials were agitating to close the paper down. Zelesney was alone in arguing to keep it open. Once again, there is an opportunity to find the two goyim; what was the source of the front page story? It was a trail to be followed.

+++

The small room in the Nazarene Hotel was cold. The blankets provided by the clerk were not enough to keep them from shivering through the night. Hamad Osta had found the room for them. Hamad had been assigned by Al Hajj Mohammad to see that the needs of Bissett and Monet were met while they were in Nazareth.

The knock on the door always caused the two catch their breath and touch the Berettas they both carried.

"Who is it?"

"I have a message for you."

"Slide it under the door."

"It is about Tulkarem."

When Bissett opened the door, Hamad stood smiling at the two of them. He seemed pleased that the coded exchange had worked and he was part of it.

"I have good news, sirs. Your pictures and report left Beirut. Do you think the Filastin will print it?"

"So far, they have."

Hamad handed Monet a copy of Ha'aretz. "The Jews did not print what you sent by post but they did print this."

The heading of the column on the first page read simply : *10,000 Pounds!* The article went on:

The hunt by the British of Andre Monet and George Bissett continues. High Commission representative Ronald Smiley announced today the reward leading to the arrest of Andre Monet and George Bissett has been increased to 10,000 pounds for each fugitive. Smiley told Abe Meyersohn: 'the increase was necessary to prevent these two from continuing to spread lies about the gangsterism occurring in Palestine. These men are aiding and abetting gangsters who are wantonly killing innocents and attacking British soldiers and the settlers.

Bissett smiled as he looked at his fellow fugitive. "That's a lot of pesos."

"And a lot of francs."

Hamad Osta stood in the center of the room. Bissett and Monet sat on the one narrow bed and read the full article together. *Why do I feel uneasy in the company of these two men. Why were they here in Palestine? What does Palestine mean to them? Did they realize what 10,000 Palestine Pounds would mean to my family? Or 20,000 Pounds? Did these two foreigners trust me?*

The British and Jews had poisoned the minds of many Arabs who are poor and desperate. Their talk of bribes and rewards and their acceptance makes us feel dirty, less than honorable. When the Jews and British offer us money it tempts us to think of ourselves that way. Why not. If the British, Jews and his fellow Arabs think of me this way, why not take the money and run. But I cannot. My family and my village trust me. Abu Kamal trusts me.

He looked at the two men, intently reading Ha'aretz. *These two men can trust me. They are risking their lives for me and me for them.*

Bissett, whose family was connected to the Middle East, looked at Hamad. It was prudent to trust no one in Palestine. He knew that. He knew, too, that he could not stay if he trusted no one. He and Andre must take risks. To believe in what they were doing, they must trust the man who stood before them.

There was a small table in the corner of the room and two chairs.

"Hamad, will you stay and have coffee with us."

"Yes, sir. I will have someone bring it to the room."

When Hamad had left, Bissett looked at Monet who seemed shaken. "I trust Hamad and you can, too."

"We need to return to Jilya. Hamad says the British have destroyed it.

"Bastards." Unlike his friend, each tragedy infuriated Monet. He wondered if he would ever be able to be a journalist again.

"It will be risky. The British will be expecting us. With the rewards, who knows how many will think the way the British do and will be hanging around Jilya."

"There must be a way to get in there. Both of us don't need to go. What we need is pictures. Kalima can find survivors for us for the report."

"It is too dangerous, George."

"What about the work crews."

"They will be from the village. The British will draft the villagers and force them to do the cleanup. They like to heap humiliation upon the destruction and killing. Teach those dirty wogs a lesson. The thought that this will only make the Arabs hate them all the more is trumped by the conviction that they will also fear them more."

"We'll talk to Kalima. I will only need to be in the village for an hour or two."

"It's too dangerous, George. We need to stay alive if we're going to do any good here."

Bissett had made up his mind. It was time to change the subject. "Andre, have you thought of what you will do when you return to France? You will be famous...or infamous."

"With the editors at Le Figaro, I know what I will be."

"There is a lot of talk of war. Sounds like there will be lots of work for journalists."

"Yes, there is a lot of talk of war by people with short memories and visions of revenge. In Europe, it never seems to end. "The important Jews in France are beating the drum for war. Not all, but many when they see what Hitler is doing."

"Always the same song. War. It's the wrong answer but the one too often written on the test paper if you want a passing grade."

"You are a philosopher, George. And what will you do when you return to Argentina?"

"I shall get richer and fatter, I suppose." He smiled at Monet. "Argentina does very well with your wars. The last one made many very rich and work was available for anyone who wanted it. I think the next one will be no different. We Argentinians have only to worry that our politicians and plutocrats might choose to take sides. There are a lot of Germans and Italians in Argentina. Even the Arabs who emigrated have no love for the English or the French. Then, again, why would they. The bankers and the other plutocrats excepted, of course."

"You've made up our mind, haven't you?"

"What do you mean?"

"You're going after those pictures of Jilya."

"Yes."

"You should remember the riches and comfort of your Argentina."

"I do. But I remember my Uncle George, too."

A knock on the door.

"Who is it?"

"I have a message for you."

"Slide it under the door."

"It is from Tulkharem."

When Andre opened the door, Hamad stood smiling at the two of them. He held a tray with a coffee pot, cups and croissants and strawberry jam. "I got them from the patisserie two blocks away."

Andre wanted to hug the young man.

Part VI

"Gonna miss you, Senator. " Everyone turned his way, and nodded.

December 1938

Robert Bruce had his driver pick up Senator Phillip Hollister in front of his Georgetown home. Inside the shiny new Packard, both were comfortable in the roomy back seat separated from the driver with a sliding glass partition if the passengers wanted to talk to the driver.

"How do you think Arach will do in front of that crowd?" Bruce knew there would be a crowd when news went out on the reason for the press conference by the two Senators and an investment banker from New York about Palestine. Actually, Palestine would be only a small part of their plan, but describing the press conference to give Palestine prominence was sure to draw the broadcast and print media like flies to molasses.

"He'll be fine. Don't let that hang dog look fool you. He won't blow you away with volume, but once they get on to what he has to say, he'll get their attention?" Hollister had been bullish about Poletsky from the start, Bruce thought--two old guys who had seen a lot hitting it off.

"Well, we're going to be the ones doing most of the talking and you'll be sticking your neck out. Me, they can all go to hell as far as I'm concerned, but they're going to hear what we have to say unless they all walk out." Hollister had put his neck out many times in his long career. Maybe this one was special, but at the end of his career he felt good about pushing for Jewish immigration and the concessions the Germans had to make. Putting it all on the table, it gave him hope. He first took office at the beginning of the Great War.

"I remember all my German friends urging me over and over to keep America out of the war. I can see Teddy now, stumping for war and pumping his fist, coming very close to calling every politician who didn't want to go to war a coward. I have to give it to him, Teddy was no coward. I know. I was beside him when he charged San Juan Hill.

"An assassin's bullet made Teddy president. I wonder what America would be like if the assassin had missed. Teddy did like to lead the parade."

Bruce looked over at him. It was a typical winter day in Washington. A brief show of sunshine early in the morning, then thin clouds that made him feel the cold dampness down to his bones. He rapped on the glass, then slid it open. "Jim, stop at the coffee shop."

Turning to Hollister, "A hot cup of coffee and nip of rye will wake me up." He touched his breast pocket where he kept his small silver flask. Getting out of the car, Bruce glanced at the sky.

"Looks like rain, Phil."

The older man nodded. He didn't like the winter weather and the cold always crept deep into his bones.

"Mary's been talking about us buying a winter home somewhere in Florida. Seems like a good idea right now."

Bruce held the door open for the older man, who entered and lifted the spirits of the sober crowd that sat at the counter and in the booths on both sides of the door.

160

"Patrick, top of the morning to you. How about two cups of black coffee and two of those stale donuts, the ones you keep in that case."

"Good morning Senators. What are you doing to the people today?"

"The usual, Patrick, spending your money one way or another. Usually don't know how we're going to spend it this early in the morning but my distinguished colleagues will think of something."

By the time they were seated, the mood in the coffee house had brightened, and there were smiling faces sour a moment before.

"Gonna miss you, Senator. " Everyone turned his way, and nodded.

For a moment, he lost his voice, then in a hoarse whisper said to everyone: "Thank you."

As they edged into their booth, Bruce did not look at his friend but grabbed a menu and began reading it.

Hollister cleared his throat and gave Bruce a back to business look.

"Lipsky and Lewis are making noises all over Washington. They want to talk about one issue."

"The Jews who supported me have given me an earful. I've gotten calls from the White House and the State Department. Couple of calls from some under Secretaries and Assistant Secretaries and old Cordell himself. The worker bees tried to make me feel I was out of my league, and after a few choice words from me, they hung up. Cordell was gracious and made it sound like he was interested. It was clear he had gotten the word about Palestine, though.

"The guy from the White House was sorely pissed that a Republican of all people was involving himself in something he knew nothing about. Well, I just told him what we were doing, and to tell the President to keep an open mind. Saving the lives of thousands of Jews was something that would never be forgotten and he was the one who could save millions of lives. He brought up Palestine, too, and I asked him if the President was willing to give all the good things up because of one issue. He ended by saying I was out of my depth and 'my friend' looking over at Bruce will not get elected if we don't pull in our horns."

"You know, Hollister, what we are proposing does sound like something thought up by a bunch of freshmen in a frat house working on a second keg of beer."

"Well, hell Senator, it doesn't make the idea worse because some young men might come up with an idea like this one. Even four sheets to the wind, they can probably think clearer than some of the people in Washington."

Bruce recalled last night's meeting with Arach. "You know, buying what Arach Poletsky was selling is not easy. I attended one of those meetings where Lewis spoke. He made a pretty strong case for a Jewish homeland and he is a very impressive guy. Nothing shady about him or what he had to say. The Jews wanted a piece of land of their own, and they have a pretty strong case for Palestine and Jerusalem. The Bible is pretty clear about the Chosen People and the Promised Land."

"When we mentioned that to Arach I have to say his response surprised me. When he came from Russia to Palestine thirty years ago, he believed the same thing. Russia was full of Zionist recruiters, encouraging capable young families and single men and women to come to Palestine, to make a home there in a Jewish homeland. This guy was a big shot, a banker who was responsible for buying land for the homeland. Sometimes we don't equate honest with banker, but we know that is mostly unfair to bankers and certainly to this guy.

"When he described his conversation with his co-worker, the name escapes me, about the Balfour Declaration he made the point better than any other way I could imagine."

Hollister kept the smile seeping up inside him hidden. His friend had finally bought the argument on the critical piece to supporting Arach Poletsky's proposal. It made both of them understand something that was always missing when he listened to Lewis, Lipsky or the Christian Zionists who talked of the Chosen People and the Promised Land.

Bruce continued:" Arach said it better than I could. There were people living there!! Arabs, some Christian, some Mohammedans and there were Jews. Only one in ten were Jews and they had lived with the Christians and the Mohammedans for hundreds of years. No one religion claimed the land for its own. It was the Holy Land but it was a land for the people living there. People owned homes. They owned land. Many had no memory of their families having lived anywhere else. To say that someone living in New York, Moscow or London had a greater right to the land than someone whose families lived there for generations turns everything we understand about rights on its head."

The Irish coffee made the senior senator feel better. He was ready to do battle. For him it was a battle with very little risk. In a few short weeks, he would say goodbye. But his dear friend would have to live with battle scars. He reached across the table and grasped the forearm of his best friend, his loyal friend, looked him in the eye and said: "Ready?"

As he opened the door, he turned and nodded. "Have a good day, Patrick."

"Take no prisoners, Senator." He gave his friend the thumbs up, who did the same.

+++

At the table in front of the podium, handouts were stacked neatly. An eclectic group representing magazines, newspapers and radio picked up their handouts and retreated to chairs as close to the podium as possible.

When everyone was seated and the sounds only whispers, Senator Phillip Hollister began to speak.

"I am Senator Phillip Hollister and with me are my friend and colleague, Senator Robert Bruce and a person who inspired the two of us to hold this press conference." He pivoted to his left, facing a slight elderly man he was about to introduce. " To my left is Arach Poletsky, a citizen from New York City. I shall have more to say about our guest later but I know he will have something to say to you.

"Thank you for coming ladies and gentlemen. I note there are a few ladies in the audience.

"The Great War cost the world dearly. In America, alone over 500.000 brave young men were killed or wounded. Many who did survive still suffer from their wounds, thousands unable to work or provide for their families. Our losses were terrible, the world's far greater. Over 16 million died and 20 million were wounded. The aftermath of that war is still with us today and Europe is again preparing for war.

"Most Americans do not want to be drawn into another war. But very forceful and powerful people in America are either urging us to join with Britain against Germany or are calling for actions against Germany to provoke them into a war. If you want to know the sentiments of those pushing for war, just observe the movies in your local theatres and the message they are sending. Read the editorials of our major newspapers.

"As members of the Foreign Affairs Committee of the United States Senate we feel it is our duty to speak to the American people of the dangers of war and" like any practiced orator he hesitated, "the opportunities for peace.

"The reason we have asked you here as the eyes and ears for America is to report what you hear and tell you readers and listeners what we propose.

"There are things all Americans who believe that war must be averted can do. We want America to have a chance to consider our proposals below and if they agree let the White House, the Senate and the House know that they support a program which can avert war and" again hesitation, "address the root causes of the crisis.

"Early in this century, Theodore Roosevelt brought two warring countries together in Portsmouth Maine, Japan and Russia, to reach of peaceful settlement of their differences. He was recognized by the world when he was awarded the Nobel Peace Prize. Like Theodore Roosevelt before him, our President must bring the parties together to avert war. To do this we must join in deliberations on the future of Europe and our President must engage in frank discussions with all the parties including the Chancellor of Germany on all issues threatening peace.

"Many historians and elder statesman and those in high positions dealing with foreign affairs recognize that the harsh peace imposed upon Germany by Britain and France sowed the seeds for another war. Those issues must be addressed. The oppressive debt burdens and land grabs imposed on Germany created instability and gave the world Adolph Hitler.

"We would like to get our message to one special group that is most threatened by Hitler's Germany: the Jews.

"Let's begin by stating that Adolph Hitler threatens peace by his aggressive moves that have alarmed the world. He has targeted the Jews as scapegoats by his demagoguery.

"One of the first steps to secure peace is getting the Jews in Germany out of harm's way.

"To begin, we suggest our President must make clear that the Jews and any others targeted by the Nazi Regime be protected from harm.

"There are many issues to be resolved in securing a peaceful settlement but none more immediate. To show the world we are committed to peace, we must do our part. Let us show the way by opening our doors to those Jews who find living in Germany intolerable. Let us call on other countries to do the same. Our best estimate is that there are 500,000 Jews in Germany. As a great nation, and one which has historically opened its doors, we will be all the better for it because we will be doing our share for peace while receiving people fully capable of making their own way.

"So, today we are appealing to the American people through you to demand that the President grab the European heads of state by the scruff of their necks to build a peace which will not fully satisfy everyone, but will be fair enough that peace can last through this century.

"If the American people do not act by insisting that the President show the way, we will drift into war. Men like Churchill in England and Hitler are spoiling for a fight and Churchill's hold card, let there be no doubt, is the United States and just as we bailed the British out in the Great War, Wall Street and Washington will ask us to do it again. To you who hear or read this, let the President and his hawks in the Congress know that you do not want this to happen, that you want a peaceful settlement.

"Tell them you understand that what Germany is doing to the Jews and others cannot continue but that you also understand there is much more at stake here. The benefits of the hard work that must be done to secure the peace is exponentially better road to take than preparing for war.

"There is one other matter which may be unfamiliar to the American people and that is the matter of Palestine. Most of you know something about the Bible and you know about the Bible speaks of the Jews as the Chosen People and about the Promised Land. Many of you have heard that Britain granted the Jews a homeland in Palestine. But most of you do not know that the British made that promise without asking the people living there, Jews, Christians and Muslims how they felt about what the British intended to do. Picture a foreign company giving away your land for someone to live on. You know how you would feel and would your feelings be justified? Of course.

"Today, we have someone who is a Jew who lived in Palestine before the British arrived. He was a very important man, his job was to buy land for the settlers as head of the Jewish National Fund. He left Palestine to become a citizen of the United States these last twenty years because he knew, as a Jew, that what was happening to the people who lived there and were being forced off their land was wrong. It was he who was the inspiration for our press conference today.

Hollister turned to Arach Poletsky. "Anything you would like to add?"

The voice the audience heard was soft, the accent shaped by his life in Russia, in Palestine, and now New York City.

"Senator, I think you cover the essential points of concern. Perhaps those here today might have some questions."

Senator Robert Bruce still had the same nagging concern about Poletsky's idea and now theirs. Does an America with high unemployment care enough about peace that they would allow hundreds of thousands of Jews into this country? What they had debated including in their presentation was the fact that negotiations with Hitler would include allowing the Jews coming here to bring their wealth with them, that in bargaining with Germany for concessions to them, we would insist on that happening. We decided to leave it out. That was an issue to be directed to Hitler by Roosevelt.

How would we sell the issue of Palestine to Lewis and others? More importantly, how would we sell the idea to those politicians like themselves who depended on Jewish money and media support? As he listened to Phil, he was mulling over two issues, peace and the Jews. Selling a push for peace would be far easier if the Palestine issue was dropped out of the package. Selling peace by selling out the Arabs sounds like the kind of thing that happened every day in Washington. He looked over at Arach and felt guilt about his thoughts.

He could read the energy in the crowd before him. Suddenly, the audience seemed to come alive and hands were raised. Now, who to call on? Certainly not the one note guy from the Times whose question he knew would be: "Are you asking the Jews to give up their birthright by not going to Palestine, Senators!?" Then again, why not? Let Arach answer and then Phil and I can elaborate if need be. He pointed at the Times correspondent who stood and asked: "Are you asking the Jews to give up their birthright, Senators."

"Mort, I'm going to ask Arach Poletsky to respond to your question."

Arach chose to stand.

"Hello, Mr. Steinberg. I read your column in the Times. If I may, I would like to answer your question this way. No, I want Jews to feel comfortable living in Palestine but I want the people who are not Jewish to feel the same way. More importantly, to establish a principle at the beginning on what Palestine is and should be. In America, we think of Palestine as a country not very green when you think of the country here in the east and in most of America. But to the people who live there it is very green when compared to much of what lies to the east and southeast of it. To speak in New York parlance, it is prime real estate. In answer to your question, who determines who can immigrate to Palestine should be the Palestinians, those who live there. The first step is for the British to grant the Palestinians a country and give those who live there the right to run their country. The Palestinians should have the right to answer your question, not America and not Britain."

"What will happen to the Jews in Palestine if that happens. Won't the Arabs throw them out."

Arach was pleased with the shift from usual discussions about Jews and Palestine which treated the Arabs as irrelevant to an acknowledgement of their existence.

"The British would grant citizenship to everyone living in Palestine today and in creating country of Palestine, the citizens would have rights. In other words, the Jews would be citizens of Palestine like anyone else living there. There is polarization, there is friction but I think you will be surprised once you find out who those Christian and Muslims really are."

Hollister spoke. "If I may interject, Arach, what I have been able to learn since Arach first talked to us is that we are asking of the people in Palestine who have lived there for generations to deal with the prejudices of the Europeans and in some ways, Americans. Those problems of bigotry and hatred are not for the Palestinians to solve by giving up their own country, but they are problems for all of us."

From five rows back, "Do you really believe America with its history of anti-Semitism will agree to take in hundreds of thousands of Jews?"

The questions sounded like an accusation to Phillip Hollister who responded: "There is anti-Semitism in America like there is hatred of blacks and even Catholics in many parts of the country. Bigotry against the Mormons has a long history. But remember that hundreds of thousands of Jews came to America during the great waves of Europeans in the lifetimes of many of us. How many of you here are Jewish and you've done pretty well and the country has done pretty well by you. Don't ever expect a short answer from me, but if I were giving one, I would say yes, they will if they know all the facts."

"Why would Jewish leaders agree to such a proposal?" The question came from a mid-western paper reporter and Bruce could read nothing into it except a request for our thoughts.

"Well, the proposal is a number of things, and the main point is that it is a way to peace should mean something to all Americans. The leading Jews who are Zionists would have to accept limits on immigration to Palestine in return for the safety and well-being of hundreds of thousands of Jews in Europe."

Fred Markey was perhaps the most highly respected journalists among the member of the press corps. He had recently returned from continental Europe. His reports all pointed to the threat that Hitler posed to the rest of Europe with his calls for Ein Volk, Ein Reich, Ein Fuehrer in English One People, One Nation, One Leader. By ending unrest in Germany and restoring German pride in their nation, Hitler had created a nation which once again threatened its neighbors. Germany was rearming, building a strong air force and a strong army and other nations were alarmed. Given his strident language and his harsh treatment of his enemies, other leaders did not believe his ambitions were limited only to uniting the German speaking peoples of Europe. Fred Markey reported all of that for his paper.

"Do you think the American President can stop Hitler?" He directed his question to Hollister, who he knew as one of the few Senators who kept an open mind about the European crisis.

"Do you recall, Fred, not so many years ago when the greatest threat to America and Europe was Russia and the spread of communism. To many of us who believed in our form of government, communism by inciting revolution through violence was a threat. In my mind, it still is and I am concerned that we are suddenly getting cozy with the Russians to stop Hitler. I think our President needs to address both threats without going to war.

"America needs to know about the millions of victims of the USSR. Read about the Ukrainians who starved to death when the

Communists confiscated and sold their grain abroad to earn foreign currency. Read about the peasants who resisted their land reforms and were loaded in box cars and sent to Siberia to their deaths.

"What we need to avoid is the formation of alliances which led to the Great War and forming an alliance with the USSR to combat the advances of Germany will only lead to war."

"Winston Churchill is demanding that we stop Hitler and any further expansion by him by force is an act of war and we must stand and fight, if necessary." Markey had the floor and Hollister was allowing him to hold it.

"Like Teddy Roosevelt who demanded we get in the Great War before it started, I can't fault Churchill by saying he is an old man who wants young men to fight his wars. I have no doubt he would be willing to fight it out with Hitler personally. And people feel somehow safe with such leaders and they trust him to protect them. But Churchill is wrong. For some slogans and feel good moments, millions, God knows how many millions will die. We have very short memories and very little imagination when it comes to wars. No, Fred, we have to stop this one. And we can, I think."

"What will we do if Hitler moves into Poland as he is threatening to do. What country will be next? Will he attack Russia and if he attacks Russia, who will be next." The reporter from a small magazine in New York was angry, and he stared at the two Senators as he asked the rhetorical question."

It was the Senator from Missouri who answered.

"If Hitler has read Tolstoy's War and Peace, I think Russia need not worry about Germany. What is most likely is that two very evil men will try to stare down the other and neither will move against the other. There are some misguided so-called statesmen who have suggested that it would not be a bad thing if there was a war between them. That is the kind of amoral thinking too often employed by major powers where death and suffering are of little consequence."

Arach worried that no further questions were asked about Palestine. Certainly, the Zionists in America would oppose the creation of a state and control of the borders of that state by its citizens. The dream that Israel would replace Palestine and the Arabs settled elsewhere would be destroyed. He felt his mood darken as he realized that such men would deal with the two Senators by discrediting them and attacking the proposals as not worthy of serious discussion. *Unless it could not be avoided, they would ignore the proposal for Palestine altogether. These fanatics, these zealots were willing to sacrifice millions for their vision and the people of Palestine would pay and pay and pay.*

The press room was empty but for the two of them along with Fred Markey who promised to join them at the Grill for a drink. Arach had graciously thanked the two Senators, shook hands with Markey, and left.

Hollister watched the old man as he opened to door leading to the street, his outline momentarily highlighted, then he was gone.

"There goes a good man. He thinks he failed today. What do you think, Fred?

"If you want me to tell you what I will say in the paper tomorrow, I don't know. I know what the true believers will say and you pretty much know what they will write or say. What this reporter can say is I need that drink but no more politicking, ok?"

"Deal."

Alone with his thoughts as he made his way to the train station, Arach Poletsky thought of one man. What will Lewis do? He knew Michael Bernard Lewis who led a useful life, a man who presidents came for advice. People who described him during his lifetime included brilliant in their descriptions at least once, often more. And he was a very smart lawyer, but more than that, a man who could shape the world around him. He liked to think of himself as a legal adviser with wide latitude to go beyond the law in dealing with his clients.

And he was the most important Zionist in the world for he had the ear of the most powerful men in the world.

I recall my surprise when I discovered that Lewis was not always a Zionist He spoke eloquently of assimilation, that Jews should be part of the great melting pot. By the time the Ottoman Empire crumbled, he was red blooded American and a Zionist. Given the respect given him by the people who matter, they see him as both and choose to see no contradiction.

What will Lewis and Lipsky and other prominent Jews in America do if momentum begins to build with the Hollister-Bruce proposal? What if they do have to choose between rescuing Jews in Germany and Jewish state in Palestine. Of course, they would argue for both, but what if they had to choose.

But Lewis has more than two Senators to think about. The British are making noises about concluding their role in Palestine as the protector of Jewish settlers and Arabs are increasingly demanding equal treatment. This must be troubling to the man whose history showed such empathy for the ordinary people, the little people and had defended their rights to human dignity. The Bill of Rights was his bible. So what about the Arabs? Are they not ordinary people too who have the protection of that same Bill?

So what will this great man do. What drives him. It is the most fundamental of forces, the tribal instinct to survive to prevail over your enemies. The Old Testament becomes not the word of God alone by a manifesto that declares the right to dominion over the land. .

I hope I am wrong.

They will attack me, of course. I may lose a few more good friends. But no matter.

***

Lewis was angry that the press conference had happened at all. The two were Don Quixote and Sancho Panza battling windmills. But such men are dangerous. Then there were reporters and columnists like Fred Markey.

Markey was a competent, very good reporter. People had confidence in what he had to say. His reports on what was happening in Germany helped the cause of getting more refugees into Palestine. Markey was useful but his Times account of the press conference made him see Markey differently. He could detect no partisanship in the article which makes it even worse. But he did, very boldly, report on the Hollister and Bruce proposal for America to open its doors to take refugees from Germany.

Lewis knew that the leaders in Palestine were not interested in taking all the refugees from Germany, only those who could fight for Palestine. But what will prominent Jews in America say about the proposal? Most will attack it as being totally unrealistic about Hitler and about America's willingness to open its doors. But some will not.

Killing what Poletsky is proposing must be done quickly. Jews able to fight must be allowed in Palestine. No one can work with Hitler and what he and the German people have done cannot be forgiven. We must isolate and damage the two Senators and keep them away from the isolationists.

***

By the time Arach reached Union Station, the steel gray clouds had grown darker and deeper and a few snowflakes were drifting down, only to melt when the touched the sidewalk. Crowds of busy people swept past him, many calling cabs which were lined up in front of the station, other racing for their trains. Departure in twenty minutes. A deep sigh that removed the tension that had been with him the whole day. It would be good to be home. A quiet dinner alone at Ricci's with a small bottle of Chianti. And to see his friends. He smiled when he imagined what Morty thinks of it all.

Whatever the mood in Palestine, the guests always looked forward to one of Emma Smythe's dinner parties. People you knew, good food and the Smythe hospitality always made you feel special. Still, when the evening began, gloom seemed to hover over them all. Two more bombings in Haifa, derailing of a train near Nablus, the massacre of Jews by Arabs in Tiberias, the bombing of two villages suspected of harboring rebels, riots reported in an internment camp north of Tiberias, and the constant movement of troops and over flights of bombers out of Jordan and Egypt. The mood of the gathering was but a reflection of the mood of all of Jerusalem.

Sarah noticed the John's mood was contrary to all the others. They were all having a drink before dinner, when John suddenly interrupted the melancholy gathering.

"May I have your attention, please?"

Everyone seemed a little surprised at how loud John was. He was usually subdued, almost deferential. He continued.

"When Leslie and Emma invited me, it was through the good offices of Sarah, who told Emma that I had an idea for bringing peace to Palestine. Well, that sounds rather grandiose, but I think sometimes grand schemes need to be tried. My plan was to get the priests, pastors, rabbis and imams to come together and pray and petition for peace."

A skeptic from the back of the room asked. "What did you hope to accomplish, Reverend?"

He looked at the older man whom he had seen at one of the garden parties that were hosted weekly by the notables, Mandate officials, or members of the foreign community. John often

175

attended such gatherings. Usually not invited, but anxious to get to know everyone in Jerusalem.

"Well, I'm not sure I was clear in my own mind what could be accomplished, but I know that the religious community has not spoken with one voice on the troubles in Palestine and I thought it was worth finding out the answer to the questions: what if they did lend their voices as a chorus, and what should be the song to be sung. So I have spent my time meeting with them individually and then invited them to attend a meeting with other members of the community.

It was Emma who spoke first?

"Well, John, tell us what happened?" Sarah smiled. Count on Emma to warm up the crowd.

John smiled as he spoke: "Well, at first there was a lot of looking around the room to see who was attending and for a while, the gathering was subdued. They did not seem very comfortable in each other's company. I could be wrong about that. I can't say I knew what they were thinking, but I did sense there was both a questioning of the invitation and a curiosity about the pastor from a tiny church taking it upon himself to invite representatives of the major churches and mosques. Perhaps the question in their minds was "Who are you to take upon yourself such a task?"

Sarah smiled at John: "I doubt that you were intimidated, John"

No one missed the fondness in her voice and the two of them as an item was a topic among their friends.

"Well, I was a little. There is so much potential energy here in Jerusalem but it is used in a provincial way with each church, synagogue and mosque. Of course, in the main, that is what each pastor should be doing for their flock, but working together I think we can do more, much more."

176

Katy Antonius had never been a woman content to be in the background supporting her husband, but had done her best to encourage other women to become active in civic affairs, to work for an independent, democratic Palestine.

"Please go on, John." Katy was wondering if much thought was given to the headmasters of the mission and other schools in Palestine. She would be guided by what John had to report.

"Very soon after the meeting began and people had introduced themselves, I sensed the mood changed, and the group became more animated. Watching the faces of some, I found them hard to read, but I'm sure some saw the need not to compromise their beliefs and mission in any way and that held them back."

No one spoke, looking at John, waiting.

"Very soon after the meeting started, I began to see the religious looking at me, wondering what was to come next. I confess I didn't know what we would accomplish, only that I prayed something would. When I thought the amenities had been sufficiently observed, I repeated why I invited them; that they were all men of peace and promoters of peace and it was their duty to show the way to peace."

"I thought a great deal about the matter of duty and I prayed over that word, knowing that I risked sounding as if I was telling them what their duties were, but for such an undertaking taking shape in my mind, I decided I should issue such a challenge. I suppose in a way, coming from a church with 120 members might be more acceptable than from one of the major religious figures in Jerusalem."

"Sarah, you know Rabbi Mostel as a friend. He was the only one to challenge my language and I'm afraid my answer was a bit long winded. Trying to read his eyes, I really wasn't able to tell what he thought of my answer. One of the things I have learned as a pastor is that dismissal of your message in not unusual so you learn to handle it without considering it a personal attack."

He looked at the small group of dinner party guests and read their faces that he should get to the meat of what happened before they had to leave. He looked at Sarah and got the same message but with a smile.

"I was uplifted by the first question, which was delivered in a positive tone of voice. It was a priest, Russian Orthodox, who asked what can we do?"

"Why?" Leslie Smythe asked."

"Because I read in his voice that he wanted to do something and to be part of it." It was Emma replying to her husband, nudging him as she did.

John nodded his assent. "I knew about the squabbles between churches and religions, but I was counting on something else, that everyone in the room cared about the Holy Land and if they were forced to examine their hearts, they cared about everyone Christian, Jew or Muslim."

"You cannot ignore the past, John, or the present. In their zeal to nurture their own, they have often hurt others." It was George Antonius who spoke, the scholarly Greek Orthodox Catholic who worked for the British.

"But the core beliefs are the same in all religions, and I want the leaders to use those beliefs to achieve peace."

"What can they do?" The questioner was Rafiq Khalidi, a teacher at the College.

"It is really up to them, whether they feel the calling to make a united effort to achieve peace. At the first meeting, it would be asking too much to expect they would make such a commitment. They would have to go back to their houses of worship and their religious bodies to consult with others. Before there is another meeting, there will be discussions among those present and whatever is to happen will likely emerge."

Emma walked up to John and gave him a hug. Leslie seemed only mildly surprised. He was used to such expressions of emotion from his Italian wife. "I think what you have done is marvelous."

There was quick affirmation as several of the guess shouted "Hear! Hear!"

The face of the pastor of Christ Church turned red. Compliments always surprised him no matter the situation.

It was a typical winter day in Jerusalem. A brief show of sunshine early in the morning, then thin clouds that made them feel the cold dampness. John looked at the letters in Sarah's hand and read what was in her eyes. "Is there something you want to tell me, Sarah?"

Sarah spoke quickly. "The one is a letter from young John. He is doing very well at Cambridge. He writes of all the talk about war. If war comes, the Nevers are always expected to be among the first to volunteer for their country."

Now he understood her mood. Her husband, her brother, and now John likely to go off to war. Why must the young and the bravest always be ready to go to war. There is nothing to say to Sarah but: "Let us pray there will not be another war." Talking now about another war made him think of what he had witnessed in the Great War. Surely those in the last war would do everything in their power to prevent another one.

Sarah opened the other letter. "I thought you might want to read this."

The letter was from Arach.

My Dearest Sarah,

I hope this letter finds you well. I hope all is well with John, the pastor sounds like a fine young man.

John paused, a lump in his throat, looked at the smiling Sarah, then quickly looked away.

I pray that something can be done by those in Palestine to end the civil war there. I have been able to get hold of the small newspapers in New York that have carried the reports from the two Frenchmen. I have also read in the Times that the British are searching for them and that the Agency has a reward for anyone who captures or kills them. It is sad to hear such news, that brave young men wanting to tell the world what is happening are hunted as criminals.

I know you are anxious to hear what is happening with the two Senators' efforts to get the President and the Congress to stop the war in Europe and to save the many Jews in Germany who are in great danger. I was present at a news conference when Senator Hollister and Senator Bruce presented their plans. I made a few brief remarks then was given the chance to explain why the rescue of the Jews in Germany must be accompanied by an end to emigration to Palestine.

Along with this letter I have included the report by Fred Markey, who is nationally known, in the Times. I think it reports what was said very well.

"The letter had been opened. The newspaper clipping was gone." It was easy to hear the anger in her voice. "Sorry, read the rest of the letter."

Men like Lewis, and Lipsky were quick to denounce the proposal to stop immigration into Palestine but thankfully did leave some room for negotiation by not rejecting the President taking a more active role in securing peace. They were, of course, not willing to even hint of stopping immigration into Palestine as a bargaining chip and wholeheartedly supported rescuing our people by increasing immigration to America.

As the two Senators pointed out before the press conference, the President is conflicted when the national interest and political gain conflict, and often is too concerned with how his actions will benefit him politically. It is a matter that is very complicated and overwhelms me when I try to understand it. I doubt if the President fully understands the conflict himself. Please, forgive my cynicism but that is the way this old man feels.

I think the two Senators have done an honorable thing; the success of their efforts is a matter of life and death for the Jews in Germany. The sentiment against war here in America is very strong, but sadly that will do nothing to stop war from breaking out. I think our President has agreed to back England if war comes. He denies it, of course, but acting as Britain's guarantor makes war more likely.

The plan that Senators Hollister and Bruce put forward is the only hope for peace and for the rescue of Jews in Germany. Let us all pray for a miracle.

I am well. Morty is doing well, although he doesn't like my stand on Palestine. He is a true friend. I have met another friend who sometimes has lunch with us when the weather is nice. Her name is Josephine. She makes wonderful sweets, always enough to share with her two old Jewish friends.

Your devoted father,

Arach

"The two senators were proposing your father's plan, weren't they?"

"Yes, but I'm sure they had more in mind."

"Does your husband's family know about the press conference and what your father is doing?"

"Most likely. In any event, I will write to them about it. Since the censors chose to remove the newspaper article, they likely know more than I do. I suppose I should explain why Arach feels as he does and that he feels there is no other way to save the lives of Jews in Germany."

"What about John?"

"Yes, he needs to know. I will write to him first. I don't want him to hear it from his grandparents because they will be angry about the plan not to ally with Britain."

+++

Herschel Feibel Grynszpan was a German-born Jewish refugee of Polish parents. On 7 November 1938, the teenager walked into the German Embassy in Paris and shot German diplomat Ernst von Rath five times in the stomach, shouting that he did it because of what the Germans were doing to the Jews. Upon the young German's death, Germans were whipped into a rage by Hitler and Goebbels. The rampage that followed quickly became known as Kristallnacht, the name given to the rampage because it left the streets covered with broken glass from the windows of Jewish owned stores, buildings and synagogues.

The Times wrote: "No foreign propagandist bent upon blackening Germany before the world could outdo the tale of burnings and beatings, of blackguardly assaults on defenseless and innocent people, which disgraced that country yesterday."

+++

Reading the Times, Senator Phillip Hollister knew their task has just become much more difficult.

The two men stared at the cold rain falling outside the Ebbitt Grill. It was warm inside, made even more comfortable by the bourbon. The street lights came on as they sat in their booth, headlights of the passing cars turning the street into glass. "I guess you read the Post this morning. Kristallnacht. What a crazy bunch of bastards. I read the remarks by the Times. Those people at the Times would have more credibility if they didn't pretend that what happened was going to lead to war as if they haven't been beating the drums for years."

"Always the cynic, Phil. Face it, Kristallnacht is not going to help our proposal. They'll be more and more calls to do something about Hitler. And the people who want us to stay out of a war in Europe are going to be even harder to convince that we can stop a war. And those who are demanding that something be done about the Jews in Germany are not willing to allow the President in the same room with Hitler or to play hardball with Britain."

"You really believe in holding all the parts together, don't you?"

"You mean Arach's proposal on Palestine, right? Yes, it will make it tougher to sell it to the Jews who want their people to be able to go to Palestine. You know, Phil, the way Arach talked about his Arab neighbors makes you understand. Yeah, for the sake the people of Palestine, I will fight to keep it in the package." Hollister paused for his punch line. "And I think the British will agree.."

"The President needs more than warm feelings for Arabs. We need to get the President to look down the road because oil is running out here and the Arabs are floating on the stuff. When the competition starts for Arab oil, helping the Arabs in Palestine gives us a leg up."

Hollister leaned back. "I've been button holing some of our colleagues. More times than not I see a light go on, then it dims, and they walk away saying they'll need to talk to some of the people who bankrolled them or they are thinking about it."

"I think we need to talk to Cordell. If there's anyone who can convince the President, it's Hull. It's hard to talk to a man who counts votes and donations every time a proposal is put in front of him."

"Be heading down to Florida next week. I think we're really going to do it this time." He looked at his friend from Missouri who did not want to drop the matter, but sometimes you got to realize you can't keep beating the horse when you know it's dead. But his young friend was no quitter so he added as he put his hands on the table. "Set it up. I'll be there.

Part VII

"It is now or never, my friends. I do not plan to go to them with hat in hand, pleading for a settlement. We must be bold. We must have chutzpah. He smiled as he thought of Yitzhak; it was his favorite word.

The raid on Kfar Giladi had lifted the spirits of Arabs throughout their world. Word that Ismael Latif was fighting beside Abu Kamal raised it even further and the few young fighting men left were joining him. Successful raids were now commonplace and reports of the Arab success were appearing in papers all over the world.

More striking was the behavior of Arab leaders who were demanding that the British and the French accelerate the march toward independence of Palestine as part of Greater Syria or an independent state.

As Churchill bellowed for war and Hitler bet on the timidity of his neighbors, the British High Command became alarmed at the uncertainty surrounding the Middle East. Italy was on the horn of Africa threatening the Red Sea passage and Arab leaders were still bitter because of the British betrayal after the Great War. Oil had become as indispensable as gunpowder and the oil coming from Mosul through the pipeline to Haifa was critical. Montgomery, Wavell and Bomber Harris needed to put down the revolt within months.

Ismael had watched their morale rise since Kfar Giladi. He knew he was a reason for that. But Ismael knew what Lawrence knew, that victories in battles were important, but the whole point was not even to win battles or the war but to gain their freedom.

Ismael avoided the isolation that afflicted most of the rebels who in their constant flight from superior forces knew little of what was happening outside Palestine. Ismael knew that the revolt could only bear fruit for the Arabs if they could somehow leverage what was happening in Europe and Asia. Britain was a colonial power and a world power and there was unrest not only by the Arabs in Palestine but in its colonies in Africa and Asia. The disintegration of the German, Austro-Hungary and Ottoman Empires and the unrest it created did not leave the French, Italians or British untouched. Agitation was rife in India and Africa had begun to stir. Now Germany had suddenly reared up to challenge the French and the British.

Britain's response to the German threat was to seek to reduce the agitation in their colonies and its mandate in Palestine. In all of this, Ismael thought, lay opportunity to create an independent Palestine which would be willing to ally with Britain in its struggle against Germany and a newly aggressive Italy. But peace for the British in Palestine must come with a price, and that price is freedom. As pressure on the English increases, so must rebel pressure be increased.

Andre and his Argentinian brother George often talked with him of such matters. Andre and George had been his source for much of what was happening in the world. Ismael also received Le Figaro once Beirut communications channels had been established. On occasion they received the London Times and however dated was full of news about ominous happenings in Europe.

Hidden by a thick pine woods, the three of them spoke softly, their faces lit by the small fire slowly dying, now only fading embers remained.

"We need to talk to the British."

Andre fixed his gaze on Ismael. "Why would they want to talk to you? They know you cannot hold on much longer."

"I think we have shown them that we can still fight and to defeat us will take time."

"Why should that matter if they are winning? They will laugh in your face, Ismael."

"It is now or never, my friends. I do not plan to go to them with hat in hand, pleading for a settlement. We must be bold. We must have chutzpah." He smiled when he thought of Yitzhak; it was his favorite word.

The smiling Arab delighted the two men, who slapped each other on the back, laughing and enjoying the light moment.

"What will you say?"

"I don't know."

George looked at his friend. "You are serious, aren't you?"

"Yes."

"Then I think you will succeed. No, I know you will succeed."

The ambush had occurred on the road from Tulkarem to Nablus on a steep incline where the road turned sharply to the left as it hugged the side of the hill. Visibility was limited to the next turn. The British were drilled to recognize danger signals and normal procedure would be to stop the convoy of three lorries and a motor car and scout around the bend to detect any ambush.

There had not been an incident on the road in over a month and as night was falling. Sergeant Johnson was tired and hungry. He thought of the hot meal waiting at the fort. He decided to forgo the normal precautions. As the last vehicle completed the turn, a feday'ee stepped from behind a small boulder and tossed a mills bomb under the motor car in front. The explosion quickly disabled the vehicle and rapid fire from above the convoy left the 10 soldier lying dead or dying. A minute and it was all over.

Johnson was bleeding from wounds as he struggled to remove his revolver. Flashing through his mind was the thought: *If I had only followed standing orders. What would they do to him?"* A young man like him stood in front of the motor car; his Enfield was pointed at him. He raised his revolver, a burst of light; he did not hear the sharp crack of the rifle and its echo through the trees below

The mounted light machine gun was removed from the disabled motor car, the dead men stripped of weapons and ammunition. Quickly, the rebels pushed the motor car off the road and watched it tumble down the hillside disgorging the four dead soldiers before coming to a stop against a cluster of pines. The dead men from the lorries were pulled from the lorries, stripped of weapons and ammunition and left beside the road. Amad, the fedayeen commander thought it unlikely that the motor car could have sent a wireless message. Assigning drivers, he sent the lorries to their new destination and ordered the rest of the men follow him to where the horses were hidden. He thought of his village for he knew he was on the list and they would suffer for what he did today.

It was not until the following morning that a reconnaissance aero plane spotted the wreckage and bodies and armored cars dispatched to the scene. The process that would follow was familiar to the combatants. Search the list of known rebels, locate their towns and villages, and punish.

The British Empire, like all empires are confident that attrition, the slow wearing down of their rebelling subjects will ultimately lead to breaking the spirit of the rebels and in submission. In the minds of the British, a tested tactic is collective punishment, where the villages were punished when it was discovered that rebels were from those villages. Noncombatants were also punished in order to deprive rebels of supplies; destroying crops and killing livestock where even a small portion of the food went to rebels. Often, in the minds of the conquerors, it was merely to teach them a lesson.

Special taxes were levied against villagers to remind them that rebellion could be costly even where they had nothing to do with the rebellion. Villagers were conscripted without pay into work bands to build fortifications and repair damaged property.

To some, it appeared as if the British were simply being malicious, which was true for such men as Purdom, but the strategy was not created because of malice. It was created to demoralize the general population and to turn the general population against the rebels, to isolate the rebels from the general population. Villages were rewarded for informing on rebels, and notables were given money and arms to fight the rebels. Old feuds were exploited to divide to weaken the rebellion.

The British expected, by applying these tactics consistently, support for the cause of the rebels would die.

But that did not happen, and it dawned on a growing number of British officials that there were wrongs being done to the Palestinian Arabs that must be addressed. And with that realization came a growing respect for their enemies, and a growing sense that what they must do was the right thing to do. In American parlance, they had come to understand that they had been hustled by the Zionists, and it was time to be both honest and fair, true to the values they wanted the world to see.

Reuters: 27Nov1938

Editor's Note: The two journalists are being hunted by the British authorities for aiding the rebels and a 10,000 Palestinian Pound reward is offered for information leading to their capture.

Andre Monet and George Bissett

We are reporting from a rock overhang overlooking the valley and the ruins of al-Bassa. We arrived at the scene twenty four hours after the British first surrounded the town. What happened in al-Bassa was told to us by survivors. We are withholding their names to protect them and other surviving members of their families.

The incident was triggered by the killing of members of a British patrol near al-Bassa. Before the killing, the commanding officer for the sector, Colonel Thurston, had warned the village chief that there would be punishment of the entire village if anything happened to British troops or Jewish militia in the area.

When we arrived' we were struck by the absence of young boys and men. Women and small children were moving aimlessly through the smoldering ruins where only the walls of burning out buildings remained.. We approached a small boy standing beside one of the ruined houses. When we approached him, he did not move. We wondered if he would talk. When Kalima asked him what happened, he told us this story.

"The sun was coming up when we heard the sound of their armored cars. When they got to the village, they scattered around. Then the soldiers began firing machine guns into the village and this went on and on. There were people lying on the ground, some not moving, others crying for help. The soldiers let the wounded lay. I could hear some of them crying for help. Then they made the other men march into a field. Then soldiers with lighted torches set the houses on fire and burnt the village to the ground. We have a small root cellar in our house, and were able to hide when they began searching for the men of the village."

We asked the young boy how old he was. He answered ten but boys his age were rounded up with the rest. He told us that since the soldiers were no longer searching the burning village, he crept to the edge of the village where he could see what was happening. He saw his father and two of his older brothers among the men in the field.

Some of the men tried to run, he told us, but were immediately shot with sub-machine guns as they ran. He made a popping noise showing how the soldiers fired their weapons.

"Then, I saw soldiers digging in the ground and planting explosives. Sometimes they do that around their own camps but did not understand why they were doing it near the village. Then a large bus appeared and drove into the field. Many of the villagers saw what was happening and tried to run. They were shot as they ran. The rest were forced into the bus by the soldiers with bayonets on their rifles. Then the officer pointed to the Mukhtar and two soldiers grabbed him and forced him to drive the bus."

The pictures show what was left of the bus. We wondered why the Mukhtar had not refused to drive the bus. Had he been told him their choices were die on the spot or take their chances?

An old woman, tears flowing on her grief filled face, told us that body parts were strewn all around where the bus exploded. After the explosion, the men that remained were forced to dig a mass grave and bury the remains of their fellow villagers. When they had finished, the young men were loaded into lorries and driven away. She did not know where they were taken.

George was reading Le Figaro which included their dispatch. They were alone in the hotel room.

"Too bad we could not have divulged the true source."

"I doubt in his wildest imaginings he could have imagined what he saw his fellows do that day.

"Must have been difficult."

"To see what his English brothers were doing or to tell us?"

"Both, I suppose."

Monet stood quickly, looking down at his partner, still lounging on the bed.

"We had better get packed. Kalima will be here around midnight. I'm going to miss this place."

"I am going to miss the croissants."

"Wait 'til you taste an Argentine chocotorta."

"I worry about you George. The Agency could get one of their newspapers to place an ad from a restaurant for chocotortas just like the ones in Cordoba."

"If they do that, I am lost."

"Ismael Latif."

"What about him?"

"Wonderful man. But I still can't look at him without thinking of the Argentine Yusef al-Dajani. He must wonder the same thing. Who am I?"

They became silent, the light-hearted banner gone. "I don't know what is going to happen to us, but I would not want to be anywhere else doing anything else and with you, my good friend. I feel very lucky."

George looked at the spare young man beside him. His face, once smooth and pink, was now lined and the eyes had lost all their innocence. He worried about his friend, worried that he too often threw caution to the wind and staying alive was not important enough.

The knock jolted George, then he smiled. Andre rushed to the door, and quickly opened it for the smiling Hamdan. "Time my friends for croissants and coffee."

Attack on Tegart Fort

REUTERS 3December1938

Editor's Note: The two journalists are being hunted by the British authorities for aiding the rebels and a 10,000 Palestinian Pound reward is offered for information leading to their capture.

Dispatch from Antoine Monet, somewhere in Palestine

In a different place, and a different world Abd Rahim al Hajj Mohammad would have commanded thousands, for Abu Kamal is a born leader. Among the important people in Palestine, even among his enemies the British and the Jews, he is known as an honorable man who fights not for glory but for a free Palestine. He disdains the Nashashibi's for their corrupt ways and the Husayni's for their personal ambitions for they stand in the way of Palestine's struggle for freedom.

His strategy is to bring all Palestinians together, to refrain from and resist the existence of factions. The bitter internecine struggles within Palestine are crippling the revolt and he refuses to engage in any actions which widen rifts between Palestinians. One of the tactics used in the revolt, and in many other revolts, is the assassination of rival leaders. When asked why he did not obey the command of Husayni to assassinate men who were accused of selling out to the British, he replied": I don't work for Husayni but for Palestine". He looks beyond the revolt to a time when differences must be set aside to build a nation.

He wears his crown uneasily, yearning for the end of the revolt and the return to his family. He is a hunted man, and his family under everyday watch, for the British and the Jews hope that his love for his family will be his Achilles heel.

We have returned from a night raid on one of the forts built by Charles Tegart, who has arrived from India to take charge of the security for

Palestine. It was Tegart who has overseen the erection of the border fence, eight feet tall, made of razor wire, and patrolled 24 hours a day. The round fort is guarded by soldiers manning machine guns sighting through turrets near the top. Abu Kamal scouts observed the target for several days, noting the paths followed by the soldiers going in and out. The British have placed mines around the fort and the paths taken by the soldiers told them where the mines were placed.

The attack began when a British patrol was ambushed outside the fort. Soldiers from the fort rushed out to assist their comrades. Kamal's men, concealed near the main entrance, then stormed the fort and fought their way inside. Explosions were heard from inside the fort as the fedayeen hurled grenades. Attempts to get inside the armory failed, and the fedayeen quickly retreated.

In less than an hour, the battle was over. Abu Kamal withdrew, carrying the wounded and dead away from the fort. Smoke could be seen rising from the fort. Two of Kamal's men were killed, five wounded, one of them unlikely to live.

There is no way at this moment to determine how many British soldiers died.

I questioned Abu Kamal after the raid.

"Was the raid a success?"

"Yes."

"But you did not capture the fort."

"No." He looked at me for a moment. It has taken some time being around Abu Kamal to speak to him and then to ask him questions which were difficult or critical. I wondered if I had crossed the line.

Then he spoke. "We cannot capture and hold what the British control. If we took the fort, to try to hold it would be asking our fighters to sacrifice their lives. There are such times when that is necessary, but trying to hold the fort would have meant certain death to my men and it would have achieved nothing."

He then added, understanding where my dispatch might be read. "If the British are listening, our message is this: we are fighting for our freedom. We will not stop fighting until we receive it. Allah will help us."

"Ha'aretz reported your story just the way you wrote it. That is a good sign. Bissett and Monet were sitting on a large boulder, catching the warm sun and enjoying the moment of peace and the presence of Monet's dispatch in the prominent Jewish paper in Palestine."

"Do you think we are making a difference; that the British will come to their senses?"

"You mean, will they do the right thing."

"Yes."

"And what is the right thing to do?"

"To grant the Palestinians and the Jews living in Palestine their independence."

"Agreed."

It was not a good day. Although it seems every Jew's anger in Palestine was aimed at the owners of Ha'aretz, he was not left unmarked. Why, Abe, did you give this gangster a forum to spread such lies. From every city, town, moshav and kibbutz comes the same bitter complaint.

He is not surprised that the High Commissioner has not sent the usual message condemning the Arab gangsters because something is happening with the British. He needs to find out what it is.

Charles Thurston is just a clerk in the political department in the High Commission but big ears and sticky fingers made him a great source over the years. Let's see what he knows and what he can find out.

He calls out to the young lady sitting at a desk outside his door. He had placed her desk in his sight because Leah is pleasant to look at. "Leah, tell Avraham I want to see him."

"Yes, Mr. Shurtok."

Lipsky could deliver a personal message to Thurston for a meeting.

His anger is like a scattergun this morning. MacMichael. Abd al Rahim al Hajj Mohammad, the gangster, the man they called Abu Kamal. Monet and Bissett, Mona, who bitched unmercifully for a thousand reasons before he left this morning. His sinuses. By mid-morning Mona is forgotten, then MacMichael is shelved. The morning sun shining through his window makes his sinuses better. That left Abd al Rahim Al Hajj Mohammad and the two Frenchmen. By noon, his focus is on the two Frenchmen, and the anger had morphed to cool determination to rid the world of those two. But how?

Landing on the beach south of Haifa, walking on the land of his birth and the birth of generations before him, Ismael was elated, yet he knew that the fight ahead would be like no other in his life. In 1918, Britain was his ally. Today, they were the enemy. And then there was Lawrence, the man they called Awrans, and the man Lowell Thomas, the American newspaperman, made famous as Lawrence of Arabia. Fighting beside Lawrence, he quickly realized that Lawrence had a mission, to free the Arabs from the yoke of the Europeans, whether they be Turks, French, or even his own, the English. Lawrence firmly believed that if the Arabs fought well against the Turks, they would be rewarded with their freedom.

The Arabs won their battle against the Turks but lost the war for freedom when the British betrayed them. It was a great disappointment for Lawrence, who had been deceived and he in turn had unknowingly passed the deception along.

But what he learned from Lawrence was to follow his star, to imagine a new world then do your very best to make it come to life. He believed in a free Palestine and would do his best to make it happen.

Three months had passed since that night on the beach and looking back, the dream of a free Palestine was still there. There had been small victories. He had come to understand the passion of the rebels, their bravery and their loyalty to their families and to Palestine.

They revolted in anger when the steady stream of Jews became a raging torrent. The attempt to protect their country peacefully by waging a general strike that failed when the British met their pleas with rejection and force. It began as a revolt of the peasants who suffered the most, and leaders like Qassam and Al Hajj Mohammad emerged to lead them.

They fought bravely and with their outmoded and puny firepower were remarkably effective. In dwindling numbers against the largest British army concentration in the Empire, they have fought.

The small fire in front of him was beginning to die and thoughts turned to the mystic Englishman twenty years ago, calling the Arabs to battle and when they asked why they should fight for the British, he would say their freedom. He thought of the irony. Why do we fight the British today? For freedom.

Ismael knew the revolt of the Palestinians would simply die like the last embers of a fire, and it would be over unless something happened beyond the borders of Palestine to change the British policy toward the Arabs.

And it was happening.

The looming war with Germany, the Italian occupation of Ethiopia, and the urgency of the British to arm and settle any differences with the people of their Empire was the greatest hope for Palestine. Only miles away inside Palestine's borders lay the pipeline from Mosul to Haifa carrying oil essential to the British. They must protect it. The British needed to come to terms with the rebels, to end the revolt.

In his thoughts, one thing was clearer than any other. The revolt must end only when Palestine was free. He must lift the spirits of those who still fought beside him, to make them understand that each day they stayed in the field was a day that made the star of freedom shine brighter.

The strategy of the rebels would have two heads. One would fight on with even greater vigor, the second open the doors to talks, to convince the British that a free Palestine would be a bulwark for their defense, and they would have the support of the Palestinians and other Arab nations.

Abdul Kamal summoned Ismael to his command post, a small room created by placing canvas over a rock overhang. Two hurricane lamps provided a shimmering light. He was sitting on a large rock fast against the wall of the cave that allowed him to rest his back. The table in front of him was covered with papers that Ismael knew the ascetic man had examined or would be examining through much of the night.

He motioned Ismael to sit. Only the two of them were in the makeshift room. As Ismael looked for a place to sit, there was silence in the room. Only the patrols were awake in the camp, the only sounds the crackling canvas and the trees whipped by the high winds sweeping through the mountains.

The older man looked at Ismael, and the younger man saw sadness in the soft brown eyes of his commander. Those eyes looked straight into his as he spoke.

"I received a message today from Tulkarem, my good friend. I have sad news. Hassan Latif, a great warrior, is dead. Your brother died in the custody of the British. He had been wounded when his squad was ambushed, betrayed by an informant. The British took him to their headquarters in Nablus for questioning."

Ismael had been unable to locate his brother since he arrived in Palestine. He had sent word to his sister Tasneem that he was in Palestine but would be unable to come to their home because it would not be safe for the family. Neither their mother Suhayla nor sister Tasneem had heard from Hassan since the Arabs brief capture of Jerusalem. They were told he had escaped during the British attack. Sarah had come by to tell them that Hassan had escaped to the north.

He thought of how he would get the sad news to Jerusalem. Their houses would be watched.

"I need to get word to my family." Ismael rose to leave. "I want to talk to them by telephone but need to make the call from a town far away from here. They might trace the call."

Al Hajj Mohammad looked surprised. "They can do that?"

"Yes." Ismael dropped his head for a moment, then looked at the Commander. "What happened?"

"Hassan and his men were part of Razzik's fighters when they occupied Jerusalem. The British attacked with three Brigades and took back the city. Hassan and his men escaped. They were on their way to join us when they were ambushed above Suffariya. Hassan was wounded. Purdom shot all the wounded except for Hassan."

"How did they know it was Hassan?"

"They were betrayed. I am ashamed to say it was a nephew of mine, Mustafa ."

"They took him to Nablus? What happened?"

"He was tortured, Ismael. We do not know how he died."

"Who did this?"

"His name is Fortson."

"You are sure it was Purdom?"

"One of the men who escaped recognized him, and heard his name."

"I will be gone for two days. I will rejoin you then."

"One thing more, Ismael. One of our informants in Nazareth overheard a drunken soldier talking about what happened to Hassan. He told his friends at the table that he had never seen a tougher Arab. When Fortson asked him where you were, he replied. 'You will not find him, he will find you.'"

"That is so, Abu Kamal. If the man Fortson is still in Palestine, I will find him. And I will find Purdom."

***

He had climbed to the highest hill above the camp. In the distance, he could see British vehicles moving along the Tiberias road. Miles away, lights blinked in a cluster that told Ismael it was a small village they had passed on the way to the camp. Listening to the wind as it rushed through the trees around him, he fought the despair eating away at his soul. Death is a terrible thing, but knowing Hassan is in Paradise, eased the torment.

.*Many think me a hero, but how much more heroic my brother, who endured torture twice to save me, and has died a warrior. Gentle, he was not born to be a warrior, yet took up the cause to free Palestine, fought bravely, and endured the worst ordeal of all, tortured until death.*

In the darkness, he spoke words from the Koran:

Think not of those who are killed in the Path of Allah as dead. Nay, they are alive, with the Lord, and they receive their sustenance from Allah. They rejoice in what Allah has bestowed upon them in his Bounty and rejoice for the sake of those who have not joined them but are left behind; that in them, no fear shall come nor shall they grieve.

Yet as terrible as my brother's death is, I can accept that, but that my family had been deprived of the right to bury him, to mourn over his grave, I cannot accept.

Wiping away his tears, he thought of his father, long gone at the hand of assassins, and was comforted that he would have one of his sons with him forever. Straightening, he worked his way back to the camp. Tomorrow he would begin the search.

***

Commissioner MacMichael welcomed the request by Sarah and John the use of the parade field for the gathering of the religious to support a peace initiative by the Arab community. It could end the revolt and the conflict between the Jewish and Arab communities. A stolid Episcopalian, he even said a silent prayer for the effort and passed the word to the Pastor Suheil of St. George's Cathedral to attend.

The request was greeted all the more enthusiastically because it was presented by his dear friend Sarah Nevers. The young Presbyterian pastor who accompanied her seemed a decent sort of fellow. He had to admit that the young man was very persuasive. He also noted he seemed to look on Sarah in a way that was more amorous than collegial. His name? Yes, John McDermott, an American with that can do spirit that can be a bit off putting. And yes, he was a bit jealous. Certainly there was nothing between he and Sarah and he twenty years older and a widower just felt some inexplicable comfort in knowing that Sarah was everyone's sweetheart and this young man, who seemed bent on some proprietary interest in her made him a bit resentful. He had to admit it was all very irrational since Sarah had not shown the slightest romantic interest in him.

From a second story window of the magnificent Government House, the Commissioner watched with satisfaction as the chairs set out on the open field were quickly filling up. It was a surprisingly balmy day for December which pleased the Commissioner all the more. He could not be expected to recognize the two notorious Frenchman taking their seats, dressed as they were in clergymen attire.

Reuters 3Dec1938

Editor's Note: The two journalists are being hunted by the British authorities for aiding the rebels and a 10,000 Palestinian Pound reward is offered for information leading to their capture.

Ecumenical Jihad

Andre Monet and George Bissett

The world should note that on the third day of December, 1938, there gathered in the heart of the Holy Land in Jerusalem the religious of all the Christian sects and Sunni and Shiite Muslims, even a number of rabbis who courageously joined in calling for peace in Palestine. Where Europe's religious leaders cry out for peace, they do it separately and cautiously, as if to not challenge the jingoism going on all about them. It was here that a boldly created council of all faiths framed a peace proposal that offered hope where hopelessness covered the land like a poisonous smog.

There was no clapping or cheers from the somber crowd, yet the energy could be felt all around these reporters. From what we were able to learn, this explosion of hope did not come from the high offices of religious leaders, but began humbly by a young American Presbyterian minister who ministers to 120 souls in a small church north of Jerusalem. With imams and Christian clerics often young like him, they took on the task of calling forth, yes, challenging their brethren of all faiths to step forward for peace.

What possessed a young, shy pastor to take on such a task? His answer: "All of the three great religions believe in peace and good will, we have a duty to help our flocks find it first and foremost here in the Holy Land. In my talks with God, I felt that was His message to me."

We have no way of predicting the outcome of this gallant fray to heal this sick land, inspired by a young preacher with a congregation of 120 souls, but it is clear that something very important happened here this day. Three speakers stood before the podium today. One Muslim, one Christian and one Jew. Each read from a text, that judging from the affirmative body language in the crowd, had been created through consultation with those who sat and listened.

The first speaker was a young red-headed priest from Bethlehem, Father Mooney. He spoke in English with a pronounced Irish lilt. As he spoke each sentence or two, he paused and a translator repeated what he said. He began by asking for the prayers of all Palestinians and for the Jews in Germany.

He then made a plea for reconciliation of Arabs and Jews who once lived together in peace in Palestine.

"Let us pray for our leaders in America, Europe and Palestine that they come to understand that we are all equal before God and it is in their hands to create a Palestine where all can live in peace."

And then, in a language all could understand, he asked all "to pray for the poor who had lived in Palestine for generations and now are being forced off their land."

The reporters could not help but note that the plea for the Jews in Germany and the poor in Palestine were intended as a message that Palestine cannot be the answer to persecution in Europe and the suffering of one group must not be the cause of the suffering of another.

The next to speak was an imam from Nazareth, Ibrihim Nassabeih. He, too, was young. Wearing glasses, thin and tall, he spoke in a soft voice and here the translation was in English.

"My message is to all Palestinians, brave rebel leaders and those who had chosen to remove themselves from the revolt or actively worked against it. Seek peace among yourselves and unite with your brothers to speak as one voice to the world. Speak of peace with the British and the Jews and offer your hand to them."

"Let us pray for the leaders in Europe and America to understand that peace in Palestine will only be possible if we all reach out our hands in the spirit of brotherhood and we all come to accept that all men are equal before God. Let us pray today that all the religious in Europe and America will join us in prayer for peace."

The third person to speak was Rabbi Mostel. The Rabbi was the oldest of the three and clearly more practiced in oratory. From America, he spoke to the audience in English. It is easy to believe that there was tension in the audience when the Rabbi began to speak. He began by speaking of God's promise to Moses and spoke of the Promised Land.

We could sense the tension among those sitting below the podium. But his next remarks surprised them.

"Only a free Palestine, where Jews and Arabs could live together will assure peace. Let us all in our own way pray for peace with justice, and let us pray for our leaders that they be granted the wisdom to bring peace to the Holy Land forever."

Dressed in our starched collar turned backwards and our dark suits, these reporters felt safe. The real possibility of discovery on the grounds of the Government House made staying with the excited crowd important, which we were able to do and soon lose ourselves in the crowds as they made their way into the streets of Jerusalem. Being reporters in Palestine for just a few months, telling the world what is happening in Palestine is to tell of small bands of men fighting desperate battles against overwhelming force. We understand the rebels, why they fight but there was the reality faced at the end of each battle or flight to escape that resistance could not continue forever. We could see it on the faces of Abu Kamal and even Ismael Latif. But you also knew that they would keep fighting, that they would never surrender, and the men under them, hungry for a return to their families and villages, would never surrender. George and I, who claim little religious fervor, found ourselves praying with the clerics that something will happen, something that will vindicate the sacrifices of these men.

So today, on the grounds of the Government House, something happened that only a pastor in a small church called Christ's Church miles from Jerusalem believed possible. An old minister who had served his congregation in Jerusalem for thirty years spoke to me as we were leaving.

I asked him what he was feeling. "Until now," he said, "there was a lingering mood of gloom, now there is reason to hope."

He paused for just a moment, then continued. "I think what happened today was something we all wanted to happen and it took young Reverend McDermott to remind us why we chose to be men of God. He opened the door for us, now it is up to us to work together for peace among all peoples in Palestine. Simply put, it makes me feel good. We all should say a blessing for the young American. God bless him."

The battle in the north grew more intense. A string of successful attacks on British outposts and Jewish settlements had emboldened the rebels, and the Agency began to sense that events were taking a turn for the worst. For things beyond its control, the Agency began to feel the wrath of the settlers who accused it for not doing enough to defeat the insurrection.

Shurtok sat at his desk, rubbing his temples. He had a headache. He thought it was in both a figurative and literal sense. Both came at the meeting of the Agency executive committee who hashed and re-hashed what was happening and all the implications for the Yishuv. But that was not the reason for the headache.

Meetings had to be scheduled with his minions and with the British including the arrogant bastard, the Oh So High Commissioner. He listened as one of his assistants, Brodsky, reported on the behavior of the Revisionists. It is the winter of 1938, in the middle of the rebellion and the Revisionists and their band of lunatics were plotting attacks against the British. The same British that at a time were supplying them with arms and Purdom was training the militias on how to fight the Arabs. Even Ben Gurion has failed to convince them that now is not the time to create a war with the British. Why do they expect him to do anything about them.

Shurtok did not like the British. And he knew that a lot of the British did not like the Jews in Palestine. There were exceptions like Purdom and Wauchope. In the past, he had enjoyed the occasions when the Mandate officials decided they had to be fair, which was becoming more and more common and see their decisions come to naught. Calls from Weizmann and Ben-Gurion to members of Parliament followed by the Mandate officials, military, police and civil service being put in their place. There were even moments of sympathy as he looked into the resentful faces of his adversaries.

Shurtok always prepared an agenda which he checked with Ben-Gurion before their meetings. Right out of the gate, when people were being seated and small talk was going on, he was ambushed. What was he doing about the two Frenchmen and right behind it, what are you doing about Ismael Latif. It was Reuben Strauss who demanded answers. Standing beside three others, it was clear that Strauss was not alone.

As calmly as he could, he explained what was being done, that the British army had been called in to coordinate the search for the two Frenchmen, only one of whom was from France. Informants everywhere were alerted and the reward had now increased to twenty thousand pounds.

He told the committee Ismael Latif's brother had been captured by the Purdom raiders and taken to Lutheran hospital and then to British army headquarters in Nablus. Zelesney had contacted the British, requesting that they treat him well since he may be useful as bait to capture Ismael or persuade him to surrender to save his brother. Major Fortson was in charge of Latif and chose to use Tegart methods to interrogate him. Hasan Latif died during interrogation. Fortson was unable to obtain any information from Ismael Latif's brother.

Strauss spoke again: "You are telling us that you are no closer to catching these two Frenchmen then you were a month ago?"

"We will find them. It is only a matter of time."

"There are rumors that we may not have so much time, Moshe" It was Ben-Gurion who spoke. There are rumors that the British are preparing another plan, another commission report."

Shurtok was angry at the committee, angry at Zelesney and Halevi and everyone involved in the search. Did they expect him to search himself!

"Did you see the Paris and London papers. The report by Monet and Bissett about the religious leaders on the Government House lawns, no less.. What was MacMichael thinking, for god's sake." Strauss's face was beet red as he stood and shouted at Shurtok.

"I think it is time to forget about the British being our ally and pay more attention to our real friends in America. I think we can count on the President. He told Felix as much." The room grew silent as they thought about Ben-Gurion's words.

"We need to talk to Ze'ev. That's what he's been telling everyone who would listen."

"What about the list?" Strauss was talking to Shurtok, apparently moving from the two Frenchmen to another matter. The list was an enemies list, persons in every city, town and village who might threaten the Yishuv.

Ben-Gurion spoke. "Moshe, I want to know every policeman, soldier and clerk who might be a threat when the time comes." Heads turned. *What did Ben-Gurion mean? If Jabotinsky uttered them, they would understand, but not Ben-Gurion.*

"Is that safe? What if the British find out?" Shurtok looked around the room. Most were visibly stunned.

"What is said here must never leave the room." Ben-Gurion's eyes seemed to stare into the souls of each one of them. "But I want that list."

+++

Purdom's men were tired. They had been following the trail of the rebels who ambushed Sergeant Johnson's convoy near Burayka since midnight. When they reached the site of the ambush, the sky had begun to lighten and daytime color restored to the land. The bodies already had been removed. The smell of death and battle remained. The twisted metal of the armored car could be seen far below the road near the valley floor. The sector commander had informed Purdom that the burned out remains of the lorries had been found near a village called Burayka. Corporal Belinsky had discovered the spot where the rebel's horses waited during the ambush. Signs showed the rebels going east, heading toward Burayka..

They reached the village in early afternoon. Traveling as always by foot, they had marched the 15 miles from the ambush site without rest breaks. Purdom paid no attention to the haggard faces and muttering of his men. He dismissed his own fatigue as he always had since he had been taught to do so as a child.

They could see the village from the road. Beyond Burayka to the south lay the wide expanse of the Jezreel Valley with its grazing land, cattle, orchards and fields of grain. Immediately beyond the last house in the village, a corral with a single cow and a goat. Chickens moved freely in the village, searching for food.

Receiving a signal from his advance man that it was safe, Purdom led the raiders smartly into the village square. Beckoning in Arabic to a small boy who watched them enter the village. "Tell your Mukhtar to bring all the men to the square."

The boy, frightened, ran off and disappeared into a stone house on the square. Soon a single man appeared, then the boy ran to the fields where the men were working. The Mukhtar, Yusef Habibi walked slowly toward the soldiers.

When the men gathered, Purdom had his Sergeant, a young settler, line the men up. As they did the Sergeant's bidding, Purdom watched, surveying the village.

The Mukhtar took his place in front of the assembly, waiting. None of the men spoke.

Purdom approached the Mukhtar.

"What is your name?"

"Yusef Habibi." The Mukhtar knew the man in front of him was the devil, Purdom. "We have seen no one."

Quicker than the eye could see, Purdom brought the barrel of his Webley across the nose of the man, who fell to his knees crying out in pain and trying to stem the flow of blood with his hand.

One of the villager's nearest the chief moved forward to help. Before he reached the Mukhtar, he was felled with a butt stroke of the rifle held by the Sergeant. The fear and loathing that moved among the Arabs produced a tension that immediately brought the raiders forward to confront them.

Purdom spoke, his voice oddly soft yet distinct. "If anyone moves, you will be shot."

"Stand up!" He shouted the command at Habibi.

Habibi rose to his feet, his legs weak as he struggled to stay erect and steady himself.

Purdom moved to face him, close enough that he felt the need to move back but dared not.

"I do not want to hear you speak until you have my permission, is that clear, Mukhtar."

"Yes, it is clear."

He felt his arm go numb as the barrel of the revolver raked his collar bone.

"When you address me, you Arab dog, you will say sir. Is that clear?"

Habibi did not want to die. "Yes, sir."

"You have been helping the gangsters that are killing settlers and British soldiers."

As the other men watched, Habibi seemed to grow smaller as he bowed his head.

"No one has come to our village." Then hesitantly, "Sir."

"What did you say?"

"We have seen no one." He looked into the eyes of the devil before him. "No one"

The sudden crack of the bullet and the Mukhtar's flopping backwards caused the village men to begin to shout and wail, yet stay frozen in place. Women began to appear, their high pitched trills filling the air.

Sensing the anger among the men, the raiders shifted their rifles with bayonets to the thrust position, pointing at the angry crowd.

Purdom moved away from the dead man toward the menacing villagers. He placed himself between the village men and his own men.

Purdom spoke so all could hear. "We know the gangsters who ambushed one of our convoys headed this way. Two lorries taken by the Arab dogs would found a mile from this village. We know they fled from the site of the ambush in this direction."

He picked a wide-eyed old man from the villages and beckoned him forward. "Are any of these men hiding in your village?"

"There is no one here, sir."

"If you tell me now where they are hiding, the men will be safe. If we search and find gangsters hiding here, your village will be destroyed and the men will be shot."

He was pleased with himself that he had picked the right man from among the villagers. The old man's hands were shaking and his lips trembled as he spoke.

"They were here, sir, but we told them we had no food, and they must leave or we would be punished."

"How long ago did they leave?"

"When the sun was setting last evening. They left as soon as we told them there was no food." Then as an afterthought he quickly added, "Sir."

Purdom turned to his Sergeant. "Search the houses and outbuildings."

He turned again to the old man. "Which way did they go?"

Beisan pointed to the north, over the steep hills beyond the road. "They went that way."

The search lasted an hour. No able bodied men were found.

Purdom looked at the old man. No matter that he may be lying, there no value in pursuing the matter any further.

Still, the village needed to know what could happen to it if they helped the rebels. The less the villages have, the less they will give the gangsters.

"Private, I want you to shoot the cow and goat", pointing to the small corral and any chickens you see." When the young man named Carruthers who had grown up on a farm in Northumberland, hesitated, he spoke sharply. "Now, Private."

He picked out Carruthers because he still was not sufficiently conditioned to take orders without question, and he knew he was a farmer's son who had spoken of his love for animals. So much the better, he thought.

"Corporal, take two of the men and set fire to their granary and the building next to it where it looks like they store something or other. Back here at 1450 hours, 15 minutes from now."

With the sounds of wailing and shouting behind him, his men spaced and in single file, Purdom moved out to the road to continue the hunt. The old man told him north, he would take his men east.

212

Looking back, he regretted not seeking information about Latif, something he had done in every town and village. When he got to the base, he would check with Zelesney. If any has heard anything, it would be him. The noose is tightening, he told himself. Soon, he would meet the Arab face to face and he would settle the matter of who was the better man.

***

Only hours after Purdom's departure, a lone man entered the village. He carried an Enfield rifle, crossed bandoliers and a holstered Webley. He stood near the edge of the village square, warily searching the surrounding buildings. He stood as if he was in no hurry, waiting for someone to approach him. The old man who Purdom had questioned was now the Mukhtar, greeted the visitor. The two men then began to walk across the square, the visitor staying close as if to use his host as a shield. The new Mukhtar began to describe what had happened, gesturing wildly and pointing to the pasture where the milk cow had been killed, now gone and butchered.

The two men then walked back to where the Arab warrior had entered the village and the feday'ee raised his hand as he faced the hills above the village. As if appearing from the earth itself, seventeen men entered the village, led by a tall Arab. As the men entered, some quickly moved to points where they could observe the countryside surrounding the village. Two men moved toward the hills where they would have a distant view of traffic on the road above the village.

It was Abd who first entered the village and now led the Mukhtar toward the leader who moved to greet the village chief. Abd spoke quickly to the leader to explain what had happened. Ismael nodded. His eyes turned to the Mukhtar.

"Peace be with you, Mukhtar Beisan. I am saddened by what has happened. My name is Ismael Latif."

"Peace be upon you, Ismael Latif. We are honored that you visit our village."

The villagers had gathered around the two men began to speak softly to each other, amazed that it was Ismael Latif that came to their village. Amidst all the despair, there was hope. Ismael had often encountered the same reaction everywhere he went, and rather than dismiss it, he welcomed it for what else could he give these poor wretches but hope.

"Mukhtar Beisan, I am sorry we cannot stay to help. How long since they left and which did they go?

Using much the same formation as his enemy, he moved his men quickly out of the village to overtake Purdom and his raiders. Although the men with him would follow him anywhere, Ismael knew he must be careful. He came to fight for his people-all of them. But his brother had been killed by two particular men, and the hunt for Purdom and Fortson was very personal. He knew, too, that his personal vendetta also served all the Palestinian people, for Purdom was the enemy of them all. Leaving the village, they had followed Purdom and his men until they reached the village of Indur. There they learned that the raiders had been met by a motorized platoon that carried them back to their base. There would be another time.

+++

Looking out his drawing room's French doors, Senator Phillip Hollister could see beyond the C&O Canal to the wooded hills of Virginia on the other side of the Potomac. Winter had scoured the leaves from the trees, and the bare trees and gray sky made it pleasant to be inside looking out. He thought of the phrase, in a figurative sense, as a member of the Senate he had always been on the inside looking out. But he wondered if the world outside knew how little comfort such a position could be, and how little power it granted. He had always been sure of himself but had never deluded himself he had the power people at home thought he had. Nor did he think that he was entirely at the mercy of events, that he could, and had, shaped them into something worthwhile.

Now he had before him a monumental challenge. A challenge that been hurled at him by a spare, gentle man so easy to underestimate. *When Jake told me I ought to talk to Arach Poletsky, I almost said no. But I had learned over the years to trust Jake, a staffer as loyal and smart as they come.* Why was he taken with Arach? How many thousand pitches had he received as a Senator? At first, it was the resolute manner of the man, and the conviction that shone through those gentle eyes. He could not recall anything before that had the monumental significance of what he and Bobby were proposing.

Bob had been a hard man to convince. He must have thought who is this guy Poletsky and why are we thinking of taking on the Congress and the White House because of him.

But Bob bought in for the whole race. Why? At first, because he is a good friend. Friendship means a lot in Washington and friendships are taken seriously. You're on top, you invite your friends up there with you, you're sinking in a storm, your friend reaches out to save you. Loyalty like betrayal in Washington is forever. You never forget your friends or your enemies.

But there was more than that with Bob. He saw what I did-the possibility that something could be done to prevent another stupid war. He'd been there. The Spanish-American War was a clean war compared to the Great War. But you still remember the dead Spaniards with their ancient rifles laying there, their dead eyes staring at you and you wondered. But the Great War when Bob served as a young lieutenant told him enough about what the next war would be like to want to do something to stop it.

The America Firsters had their own idea about war-stay out of it. People like Lindberg argued for letting the Europeans fight it out and Norman Thomas thought that war was just something cooked up by bankers and he was against war, period. Norman

Thomas was closer to the truth but neither Lindberg nor Thomas knew what they were up against. Our President, his admirers like to say when he did something devious, was a complicated man. Well, maybe, maybe not. What is clear about Roosevelt is that he is always counting votes but sometimes in a pretty sneaky way. He counted on the people who could get him votes and the things he could do to get him votes and I don't think he cared very much about the people who actually went to the polls. He would get the people's votes through his friends and he would return the favor by giving them what they wanted.

Watching the President twenty years after the Great War, he's giving out signals that he wants us in a war if it starts in Europe and he wants us on the side of the English. Like so many in the East he is an anglophile. But he is first and foremost a politician whose political success depends on money and bright people around him and they're going to want us to jump in with both feet if Britain gets into war with Germany. The propaganda blitz has already begun and Hollywood and the New York press are leading the way. Hitler's treatment of the Jews makes America's entry into the war all the more likely.

***

They were having a drink in Bruce's office and rehashing the day when talk turned to Poletsky. The trigger was an article in the New York Post which included some harsh remarks about Arach Poletsky.

"Traitor is pretty harsh. The poor guy must be going through hell." Bruce started the conversation.

"I talked to him yesterday. Seems some of his friends, or former friends, don't show up to play chess anymore."

"Maybe they're tired of losing."

"I think he knew what he was getting in to but I am sorry to see it happen."

"He told me he still has Morty and Marty, the two M's he calls them. They still come to the park but they still shake their heads at their strange friend."

"Sometimes someone comes along and gets in Arach's face and Morty jumps up and offers to fight the guy. Then he turns to Arach and says: 'See what you have done, you schmuck."

"I don't know if you have noticed, Phil, but our social calendar is pretty empty these days."

"Well the America Firsters are furious because we want to bring in a couple hundred thousand Jews and the bankers and the movie makers are mad because we want to stop Jews from going to Palestine."

"You know, Phil, the America Firsters are the most blind of all yet our biggest opportunity. They don't want war. They don't like the English. We need to convince them that by opening our door America has the opportunity to bring some of the smartest, best educated in Europe here. Underemployment is not going to last forever and America is going to start to grow again, and all these talented people are going to make things even better."

"Bob, I have a meeting with some of the Firsters tomorrow morning in the conference room down the hall. Want to sit in. Arach will be there. Tell them what you just said."

"Is that a good idea having Arach there?"

"Yes, they need to see a Jew in the flesh; the kind that will make America a better place."

Part VIII

"My name is Margaret Larsen and I am a member of Women for Peace."

Jake had done a great job of bringing the anti-war groups together. As Bruce and Hollister surveyed the crowd, he could see the air of confidence and resolve on all their faces. Americans, they knew, didn't want Americans dying for Britain and France again.

It was Bruce who agreed to address them first and Hollister would be there for additional remarks. Then Arach to address his reasons for including Palestine.

"Good morning, ladies and gentlemen. It is good to see the women of America represented here. No one hates war more than the mothers and sweethearts in America, and that has always been true. I know there voices will be heard as talk of war grows louder.

"I am Bob Bruce and I'm afraid I can't claim to be from the line of the Scottish hero. My mother is a Scottish romantic. With me is Senator Hollister. Phil has been my mentor since I first came to Washington and a good friend. With us is Arach Poletsky, whom I think has offered some new ideas on how America can prevent a war in Europe. He is here to answer any questions you have about Palestine. Why he is here will become clearer, I hope, as the morning goes on.

"I want to thank you all for coming and for giving Senator Hollister and me the opportunity to tell you of our plan to prevent a war in Europe. We agree with you wholeheartedly that America should not be drawn into another war. Make no mistake, there is a danger danger that there will be a war in Europe. I know that many of you do not think we should have been drawn into the Great War. The war to end all wars, remember. Well, I think we all know differently. If we don't want our country in another, we are going to have to work real hard to prevent it.

"We call our plan Lasting Peace. The big question we have before us is how we keep America out of war in Europe.

"President Roosevelt has assured you that our men will not fight if Germany and England go to war. I think our President knows that the great majority of Americans do not want to go to war, to fight someone else's battles.

"If we accomplish nothing else this morning, I hope we can convince you that if there is a war in Europe, America will not sit on the sidelines. Just as in the Great War our men and women will fight and die for some noble cause yet to be determined. Rest assured it will not be determined by me or Phil or any of you.

"The beginning of the propaganda blizzard has already begun. Already, young men have joined the Lincoln Brigade to fight the Germans in the Spanish Civil War."

"Hollywood has filled its theatres around the nation with anti-German films and we see the Russians being humanized and "nobilized" if there were such a word. Gradually, the Americans are being made to take sides which must happen if we are to go to war. The sentiment, as you know, is already overwhelmingly pro-British and French and anti-German. Anti-Russian or anti-communist sentiment will be harder to overcome, but it will happen and is happening now.

"The point we hope to make, ladies and gentlemen is that there are people in America, powerful people who are pushing us to war. Perhaps it is more accurate to say that they are preparing us for war by aligning us with England and France, two of the three major countries in Europe. The bond will be made so strong that any

219

attack on either by Germany will bring us into the war. Whatever you do and say, you who feel strongly about America staying out of war will fail if a war breaks out in Europe. However it is done, it will be done.

"War for America can only be prevented if we prevent the war in Europe."

Bruce looked out at the audience. A veteran, and all-state football player, he was rankled when the hawks talked about the peace movement. They wanted to paint us as milquetoasts, he thought, and it made his blood boil.

"I want to say one other thing. There has been a lot of talk about the peace movement being a bunch of pacifists. Well, we're not because we're going to stand up to the hawks in this country, and if they want a fight, we'll give it to them. We'll do it with facts and faith in our cause, and we think the people will join us, to fight alongside us."

There was scattered applause but it was drowned out by people in the room began shouting at Robert Bruce about his emigration plan. It took a few minutes for the crowd to settle back.

When people were back in their seats, it was Phillip Hollister's turn to speak. Before him was a tough crowd and he found himself saying a silent prayer that they may listen to what he is about to say and that it will move them.

"Some of you may know who I am. I have been a Senator since 1916 when the winning Presidential candidate promised America that no American boys would die on foreign soil. One year later, troops were being loaded on ships bound for Europe to the sounds of marching bands and cheering crowds."

"Bob told you America will not stay out of a war in Europe. If a war does happen, I hope he and I are wrong, that we can stay out of a war.

"He also ended his little speech with the comment that the only way to keep us out of a war in Europe is to prevent one from happening. I agree with Bob. Of course, he ended with a little fighting speech, because anyone who knows Bob knows he is a fighter. So am I, and I know you are, too.

"We believe it is possible to stop the war in Europe. It will require a President who does not simply wait for a war to start then get us into it, but to show the flag now by knocking heads together in Europe and including some chin to chin discussion with the German Chancellor, Adolph Hitler.

"But Hitler is not only one in the march to war in Europe. That belligerent fellow Winston Churchill is practically rolling up his sleeves and calling Hitler out in the street.

"Well, why do these two act the way they do. Don't they understand that millions would die? Don't they understand the precipice they are walking beside; that below are the fires of hell. Well, America has got to do something about that.

"So what we are proposing is that our President of the greatest country on earth take a stand, that he offer himself as a mediator to resolve the issues that seem intractable merely because the adversaries choose to make them so.

"That he engage Hitler, listen to what he has to say, do the same for Churchill and the other leaders, and then propose solutions with sticks and carrots.

"To curb Churchill's appetite for war, let the President make clear that he will not back England if it declares war but that there are carrots in his bag if England agrees to negotiate in good faith.

"To Hitler, he must immediately desist in his treatment of the Jews and make a pathway for them to leave Germany with their assets and he must participate in good faith negotiations to resolve the boundary problems which were created after the Great War. Again, carrots are available in the form of trade agreements and other matters if he agrees to negotiate in good faith.

"This is an appeal to you to join other groups who want peace for the good of mankind and in our nation's interest to call on the President to be a leader for peace.

"Let me stop to make a special point, perhaps the key to keeping us out of war. By bearding Hitler regarding the Jews, we must be willing to do our part. As many as 500,000 Jews are expected to want to immigrate to countries where they are welcomed."

Two men rose and began to collect the papers in front of them. The Senator walked over to them.

"Please, here us out. Let us finish. We will be glad to answer any questions you may have and listen to anything else you have to say."

The two men sat down and the Senator continued.

"There is another part of the plan which is essential. While we are proposing that the Jews being persecuted in Germany be offered homes elsewhere but we also are proposing that the émigré's not be allowed to immigrate to Palestine in numbers so great it will overwhelm the people that live there now.

"Although Arach Poletsky can answer any of your questions about this part of the proposal, any additional immigration into Palestine in large numbers threatens to spark a war which will not end in our lifetime and perhaps will be endless, This would mean that the Holy Land, sacred to three major religions, would never know peace. As inconceivable as it may be to you now, there may come a time when we, too, would be shedding blood in the Holy Land."

One of the men who started to walk out earlier shouted.. "What does Mr. Poletsky think of such a proposal? We understand he is behind this."

Arach stood up slowly and looked around the table at those present, then at the audience in the room.

"I am a Jew, as most of you know. I lived in Palestine for ten years before I decided to come to America. I did it with great regret because I left my daughter and son who chose to stay. I left because in good conscious I could not be part of an effort to remove the people who had lived there for generations to make room for my people."

"Why do we have to take "your people" in? Why can't they go to Palestine?"

"Let me tell you, many Jews, probably the majority, feel the same way. If the land was empty of people, as some would like you to believe, that would be an acceptable plan. But there are people there, just like you and I who love their land; they are already bitter that over 500,000 Jews that have come into their country, invited not by the people there, but by the British."

Another spoke, this time in a moderate voice. "Our country is struggling to get back on its feet. We can't afford to take in another five hundred thousand."

Robert Bruce spoke, not wanting the burden of the answer to fall on Arach's shoulders.

"The Jews who would be coming to America would not be without assets under our plan, and we think the Jewish community here would do more than their share to help. Please remember these are some of the brightest, hard-working, educated people in Europe. Such people would not be a burden but an asset. Our country will not remain underemployed for much longer if history is any guide. When the country begins to grow, the skills of these people will be needed."

The room seemed suddenly to become silent and the three tried to read the mood of the people in front of them.

Then a lady, tall and broad shouldered rose to speak.

"What can we do to make your plan work? My name is Margaret Larsen and I am a member of Women for Peace. We are opposed to America going to war and Senator, your contention that America cannot stay out of war unless it can help prevent a war in Europe is a point I will take back to our organization. If the success of achieving peace is dependent on finding a home for Jews now living in Germany, I think that is also worthy of deliberation."

"When you invite the Jews, you will be inviting agitators and speculators just like what occurred in Russia and Germany. That is why they are hated in Germany." The angry questioner shouted from the back of the room.

Robert Bruce looked at Arach who betrayed no reaction to the comment. He knew he had heard all this before. It was time to take risks.

"I would like Mr. Poletsky to respond to your remark, sir."

"Among my friends in Russia, there were those who worked to overthrow the Czarist regime. And there were speculators who selfishly exploited the people in Russia. In Germany, the same thing has happened. There are Jews in Germany enamored with communism, who believe that a capitalistic society like ours exploits the people. There are speculators who have exploited other Germans at a time when the German people were suffering. I can only answer by saying that this is a very small minority of Jews, the great majority are hard-working honest people like you. And by the way, many others were involved, too. For that small minority, probably less than one percent, keep in mind that America is not Russia or the Germany after the Great War but a strong country with laws to deal with exploitation by anyone.."

Another spoke up. "What's wrong with allowing them all to go to Palestine? From what I read, that's where they want to go."

"I can only ask you to consider those who have lived in Palestine for generations will be forced off their land and will become second class citizens. Try to imagine what it would be like if you were told that thousands of people, far richer than you and able to buy up the best land, real estate and businesses were to come to your community. Try to imagine that the government would have rules that protected the 'settlers' by using force against you if you protested."

"You make a good case, Mr. Poletsky, but why are we addressing the situation in Palestine when our main concern is keeping America out of a war in Europe?" It was tall, older man, wearing a rumpled suit and holding a pipe in his hand, who stood to ask the question. Hollister guessed he was an academic from one of the universities in the area. Sometimes he was impatient with such men, who seemed to enjoy their mellifluous voices. This time he was not for he opened the door.

Phillip Hollister stood to be heard.

"What I am about to say is about the elephant in the room. It takes up a lot of space and people keep moving back to give it room, but nobody wants to say it is there. People who dare to point to it usually are asked to leave the room. So those in the room feed the elephant but everyone in the room knows that they cannot tell anyone it was there.

He looked around the conference room at the faces. He had their attention.

"Arach, I hope you understand what I am about to say." Hollister put his meaty hand on the bony shoulder of his friend.

"The success or failure of our effort to stop a war in Europe depends on the support of the Jewish community in America and Europe." He could see the people now leaning forward, sensing the import of the moment.

225

"The Jews are not the leviathan described in the Protocols of the Elders of Zion, which has been labeled a forgery, but they are a very powerful force with very powerful weapons. What are those weapons? They're easy to describe. Unity, despite their internal differences. Talent to accomplish great things. Money from the many that are very wealthy. Enormous power in the propaganda arena through entertainment, newspapers and broadcasting. These things make their support for peace essential. That power is now focused on Germany where Jews are being persecuted and threatened with imprisonment and even death. And they are calling for war."

Someone shouted from the back of the room. "Hitler is a madman. He must be stopped."

Hollister answered back. "More important than stopping Hitler is stopping the war."

The same person, now standing in the aisle, shouted. "Hitler is the cause of any war."

"If you want war to stop Hitler, you will get it. Millions will die. What do you think will happen to the Jews in Germany? What will be the outcome of the war? The last Great War laid the groundwork for the next. Will the next be any different?"

Robert Bruce stood up then. "War is a real possibility but perhaps for the first time let us turn our attention to creating peace. Let those who have the power to take us into war use it to create peace. The differences with Hitler seem intractable but actions can be taken to bring war or peace. God endowed us with the power to think and to choose."

The meeting ended with the silent departure of those invited. Only when they were out of the meeting room, could they be seen forming small groups joined in animated discussion.

The room was empty but for the three of them. Two Senators and an investment banker sat silent as they listened to the sounds outside the meeting room, each trying to cipher what they meant .

Arach turned to Phil. "I think you overestimate the power of the Jewish people, my friend."

"Perhaps you would see things differently if you served in the Senate for twenty years. I think we need to be honest about power. At this point, it is very dangerous."

"So you do blame us."

"This is getting us nowhere. We have a challenge before us, Arach. Can we stop this war? Will the Jewish community help?"

"You are right, my friend. The question is: will the Jewish community help. Perhaps we should drop the matter of Palestine."

Bob was listening to the exchange, "I think that would be a mistake. The Middle East will someday be our main source of oil. If we can't bring peace to Palestine, we will have to face another war for the Holy Land. Do you really think that is the best course to take, Arach." Arach could sense the anger in the younger Senator.

"No, of course not. I am sorry. I should not have said what I did."

For a moment, the three were silent until Hollister stood up and shouted: "Turn the ship around. There's a storm brewing."

Then Bruce stood. "Hell no. Break out the sails, full speed ahead."

Arach had to laugh at his two friends.

"Well, well, what are the three musketeers up to this cold wintry day. Think you hit anything?" Markey had a big smile on his face. The three looked out to see the reporter in the rumpled suit walking toward them.

"We always think we hit what we aim at. The question for you is what you think and what you will write about."

Switching similes, the reporter responded. "I'm still trying to figure out what you three mad dogs are up to. Those people in the audience are so hide bound that radical ideas like yours just leaves them shaking their heads. Take in five hundred thousand of anyone, talking to Hitler, telling Churchill we won't back his bellowing for war, and then telling the Jews to help us when we want to place Palestine off limits."

"I always feel better after we talk to you. Did you talk to that tall blonde lady?" Hollister, always with an eye for beautiful women, was impressed by what she had to say.

"Yes, I did. She has a lot to say. Professor in Madison. How did you read the audience, Arach?"

"I don't know but I think they were listening."

"Do you have some time to talk later, Arach?" Arach nodded

"There were people in the audience who speak for a lot of people, so we need to keep our fingers crossed." It was Hollister who spoke.

"Any luck with Secretary Hull?" Bruce was looking at Hollister, a good friend of the Secretary.

"He's got his ear to the ground. I think he's listening but waiting for a signal from the White House. The people closest to Roosevelt are dyed-in-the wool Zionists but we shouldn't give up on them. The point about the effect of a war on the Jews in Germany is compelling. "

"What about Lindberg?"

"I think he's burned his bridges but he does make up his own mind and a lot of people listen to him. He's going to be for talking to Hitler but his support for immigration would be a shocker. Still, you never know."

"Too many people with their feet in cement on this one." Bob seemed the more pessimistic of the two senators this morning, and it surprised Markey.

"You don't sound very hopeful."

"I still am. We just need a jackhammer."

Hollister smiled at the three of them. "Maybe we need to get them moving before it hardens.

Fred interjected. "How about the Vice President, Bob, he's always available. Probably doesn't even have an appointment calendar."

"Smart-assed comments like that Fred don't make me feel any better. I happen to like the guy."

"If you want to get to Roosevelt, Cactus Jack is not your guy. Roosevelt is still smarting over Garner's opposition to stacking the Supreme Court."

"But he's in tight with the Congressional Democrats and that may be important down the road."

Fred started to leave. "I need to talk to Arach."

Phil looked at him. "You overheard my conversation with Arach, didn't you?"

"I confess. I did. I wouldn't repeat it around Washington. You're in enough hot water already."

"No matter. I'm a short timer."

"Doesn't make any difference."

"Well, Fred I won't ask you what you are going to write. By now your editor must be wondering about the company you keep."

Markey looked at his watch. "Meet you at the bar next to the funeral parlor on Pennsylvania. Always wondered why we picked that one."

+++

Tonight, the crowd inside the Tel Hai meeting house was loud, there were shouts across the room, and people moved about quickly, forming clusters that would fall away and new ones would form. There was news that the British were going to end the immigration of Jews and close the borders.

Most of the people in the settlement of Tel Hai were immigrants themselves and had relatives who were planning to come to the Yishuv when they had the opportunity. Many had applied for exit visas that were being held up on matters of how much of their wealth they could take out of Germany.

Some were slipping into the surrounding countries, hoping to get to Palestine from there. Now came news that the borders were to be closed and there would be a nation called Palestine.

Avi and Shlomo were late to the meeting. They had received new instructions from the Irgun and it had taken more than an hour to learn how to use timed explosives with a new triggering device. The first target using the device was to be a hiring hall near the Haifa port, where Arab men gathered looking for work on the docks. The device would be attached to one of the heavy benches in the waiting room.

The two were now wanted men. The British had connected them to the Haifa and Nablus bombings. The Irgun had arranged for them to leave their rooms in Haifa and be taken in at Tel Hai.

The leader chosen by the settlement was a tall Russian, and some said he reminded them of Trumpeldor, the courageous former Russian officer who had taught the settlement how to defend itself and had been killed defending the settlement almost twenty years before.

"The news today is not good, my friends. The Agency reports that there are rumors of a new British announcement that the Mandate will be ended and Palestine will be a new nation. The rumors about immigration are correct, that it will end or reduced to a pitifully small number each year.

"I never trusted The British. We must find a way to prevent the British from issuing such a policy. Ben-Gurion has left to see our friends in London. He has been in touch with our friends in America.

"What about their promise? They can't break such a promise." It was a young woman near the front who shouted at Schmuel Rabin, whose face hid his annoyance at Rhea Hemmelman who seemed to blame him for the news.

Another spoke from his seat. "They can and likely will." Levi Strumpf had been a school teacher in Regensburg who witnessed what was happening in Germany during the 20's and left.

"What shall we do if the British issue such an order. What will the Arabs do to us?"

"I think we will have to fight." David Weill was one of the new German immigrants, young, physically fit, and ready to fight.

Strumpf looked at the young man who spoke. So many of the new settlers were young, few families were among the new immigrants. Weill came to Palestine, angry at what had happened to him and his friends in Germany, and spoiling for a fight. To him, the Arabs had become Germans and he would make them pay. He was a new recruit for the Irgun.

Strumpf noted that Nelkin and Yellen were getting a lot of attention from the new Irgun recruits. Most were young men trained by Jews who had fought with the British Army or were trained by them. Did the British know what they were doing? He sometimes wondered.

Strumpf recalled the stories about his uncle, who was killed almost two decades ago. His father told him that Benjamin Strumpf had been killed by an Arab assassin. The assassin's name was Ismael Latif, the same man who had returned to Palestine to join the rebels.

Recently, he had visited an Arab friend, who recounted the story of Ismael Latif. He saw in the eyes of his friend that he was a hero, someone who lifted the spirits of the Arabs and gave them hope. He felt no animosity for this man and found himself wishing he could and talk him. He kept his thoughts to himself.

The excitement subsided as Rabin took up the rest of the agenda. Weapons were discussed, a letter from the Agency discussing new assessments on Tel Hai and others matter regarding the management of the settlement. The guard roster was posted on the board behind Rabin. The incident at Kfar Giladi was touched on, bringing the settlement up to date on progress in capturing or killing Arab gangsters roaming the north. Rabin read a dispatch from the Agency requesting that members of the settlement keep their eyes and ears open on any word about the two renegade reporters. They were reminded that guards should accompany trips to Haifa to pick up shipments at the port.

As the meeting ended and the settlers began to move to their quarters, the tight group of men who were members of the Irgun stayed together as they left the meeting house, talking in low voices. Avi and Shlomo were in the center of the group and seemed to be doing most of the talking.

***

The three story stone building seemed large among the smaller ones surrounding it. It was part of the Jewish section of Haifa which was quickly expanding from the flat land around the horseshoe harbor into the hills which rose steeply and then crowned by majestic Mount Carmel. The building was one of the first built by the settlers in the early 1900's and had fallen into disrepair, now occupied by itinerant workers or immigrants looking to earn enough money to move to more livable quarters.

Avi and Shlomo both had lived on the third floor toward the back of the building, where the steep sides of the mountain seemed but a stone throw away. Two days before this cold and sunny day they had left for Tel Hai, warned of the police raid.

The usual sounds of the busy harbor were suddenly pierced by the pulsing sirens of three police vehicles that quickly discharged men who began running to the exits of the building to block any escape. Two stairways led to the third floor. Four police officers climbed each set of stairs, then took up positions on the landings, their eyes directed to the two doors where they were informed the suspects lived.

Sergeant Murray wasamongthefirst to reach thelanding. Motioning for a man to post on each side of the door, short 10 gauge pump shotguns at the ready, sturdy men stood in front of each the doors.

"Now." The command issued in a low voice unleashed the two men who in unison kicked in the doors and the men beside each door burst in the rooms, their shotguns cocked.

A lone man stood wide-eyed, speaking quickly in Russian. The next room yielded the same, a frightened immigrant pleading in Russian for his life.

The Sergeant looked at the two frightened men and through the Russian interpreter that had been called in, learned that both had arrived a day before, and the rooms were empty when they arrived.

"They must have been warned, sir."

"You're right, Corporal. See what you can find out from the manager."

He called into the hallway. "Simmons, talk to the neighbors. We only have one Russian interpreter and it may take all day. Ivan says he also speaks German so we may be able to make do with only one.

Murray went back into the rooms. He looked around the first. A sink. A bed. A chair. That was it. He guessed the window sill could be used as a table and desk. There were hooks on the wall to hang clothes. He knelt and looked under the bed. Trash, nothing else.

"How long had the two of them lived here? Two believers who seemed oblivious to their surroundings. A bed, a sink and a bathroom down the hall. What more could a zealot bomber want? And they had each other to share in their cause, to take away the loneliness." Murray had a habit of talking to himself as if there was someone else there. His men had come to understand and left him alone unless it was clear he was speaking to them.

Murray thought about the way he received the information that Avi Nelkin and Shlomo Yellen were there. It had come from Intelligence. There was an unwritten rule not to ask intelligence operatives where they got their information unless they offered the source. Obviously, the intelligence was poor in this case, and old. Someone had fed our people information. But why? Double agents were common in Palestine and planting useless information almost the norm. What if someone in the Yishuv decided to give the two to us? The more he thought about it, the more convinced he would never know the answers.

A good night's sleep, a letter from Glenda, and the beautiful city on the blue green Mediterranean cleared his mind. Time to do a little brainstorming with a few of the officers, to try to out think and out guess the enemy. In the last several months, it had become clear who the enemy was.

The underground was active and bombings clearly were intended to frighten the Arabs, to make their lives so miserable that they would leave Palestine. There had been rumors that Jabotinsky was speaking out against the British, and increasingly intelligence was hearing reports that the Irgun was planning attacks on the British.

When Murray first heard these reports, he was not surprised. All hell could break loose. He wondered if his superiors knew that.

He didn't have a lot of men and he had to place them where they would do the most good. Working in Haifa, he saw his job of heading off bombings and shootings. It had been months since the last bombing in Haifa but the success Abu Kamal was having to the north and east might trigger another bombing in retaliation.

Haifa was a likely target. Densely populated, the impact could be especially deadly. He had considered a number of possible targets. The bus terminals, the railroad station, marketplaces, churches and mosques all were potential targets. What had he missed? Schools? A possibility. The docks? Neither side wants to shut down the port.

The hiring hall. Hundreds of young men gather there each morning looking for jobs on the docks. He had been there several times, young males looking for work often get in trouble and he and his men had been there to find someone who had been accused of a crime.

Young Arab men, many from the mountains, desperate men, prime candidates to join the rebel bands. A bomb could be deadly to the body and the spirit of the revolt. He would concentrate on the hiring hall.

***

The plan was simple. The hall was guarded by two armed guards when the hall was closed. Two men dressed in uniforms of the local electric power company would present themselves at the main

235

door and inform the guards that they were called by the office manager that there was a problem with the power; that the power box and the circuits had to be checked.

The box was located inside in the rear of the building. One of the men was to request the help of both guards, sending both to locations on the second floor of the building to check the electrical outlets. The other man would plant the bomb in the center of the hall under one of the benches timed to go off thirty minutes after the hall opened in the morning.

The backup plan, if the guards refused to cooperate was to murder the two guards by shooting them with revolvers that were equipped with sound suppressors. The intruders would attempt to open the safe to make it appear a botched robbery.

***

The wide street leading to the harbor was empty of vehicles and people. The stillness was broken only by the barking of a dog, quickly silenced, and shouts that would come and go. The gentle wind was cold and the air damp from the bay, the placid water slapping the walls of the docks in a steady cadence.

Ahmed Beisan was standing in front of the hiring hall, having completed his circle of the building; stopping to survey the dimly lit harbor. From where he stood, he could see the warships in the bay, only outlines this early in the morning, and the freighters fast against the docks.

He had worked as a guard for six months now, and thanks to Allah there had been no violence during the nights since he began. The mornings were different, when hundreds of men forced themselves into the hiring hall, pleading for work. Sometimes, when but a small handful were hired and hundreds were turned away, the anger would spill out into the streets, and mounted police with their batons striking indiscriminately would disperse the crowds.

His cousin had told him that there was more work than ever on the docks but the fellaheen that had been forced off their land by new owners, falling prices for what they grew and then the droughts produced more people looking for work than there was work to be had.

Something else made them bitter. The men from the Jewish union were given preference when there were jobs to be had, and when Jews and Arabs did the same work, the wages for the Jews were greater. Because of union protests, the British declared that the owners must pay at least a minimum wage, but the Arab unions quickly discovered that the minimum wage for Jews was higher than for Arabs.

Still, he thanked Allah that he could provide for his family and he avoided joining with others in protest for fear he might lose his job.

He was about to unlock the entrance door when he heard the whine of an engine. A van marked Haifa Power Company pulled to a stop where he stood. He unbuttoned the flap on his revolver as two men with large tool bags got out of the vehicle and approached him. As he was trained to do, he noted the appearance of the two men who he decided were Jews. The taller one approached him addressing him in Arabic. The short thick one moved in behind him

"We have a report that there is a problem with the electric connection from the power company to this address. We will need to do some checking inside."

"May I see your cards, please?"

They quickly pulled out their identity cards with Haifa Power Company printed across the top.

"And you are?" Ahmed looked at the man with the card with the name Avraham Lisky.

"It's on the card."

Ahmed Beisan looked at the thin one, who could not wipe the smirk from his face. He waited.

"Avraham Lisky."

"Thank you" and handed the card to him.

He noticed that the shorter man seemed nervous as he took his card.

"Ruben Gordon."

"Thank you. I am required to check everyone's identity." He turned to unlock the door, while turning his body to observe the two men. Then he remembered.

The two men walked to the center of the waiting area. Avi turned to the guard who showed no sign of alarm. He decided the guard was not suspicious. This would be easy, he thought. He smiled at Shlomo, bothered by the beads of sweat on his partner's forehead—trying to calm him.

The guard now approached. "My name is Ahmed. There is another guard in the building. Dahud will have to accompany you." He looked at the two men. The short one who called himself Ruben was nervous. Such men are especially dangerous, he thought. "I will just be a moment."

When the Arab was gone, Shlomo spoke quickly in Russian. "Let's plant the bomb before he comes back."

"We'll wait."

They waited and Avi regretted his decision not to plant the bomb. Five minutes passed. Then they heard footsteps. It was Ahmed returning without the other guard. Something was wrong. Avi touched the Berretta holstered beneath his arm. He nodded to Shlomo.

Shlomo reacted first, reaching for his weapon as Ahmed, seeing the movement, ran for cover. Avi had his weapon out and fired quickly at the fleeing guard. Beisan heard the deadly whisper of the errant shots as he dove behind the counter and drew his Webley.

The assassins separated, moving quickly to flank him. Dahud was somewhere out there. Dahud had made the call to the police station. It was not always possible to get through this early in the morning. He heard a sound to his right. They were trying to get behind him. Fifteen feet behind him was a heavy desk close to the rear wall of the building. Firing as he went, he sprinted and dove behind the desk, hearing the soft thud of bullets striking the desk. He could hear the siren now and the screeching of brakes.

To the left, the pop, pop of a Webley and the cry of pain from one of the two. Then he heard running and knew one was trying to escape. He rose to see Dahud moving cautiously toward the fleeing Jew, now trapped between the guards and the British police.

To his front, the British uniforms moving toward the door, he looked down at his friend, lying in a fetal position, crying in pain from a stomach wound. Blinded by rage, Avi faced the Arab, firing wildly. Dahud, an Ottoman Army veteran, now stood, legs apart, and fired twice, both bullets striking the chest of the young man. It was over.

Two British policemen entered the building, cautiously surveying the scene. Ahmed and Dahud moved to the center of the room where the policemen now stood.

Ahmed pointed toward the two tool bags.

The Corporal in charge spoke loudly so everyone could hear. "We need to clear the building. Anyone else in the building?" Both guards shook their heads no. The Corporal looked at the two fallen men, one being attended to by a medic. He shook the hands of the two guards. "Damn good work, gentlemen." He looked again at Avi and Shlomo. "These two murderers are responsible for at least a hundred lives, men, women and children. We'll get the bomb team to take care of those bags."

As the two Arabs and the policemen walked into the street, men like gray ghosts in the dark, began to form in front of the hiring hall. Ahmed took Dahud's hand, the two cousins moving to the other side of the street. There was still two hours to go on their shift.

***

When Hamish Murray arrived in the morning, he was greeted with the news. Nelkin was dead and Yellen was in hospital, not expected to live. The job had small satisfactions, he thought. Alerting the hiring hall had paid off, thanks to the two guards.

He thought how the situation unfolded. Ahmed Beisan had noticed the heavier one was nervous, and decided to check on them. Although their faces were different, the size and build of the two fit the description the police had given them. When Ahmed went to look for Dahud, that's when Shlomo panicked.

Murray thought about the two guards. When members of the Irgun are killed or captured, the defeat is often treated as an assault on the Yishuv and some act of revenge follows.

"Corporal, warn the two guards at the hiring hall. They may be targeted."

+++

Bissett and Monet were standing on a ledge on one of the hillocks south of Mount Tabor looking out over Jezreel Valley. They were camped in a small cave cut into the hillock. The camp was just below them on a bench that rimmed the south side of the hillock. The wind was warm this morning, coming from the south. Osta had found them a bag of rich black coffee from Ethiopia which they savored as they talked.

"I talked to John McDermott yesterday."

"Be careful, Andre. Very likely someone is tracking the Pastor."

"I went there after dark and the rain made it hard to see more than ten meters in front of you."

"Anything new?"

"You heard what happened in Haifa. Seems they were the same two who planted the bomb in Nablus,"

"Do you think Sergeant Hamish Murray would talk to us?"

"Not officially, since we are wanted criminals, but even in secret it would be too dangerous for you and for him."

"I have heard he knows a great deal about what is going on in Haifa."

"Forget that one, Andre."

"I heard there is to be a religious gathering in Nazareth. Sarah and John are looking for trouble by going there."

"I think they know that. John is a strange fellow. Seemingly a gentle fellow, but a bomb thrower inside."

"Kalima is going to try to arrange something with the Ghost of Sheik Qassam."

"Aref Abdul Razzik, sounds like quite a man."

George handed Andre a paper. "It's a communication from Razzik. Look how he signed it"

"The Ghost of Sheik Qassam., looks like he's taken by the title."

"Osta gave me a newspaper clip with a poem the British soldiers have made up about him."

George handed it to Andre.

> *Aref had a little mare*
> *Its coat as white as snow*
> *And where that mare and Aref went*
> *We're jiggered if we know.*

"Sounds like something written by some soldiers who are not sold on fighting Palestine Arabs."

"Not like Purdom."

"No, if they're like the French soldiers, they joined the army for three meals a day, a bed, and a few francs to spend on Saturday night."

"Pretty much a class thing, I guess. The officers are taught to believe in their cause and many have a little Purdom inside, although he's one of a kind."

"Kalima told me that he thinks Ismael will go after Purdom and the jailer who tortured his brother. I guess you have heard the stories of what happened after the death of his father and the death of his friend, John Nevers."

"There are also rumors that Purdom questions Arabs in every village he enters about Ismael. British soldiers say he is obsessed. Of course, they also believe he's insane and stays in Palestine because the Jews protect him."

"Well, most of the world knows of Purdom thanks to the Agency and Abe Meyersohn. They're trying to make him a hero in Europe and America."

George returned to the Ghost of Sheik Qassam.

"So, do you think Kalima will be able to arrange for us to join Razzik?"

"Yes. Whatever we ask, Kalima gets it done."

Andre looked at this friend. "We're starting to get reckless. There are a lot of people looking for us."

"You're right."

They turned to see Kalima climbing toward them, waving a hello.

+++

They followed the folds of the hills as they rode south; one hundred men led by Abu Kamal to rendezvous with the forces of Aref Abdul Razzik. Both leaders had accepted the plan presented to them by Ismael Latif to attack the area command of the British Eighth Infantry Division. Over three thousand men operated out of the Nablus sector to cover the area surrounding Nablus and Tulkarem. The base had never been attacked since its establishment in 1937. By any reckoning, the number of soldiers at the base exceeded the rebel forces in the field throughout Palestine.

The British base was located on the north side of Nablus. A series of roads ran from the post to the main roads leading in all directions. It was from this base that armored vehicles moved to attack rebel concentrations. But foremost was its communications center, able to quickly reach units in the field and the airfields in Jordan and Gaza. Early in the revolt, rebel groups suffered large losses when they found themselves faced with bombers and reconnaissance aero planes, and coordinated ground and air attacks. Abu Kamal and the Ghost of Qassam were forced to adjust their tactics, hitting targets with small groups that could quickly fade into the countryside,

Now the small army of Al Hajj Mohammad who the men affectionately called Abu Kamal moved south to the rendezvous

243

in squads, divided to avoid alerting informants of a larger force on the move. The squads would then rendezvous in a seldom traveled ravine three miles from the British base. There Abu Kamal would meet with Razzik, whose men would be camped one mile to the east.

Abu Kamal and his men traveled by night. On the second night all the men reached the ravine. The narrow space between the hills that seemed close to touching each other provided but little protection against the cold winds coming from the north, the men's discomfort made worse by the order that there were to be no campfires. Veterans all, they had come to accept such conditions as part of the struggle to free Palestine from the British and the Jews.

All sensed that there was to be a great battle and many of their comrades would be lost. They had seen their numbers dwindle as the intensity of the British counter-insurgency increased. Still, desertions were low and few would give up their fight for the Palestine where they were born and raised. Like before other battles there was little talk among the men. Some prayed. Some thought of home. Others worried about their wives and children. As the checked their equipment and cared for their horses, a small group of men led by a man on a white mare entered the east end of the ravine. In low voices, the news raced through the camp and they stopped to watch Ghost of Sheik Qassam pass among them.

Ismael had decided on the attack for two reasons, one to lift the morale of fighters everywhere in Palestine if they achieved victory, the second by showing the British that the Arabs can and will pressure the British to reach a settlement rather than continue to fight a war with no end in sight.

Not too many months before when Montgomery put the Eighth Army Division in the field, it seemed time was running out for the revolt very quickly. But with Ismael's arrival things changed. Small victories happened more often. The fedayeen were having greater success in eluding the British.

Most importantly, the international tensions created a sense of urgency by the British to settle differences in the Commonwealth countries and the Middle East, to assure the continued flow of oil to power their planes, ships and tanks.

Razzik was a man still full of strength and energy. Like Abu Kamal, he was a veteran who knew how to lead and to fight. The British had put a price on his head large enough to make men rich. There been many stories of Razzik's mastery of deception and illusion, of making the British think he would strike here, and discover he had struck them there. Among the British enlisted men and many officers, there was admiration for they saw him winning against great odds and always eluding traps laid for him. Among other British officers who had often been humiliated by his behavior and by the Jews who did not want Arab heroes, they wanted him not only dead and but gone, denied a hero's funeral.

A single tent was set up for Abu Kamal and Razzik to meet. Covered with a second layer of dark canvas to prevent the lighted interior from being seen from a distance, Abu Kamal stood at its entrance to welcome Razzik.

"It is good to see you, Commander Aref. I hope your family is well."

"It is good to see you, Commander Abd. Word has reached me that you saw your children recently. How fortunate you are but you must be careful. The British and the Hagenah will try to bribe traitors among us to betray you."

"We all are prey to such jackals, even you, Commander."

"With our two hundred and their three thousand, your plan carries great risks, Commander. But I am sure you know this and there is more to learn about your plan."

Abu Kamal thought at this moment, he should give Ismael the chance to respond, but no, he must hear it from me.

245

"The perimeter of their base is protected by two eight foot fences made of razor wire. It is fifty feet between the two fences, with men in armored cars patrolling the inside perimeter every half hour. There may be trip wires beyond the outer fence which can ignite flares if stepped on."

Razzik was looking closely at Abu Kamal. None of what was said surprised him. Where was this leading?

"The attack must be at night, preferably shortly after midnight when the camp is likely to be the most silent.

"The attack must be selective and create the greatest damage with a small force. Three targets were selected: the motor park which includes a petrol storage depot, the ammunition depot and the communication center.

"We were able to obtain a map of the camp which shows where the three areas are located. The ammunition depot is too well protected to risk an attack. That leaves the motor park with the petrol storage depot and the communications center.

"The main gate is located on the south side of the camp, two hundred yards from the main road. There are gates on all sides of the camp. As you can see, Commander, the closest gate to the motor park and fuel depot is the main gate. The communications center is located the same distance from all the gates and less than one hundred yards from the motor park.

"The main barracks where the soldiers are quartered is located east of the communications center approximately 100 yards to the east.

"We will enter the camp through the main gate. We will use British vehicles, one armored car and four lorries. We will need fifty men."

Abu Kamal watched Razzik raise his eyebrows and knew the question before it was asked.

"One hundred fifty men will create a diversion after the vehicles are inside the camp and after the attack on the two targets begins. You will attack through the east gate here and set up a perimeter just inside the gate. You will hold your position until we signal by flare to retreat. You will have to decide how close the horses can be placed to the camp to avoid detection yet still allow the men to leave the area quickly."

Razzik was watching Abu Kamal, silently wondering how he had underestimated his fellow commander's ability to plan such a complicated operation. He glanced quickly at Latif, wondering and concluding who was the source. He remained silent, seeing that there was more to be said.

Abu Kamal; continued. "The fifty men who will enter the front gate will be dressed as British soldiers. The critical members of the attacking unit must be able to pass as British soldiers. We will need at least ten men who might not immediately be recognized as Palestinians. The main gate entrance likely will be well lighted but still less light than daytime. The plan takes into account that the guards are not likely to let the convoy pass routinely and they will have to be eliminated quickly and silently.

"We know the British are thorough and even a night raid like this one will not take them totally by surprise and we can expect them to react quickly. That is why the attack from the east must come off before the attacks on the motor park and the communications center. The leaders inside the camp must believe the attack is coming from the east. The plan is to destroy the communications center, the petrol depot and the motor park as quickly as possible and exit the main gate.

"When the main gate has been cleared and the convoy begins to move inside the camp, my command will fire a flare. That is your signal to attack. If all goes well, a second flare to let you know we have left the camp. Once we have withdrawn, each command will make their way back. My men that are assigned to you will make their way north.

247

Abu Kamal put his hands on the shoulders of his fellow commander. "Success will depend on speed and timing and Allah's blessing, my friend."

Razzik was impressed but unconvinced. "Where will you get the armored car, the lorries and the uniforms for the men?"

"The Levant is swarming with arms dealers. They have their ways of getting their hands on anything you need if you have the money. Several Zionist banks reluctantly handed over enough money to pay for what we need. During the offloading of British equipment, some managed to be diverted to our dealer and we have not only lorries, an armored car, and uniforms, we have sub-machine guns, ammunition and grenades.

"When this is over, I will need the name of the arms dealer."

Abu Kamal smiled at Razzik. There are other dealers that we know. This one has disappeared. He couldn't be trusted and might sell information to the British."

"Will the British be suspicious when a convoy arrives early in the morning?"

"We have been observing the traffic at night over the last week. It is not unusual, with the reinforcements coming off the docks in Haifa, for convoys to arrive in the early morning hours."

Ismael watched the two men, wondering whether there might be disagreement. Who would lead the convoy? Who would lead the attack on the east gate? He was relieved when the two quickly agreed that Abu Kamal; would lead the convoy and Razzik the attack on the east gate. He remembered the delicate task that Lawrence had to perform before each action when such decisions had to be made. A careless remark between proud men could be enough to abort a mission.

Fifty of Abu Kamal's men moved to the Razzik camp. The fifty chosen for the convoy had been briefed by Kamal's lieutenants on the mission and given briefings on the new automatic weapons and the use of mills bombs which everyone would be required to attach to their crossed ammunition belts. Included in the weapons were Sten MKII's, sub-machine guns that could be mastered quickly by his men and assigned to the most experienced of the fighters. A mounted Bren MKI on the armored car would be operated by Kalima, with Abd as his replacement. The high explosive fragmentation grenades were easily mastered by all the men, and Ismael personally instructed the men in their use.

Kalima came looking for Ismael. "I think we should consider homemade incendiary bombs, Ismael. They are being used in Spain. Bottles filled with petrol and ignited by a cloth fuse which are lit and thrown at the target."

Ismael nodded. "We will use them after rupturing the gas tanks and the petrol drums. We'll need at least fifty."

***

Darkness would be complete soon. In four hours, 0030 hours, the men under Abu Kamal would begin to leave the camp and move with their weapons to the rendezvous on the main road three miles from the main gate of the British camp.

Ismael was not surprised when two donkeys appeared out of the mist that blanketed the ravine carrying 50 bottles already filled with petrol together with fifty tightly bound cotton fuses. Kalima, walking alongside the lead donkey, waved and smiled at Ismael. Shaking his head at the wonder of this young man, he saluted the young warrior.

The two ajnabi knew that what was before them was different, different in the size of the force involved, different that the two greatest leaders of the rebellion had joined together, and different because there was far more danger to them personally than anything that had happened before.

As they traveled south to rendezvous with Razzik, each collected their thoughts about what was happening and how it could be that they were accompanying these brave men whom they really did not understand in a place so far removed from their lives to date that each could ask themselves: Is this really happening? Am I really accompanying Arabs to battle in the Holy Land? Am I really here and is everything around me real? Or can I wake to a warm bed among my friends and family? But each knew he could not go back and what they started they must finish. Each possessed the admixture of bravado, fervor, foreboding and resignation that possesses those going to battle.

"It is the beginning of summer in Cordoba. After the bustle of spring and it rebirth, life seems to slow as everyone adjusts to the hot summer." Bissett adjusted the scarf around his neck to keep out the cold wind at their backs.

"It is not so different than Paris. More rain, less sun but the weather is much the same. But it is Paris whatever the season and I miss it. I lived in Montmartre." He looked at his friend. "You must have been to Paris."

Bissett nodded, ending the conversation.

A flip of a coin decided who would enter the base with the convoy and who would join Razzik in the diversionary attack on the east gate. Both were torn as to which was most important, for neither had been with Razzik on any of his raids yet the attack by Abu Kamal was clearly more critical. Andre Monet would join Razzik, Bissett would accompany Abu Kamal.

Andre was relieved that the Ghost of Sheik Qassam welcomed him andprovidedhimwithayoungwarriorinterpreterwhospokefluent French. Razzik, despite the rising tension, graciously answered his questions. Andre began to form in his mind the beginning of the dispatch he would send after the attack.

The men began to move; only the muted sounds of horses' hooves interrupted the silence. Ismael moved to the front with Abu Kamal. Both commanders knew of the importance of this mission, both trying not to think beyond their mission tonight.

To their east, Monet watched Razzik's men prepare for battle, checking their rifles and their bandoliers, feeding and watering their horses. The two tripod mounted Bren MKI machine guns were inspected and loaded on horses.

Two miles from the main gate, the troop of Abu Kamal's fifty men moved their horses behind a step hill abutting the road to the British camp. The horses were hobbled and guarded by two of his warriors. They found the uniforms and helmets in crates already opened. Quickly the men removed their clothes and put on the uniforms, sometimes exchanging among themselves to obtain a reasonable fit. Ismael found the uniform and hat that he would use as the officer in the armored car first to enter the camp. The distance to the road no more than one hundred yards, the men waited.

They heard the whine of engines and started to move. Ismael quickly stepped in front of the men and raised his hand.

"Wait!"

The sound grew louder and two armored cars passed moving toward camp. Al Hajj Mohammad looked at Ismael Latif, grateful that he was with them.

The high pitched sound of vehicles, this time louder than before brought the men to full alert. Five vehicles approached, led by an armored car. This time they waited until the vehicles stopped and the drivers exited the vehicles and signaled.

Moving quickly, the men climbed into the lorries. Four men climbed into the armored car. The bottles filled with petrol were loaded in the last lorry.

Abu Kamal, also in an officer's uniform, signaled from the side of the first lorry for the convoy to move. He climbed in beside the driver who had shaved off his beard and the sound of the engine and shifting gears filled the air as the attack began.

To the east, Razzik had moved by horseback within a half mile of the east gate, protected by the hills to that point. Leaving their horses, they began to move on foot, carrying the two machine guns, the men armed with Enfield's, some with grenades. One hundred yards from the gate the folds of the land still provided cover. Beyond that to the edge of the first wire fence was open ground. Razzik ordered one of the machine guns to be mounted and trained on the guard house inside the fence.

To move one hundred yards after the flare was seen would take less than 30 seconds if there was no force confronting them. Two sappers were now working their way toward the outer fence, their task to place gelignite in front of the gate to blast an opening through which his men could move. The gelignite would be detonated by machine gun fire from the second machine gun.

Aref Abdul Razzik had been in many battles which were preceded by carefully crafted plans covering every contingency. What happened when battles began seldom followed the plans. The truth, Razzik knew, is that it is impossible to cover every contingency and too often one that no one thought of comes into play.

By his reckoning, Abu Kamal's forces were on the road and only minutes remained before he would be seeing the flare. The sappers by now had planted their explosives and were working their way back.

Suddenly, a sound caught the ears of the men prone, waiting to rise up and attack. It was a lone vehicle heading for the gate. If the gate opened, an attack was the best chance of getting inside. If he relied on the explosives, there was the chance that the gates could not be breached and his men would be exposed to a counter attack.

He made his decision as the vehicle approached the gate. He turned to his machine gun crew. "When the gate opens, commence firing at the gelignite, the lorry and the gatehouse."

Excitement filled the air as the men pointed to the sky. A flare rose and in a slow arc began to descend and light up the sky beyond the camp. Razzik could not believe what he was seeing. At the moment the flare still lighted the sky far to the west, the gate opened.

The sound of the machine gun sighted on the lorry and the gate house and the exploding gelignite drowned out the shouts of the men charging toward the gate, firing as they charged. To his right, Razzik could see lights go on where the barrack tents were located.

***

As the convoy approached the gate, Ismael could see one of the guards walk to the switch that opened the gate. Body language spoke of a young private bored by his duty which had been the same uneventful watch every night.

He barely glanced at the officer who handed him his identification papers and waved the convoy through. The young man from far off England was blissfully innocent of the quick death that came to him silently, nor was the corporal in the guardhouse who looked up from the letter from home to see the shadow of a man who ended his life without a cry. The two dead men were pulled into the guardhouse replaced by two Arabs dressed in the same uniform.

The convoy rolled into the camp heading for the motor park. The armored car and the first lorry veered to the right toward the communications center. The three remaining lorries headed toward the motor park and the petrol depot. Above, Bissett watched as the flare rose, seemed to stop, then burst to illuminate all below it.

Ismael leaped from the armored car carrying his Sten sub-machine gun, firing short bursts as he headed toward the tented communication center. Two of Abu Kamal's men moved to his right and left and fired into the tent. Two men emerged from the tent, also armed with sub-machine guns, firing in the directions of the attack. One of Abu Kamal's men went down before the two British soldiers went down. Running low, Ismael tossed a grenade through the tent opening, retreated and dropped to the ground, leaped to his feet after the debris was clear, then entered the tent, firing as he did.

No one was still standing, and three men lay on the floor, their bodies torn by the grenades. Replacing a clip on his weapon, Ismael sprayed the equipment, rendering it useless and likely beyond repair. Pulling a grenade from his belt, he placed it next to the largest piece of radio equipment, removed the pin and dashed from the tent. He shouted at the other men: "Down!" and dropped as the explosion sent debris flying.

Abu Kamal had set up the two machine guns facing the barracks, traversing as they fired. Fire was being returned now. Soon it would be intense.

Behind him, Ismael could hear the steady staccato of the Stens, the men firing at any motor park guards but also directing their fire at the petrol tanks. Others were systematically firing into the park vehicles, aiming to rupture their gas tanks. There were over a hundred vehicles and forty men to destroy them. As the men began to retreat from the motor park, a squad of ten stayed behind to fire the gas filled bottles and toss them into the vehicles.

Abu Kamal now saw the danger to his men if fire reached the gas pouring on the ground from the huge tanks. Vehicles were exploding in flames now and any minute the flames would reach the gas pouring from the tanks.

He passed the word to retreat. Ismael was beside him now, aware of the danger to the men still tossing gasoline bottles into the vehicles. Suddenly, Abu Kamal ran into the burning motor park, shouting at the men to get back to the lorries.

Ismael saw the danger to the men and ordered them into the lorries and the armored car. The men hesitated, their leader still in danger, yet they obeyed. The entire motor park seemed to be in flames as vehicles that had not been firebombed were ignited by the heat of those already burning.

In every battle, decisions had to be made to preserve the group. He now had to make a decision. If the petrol tanks exploded, no one would survive. He knew it was only a matter of minutes, perhaps seconds, before the petrol tanks exploded. He knew what he had to do. Suddenly, like spectral apparitions, men began to pour out of the flames. Two were dragging their leader. The clothing of the men were smoldering from the heat.

Abu Kamal shouted: "There is still one man down!"

Grabbing Abu Kamal's arm, he pulled him into the armored car. Checking again to see if anyone in sight that had not reached the lorries. He saw no one and ordered the convoy out of the camp. Outside of the camp, he fired the flare and watched it soar above them then begin its slow descent. The road rose above the camp as it wended its way west then northwest. Below the fires were still burning and the army vehicles looked like tortured skeletons of ancient creatures. Ismael glanced quickly at Abu Kamal, then turned away. He prayed his commander would understand what had to be done.

Razzik turned to one of his men as he pointed at the sky. The flare was descending. He felt the tremor before he saw it, a huge orange and gold cloud ascended from the earth as the petrol depot exploded. The firing on his positions was becoming more intense as he ordered a retreat. He thought it ironic that this time there would be no pursuit. No communications and no vehicles. As they drew clear from the British soldier's weapons, he did a quick count of those left behind and the wounded that had been dragged from the field. Twelve men were left on the battlefield, presumed dead and fourteen more suffered wounds, only two so serious that the warrior's life was in jeopardy. He glanced at the Frenchman who had been with him throughout the battle. He could see the fear in his eyes when they advanced but the young man never left his side. Such men who risk their lives for another's cause are men he did not fully understand. Yet Monet would be remembered and if Allah grants us victory, we will tell our children about him and they will tell theirs.

+++

On the road to the west, five vehicles could be seen burning. Discarding their British uniforms, the men mounted their horses and headed north. Ismael saw his friend from Argentina walking toward him. His face was covered with soot and his uniform reeked of smoke.

"Well, my young gaucho, you have your story. What was your understanding with Andre. Will he file the story himself or will he wait for your photographs?

"He need not wait. I doubt they are very good. He will need my account of what happened inside the post."

"You are a good photographer. They will be like the others."

"Ismael, I have never been so frightened as I was tonight. Until your commander pulled me out of the motor park, I was convinced I would die."

"Well, you're here, my friend. Your uncle would have been proud."

Ismael felt embarrassment when the eyes of his young friend filled with tears.

"Thank you. That means so much to me to have you say that."

"They ran him down with a motor car, didn't they?"

"Yes." He would say no more about the assassin leaving the motor car and stabbing his uncle with an ice pick in his ear hole to avoid detection, to make it look like death was caused by the collision. George didn't need to know.

As they walked toward their horses, Ismael putting his hand on his friend's shoulder. George looked at his friend. "Do you think this will help Palestine find peace?"

"It gives us reason to hope. I think they are ready to listen."

"What happens now?"

"We will have to be quick and nimble. General 'Monty' does not like to have his nose tweaked. Many innocents will suffer because of what happened. Much depends on Andre and you, George."

Abu Kamal approached them. "The men will form units of five or less and proceed north by different routes. Runners will make contact in a week to form up as a unit." He looked at Ismael.

"May Allah protect you, Ismael. Pray for peace."

"Do you want me to go with you?"

"No, it is best the leaders be separated."

Ismael nodded, knowing it best in the event some of the units are discovered and relieved that his commander had understood.

They rode south through a rocky land where tracking was impossible, then turned west then north. Soon it would be light and they must find cover.

They could see the light forming on the rims of the hills to the east.

"I hope Kalima is with Andre." Bissett was worried about his friend.

"I'm sure Razzik will get him away safely."

"What should we write, Ismael."

"I think you can tell them about Nablus, but you need to include a plea for peace."

"What will you do now?"

"There is something I must do in Nablus. Then I will spend the next week talking to Arab leaders in Palestine and finding a way to talk to the High Commissioner."

"Have you thought about Sarah Nevers?"

Ismael felt his ears burning and he wondered if his face betrayed his feelings for Sarah. He quickly realized what George was asking.

"Yes, and Pastor McDermott."

Aware that the light was quickly coming to the land, one of the men pointed to a cut between the gray hills to their right and they turned to seek cover for the day.

+++

Major Jonathan Fortson had hoped to be assigned to one of the three coastal cities in Palestine. Instead he had been assigned to the sector headquarters in Nablus. Still, he had comfortable quarters where he could walk to work and the food and drinks and the officer's club were quite good.

The Major realized he had been a disappointment to his father, a Baron. The senior Fortson was a major partner in Lloyds of London and has sizeable shares in Argentinian railroads. An officer who distinguished himself in the Great War, he expected his second son to do no less. Young Fortson did not object when he was enrolled in Eton nor did he object to Sandhurst. Some might have resisted being managed in this manner, but young Fortson decided the rewards of staying on the good side of the Baron far outweighed the loss of freedom to be his own man. Truth be known, he had no wish go do anything else.

The Major had been commissioned in 1931 and had moved from post to post in the Empire, sometimes by pulling strings, but others at the request of his commanding officers who found him insufferable as a person and mediocre as an officer. The revolt in Palestine that began in 1936 created a demand for officers for all sorts of jobs that the military must perform in putting down an insurrection.

It was in India that he met Charles Tegart, who had established himself as a security specialist, one who could secure areas from the gangsters that called themselves freedom fighters. One of the specialties was the extraction of information from captured rebels. A student of past empires, he had researched the ways that information was obtained from persons determined not to divulge it. Breaking limbs, cracking bones, burning the most sensitive parts of the body, notably the eyes and the genitals, worked well, as did water torture, a seemingly innocuous form of torture since it did not inflict excruciating pain. Instead, it created panic from the fear of drowning, of being denied air to breathe. It seldom failed to produce results, which often proved unsatisfactory because the victim would confess to anything and provide information just to have it end.

Tegart had derived great satisfaction in "breaking" a man, one who stood defiant in front of him, refusing to tell him what he wanted to know. When he had finished his work, standing before him was a "broken" human being unlikely to ever recover his self-image as a man. There were times when he had failed, and when he did, he saw no need to honor the brave man, but more often than not had him shot or ignominiously hanged.

During his work in India, a jaded young captain had been assigned to him. It was made clear that accepting Captain Jonathan Fortson was not a choice. He was prepared to tolerate the tall young man who seemed to slouch even when he was called to attention. But he notice something he looked for in men under him, sadism, the enjoyment of inflicting pain and humiliating the Indians they had captured. He noticed something else, that the man had no soul. At the end of the most brutal treatment of a prisoner, he seemed not to care at all what had transpired, but most likely would walk away from the prisoner discussing the evening's entertainment at the club or the officers' brothel. Such men were valuable because they were dependable. The horrors they inflicted and witnessed seemed to touch their hearts only in a twisted way; they enjoyed breaking men. Tegart, never quick to judge himself, nevertheless judged Fortson as a man who saw the degradation of his victim's as the pleasure of his own degradation.

It was no surprise to anyone in India that Tegart took Fortson with him to perform the macabre in Palestine. Tegart would oversee security, but he wanted Fortson there to carry out his wishes. Nablus was an area of intense rebel activity, and Tegart assigned his protégé there. Fortson had hoped he would be rewarded by granting him the right to command men but Tegart knew his man and had other ideas.

Fortson was bitter about the news. He had no command but an assignment as a specialist, doing what he did in India. He saw little difference between the defiant Indians and the equally defiant Arabs. The task would be the same; to extract information by whatever means. His fellow officers knew what he did, and they kept their distance whenever they could, sensing that by socializing with him they might discover something they did not care to know about.

His treatment by his fellow officers in Palestine was no different than in India and found it produced no resentment toward them. Nor did it make him feel the worse about himself. He was doing something essential, more important than what most of the officers were doing; doing more to end the revolt than most. And he enjoyed his work, something he would never tell anyone lest it be Tegart, who understood.

When his self-satisfaction and self-importance were at their highest after a particularly satisfying day, he would be jolted by Hassan Latif's words. "You will not find him, he will find you." The black eyes looking into his soul, the last words of a dying man. Neither would go away. On the streets of Nablus, on his way to the club or the brothel, he would be watchful, sometimes turning if he heard a strange sound, snapping the flap on his Webley holster. As often as he could, he would invite himself to accompany other officers on his night time trips.

+++

"Two Frenchmen and the Arabs are winning the propaganda war. How can that happen, Abe?

"With the British and the Yishuv after the two, how can we not find them? It is a tiny country and we have informants everywhere, the British are becoming more numerous than flies, and our people are looking everywhere, and still they send their lies and half-lies out to the rest of the world."

"Andre Monet is a very good journalist and his partner has the genes of a great newspaper man."

"We didn't have a problem getting rid of his uncle."

Shurtok decided to change the subject. "We are watching Sarah Nevers and her boyfriend Pastor McDermott."

"Is that true?"'

"What they're doing is dangerous."

Shurtok leaned forward in his chair, his eye catching something on the street below. "Miss Poletsky has been a disappointment. Like her father who has stirred up a hornets nest in New York."

"I knew Arach but I never understood him. Sarah I do understand."

"The Filastin has a piece about another religious gathering, this time in Nazareth. Do you know anything about a Father Michael?"

"Twenty years ago he caused the Yishuv a great deal of trouble. He's blind. He had the bad luck to be on the same train as the Syrian, Yusef Shukri."

Meyersohn smiled. He loved the side angles to the story. "You know his servant killed Shukri. He never got out of Deraa. We never recovered any of the money. If we had waited a few days before paying him, we would have saved a lot of money."

"Well, our priest is at it again. He's asking all the religious in the north to gather in Nazareth to demonstrate for peace."

"Which brings me back to the two Frenchmen. I know, I know, one is from Argentina but the other lived in Paris and Bissett is French, too, as far as I'm concerned. They were in Jerusalem at the first gathering dressed as priests. Right under your noses."

"If they are in Nazareth, we'll get them." He never really liked Meyersohn. Now he hated him.

Part IX

"What the hell is an Arabist?"

Throughout the nation, the airways, movie theatres and newsstands were filled with talk and visions of war clouds in Europe. Communism left the stage as if it had never been there, but fascism was center stage. Slowly at first, now like a rushing torrent, propaganda created sides but the battle in America was not about taking sides but staying out of the war in Europe or not. But those who were against going to war and that was where most of America was could feel they were slowly being drawn into the vortex, powerless to stop the move to war.

To many astute observers it was clear that the most powerful man in America intended to lead America into war while denying he was not. Advisers like Lewis and Lipsky saw war as the way to save the lives of hundreds of thousand Jews now in peril because of Hitler. They had assured the President that the people would follow him if he made his case to the people. But the political animal that he was, he was not so sure and was cautious about the power the people possessed if they chose to use it. Sometimes he laughed to himself about what Lincoln had said about fooling the people but deep inside him he knew that the power of the people could be real.

The President knew his advisers, the ones on the books and the others, and knew they were either solidly behind him or would not stand in his way. This meant that information about the war sentiment in the nation didn't always reach him through these advisers, so he found other ways of feeling the peoples pulse. One way was to read the small town papers or the second paper in the large cities to find out what people were thinking. In this way he got the sense of the distaste for war that the people had. In the major papers, Fred Markey's columns caught his eye.

When Markey reported on the news conference at the press club, he paid attention to what Hollister and Bruce had to say. Neither were the powers in the Senate but they were smart and hard to buy. It was hard not to see that these two men, and their advisor Poletsky, were presenting something very powerful if he and the hawks were not successful by killing it with silence. Yes, his advisers assured him that these two spoke for no one, but what about the people. Did they speak for them?

Early morning, nobody around, a time to clear his mind. Outside, the sun was shining, turning the color of the granite sides of the Washington Monument a soft rose color and the Tidal Basin beyond a blue green. With a steaming pot of coffee beside him, he thought of these moments as his alone. He picked the Times for the news, to count the times his name appeared and to read what the editors and the columnists had to say. Markey was always first.

Yesterday morning, Senators Hollister and Bruce met with national organizations against America getting into the war in Europe. Among those represented were The America Firsters, the Norman Thomas movement, and Women for Peace.

No one at the meeting seemed to grasp or accept the essential point made by Senators Hollister and Bruce that the only way to prevent Americans fighting in Europe is to prevent war breaking out in Europe.

The plan called Lasting Peace has been reported by me and others before. But at the meeting it was clear that those in the audience and others are having trouble accepting America's role as peacemaker, a role that another Roosevelt took on early in the early twentieth century when Russia and Japan were at war. He won the Nobel Prize for his efforts and no doubt the gratitude of the thousands of young Russian and Japanese men whose lives were spared.

By making that clear, the two Senators threw down the gauntlet; if you are serious about keeping America out of a war in Europe, it can only be done if a formula of give and take prevents war from breaking out and the creation of that formula depends on America's leadership.

The audience seemed stunned and puzzled when the Senators pointed the essentiality of providing a home for Jews in America, despite the strong case made by the two Senators that such an act, which might be an act of compassion, was a key to preventing war in Europe.

When Senator Bruce explained that this was not only an act of compassion to open our doors but that we would be receiving a group of people who are well educated and would be an asset to the nation there were murmurs in the crowd. He acknowledged that the large number of unemployed in America makes accepting hundreds of thousands of additional workers a challenge, but the immigrants would bring much of their wealth with them and can support themselves.

From the audience came the question: why not send the Jews to Palestine. The answer came from Arach Poletsky, who was instrumental in proposing the Jewish emigration plan. Palestine should not be an option because it cannot absorb any more Jews without forcing the Arabs out of their own country. This would mean endless conflict.

No group, with the exception of Women for Peace would concede the merits of the Lasting Peace plan. Only Margaret Larsen, chairman of Women for Peace and the only organization that sent their leader, said she would take the plan back to her members.

Lasting Peace calls on the President to lead the battle for peace. The Senators repeatedly made clear that he alone has to bring *the parties together. He alone can alter the course that Europe is on by engaging the parties and finding a formula for peace.*

At the end of the meeting, I talked to Rolph Jorgensen, Professor of International Affairs at George Washington University.

"The plan is radical but well-conceived. But what is being asked makes Americans wary. We were drawn into the Great War after it started. Now the Senators are asking that we impose ourselves before a war has started. This makes people suspicious. But the purpose of the plan to stop a war which will kill millions and wreck Europe is worth the effort, and I would hope the President will discuss the plan with the two Senators and the entire Congress and give it serious, very serious consideration."

The Professor should have addressed the audience.

Two paragraphs struck the President. One, that his cousin won a Nobel Peace Prize for doing what was being asked here and the quote by the Professor. Clearly what is being proposed would be a dangerous shift from the course he is on. The people, that abstraction he used in his powerful fireside chats to persuade and intimidate are real and that worried him. What if the people......

Something else about the war in Europe he could not ignore. Already, Detroit and Pittsburg are hiring to build a war machine and the demon of unemployment is on the defensive. Jobs are being created by the thousands and jobs mean votes. Peace is an ideal but jobs and happy corporation presidents and Wall Street bankers are real. He finished his coffee, watching the black servant approach.

He spoke to the Negro: "Let the peacemakers tell us how to create jobs and get America back on its feet." He looked at Moses, who was used to such remarks and trying to decide how to respond and get back to the kitchen. "You're right about that, Mr. President." Moses found that seemed to work just about every time.

The President watched Mose leave, content that Mose worshipped him. He had time this morning to reflect on his future. Presidents served only two terms. But who could better steer the country through these troubled times. Some things you keep to yourself til the right moment.

+++

Seth Morgan began broadcasting way back when. He wasn't there when radio broadcast began, but people still called him one of the pioneers. Seth and Sam Watkins had been friends for a long time, and there were two of the six who got out of the house every Thursday night for a serious game of poker. Sam arrived early, wanting to talk to his friend in private.

"See you got yourself in hot water with your advertisers, Sam." Seth saw his friend chomp down on his cigar and squeeze his bushy eyebrows so close they form a single line across his broad and florid face.

"Couldn't help myself and that damn professor from Oberlin got to chewing at me."

"You mean President King or at least he used to be."

"That's the guy. Someone called in to the station and called King an Arabist."

"What the hell is an Arabist?"

"Well the fellow, whom I think was a professor at Oberlin, said it was somebody who takes the side of Arabs all the time."

"Did the Professor give any details about why he thought King was an Arabist?"

"You know Henry was on a commission that Wilson sent over to Palestine along with a big shot from Chicago named Crane to find out what was going on. As I understand he went over thinking the Jews were in the right and came back thinking they were not."

"Right about what?"

"We're getting in too deep here. As simple as I can say it based on the little I know, Henry and Crane found out there were people living there and didn't want to be pushed off it by Jewish immigrants."

"So that makes him an Arabist?"

"'Fraid so."

"So what you're telling me that friendship got you in trouble? Come on, Sam, there's more to it than that. You were trying to be a real journalist and print what you think the people should read. Heard about those two in Palestine riling everybody up here with the reports about what's happening to the Arabs there. Damn good writing by those two Frenchmen. There are times, in moments of weakness I wish I was in their place, writing the truth, evading thousands of British troops."

Seth reached for the bourbon in the center of the table, offered to pour to the people around the table, and poured one for himself. Then he smiled. "But then what about my poker buddies and those big pots I win every week." Concern was written on his face as he looked at Sam. "So what are you going to do?"

"I guess a mix of sensitive mea culpa mixed with a dose of righteous indignation, maybe a little flag waving and hope we don't go broke."

Sam took the cards; it was his turn to deal. In the poker ritual of trust but verify, he pushed the cards over to Sam Weinstein. "Cut."

Sam Weinstein looked around him. His family had settled in Cleveland fifty years ago and he knew a lot of people. There were moments of tension among friends when someone made a stupid remark, but people got along. Everyone at this table accepted him without reservation. Yet even Sam Watkins doing his job hurt him. Some of his family was still in Germany.

The conversation shifted seamlessly to the weather, which was colder than usual, local politics and sports, topics that everyone had something to say about, and no one had their feelings stepped on.

Everyone had left and Sam Watkins and Seth were cleaning up. Sam looked at Seth, acknowledging the tension they felt tonight. "Sam's house next week, huh?"

Sam nodded. Of all his friends, Seth had been the closest. They both were in the broadcasting business. Seth had been extraordinarily successful with his radio station. Much of the air time was filled by music but at six o'clock every evening except on weekends, Seth gave out the local and national news and he invited people to talk about it. As the number of cities that picked up the station increased, advertising revenues increased and things were looking good. While he and the others were doing well, Seth was on the edge of becoming a rich man.

"I think Sam was upset. He's one of my best customers."

"Mine, too." Sam said. But I didn't get in the newspaper business to make money. There are stories around where large groups of Jews pulled advertising and the stations and papers gave in. I hope it doesn't come to that."

"Has Phil talked to you lately? This Lasting Peace thing is starting to get some life."

"You know Seth, Lasting Peace sounds bizarre—maybe pie in the sky is a better way of describing it, but dammit it's the only thing that makes sense if you really don't want a war."

"Sam, you know that Roosevelt has his tailor fitting him with his Commander-in-Chief uniform. He's doing everything he can to get us into a war if it starts and will do nothing to try to stop it."

"Well, Roosevelt is a politician first and a statesman second, and you can bet he's paying attention. He'll try to manage the people's sentiments, but if the bus comes rolling at him, he's not going to stand in its way and be run over, he's going to jump on it and take the driver's seat."

"Which brings me back to Sam. Phil is going on the air at my station and there's a rally planned next week at the baseball park."

"I know, there will be a piece in the Herald tomorrow. Chris is on it and it's going to be front page. He'll do a good job."

Sam walked Seth to the door.

"So how much did you take us for tonight?"

"I did okay."

"You got me for 50 cents this time. I guess there's no way to open for less than a penny?"

"See you next week, Sam."

+++

Jonathan Fortson was pleased with the news. He was being reassigned to the Acre prison-only minutes from Haifa, a more cosmopolitan city with Europeans, theatres and good restaurants and better living quarters.

Tonight he had celebrated his good fortune at the club and decided to return to his quarters early to pack. He was scheduled to leave by train in the morning. He didn't know how many scotch and sodas he had, but he knew he was drunk. No matter, he would soon be in his quarters, and he would feel fine in the morning.

The distance between the club and his quarters was less than one hundred yards. There were street lights in front of the club and his quarters, but between enveloping darkness. For days after Hassan Latif died, that hundred yards was like a dark abyss and he usually persuaded a fellow officer to accompany him. But the evening was early, and none of them wanted to leave.

At first, he could only hear his own breathing and footsteps. He unsnapped the flap on his revolver and began to walk quickly toward the light. Suddenly, the shape of a tall man stood before him. As he grasped the handle of his revolver, he felt a sharp pain as the dagger passed through his rib cage and pierced his heart. As he began to fall, he felt the dagger leaving his body as the man whose face was shrouded in shadow seemed to be looking at him.

"Ismael?" Suddenly he was cold sober and he opened his mouth to scream.

"Just as my brother said it would be, Major."

Fortson eyes grew wide as the terrible realization struck him. He was dying. "How can that be?" Ismael stood before the man he had sworn to himself he would kill and held no grief for the one who tortured and killed his beloved brother. He watched his enemy drop to his knees, struggle as if to rise, fall heavily on his face, then lay still.

It was not until two hours later when the other officers leaving the club found the body face down on the dark street. Ismael Latif had left the city and on his way north to rejoin his comrades.

***

Father Michael thought every Wednesday a wonder. It was a day everyone at St. Stephen's knew the Father wanted to be to himself, to pray, to read and to relieve his mind of the big and small problems of the parish and the school.

Father had one of his older students build a bird house which was placed outside the window of his study. This morning he listened to the cheerful song of a small wren that had come to feed. He came to know the names of birds by their songs, with the help of a bird watching English missionary who would sit with him and name and describe the birds and then imitate the sounds of the birds. He marveled at this friend's talent. Father would connect the sounds with John Murdock's descriptions. This morning he had already been visited by finches and doves: he would ask Hani if there was enough food laid out on the window sill for them.

On his lap was a copy of one of Chesterton's delightful Father Brown mysteries in braille, sent to him by Trevor Markham, his friend for the last eighteen years. He thought about the Major, who was the military administrator of the area around Nazareth then, and he could see him clearly in his mind. He had been blinded a short time after the Major arrived in Nazareth.

He ran his fingers across the letters of the book, and thinking what a wonderful gift Louis Braille had given all those whose eyes could not see. He was grateful for the time when he had the gift of sight and the memories of when his eyes could see made Lord Chesterton's book even the more delightful.

He sensed the door to his study was opened even before his housekeeper Hani spoke. He could sense her irritation when she spoke. "Father, you have two visitors. I can ask them to come back tomorrow."

"I know, Hani that you would not be talking to me unless you thought I would be irritated with you if you turned them away."

"Well, Father, they are from Jerusalem, an American and Sarah Nevers."

"Send them in, please."

He heard the two enter the room. "Sarah, it has been a long time."

"Hello, Father. I want you to meet a friend of mine, Reverend John McDermott."

John stepped forward, placing his left hand on Father Michael's shoulder and shaking his hand. John was told the story of Father Michael, Amin al-Dajani and Yusef Shukri and the stolen will, and how Ismael Latif had recovered it and given it to Sarah's husband. Sadly, the will, which would have negated a huge land sale to the Jewish National Fund had cost John Nevers his life.

Sarah and Father Michael had been in touch over the years. The first visit was soon after John's murder. Sarah had visited Father Michael after she was told the full story including how Father Michael had been blinded by an assassin's bullet. At that time she told Father that Ismael Latif had safely left Palestine but did not know where he was. Her second visit was to inform Father that a letter arrived from Argentina. And now all Palestine knew that Ismael Latif had returned.

John spoke. "Father Michael, I have a small church north of Jerusalem." He smiled. "Actually, it is very small; only one hundred twenty souls some still not sure whether Jesus was a Prophet or the risen Christ."

Father Michael smiled as he reached out and touched the young pastor's chest. "I understand that you are doing more than just watching over your small flock, Reverend."

"Please call me John."

"Then you must call me Michael." The smile left Father Michael's face as he spoke. "What you did in Jerusalem gave us hope, John. I don't know if many of us who have lived so long in Palestine could have done what you have done, or even tried."

"Thank you, Father" er..."Michael. What happened in Jerusalem can happen in Nazareth, Haifa, Tiberius, Jaffa and in every town and village in Palestine."

Sarah spoke. "We need your prayers, Michael, but we also need your help in creating the same kind of religious community that came together in Jerusalem, to pray for peace as a group and to call out to the Arabs, Jews and British to bring peace to the Holy Land."

Father Michael stood silent for a moment. He thought of all his friends in Nazareth. He thought of his school which was open to all. And he thought what young John McDermott asked. I pray, sweet Jesus that it can be done. For peace and love in Jesus's name. Amen.

Father walked past them to the door, beckoning them to follow him to a small table in the rectory kitchen. He beckoned them to sit.

"Hani makes wonderful coffee and only this morning, she purchased some croissants from the pastry shop just down the hill from here."

While the housekeeper, smiling contentedly at Father Michael's praise, busied herself setting out the coffee and croissants, the old priest leaned forward, placing his hands on the table, turned to the young pastor and spoke.

"Well John, we will begin the quest. What do you want me to do first?"

+++

From where the three of them stood, they could see the ruins of Capernaum and the silver sea beyond. During the night, a light snow had fallen on the hills to the north, causing them to glisten and highlight the green of the cedars that grew on their slopes. They had made the journey from Nablus in two days, watching the planes circle overhead during the day and hearing the armored cars moving in convoys on all the passable roads. Andre had joined them yesterday; bringing them up to date on the story he had written and was on its way to Damascus where the French news service Agence France-Presse had an office. A few hours after Andre arrived, Ismael rode into camp astride his spirited black stallion, a gift from a wealthy merchant in Tiberias. Like the great stallion that carried him twenty years before, he called him Mukhtar.

George recalled what happened after the raid. When they began their journey north after their attack on the camp, Ismael had reined in his horse after they were well clear of the British camp.

George recalled his words. "I must return to Nablus. I have business there." Abd, Kalima and George watched him go. The three were silent as they watched him ride away, gone into the night. It was George who spoke. "He's going after Fortson. Godspeed, Ismael." The other two nodded, and they turned to continue their journey.

**

Now he had returned. The sun was warm as they stood in the opening looking toward the sea. They felt safe as planes flew high overhead and the roads were almost empty of military vehicles.

Kalima broke the silence. "I will go to see Osta in Nazareth tonight. He will have word of where Abu Kamal is."

Listening to Kalima, George marveled at the young man and the change that had come over him since the first night on the beach. *He has protected Andre and me. He has led us to the stories we have written and always he seems to know what to do. If he lives through this, he will be a leader.*

Ismael lowered himself on his haunches, looking out across the water to the Golan Heights and Syria and watching the fishermen cast their nets. Close by, he knew there was a Jewish settlement, where armed men made their night time sorties searching for us. He turned to George. "Someday soon I hope you will be able to walk without fear among the ruins of Capernaum where Jesus walked and where the fishermen followed him to become fishers of men. It is a holy site for us too, George."

"Until I walked among your people, Ismael, I did not understand how close we are and should be. I mean the Christians, Jews and Mohammedans. Yet we are not close, are we?"

"When I was a boy living in Jerusalem, our neighbors were Jews. The Poletsky's had two children. We did everything together with the approval of my father and their father. The daughter Sarah married a British officer. "He paused then. "Her brother was my best friend growing up. He gave his life for me."

The four who listened were silent as if to speak would desecrate the solemnity and grace of the moment.

"I will be leaving you today to go to Jerusalem to see Sarah and John McDermott. They have performed wonders in gathering the religious of all faiths to pray together for peace. I hope they will let me join them in their journey."

Abd spoke quickly. "You will not have to travel so far. The two of them visited Father Michael of St. Stephens in Nazareth. They might still be there."

"Father Michael is a wonderful man, loved by everyone. I have wanted to meet him for a long time."

Kalima spoke for the four. "Let us go with you."

Ismael smiled at them, feeling gratitude for their loyalty, and shook his head. "It will be better if I go alone. He looked at the two Frenchmen. "We need you." He looked at Kalima. "Keep them safe, my friend."

"When will you leave?"

"Tonight. I want to be there before sunrise."

+++

Abu Kamal was devoted to his four sons. Whenever he could, he would arrange to visit them at some location away from his home. His enemies knew this and watched his children.

All of Palestine had heard of his brilliant assault on the British camp in Nablus. They knew that Ismael Latif was with them, but still they recognized that Abu Kamal and Razzik had won a great victory, one to boost morale and become part of Palestine legend and history.

For a week after the raid in Nablus, Abu Kamal's army melted into the mountains, hiding in small groups, waiting to be called together for yet another attack on the settlers and the British.

Abu Kamal had not seen any of his children in the last two months. Summoning one of his lieutenants, Tewfiq Beisan, he asked him to arrange to meet his youngest son, who was his favorite and needed to see his father. It was a seven hour ride to Dhinnabi, where his leader's family lived.

Nassar Shamout had been sent by Ersheid to search for Abu Kamal. For fear of being ambushed in his search, Shamout had found a copse of oaks with a view of the high hills surrounding the valley. He was not anxious to travel into those narrow passes between the hills. At the end of the first day, he would report to Ersheid that there were no signs of Abu Kamal in the area he searched. He had described what he found in the narrow passages into the hills where he chose not to go.

The second day, he had found a grove of banyan trees and oleander bushes high enough to view the hills to the north yet the cover thick enough to keep him well hidden. It was mid-morning when a lone rider emerged from the hills and rode onto the road leading east. Lifting the binoculars, he focused on the rider. He knew the man.

He was from his village. He had left the village to join Abu Kamal's rebels. Giving him a wide lead, he followed. He was heading toward Dhinnabi where the rebel leader's children lived with his sister.

When Beisan entered the village, he stopped the first man he saw. Shamout watched as the two men talked, keeping himself hidden behind a sheep shed. From where he stood mounted on his horse, he could see the length of the main street. It was on the main street that the children lived with the sister. After some time, the rider rode his mount between the houses and disappeared. Shamout would wait.

The cold winter sun was falling rapidly toward the hills in the west when two riders appeared from a side street. One of the riders was Beisan, the second was a small boy Shamout decided was one of the sons. Shamout moved to the back of the shed away from the road and watched the two men pass. When they were almost out of sight with the naked eye, he followed using his binoculars to keep them in sight. The sun was touching the tops of the hills when the two men turned into a narrow passage, the same one that Beisan used in the morning. He had seen enough. He did not dare follow the two men into the hills. Instead he would report where they left the main road and entered the hills.

The call was made by radio from Ersheid to the commander of the northwest sector. The area where Abu Kamal was located was circled on the map, the perimeter extended to assure that they would have their prey encircled. The operation would have to be undertaken with infantry armed with light weapons, using aerial reconnaissance to assist. All roads leading in and out of the area would be covered, with troops held in reserve at strategic points on the perimeter to be able to move quickly to the area where the rebel leader was spotted. The operation would be performed in daylight, commencing at 0600 tomorrow.

**

Al Hajj Mohammad had killed both of his brothers. Now it was his turn to die. His only regret was that he could not do it himself, that the British would kill him, instead. There were rumors that Ismael Latif might be with al Hajj Mohammad. Farid Ersheid understood that if the British killed either man, he would die as well if he stayed in Palestine. The British commander had assured all the leaders of the peace bands that they would be given passage out of Palestine and be settled with their families in one of their Commonwealth nations. They had paid him well but he did not trust the British or the Nashashibi's. It was not safe to trust anyone outside of the al-Barqari tribe.

Abu Kamal was happy for his son, pleased that he was doing well with his lessons at the kittab and that the others were doing well. Abd knew they called his father Abu Kamal but the British called him Al Hajj Mohammed, commander of all the Arab fedayeen in Palestine. It was al-Hajj Mohammad to those who were slowly closing the circle around his camp.

The victory in Nablus had not been without cost. Ten of his men were dead or missing. The intense hunt for his small army made him delay bringing his scattered forces together. Only twenty of his men were with him now.

At the first touch of dawn, his son Abd al-Jawa had departed alone. Old enough to travel alone, Abu Kamal felt no concern for his safety as he watched the young boy until a turn in the trail and he was gone.

A squad of riflemen had been moving along the trail when the point man signaled them off the trail. Abd al-Jawa walked his horse down the trail toward the soldiers then passed. He sensed no danger around him, his eyes on the trail ahead. Waiting until they were sure the small boy no longer could see or hear them, they formed back on the trail sure now their quarry was close. The squad leader motioned them to move.

Abdul was only sixteen when he left his village to join the rebels. Two armed men on horseback had entered his village two years ago and talked to the Mukhtar. The men of the village were called together and the two men, with rifles and revolvers attached to their belts spoke to the men, telling them that the Arabs had risen up to take back their beloved country from the British and the Jews. They needed brave men who would drive their enemies into the sea or beyond the Jordan.

Abdul had never learned to read or write but he knew of the peasants who had been driven from their land and the Arabs who had been killed by the British and the Jews, some hung, others sent to camps never to return. When the told him he would have a weapon and a horse, he volunteered.

He had been fighting for Abu Kamal the whole time. Their leader was a brave man who led his men into battle and was kind to him, although he had been punished when he did not do exactly as he had been told. Still, he was proud to be a feday'ee. Once, when he had traveled through his village, all the young boys came out to greet him, and that made him proud.

He was one of the men who were sent to Commander Razzik to attack the British camp. Disappointed and uncertain when separated from Abu Kamal, he would fight for Razzik to make Abu Kamal proud of him. When he returned, Abu Kamal had spoken to him, telling him he had done a great thing, and he was proud of him.

He did not like sentry duty. Being by himself made him afraid at first. He tried to imagine what he would do if he was confronted by a settler or a British soldier. But he had often served as a sentry and had never been confronted by an enemy. He had found a boulder at the edge of the trail where he could see down the trail for over twenty yards. He leaned his rifle against the boulder so he could quickly lift it to fire down the trail.

Abdul was not sure what he heard but the sixth sense that comes with battle made him start. Suddenly alert, he looked down the trail where it disappeared from view. Carefully, he released the safety on this Enfield, and wrapped his hand around the stock below the trigger guard.

The soldier was tall, holding his rifle across his chest, and moving silently. Abdul Alami felt his heart jumping in his chest. Rising quickly, seeing the startled look on the point man's face, he fired into his chest. Almost immediately men behind the fallen man moved forward and off the trail, searching for him.

One of the soldiers pointed at the boulder. They knew where he was. The boulder stood alone next to the trail and there was no way to retreat without being seen. He knew the shot would warn the others, that he had done what his Commander had asked of him. He began to pray.

The camp was alive now with the sound of gunfire down the trail. The firing was intense. Then the explosion all knew was a grenade. Then silence.

Abu Kamal stood in the center of the camp. As was done every morning, the horses were saddled, ready to carry their riders to attack or to safety. There were three trails leading into camp. Abdul had guarded the first. The second led north, the third to the east.

Seldom was the option when attacked to stand and fight. They would be overwhelmed. Escape but which way. Should they separate and use each of the open trails. Then they heard firing on the trail leading north leaving one option. Kamal considered the trail to the east. It led quickly into open country where they would be exposed to aero planes with their bombs and machine guns.

His lieutenants had gathered around him, looking at him always as their savior in times like this. There would always be that time, he thought when they could not be saved. He had known it would come, and in his bones he felt this was the time. Abdul had fired no more than three hundred yards from them.

Abu Kamal pointed toward the men holding the horse and shouted. "Move them over there, out of the line of fire" In that moment, all knew what was about to happen.

The shape of the camp was like the bottom of a bowl. Surrounding the bowl were three heavily wooded hills from which attackers could fire into the camp.

Pointing to his lieutenants, he then quickly separated the men into three groups. "Carry what ammunition you can and take positions up there." He pointed to the surrounding hills.

There were four sub-machine guns in camp. Selecting three of the men who were familiar with the Stens, he stood before them, looking each in the eye. "It will take some time for the men to get in position. You will have to give them that time." There were always these moments when duty required the certain deaths of men, and he knew this was one of these moments. "Awad, take the trail to the west where Abdul was. Aref, the north, and Mohammad, the east." They will be coming soon. He touched each on the shoulder. "We will meet again in Paradise. Go quickly." He watched the three move down the trails then followed his men up the slopes.

Word reached the British command post in the valley that contact had been made. They had him! The command was given to tighten the circle, to move the perimeter closer to the enemy. The small enemy force had dug in on the hillsides around their camp, and the attackers were taking heavy casualties. Orders were transmitted to pull the troops back from the enemy positions. Orders to the Royal Air Force at Amman to clean the enemy off the hills. Spotters were placed on nearby hills to guide the planes in their attacks.

Colonel Pearson was given the assignment of coordinating the attack. He had been in Palestine for only six months but had experience dealing with insurgents in Rhodesia and South Africa. He was not a sadistic man by nature and often ended his days feeling guilty fighting virtually defenseless natives. In Rhodesia it was often spears against machine guns. The image of Africans charging a machine gun, armed with spears and leather shields bothered him but did not prevent him from very good at his job.

In the short time he had been in Palestine, he knew that the fight was not quite so one-sided, and the enemy quickly learned to use explosives and automatic weapons but the asymmetry still was stark. It was made all the more so by the aero planes and wireless communications.

Pearson spoke to a young captain standing beside him in the commander's tent. "Do you think there is any chance al-Hajj Mohammed can be talked into surrendering?" He was asking himself the question really and he knew the answer. When the young man opened his mouth to answer, Pearson stopped him. "No, of course not. Prisoners don't fare well with Tegart. And al-Hajj Mohammad is not that kind of man."

Pearson's show of admiration for the enemy leader surprised the young captain, who thought it showed weakness.

***

Most of the morning and into early afternoon, the firefight between the British infantry and the rebels continued. There were intervals of intense firing by the men below but no moves to advance up the hill. Reduced to sniper on both sides, casualties were light. .

The interlude allowed the men dug into the hill time to pray, some for a miracle but mostly for a gallant death and a rise to paradise.

Abdul Ahmed had been with Abu Kamal the longest. He was the one Kamal trusted for his loyalty, his skill and his courage. It was he who approached his leader. "You must try to escape. When it is dark, you can make your way to the west and slip past the British. If we continue to fight, they will have no way of knowing you have left."

"I cannot do that, Abdul. I cannot leave you. These men have fought with me and me with them. That is the way it is to be."

"The planes will come soon."

"Have the men dig in as best they can."

As they talked, the drone of the planes could be heard in the distance. It grew louder and louder until it seemed to be in the trees over their heads. The explosions shook the hillsides and fragments of rocks, trees and bodies seemed to fill the air. Those still alive were about to raise their heads when a second wave tore into the side of the hills, killing most who survived, and leaving those still alive numbed and disoriented, struggling to gain their bearings, looking around them with unseeing eyes.

Minutes after the last bombing run, infantry armed with sub-machine guns and grenades began to advance up the hills, killing those who were alive but still stunned into helplessness. They passed among those still writhing in their death throes, those few like al-Hajj Mohammad who returned fire until mercifully dying fighting.

Walking among the dead, a young officer stopped beside the body of Al-Hajj Mohammed and honored him by covering his battered face with his handkerchief.

The Colonel received word of the rebel leader's death. "Captain, I want you to see that al-Hajj Mohammad is taken back to his village for an honorable burial."

"Sir, we were told to burn his body."

"You do that, Captain, and you will answer to me. This is personal, Captain, between you and I. Do you understand me"

"Yes, sir. I do. And sir, thank you."

+++

Radio had always been Seth Morgan's first love. From an early age, he dabbled in building wireless transmitters and receivers but his imagination soared when he grasped the power of broadcasting voice through space that millions could hear. Listening to KCBS in California, it occurred to him that a lone man in Cleveland with some technical knowledge and a small amount of money could do the same thing. And he did it. KMBS became a reality and it grew. Affiliation with one of the major networks coming out of New York and the number of listeners kept growing and growing.

What made it grow was the attention Seth gave to content and an ear for what the people out there in America wanted to hear. Seth was an avid reader of news and he regularly scanned newspapers from all over the country. He paid attention to the major papers in cities like New York, but he also received copies of small town papers from around the country. What were people thinking about?

Every evening during the week, Seth told them what people were thinking in America and he encouraged people to call in and tell him what they thought. Seth was never patronizing, it was his nature and it was shrewd business. What people had to say mattered.

He talked to people in the good times in the late twenties when his station first went on the air, and he talked to them during the bad times which seemed to linger for millions out there. Someone once called him a poor man's Will Rogers, but he wasn't that. Seth didn't have many wise sayings for his audience, just what he saw going on and a touch of what he thought about it.

He thought about his next broadcast as he scanned the stack of papers piled on a table next to his desk. Times were getting better in places like Detroit and the shipyards. Easy to see it was the talk of war and it was more than talk or Detroit wouldn't be building tanks or Seattle building destroyers. Some people in Washington were set on going to war.

But there were a lot of people out there who saw what Washington was up to and were determined to stay out of the war that was looking more and more likely in Europe. Seth saw the pull on America, on the one hand they didn't want our sons to go to war, on the other they saw that millions were being hired and people had money in their pockets and they were stirred by all the talk of Hitler and Mussolini as madmen.

In his broadcasts, he paid attention to what he read, trying to tell his audience what he saw. He started getting more calls from advertisers who were aware that Seth Morgan was being listened to, that he was a voice they trusted. Advertisers latched on to the trust that Seth had earned over the years and figured maybe a little of trust would rub off when they sold their products on the air.

Seth got a lot of phone calls, which he had a very pleasant young lady answer, and a lot of letters. Some were pretty nasty because they thought their view of things was being given short shrift. Most came from the pro-war crowd and they were not only nasty but patronizing. What does and uneducated bumpkin from Cleveland know about what was happening in the world.

Seth never answered the letters or called the callers back unless it was a business matter.

Times were good for KMBS and Seth Morgan. While millions scratched for a living in the '30's, he made a lot of money. A bachelor raised to be frugal, he deposited the money, made some prudent investments or put it into some improvements at the station.

But what Seth read and commented on began to weigh on him. Seth was a Quaker and peace was a major tenet of his beliefs. He wondered if he shouldn't begin to take sides against the war. Not just America getting into the war but war itself. He always read Fred Markey in the Cleveland Herald, Sam's paper. From the first article about his Senator and Senator Bruce, he began to see the plan they proposed as the only one that made sense, for he, too saw that only by stopping a war in Europe could Americans be kept out of war. But that was not the persuasive argument to Seth, and he told Sam this, it was that it was a way to stop a war that surely will be even more terrible than the Great War whether America was in it or not.

His mind turned to the new movement called Lasting Peace. It was a call to take the plan of the two Senators to the people, and for the people to use their power to get the leaders to take the plan seriously and to make it work.

Seth knew that he was walking on dangerous ground, just as Sam knew. Sam's paper depended on advertising like the station and it was no secret that the most expensive advertisements came from those who were pushing to stop Hitler by going to war against Germany.

But the plan also would offend the leaders and the followers of America First because it called for giving hundreds of thousands of Jews a new home in America. Lasting Peace would have to persuade many who were suspicious of Jews and many others who wanted to stop immigration of anyone from anywhere.

Thinking about it made him smile. Why bother? It was the Quaker in him that made him decide.

***

Seth Morgan was a confirmed and comfortable bachelor. His life was his station, and his Thursday night poker games. Outside of his mother, who died ten years ago, there were no serious personal relationships with a woman. There were, of course, women that worked for him, women he knew in the Society of Friends, and others. He had to admit that aggressive women who saw him a sort of security blanket intimidated him. He liked his life the way it was, which in his mind was close to perfect.

So when he met Margaret Larsen, he was surprised at his reaction to her. Seth was not a large man, several inches under six feet, and slight, he never seemed to gain weight. Margaret Larsen was just an inch under six feet, broad shouldered, blonde hair and Nordic blue eyes.

Seth could not decide whether he thought her beautiful or handsome but in his eyes she was certainly one of them.

When Margaret walked into the studio and saw this slight man with the keen eyes looking at her so closely, she smiled and extended her hand, taking his firmly. "I'm Margaret Larsen and thank you for seeing me."

Why was he nervous? Pull yourself together. He did and then had to ask, "Is it Miss or Mrs."

Margaret Larsen smiled at him, amused and flattered by his discomfort. "It's Miss."

"Everyone calls me Seth."

"Margaret is fine, too."

"Margaret, I wonder if you might appear with me on my six o'clock broadcast to talk about Lasting Peace."

Seth suddenly saw a different side of Margaret Larsen when she looked at him. "This will be a first for you, Seth. Why did you choose Lasting Peace to do this? You have always been careful, I understand, not to take sides."

"I know. It was not easy. It has risks, you are right about that."

"How would such a broadcast be done?"

"I can assure you of one thing, I am on your side. I will introduce you, say something that lets the audience know where I stand but in a modest way, let you speak about Lasting Peace for ten minutes, then I will ask some questions."

"Are you thinking of doing it this evening?"

"Oh, no. But we can do it tomorrow, if you are agreeable."

"That would be wonderful."

"OK, then. If you will be here at noon-lunch will be served here-we will rehearse. That should take about an hour, maybe more. I will ask the questions but I want you to hear them and make any suggestions about the questions I ask or add any you think I should ask."

Margaret Larsen stood, smiling at this man so full of surprises. She surprised herself when she felt the tears began to well up and in a hoarse voice said "Thank you."

Damn, I'm embarrassed, he thought. "You're welcome, see you at noon tomorrow."

He watched her leave, taking care to smile at Judy, say something to her he couldn't hear and shake her hand.

It was pure Judy after their visitor left. "Gee, boss, she's really pretty." She looked at him the way she always did when a good looking single lady passed her desk. At first the look was hopeful, then of disappointment and sometimes pity.

Judy's right. She really is pretty.

***

The broadcast began with the Set's soft voice introducing the topic and his guest, Margaret Larsen, the Chairman of Lasting Peace.

Margaret, in a warm but commanding voice stayed within the ten minutes.

Seth remembered thinking, Thank Goodness Margaret kept her remarks to ten minutes. And then came the response that overwhelmed the station switchboard. Almost three hours passed before Seth was forced to close down the switchboard and announce to the audience, "That is all the time we have. To all those out their listening to KMBS, thank you for listening and goodnight."

He looked at the pretty lady, still smiling yet exhausted, and knew he was part of something very big, very big.

+++

The higher ups in the World Zionist Organization and its many offshoots all over America were divided. Among the millions who listened to the broadcast were those who praised the proposal as a way to save the Jews in Germany and stop the war that was looming over the Continent. Among them were those who opposed the war on humanitarian and practical grounds, practical because they knew the Jews would suffer more if war were to breakout. It would loose anti-Semitism all over Europe that was controlled during peace time and unleashed whenever there was chaos.

But there were others who believed rationally or irrationally that those persecuting the Jews must be punished, whatever the cost. They believed, too, that denying emigration to Palestine was a dagger at the heart of the Jewish nation in diaspora. And those same people thought that once this was "all over", when God had punished those who killed or otherwise persecuted the Jews, then all would be right on heaven and earth. Clearly, the latter group, the unabashed Zionists had the ear of the President.

But the first group, unlike in the past, chose not to be silent but to join with others in Lasting Peace to urge the President to take the lead in stopping the war in Europe. In letters, calls, visits and petitions their voices were heard.

They were heard everywhere, standing side by side with those who were part of Lasting Peace, and the President, alone with his pot of coffee listened. There was a way to that third term without war.

***

Professor Margaret Larsen was sitting at her desk, struggling through Aristotle's theses on being when the phone rang.

"Hello,"

"Margaret, this is Seth. I wanted to know how you were holding up? You must be exhausted."

"I'm fine, Seth. Are you doing OK?"

"Well, I had a lot of complaints about meddling in national affairs and such and there were threats of withdrawing advertising. I think once Lasting Peace began to snowball, advertisers decided it best to ride the bandwagon."

"Seth, your little training session on how to reach your Congressmen and Senators and the White House was wonderful. It seems to be working."

"Here in Ohio they're talking about Hollister for President and I heard they are doing the same for Bruce in Missouri. It's amazing. What has happened, Margaret? It's like there was a magic button that no one could find and suddenly there it was."

There was a moment when neither spoke. "Margaret, are you still there."

"Thank you for calling, Seth."

291

Seth knew he had been found out. "OK, Margaret the truth is I just wanted to hear your voice and talk to you. Lasting Peace makes it easier."

"I'm glad you called. Most men look at me and run."

"Well, I know you're busy. Judy, says high."

Margaret laughed. "Well, you tell that sweet lady high back."

"Goodbye, Margaret."

"Goodbye, Seth. And Seth, call me Maggy." She hung up and picked up her book. The man is full of surprises. She smiled when she thought of Judy who had whispered in her ear: "I think you two would be perfect."

***

There was a lull in the day and Abe Meyersohn had time to look out his window and muse. The Revisionists were the bad cops in the good cop, bad cop routine. While Ben-Gurion presented the reasonable face of Zionism, Ze'ev Jabotinsky was the no holds barred side of Zionism. But with Zionism, the objective was the same: to get as many Palestinians as possible out of Palestine and as many Jews in. While the Jewish Agency might rail against the violent Revisionists and its assassins, the Irgun, such condemnation was equivocal and the Irgun was left to commit violence against the Arabs.

The battle against the rebels had been going well and the British had been doing their job. Now there were setbacks with the arrival of Ismael Latif, and things were changing. Then something new and unexpected, the gatherings of religious praying for peace. In more secular nations, like most in Europe, what the religious did was of little consequence. But in the Holy Land, which the Christians like to call it, it was a different matter. Something had to be done or the dream of Eretz Israel would be only that.

Part X

They did not see the two men with field glasses surveying their work, satisfied that they had done their job well.

"This is a beautiful spot, Father." Sarah glanced at the Father then worried that he was unable to enjoy the beauty in front of them. She was looking down into the valley, the bright red tiles of the roofs, the white buildings adorned by cedars and other evergreens that poked their crowns above the skyline. Below Father's window there was a small flower garden, a statue of Jesus in the center and surrounded by the flowers of Galilee: irises, asphodel, ranunculuses, narcissi, cyclamen and anemones, the colors of the rainbow.

"How do you like the garden? The statue of Jesus was given to me by one of my former students. Hakim is a wonderful sculptor. I do miss seeing the beauty that the eyes can see, Sarah, but having my sight once allows me to imagine what you are seeing and imagination can be a wonderful thing. I suppose in many ways it can be better than seeing things as you do. John and Sarah, God has allowed me to accept what happened and be at peace. But it is not my peace we are concerned with, is it? It is peace for millions of souls in Palestine."

Michael heard Hani's footsteps and listened as she sat the tray with coffee and croissants on the table. After his housekeeper had poured the coffee he smiled: "Thank you, Hani."

John stood quickly to hand the coffee to the other two. "There is butter and jam for the croissants, Father. Can I fix one for you?"

"Please, John. Butter and jam. Hani makes wonderful strawberry jam. And please, call me Michael."

Hani appeared at the doorway. "Father, you have a visitor."

"Does he understand I have guests?"

"Yes, Father, but he said he thought you would want to see him, that it is important."

Father Michael put his weight on his cane and started to rise.

"Please, Father, do not get up."

Sarah stood and gave out a cry. John looked at Sarah and then at the visitor. He watched Sarah rush past him and give him a hug. "My God, Ismael, you look just as I had imagined—just the same."

"And so do you." His words were charged with all the memories and the affection the three of them felt for the other. "It is good to see you, Sarah."

Aware of the other two, Ismael turned to Father Michael. "It is such an honor to meet you finally, Father Michael. I have prayed for you often. The people of Palestine owe you so much."

"You are taking a great risk, Ismael, appearing in broad daylight in Nazareth."

Ismael did not answer but turned to the tall man who seemed embarrassed at not having any connection with the visitor. He put out his hand. "I am John McDermott."

Ismael took his hand. "What you and Sarah are doing is the most important thing to be done now. The force of arms will not deter the British or the Zionists, but what you are doing can."

"I hope that means you will stop the fighting and killing."

295

"Not yet, John, to stop fighting now will be telling the British that we surrender unconditionally. Then things will simply stay as they are and that it is not what you, Sarah and Father Michael are fighting for. I hope you all understand that."

Sarah spoke: "The British are landing more troops every day. They are training the settler militias and arming them. Surely, you do not expect to win."

"The people of Palestine cannot defeat the British and the Jews, but we must make them accept that they cannot defeat the people of Palestine, that the struggle will never end unless they end it. On all sides, everyone knows what will end the revolt. That is a nation with borders and the rights of people within them."

Father Michael spoke. "Hani, would you bring another cup and some more of those croissants. Ismael, I am so pleased to meet you at last. Please have a seat." He could not see his visitor but could imagine him. Clearly, judging from where his voice came, he was tall. He spoke in a way like Trevor, where command came easy.

"I know you are pleased to see Sarah, Ismael, but I think you have other matters in mind judging by the risk you took to come here."

"I want to join with you to end the revolt and build a free Palestine."

Father Michael let John McDermott know that it was for him to reply.

"We can't be associated with violence."

"I understand Pastor. But there will be a time when we will ask the religious of Palestine, Jew, Christian and Muslim to join with those who are sacrificing their lives for peace."

"I don't see when that can be, Ismael."

It was Sarah who spoke then. "John, I have known Ismael since we were children riding our horses to Bethlehem, standing on a hilltop looking out over the Jordan River. No one loves his country as much as he or fights so fiercely for the land and peace."

John looked at Sarah and his heart sank. Sarah was in love with this man. She had always been in love with him and her feelings would never change. But what kind of love was it? And that thought gave him hope.

Ismael stood to leave. He had said what he came to say. Sarah had turned from them and she was crying. Only Ismael understood that seeing him brought all the bittersweet memories back. Ismael looked at John. The message was clear. Are you going to stand there like a clumsy oaf or are you going to comfort her. The gratitude John McDermott felt at that moment overwhelmed him as he moved to comfort his dear Sarah.

When he turned, Ismael was gone. Father Michael had led Ismael to a side door, entering into a small garden and then into a narrow street. "Please say my goodbye to Sarah for me. Tell John. I will pray for him and all the religious. Pray for me, Father."

"I will, my son." Father heard the soft creak of the door hinges and then his visitor was gone.

+++

The crowd of the religious was growing as the sun rose over the playing fields of St. James Academy. Winter had come but the grass was still green, though the trees had lost all their leaves and only the pines, spruces and cedar kept their adornment. Today the crowd differed from that in Jerusalem, for sitting where they could and standing when they couldn't were hundreds of off duty British soldiers and civil servants along with thousands of ordinary citizens of Nazareth and surrounding villages; all speaking with their feet for peace. Facing the crowd were the leaders of the religious communities, coming together to pray for peace

Sarah and John chose not to be in the chairs and the long table facing the crowd, but to be in the crowd. The religious leaders were a mix, some like the vicar of the Episcopal community was the most senior, serving Nazareth since before the turn of the century. Others were young, sent to serve in Nazareth in the last few years and serving their first congregations. Some seemed uncomfortable as they sat facing the enormous crowd, for they had chosen to serve only their congregations and live inside a tight community, where others were by nature ecumenical, and went out of their way to visit their fellow religious, impervious to differences and open to fellowship.

But all had come, all came because they genuinely wanted peace in Palestine and they differed only in how conditional their commitment was. Wariness was like breathing, it was part of being human, and trust was a fragile thing and it depended on the acceptance of love as the guide in one's life. Unconditional love for everyone you meet, and that, to everyone in that huge audience, was asking a lot.

It was Father Michael, this frail little man, after all the convocation prayers were uttered, who stood unseeing before them. No rabbi, priest or pastor was more suited to the task not by what he would say but by what he had done in his lifetime. No one welcomed the other religious into his life more enthusiastically, no one reached out to them more energetically and no one expressed unconditional love for all men more than the little priest.

He stood before the large crowd, the microphone in his hands. "My friends, we are all servants of God. And we all pray for peace and we all believe in peace. The holy days will begin in your houses of worship tonight and I ask each of you to stand before your congregations and ask them to pray for peace and from this day forth become witnesses to the cause of peace in Palestine. Like Jesus's disciples, we are fishers of men, and as fishers of men we must ask each person we meet to treat their neighbor with love and compassion, to forgive, and where there is hate, offer love."

Father Michael continued: "Let us pray also............ " The explosion so sudden the podium disappeared in smoke, flames and flying debris and parts of human bodies flew in all directions, showering the audience and causing them to panic as they rushed away from wreckage. Some of the young men far to the rear began to move forward, to help those injured. Some were British soldiers who bravely stepped forward risking the wrath of the crowd that had begun to reassemble far from the center of the explosion.

A young sergeant began shouting in English at other young men, trying them to understand that there may be other explosives planted at the scene. Calling together other soldiers and several young Arab men, he gave them quick instructions on what to look for.

In the distance, there was the wail of sirens growing louder. First to arrive were armored cars, soon followed by ambulances that quickly moved among the wounded and dead and began treating the wounded and collecting the body parts that had landed as far from the podium.

John and Sarah were sitting together in the third row. The concussive force had thrown them backwards; amazed they were not hit by the shrapnel driven by the blast. Dazed, they worked their way to the open fields and then turned to look toward the podium. Only a crater, some thirty meters across remained on this Thursday morning where the silver gold sun shone brightly in a Dresden blue sky.

The bomb had done its work. Except for the few who were visiting elsewhere the leadership of the religious community in the place where Jesus lived as a boy were gone.

As they watched two young Europeans were moving among the wreckage. One had a camera.

They did not see the two men with field glasses surveying their work, satisfied that they had done their job well.

Neither John nor Sarah spoke as they made their way toward the rectory of St. Stephen. They would have to break the news to Hani, the other priests and teachers at the school.

The two men they had seen taking pictures had caught up with them. Andre spoke. "May we have a word with you? We are reporters. My name is Andre Monet and this is my partner, George Bissett."

Sarah looked at George. The resemblance was striking. "I knew your uncle. He was a very brave man and my father's friend."

"After what has happened, what will you do?"

John knew what he had to say would soon be known around the world. When he had recovered his bearings after the explosion, he had asked Sarah the same question.

"We will continue to work for peace and continue to call on the religious leaders everywhere in Palestine to speak for peace. Some will be frightened but more will join us."

"Misses Nevers, would you add anything?"

"I think what happened here this morning will awaken many people to the dangers of people who are so committed to their cause that they would kill innocent people to get what they want."

"And what do you think they want."

"I think they want all of Palestine and all of the Arabs persuaded or forced to leave."

"Do you think what happened today was done by the Jews?"

"By Jews, not all Jews, but a group of zealots who think they are following in the footsteps of Simon Bar Kochba."

"Who is Bar Kochba?"

"He was a leader of the Jewish revolt against the Romans in the second century."

"Arach Poletsky is your father, isn't he?"

"Then you know about my father."

George nodded. "He has become well known in America. Do you know what he is doing?"

"Yes, he has written me. In his last letter, he was very hopeful about the success of Lasting Peace. I am hopeful, too."

"Does he know what you are doing?"

"Not altogether, but I know he would think we are doing the right thing."

Andre grabbed George by the arm. "There are British soldiers ahead. We need to leave."

George tipped his hat to Sarah and John and hurried toward an alley leading away from the soldiers.

***

"Ben Gurion is furious. There was a big blow up with Weizmann. He was on the phone from London for an hour. He won't take Jabotinsky's phone calls. It's a disaster, Abe. A disaster."

Abe Meyersohn looked at the man sitting in his huge chair behind his glistening olive wood desk. He looked smaller. A man who seemed so sure of himself now looked genuinely miserable. In many ways more analytical than the other leaders, he saw clearly what the Irgun had done. What the massacre in Hebron had done, the massacre in Nazareth has undone.

Jabotinsky was not without his followers. His solution was simple, to terrorize the Arabs into submission. Ben Gurion and Weizmann were always sure of themselves, that they could control any situation or anyone and that is how they viewed Jabotinsky. They saw what he did as despicable but never openly challenged him because they were not sure they would win. Nor did they totally disapprove since the goals of Ben-Gurion and Weizmann were little different than those of Jabotinsky and the Revisionists.

"And now the sacrilege in Nazareth. MacMichael is furious. Montgomery is furious and threatening to disarm all the militias."

"I'm sure Purdom would approve of Irgun's act. He's a damn fascist just like the rest of them." Shurtok was bitter. He knew he was a much to blame as anyone for winking at the Irgun leaders and this would be on his head, too.

Abe lifted himself in his chair and tossed a copy of Le Figaro on Shurtok's desk.

The pictures were on the front page.

Shurtok tossed the paper back. "I know. First the two Frenchmen. Now Ze'ev. Coty must wish he had his paper back to do his Jew bashing."

Abe looked at Shurtok. A smile was on his lips but his eyes were cold. "This is not about anti-Semitism, Moshe."

Shurtok leaned back, turning his head enough to see the cold rain falling on the sidewalks below. "It is up to our friends in America now."

+++

Command of the Arab revolt now fell on the capable shoulders of the Ghost of Qassam, Sheik Razzik. It was Ismael who convinced the remaining commanders of Abu Kamal's fighters to join Razzik.

Despite the loss of Abu Kamal, spirits were still high and the will to fight still strong. Abu Kamal had depended on Ismael to plan operations and to execute them. Ismael knew he would be expected to serve Razzik.

But still smoldering inside him was the death of his brother Hassan and despite his awareness of his responsibilities to all the people of Palestine, he must find Purdom. He had the word passed throughout the north that anyone reporting the sighting of the British officer was to get word back to him.

He had finished his morning prayers and preparing for his day, when a young boy entered the camp. Approaching one of the men who stood nearest the edge of the camp, Ismael watched him talking excitedly to a young fighter, not much older than he. The young fighter pointed to Ismael, and Ismael stood waiting as the young boy rushed up to him.

"What is it, young man? What is it you want to tell me?"

"I have come from the village. A lorry driver told the Mukhtar that Purdom and his men have been spotted in the hills above Sanur."

That means they are close. We are five miles south of Dhinnaba. Sanur was ten to the north of the village. He looked at the boy, no more than ten or twelve. Boys his age were proud to be chosen to carry messages to the rebels.

"Did they tell you how far from Sanur Purdom was?"

"They told me to tell you they were near Sanur."

303

"What is your name, boy?"

"Jamal, sir."

"Jamal, this very important. Tell the Mukhtar that we must know where the British commander Purdom is now. Tell him to send out boys who are brave like you to find him and then get word to us."

Kalima was standing beside him. Ismael turned to him. "Bring the men together." There were twenty altogether. All had been with al Hajj Mohammed since the rebellion began. All had killed men in battle, most in hand to hand combat. Though expert horsemen, years of combat made them fit to travel fifty miles a day on foot, and they could live on the land for weeks.

Kalima and Abd had told the others of Hassan and who had captured and tortured him. They were told the torturer was killed by Ismael's hand and they were after the man who ambushed Hassan and his men. The same man who killed old men and children, burned houses and killed livestock and humiliated the men in front of their wives and children.

The stood in a circle with Ismael in the center. Their leader had scratched out a map that all could see.

"We have word that Purdom's band was spotted near Sanur. If he repeats his tactics, he will attack either Sanur or Dhinnaba.

"We all know something of this man's tactics. Some say he is mad, even among his own men, it has been said. We know he is vicious, and he uses terror to frighten us. But he is also smart and tough, and so are the men with him. We know that he most likely will attack at night. We also know how to fight at night. We will defeat him by being tougher and smarter; we will see the end of the man the Jews call Shammah."

Ismael then pointed at the map. "We are here, south of Dhinnaba. Purdom and his men were last reported to be here just north of

Sanur. I have sent word back with the boy. The Mukhtar will send out scouts from the village. If they spot them, get word back to us. If they bypass Sanur, they will travel south to Dhinnaba; it would be two hours of quick march travel to their target. We are less than an hour from the village traveling by horseback. If they repeat their tactics, they will be on foot without support or contact with other British units. I cannot predict what Purdom will do. It is possible he is looking for us. If he is, Dhinnaba might be the bait." He continued. "He will attack the village and quickly retreat. He knows we followed him after he attacked the last village. He will expect to do the same and he will be waiting for us."

Word was sent out through the Peace Bands and the paid informants that Purdom would make whoever provided information that would lead him Latif very rich. Purdom did not depend on the British to provide the money, but the Agency would. His superior officers never really liked the way he operated, yet turned their backs because any criticism of him, and the Agency would come to his defense and his critics likely to be dressed down.

As an officer, Purdom demanded authority, but never felt subject to it by the men above him. The Zionists saw Purdom as the most important man in the British Army because he was obsessed with punishing Arabs who threatened the Jews and because he had committed himself to training the fighters for the new Israel. Smart and quick, he saw clearly that he had placed his loyalty to the diaspora Jews above that to his King but that he would never have to pay the price for his disloyalty. He knew instead that he would be rewarded by the very nation he defied.

His camp was well hidden among the pines that grew on the steep hillside. His men busied themselves with checking their packs, and cleaning their weapons. Some could be seen running their whet stones across their bayonets, stopping to run their thumbs gently across the edge of the blades, then return to the rhythmic sharpening strokes. Twelve men, six from the Hagenah, and six British soldiers. Like the biblical Shammah, he disdained large troops of men to fight, and chose among the very best who could separate themselves in small bands from the main body and stay in the field for weeks.

The raid on the Nablus camp by Razzik and al Hajj Mohammad gave him a grudging respect for his enemy, and men like al Hajj Mohammad and the ghost Sheik Razzik. Al Hajj Mohammad was dead because his own people had betrayed him. A brave man among the despicable Arabs who would betray their own for pieces of silver. It was inconceivable that among the Jews in Palestine, such a thing could happen and that only added to his hatred.

What would Shammah do, he thought? He must deceive Ismael and draw him into a trap that will destroy him. He knew that Ismael Latif was hunting him, he had already killed Fortson. No one would admit that it was Ismael that killed Fortson, but he knew. Ismael was a leader who undoubtedly planned the raid of the camp and while the others escaped into the hills and mountains, Latif had crept into Nablus and killed his enemy. He had no doubt what happened, that Latif had faced Fortson, allowing himself to be recognized, then plunged the dagger into his heart.

The first step had been completed. He had exposed his raiders to be seen by scouts looking for him. His own paid scouts from the Ersheid peace band were scouring the countryside.

Purdom sensed that his enemy was near; that the time had come.

***

"We will be travel north to Dhinnaba and set up a camp and corral for the horses. Mustafa and Aref will load the pack horses." He looked at the two men." Pack two Bren guns and forty ammunition clips. Each man should carry extra ammunition and grenades. We do not know how long it will take, but take enough provisions for a week. This may be our best chance to find Purdom, we will make the most of it."

As men began to move about the camp, Ismael pulled his prayer blanket from the back of his horse, knelt facing Mecca and began to pray. Others did the same.

They began moving north, the winter sun set low on the horizon to their west. "Two hours before dark, Ismael spoke to Kalima, "we must find our camp within the hour." Kalima nodded, turned his horse and began relaying the information to the rest of the men. As they left the hills and came upon the broad plain, the cold wind from the sea bit their faces and caused them to lower their heads and hunch their shoulders. In pairs they moved, keeping distance to avoid making them easy targets in an ambush. On his black stallion, Mukhtar, named after the one he rode almost two decades ago, Ismael periodically broke from the group and rode to the crests of surrounding hills, with his binoculars scanning the surrounding countryside.

Seeing Dhinnaba in the distance he led his men to the west of the village. Abd, who had ridden ahead returned to report he had found a sheltered area for the camp with a running stream and forage for the horses. No sooner than the men had dismounted, Israel ordered men to high points around the camp, to be relieved ever four hours.

∗∗∗

It was dark; there was no moon, when the twelve men began to move. Purdom was certain that his squad had been spotted by scouts who had reported the siting to Ismael. As a commander, sometimes your intuition must be your guide if there is nothing else. He trusted his intuition, and some of his greatest triumphs in the Sudan and now in Palestine resulted from anticipating the moves of the enemy.

Latif was somewhere nearby; he knew that from the bits of intelligence he had received. Having spotted his raiders near Sanur, Latif will expect the squad to raid Dhinnaba, the home of the now dead al Hajj Mohammad, to punish the village for supporting the

307

rebellion. The Arab leader will set up an ambush north of Dhinnaba and wait for him. But wait. Latif would expect that I would anticipate the ambush to the north and instead wait for me after I left Dhinnaba, heading south on the way to our base. That is what he would do and he respected Latif enough to know that is what he would do. It was now clear. He would order his men to bypass Dhinnaba and search for Latif to the south.

By now, informants may have found the location of the Latif's camp. He knew there was the possibility that the force under Latif's command was considerably larger than his own squad of twelve but his men were capable of destroying a much larger Arab force. In such moments, his mind drifted to the Bible and Shammah's deception that had won the day against the Phillistines. He would do the same.

Purdom's new plan meant that his men must be on the march for an additional hour or more tonight. He expected that of his men and they had learned to expect the impossible of themselves. They could see the lights of the village. They followed their commander as he turned to the west.

As they began to move west, Purdom raised his hand halting the column. He moved away from his men. Something bothered him. Then he realized what it was. This man was hunting him. No one had ever challenged him in this way. He looked at the total blackness around him, then returned to his men and signaled them to follow.

The camp was now silent. What had he learned from the British twenty years before? To take every precaution, to think through every possibility, and never underestimate your enemy. Ismael had no way of knowing where Purdom and his men were at this moment. At this moment, he could only secure the camp, order total silence, and wait for word on the location of Purdom. A long time ago he had learned to trust his sense that danger was close. He felt it now.

Softly, he moved about, selecting men to double the sentries, each additional man to pair up with those now on guard. Any sign of danger, one sentry would remain at the post while the other reported back to him.

The silence was near complete, so much so that the slightest sound, the shuffling of one of the horses, footsteps, the shifting of sleeping men all seemed magnified in the darkness. Ismael could see his breathe as he moved about the camp, knowing his men yearned for the warmth of campfires yet understanding there could be none.

Ismael heard the sound of running feet before he saw the sentry approach.

"Someone coming down the trail!"

Ismael was on his feet, everyone in camp now fully awake. Ismael spoke softly to the sentry. "How far away?"

"Maybe two hundred yards. They are moving fast. I couldn't tell how many."

They were camped above and west of the trail which ran south and north. Within minutes whoever was on the trail would be below them.

"Kalima, take six of the men south and set up your men to cover the trail from the north. Quickly."

He watched Kalima and the squad running; then ordered the remaining men to take up positions covering the trail.

***

Moshe was a sabra, born in Palestine and fluent in Arabic. He was only eighteen when he joined the Hagenah. Toughened by hard labor, he had excelled during weapons training. When the Agency and Purdom decided to join forces to form the raiders he had been selected to be part of them.

Night fighting was frightening at first, but soon he learned how to see at night and he became one of Purdom's best men. Tonight, he was on point, a dangerous place to be at night, yet he was proud that he was considered one of the best. Like his friends, he yearned for the day when Israel would be free of the Arabs and the British and he would be part of the new army.

They had been marching for almost three hours and his feet were hurting. He could feel the blisters forming and some already ruptured. But Shammah showed no mercy and Moshe expected none. One day, he would be in the same position and he would be like their commander.

He stopped when he heard it. The sound like a rock breaking loose and scraping the ground as it moved. He raised his hand signaling the column to halt. At his signal, men immediately crouched into firing positions. He waited. Silence. Could have been an animal. He knew the must get to their position behind the Arabs before daylight. The young settler stood and motioned the men forward.

From where Ismael now stood, he could see the point in the trail where it angled to the right. That is where Kalima would be. He watched the first man in the column stop and crouch. He had heard something. They would wait. If there was any sign they were discovered he would begin firing and his men would follow suit.

The freedom fighters had seen photos of Winston Purdom. They knew he was tall and thin, whose eyes and thin lips betrayed the cruelty he possessed. The column was passing below them now. Ismael saw him. He was in the center of the column, stepping smartly as if an evening stroll, swinging his head slightly, taking in all around him.

The shot startled Ismael. It was too soon, but no matter. Suddenly shots rang out from above the trail and now from the front where

Kalima and his men were. No more than a minute and everyone on the trail was down. The firing continued into the now still column until they heard Ismael shouting to cease firing.

Cautiously, Ismael's men walked onto the trail. Purdom's men were dead or dying. The rules of this barbaric war were clear. No prisoners. Each man, alive or dead, was shot in the head. To avoid early discovery and then pursuit, the dead men were taken off the trail far enough that they could not be seen by anyone on the trail, nor by air. All but one was accounted for. Somehow, Purdom had gotten away.

Anger swept over Ismael. They had lost him.

+++

When the first shot was fired, he had dived for cover. Within minutes, the ambush was over, and he could hear the shouts in Arabic and the single shots, one after the other. Had anyone else escaped? No matter, the task ahead is to escape and finish what he started.

He had moved away from the trail, putting as much distance as possible between him and Latif's gang and now he took his bearings. To the east lay Nablus and the British Army. He estimated two hours before light. He would circle above Dhinnaba, then travel east until he reached Nablus. He was tempted to head toward the main highway running to Nablus, but that would be too risky. He was a wanted man by the Arabs and they would be looking for him. Moving around the villages and walking through strange country, he estimated he would be behind the British lines in three hours.

He was not tired but the fury within him grew when he thought of the humiliation of losing every member of his squad and having to explain how he allowed his squad to be wiped out and how he alone managed to survive. He had time to think as he walked and he was able to convince himself that he would be given a second chance to find Ismael. He wondered if it was true about Hassan's last words. "You will not find him, he will find you." He thought of the words with a mix of fear and hate and although they had been uttered to Fortson, he knew they were meant for him, as well.

He had been travelling for two hours. The sun touched the horizon and now in his eyes as he headed toward Nablus. Moving from cover to cover, he had emerged at the edge of an open field when he heard the sound of a cantering horse, then a rider appeared with the sun at his back.

Ismael knew Purdom would head east to the nearest army base near Nablus. He would not use the main road but keep to the base of the hills that framed the south side of the valley. Mounted on Mukhtar, Ismael moved at an easy gallop until he knew he was well to the east of his quarry. Selecting a hillock, he scanned the land to the west with his binoculars. The sun had risen at his back when he saw the lone figure moving carefully toward him.

The silhouetted figure with the sun at his back was a large man, erect in the saddle. Seeming to be in no hurry, the man dismounted and moved so Purdom could see his face. Joshua Purdom knew then he would not have to explain anything to his fellow officers. Ismael Latif was walking toward him, close enough now that he could hear his enemy's footfalls. The British soldier felt a sensation new to him, that of fear. He unsnapped his holster flap, and his hand trembled as it gripped his revolver. Close enough to touch his enemy, he looked into the eyes of the man he swore to kill.

***

It was a story that the people of Palestine would cherish forever. For his strength gave them strength and hope. To many of the British officers and men in Palestine, they felt better about themselves for one of the very worst among them had been killed.. To the zealots of the Irgun, it was a defeat for they had lost their hero and who among the British would take his place. To the people of the world who read the story by the two Frenchmen, it told of a dark side of the revolt in Palestine that they had been told too little about. To Sarah Nevers, it was a relief that Ismael was still alive and to John McDermott, there was hope that such men would not always be the story, that men of peace and good will would take their place.

Part XI

"The poker ended early. It was Seth's turn to be host and he had offered the usual of bourbon and ham sandwiches and Seth, as usual, playing close to the vest and won one dollar and thirty cents."

For the first time in twenty years, Murray's wife called to say that he would not be able to make the Thursday night poker game. When Seth asked why, Pearl had said she couldn't say but they shouldn't expect him next week, either. Bob Bruce happened to be in town, so he agreed to fill in. Sam Watkins was pleased to hear that Sam Weinstein would still be there.

"Lasting Peace hasn't been that for our poker playing crowd."

"They'll get over it. Besides, they have to advertise somewhere."

"There you go with the 'they' again. All the time putting people in bottles with labels on them."

"You're right, Seth. Sorry Sam." Sam the editor was looking at Sam the car dealer.

"I feel bad about Murray. He's a great guy. Must be feeling some heat. You know who Pearl's brother is?"

"Yeah. Poor Murray on both counts." Sam the car dealer mumbled through teeth clenching his cigar.

"I'll go by and see him at the store. Talk to him about an advertising special or something. Try again to get him to join us."

"You know anything about poker, Bob?"

Bob put his hand on his stack of pennies. "How do you think I pay for all those billboards, Sam?"

***

The poker ended early. It was Seth's turn to be host and he had offered the usual spread of ham sandwiches with bourbon and Seth, as usual, playing close to the vest and won one dollar and thirty cents.

Bob Bruce stayed behind to chat with Sam and Seth. He was in town to raise some money for the primary in the spring, talk to the Chamber about Lasting Peace and agreed to join them because he told them he needed a break.

Sam looked at Bruce; "Little chilly tonight, Bob. Sorry about that."

"It comes with the job, Sam. Phil and I stuck our necks out, so we gotten use to the cold stares and hot words."

"When you've got the President climbing up on the fence and leaning your way a little, Lasting Peace has come a long way."

"Thanks to Seth's girlfriend."

Sam and Bob looked at Seth, who had turned a bright red. He started to speak when Bruce put his big hand on his shoulder. "That is one remarkable woman. And she is shrewd. Lining up all the male co-chairs and bearding the lion's den by going to see Charlie Lindbergh were moves any politician would envy. I'm sure the President was impressed."

"You know he was. He invited her to the White House the next day."

They all seemed to enjoy Sam's remark. There the three of the stood, participants in something that could be one of the most momentous times in history, knowing they were a big part of it, and savoring the moment among friends.

"How about one to brace yourselves?" A light snow was falling outside and it was well below freezing.

"Sounds good to me, Seth. I need something to wash down those awful ham sandwiches. "Sam winked at Bruce. "I hope Margaret is a good cook."

+++

They agreed to meet in Philadelphia in a small back room in Bookbinders, began as an oyster bar by Sam Bookbinder late in the nineteenth century, now a favored haunt of Jewish elites.. They were the most powerful Zionists in America and therefore the most powerful Zionists in the world. While continental Europe was where the World Zionist Organization was born, and London was where Balfour bequeathed settlement rights in Palestine, world power had shifted to the United States during the Great War and Zionism's power with it.

They were here to discuss Lasting Peace. Among these men there was no need to spell out the issues or the stakes. What they had to face was staring boldly at them. It was the lives of hundreds of thousands of Jews that were in peril in Germany and throughout eastern Europe.

Lasting Peace was offering a way, one that could work to save the lives men, women and children. And it promised the saving of millions of other lives of Gentiles and their fellow citizens in America. But Lasting Peace came with bitter medicine, the end of immigration into Palestine, and the end of their dream for the nation of Israel.

To any observer, the choice might seem bizarre. Why would you consider sacrificing millions of lives to create a nation on land taken from the people now living on that land? In the name of humanity, why would such a choice even be considered? Yet that was the choice and powerful men left that meeting still willing to sacrifice lives for a dream. They would hide their choice with words, but they made their choice just the same. They had only to convince one man and that had not been difficult in the past.

The Times covered the awful tragedy in Nazareth. They had hidden the story of Palestine by distorting it in the past, now this was no longer possible. They denounced Irgun as an extremist group and quoted the horrified Ben-Gurion as if he was speaking for all Palestinians and somehow were unable to find anyone among the church leaders in Palestine who were quotable. But even the Times Editors could not control the story because the two Frenchmen, as they came to be called, sent their reports with photos all over the world, and this time, the Times had no choice but to tell the full story. And in telling the full story, Lasting Peace and its two part solution to the plight of the European Jews came into play.

In London, the many bureaucrats and politicians who had firsthand knowledge of what was happening in the Middle East were suddenly energized to tell the real story and recount the impact of allowing unchecked immigration into Palestine. The people of Palestine were made real to a public that had given them little thought until a single act turned night into day. And in so doing, White Hall and 10 Downing Street were called to account in Parliament.

I had been briefed about Margaret Larsen and was prepared to listen to someone that seems to be the main reason Lasting Peace got off the ground and now has the support of a majority of Americans. She's coming in to see me this morning.

We were going to war. I saw the danger of Hitler and Mussolini and what Hitler was doing to the Jews and our friend England was in danger. I knew the unspoken reasons for war, too, that war creates

317

jobs and prosperity and no one seems to have a better way than by preparing for war and war itself.

Hitler was a megalomaniac who loved the spotlight. Some of my own enemies said I was, too. I attacked Hitler at every opportunity and don't apologize for preparing America for war against Germany. Now the people were saying no to war, and more important, they were telling me that my job was to stop a war from happening. I am irritated as hell at Hollister and Bruce and the Jew from New York, who started it all, at least the part about not letting the Jews go to Palestine. Going around telling everyone the people want what they're selling. Well, I am the president and I will decide what they want, and what that is.

But I have to admit that Margaret Larsen and the three of them have me thinking. Is what they're proposing so bad?. My cousin Teddy won the Nobel Peace Prize over thirty years ago, getting credit for a peace treaty between Russia and Japan. I want that third term. War will get it. Peace won't.

He thought of his talk with Mose this morning. He asked Mose what he thought of Margaret Larsen.

"She's a handsome lady, Mister President, and smart, too."

"Well, what do you think of Lasting Peace?"

"Well, Mr. President, I read the Post and they don't think it's much. But I talk to the people in the kitchen, and they think those people are right."

"So you think I should butt heads and stop those people in Europe from going to war. Sounds like a pretty tall order, Mose."

Mose laughed and the President laughed with him. "Well, Mr. President, I know you're gonna do what is right for all the people, but if anyone can stop a war over there, it's you."

Then there she was. Her stature, her smile, her demeanor and intelligence filling the room.

She entered the Office, accompanied by a dozen of my aides and advisers. I knew why they were there. They were afraid I would do something rash, which means something they don't want. Beyond my back, I'm sure they talk about my weakness for beautiful women.

A nod of his head and all the advisers left the room, each looking back hoping they would be the one asked to stay.

They started off with small talk finding that neither had any mutual acquaintances and Margaret Larsen's opinions of people the President mentioned were mostly positive but never negative. Quickly, the President decided that they needed to talk about Lasting Peace. He knew the onus was on him because he had asked to see her. He was impressed that she did not immediately begin selling Lasting Peace.

"Margaret, you know the situation is serious, and Hitler has got to be stopped."

"I understand, Mr. President."

He was surprised she didn't follow up with a call for him to take on the task of stopping war.

"I don't think the American people are completely sold on taking in hundreds of thousands of Jews or anyone else when there are so many that are unemployed."

"Thepeoplewhohavejoined Lasting Peacewillsupportimmigration if other nations are willing to open their borders, as well."

"Hitler has not been willing to compromise. When England talks of compromise, Hitler sees that as weakness."

"Some in Lasting Peace have experience in foreign affairs, and they think you and the United States can achieve peace if it becomes an honest broker. Wherever our sympathies lie, each party must be allowedtoparticipateinaprocessforpeacewithoutpre-conditions."

"That would mean abandoning our friends."

"We think it would be saving them from themselves. Pounding the war drums on either side needs to be stopped and that is where you, Mr. President, need to start. Always foremost in the minds of the leaders of Europe should be the terrible cost of failure."

"Many of the people who make up Lasting Peace are isolationists, who want to hide their heads in the sand, and frankly, many are anti-Semites."

I had to bite my tongue. I met a lot of people traveling the country who accepted Lasting Peace by shedding their prejudices against being involved in foreign affairs and foreign wars and who had misgivings about hundreds of thousands of Jews coming to America. But the overarching purpose to stop a war which would drag America in and cost millions of lives persuaded them that the plan of Lasting Peace was the only way. Now, this politician is pigeon holing people he knows nothing about or worse, that he doesn't care to know.

"Mr. President, Lasting Peace is not isolationist but anti-war and we are willing to take in hundreds of thousands of Jews to protect them." She hoped her anger did not show in her voice or in his expression. She was even able to force a small smile.

"Margaret, I am glad I asked you to drop in to chat."

She looked around. This was the room and there is the fireplace. She smiled and the President wondered why.

She knew the meeting had ended. "Mr. President, I want you to know that I am grateful to you for seeing me and letting me talk about Lasting Peace. If you do engage the European leaders in a search for peace, you can be assured we will support you in any way we can. We will need your powers of persuasion to assure the American people that opening our doors to the Jews in Germany will be in everyone's best interest."

Smiling as he put out his hand to say goodbye, there was a lot to think about, a lot of uncharted water.

I watched from the doorway as Margaret Larsen breezed by the now standing assistants and advisers, smiling at each of them as she left. I looked at their anxious faces and nodded. They followed me inside, the last one closing the door. I had a lot to say and they had a lot of listening to do.

+++

If one were very important, it would be possible to visit all the people who ran the British Empire in a day, and not be rushed. Walking through Westminster, one could visit with the resident of 10 Downing Street, talk to the Colonial Secretary and take in the Exchequer and military top hats and still have time to admire Big Ben and Westminster Abbey. Although all could talk to you about the major parts of the Commonwealth, they would point out that even in South America, they had the Falkland Islands and some interest in Antarctica. If, after talking to all of these important people, you had time to reflect, you would be struck by how much time was devoted in their discussions to Palestine. When things were going well, and the Empire was secure, discussions were of a hopeful nature in Palestine although there were some rough edges. But now, in the beginning of 1939, the mood toward Palestine was very different.

Perhaps the turning point was the Irgun bombing in Nazareth, when Europeans died alongside Palestinians but the slow awakening had begun before. Since the turn of the century, the British view of Zionism was positive, particularly among those who ran the Empire. Lord Balfour had treated the notion that the Arabs should be consulted about a Jewish homeland in Palestine with open contempt. He had no intention, he had said, in consulting with the Arabs, Christian, Muslim or even Jews who lived there.

But times had changed, as immigrants began to pour into Palestine, and the notion that Jews and Arabs could co-exist was vanishing. The Arabs began to push back and the Jews more and more were discarding any pretense of a state governed by Jews and Arabs. They wanted it all, the only difference between Ben-Gurion and Jabotinsky was in the methods used to get there.

While the intentions of the Balfour Declaration, if one reads the words, was a state where Arabs lived side by side with Jews, it was clear by the early actions of the British that Arabs property and civil rights were secondary to Jewish settlement.

Twenty years later, the British had awakened to the dangers of unbridled Zionism. Immigration had to stop, the people in Palestine should be granted the right to govern themselves, and the people of the nation of Palestine should, as any nation, have their own immigration policy.

Yes, the British had awakened but the rule of law and not mob rule that held the British together was still solidly in place, and elected members of Parliament determined what was in the best interests of their constituents. This meant some constituents had their interests tended to more than others, and those constituents that could assure the member's re-election and grant other benefits were treated differently. Such skewed treatment of the members' interest was at play regarding Palestine, and Zionists were busy lining up votes to oppose the White Paper.

But others were busy, too. The emergence of oil to drive industry and the military made the Arabs important and British Petroleum delivered the message to the members of Parliament and to 10 Downing Street and important people up and down Whitehall Road. The Ministry of Defense, facing the possibility of war and anxious to maintain good relations with the Arabs, and the Foreign Office, sensitive to relations with all the Commonwealth nations, argued for an end to Jewish immigration and a pathway to an independent Palestine. The authors of the White Paper also took account of those who had worked for the Mandate Administration and from the increasingly articulate Palestinians raising their voices against unchecked immigration and the failure of the British to announce a plan for independence.

Malcolm MacDonald had a target on his back. He was the author of the White Paper. It was called the MacDonald White Paper. It was he who managed its production and he who would introduce it to Parliament amidst the unruly din of an energized Parliament. It would be his job as Colonial Secretary to make the presentation to Parliament and along with his Prime Minister, Neville Chamberlain, gain the approval of the House of Commons.

He was working at his desk when his secretary approached him. "What is it, Evan?" Evan Longman felt his body stiffen at the tone of his boss's voice.

"You have three visitors, sir."

"Can you handle whatever it is, Evan? I really have to go through these papers."

"They say they are from Palestine, sir. One is a lady you may know. Her name is Sarah Nevers. There is a Pastor John McDermott with her and the third is Yusef al-Dajani."

Yes he knew Sarah and her family. The Pastor's name rang a bell. He remembered, he is one of the leaders of the religious demonstrators. The third anyone in the Foreign Office familiar with the Middle East knew of Yusef al-Dajani, the name Ismael Latif was given to him to get out of the country in 1920 and the name he used to reach Palestine four months ago. Wanted by the British in Palestine, he was amazed at the daring of this man, gambling that the name al-Dajani was not on the wanted list.

323

"Send them in. No phone calls, no interruptions unless it is the Prime Minister."

He stood up and came around his desk as his three visitors entered. "Hello, Sarah. You are beautiful as ever, no, more beautiful. Some of my school boy chums were talking about John just this week."

"Malcolm, you may have heard of John McDermott."

"Pleased to meet you, John. Is this your first trip to London?"

"My second, sir. My first when landing here in the War."

MacDonald turned to Ismael. Only the worst of men thought ill of this Palestinian fighter. Officers who had been in Palestine cursed and praised him, often in the same conversation. He was wanted for one murder eighteen years ago when he cut the throat of Reginald Wilkins, and the murder of two officers, Purdom and Fortson, in recent weeks.

MacDonald put out his hand and Ismael took it. "I know who you are, Yusef al-Dajani. I'm glad you came although I don't know the purpose of the visit."

"I am pleased to meet you Mr. MacDonald and thank you for making me feel welcome."

"Well, I know it takes something very important for Sarah to leave her school." Macdonald looked at the three, inviting any to speak. Then, embarrassed for letting them stand, he beckoned them to sit at the round table near the window and a view of Big Ben.

Sarah broke the ice. "We came to tell you that the Palestinians, those living in Palestine now, support what the position of His Majesty's Government contained in the White Paper"

"You've seen it?"

"Yes."

"How wide is the support? I am pleasantly surprised that the White Paper has been read in Palestine, by the way."

"The support among the Muslims and Christians is virtually unanimous. There are a few notables who may support whatever the Yishuv supports. That is, frankly, because they are corrupt and are being bribed." It was Sarah who spoke.

MacDonald looked at the two men.

"I'm not the one to speak to that, sir. I am still and outsider with a very small congregation; less than 200 souls. And that is on religious holidays."

"But you have been the one who brought all the religious together."

"Only partly, and while I cannot speak for the religious, among them is a great concern for peace and I agree that what the White Paper proposes is the only hope for peace."

"And what about you, Yusef?"

Ismael smiled at this man whom he instantly took a liking to. He thought: "He knows who I am and yet he knows my only protection while in England is to continue the charade."

My English is still poor, Mr. MacDonald. May I speak to you in French"

MacDonald looked at the tall Arab in front of him. He was dressed in a western suit with waistcoat. He had to contain his laugh that sometimes welled up when totally unexpected happened. He replied: "Assurement."

"There was a time when the people of Palestine would have voted for a greater Syria. Circumstances have passed us by. Now the people of Palestine want a nation with the Jordan on the east, Syria and Lebanon to the north, and Egypt to the south."

"What would you say to the Jews who have immigrated since the Balfour Declaration?"

"That they may be citizens like any other Palestinian."

"What assurances can you give them that will be the case?"

Ismael broke out in a great grin which was contagious as the others smiled without knowing why. "I think we are moving too fast. First we need the Parliament to approve the White Paper." And then he added when he saw the frown on the Colonial Secretary's face. "I think that would be agreeable." He then added: "There are great challenges, your excellency, not only among Jews and Arabs, but within the Jewish Yishuv and among the Palestinians."

"You think you can succeed."

"I'm not sure I understand the question. I am only one man."

"I think it is fair to say, Yusef, that you speak for those who supported the revolt, so I ask you in that capacity do you think the people of Palestine can succeed?"

"I think we can but more importantly, I think we have a right to try."

"So John McDermott, what you did was extraordinary. The religious of Islam, Christianity and Judaism demonstrating together for peace. Try that among the Roman Catholics, Greek Orthodox Catholics, Anglicans and Methodists in England and no one would believe it was possible. And after the obscene violence in Nazareth, the crowds in Haifa and Jaffa were even larger."

"Perhaps because at the core of all of us is the yearning for peace with justice."

Sir Malcolm looked at the young man and offered a small smile. "Perhaps you are right."

It was almost noon when the meeting ended. Evan Longman had a stack of messages and angry callers and visitors as his boss talked to the three visitors. Most of the people who passed through his portal were pasty or ruddy faced with corseted stomachs. The three visitors were deeply tanned and trim. The tall dark one made him uneasy although he seemed pleasant enough; the other man looked like a minister with his forelock almost covering his eyes and his clothes seeming to hang on his body. The woman, he recognized the name, was striking. And when she smiled at him, he melted before her. It was a remarkable morning, one he would never forget. He knew he was sworn to secrecy in his job, but perhaps at the pub during a game of darts with an ale in his hand, he might drop a hint or two.

Malcolm MacDonald's luncheon with his father was in less than half an hour. In his head, the words kept coming back to him; words he will never forget.

But, with the Royal Commission, His Majesty's Government believes that the framers of the Mandate in which the Balfour Declaration was embodied could not have intended that Palestine should be converted into a Jewish state against the will of the Arab population of the country.

He will repeat those words in some form, perhaps verbatim, from the bench in Parliament. These are honest words, words that should have been spoken by his government years before, and words that will be bitterly denounced by Churchill who shows such slavish obedience even when right in every sense for Britain and the people of Palestine is involved.

How fortuitous the three visitors this morning. When so much controversy surrounds any issue, there are always doubts. Sarah, John and Ismael erased those doubts. Yes, Britain is doing the right thing for our national interest; we also are doing the right thing for all the people in Palestine.

"Hey Arach, you see this." Morty was shaking the paper in Arach's face and Arach was laughing, not that he knew what Morty was talking about, but Morty's antics always made him laugh. "You see what the British are doing. I hope you're happy, you schlemiel."

When he handed the paper to Arach he had turned it to the foreign affairs section. He then stood and jabbed his finger at the headline.

Parliament to vote on the MacDonald White Paper.

Arach had seen the Times and the editorial attacking the British action. Arach also had heard from Sarah about her visit with MacDonald. He was amazed that Ismael had been with her, along with the young man, McDermott.

"Morty, I know how you feel. But you can't ask the Arabs to solve Europe's problems. Unless immigration stops, there will be endless war between the Jews and Arabs. The Arabs are being forced off their land. Some of the families have lived there for hundreds of years."

"What about your own, Arach. What about all those who need a home. Where will they go?"

"I think the President has an answer to that, one that can save hundreds of thousands of lives. It is up to him now. The people of America understand. I think the President understands, too."

"I don't trust the people of America."

"Remember how you got here, Morty. Americans opened the doors once, they will do it again because they have more sense than our leaders."

"You're talking about the Jewish leaders?"

"Yes, I am."

"My friend, I don't understand you."

"But we're still friends."

The board rested on the bench between them. Morty smiled. "Your move."

+++

As the President took his place, moving his wheel chair to the table, he looked around the room, offering a smile and a nod to each of the Secretaries.

Speaking without notes, he began. "Tomorrow evening, I will inform the American people that I have decided to offer my services and the services of the entire government of the United States of America to prevent a war breaking out in Europe. I will talk to the American people to explain what I plan to do and why. The reason why I shall engage all the leaders in Europe is that another world war with all the great advances in weaponry that have occurred since will be a holocaust far, far greater than the Great War.

I will seek to explain to those who want to keep America out of a war in Europe that we will only be able to do that if we stop the war in Europe. In the utmost secrecy, Cordell has engaged in preliminary steps which will assure that no stone will be left unturned to achieve a peaceful settlement in Europe. For the last several weeks, I have been in touch with the leaders of the Lasting Peace movement, and their remarkable grass roots effort, and I am fully confident that they speak for the majority of Americans who want their President of the United States to work for peace. I need the support of all of you in this effort and that is what I am asking from you as I go before the American people tomorrow."

The President stopped then but only for a moment. It was not time for questions and comments yet.

"There is time to get word of my talk tomorrow in the papers and to the broadcasters. What we will release to them will be a statement of my concerns about war and my intentions to unveil a plan to prevent war in Europe. I will go in greater detail when I address the American people."

The Cabinet was stunned. As were his advisers who sat along the sides of the room near the President. Everyone but Tommy the Cork, who alone knew what the President would say and Cordell Hull, who was doing the back channel work through Ford and IBM to test Germany's receptivity. The Cabinet meeting followed the normal pattern for Roosevelt and the agenda was sent to the members in advance. No surprise's had been expected. When the President entered the room, the usual protocol was observed and the Cabinet members glanced at their notes and whispered to their aids about the things that were on the minds.

"Tomorrow, I shall suggest to the American people that they urge the Congress to support the plan I will describe to the American people. All of you will be asked to deal with Congress and ask for their support. I will know better after tomorrow night what our message to Congress should be and how you can help deliver it. I have no way of knowing the sentiment of the major papers and broadcasters will be, but we should expect some headwinds. The naysayers will be out in force, as usual, and we will have to take them on with the aid of our friends.

"I know many of you have important issues to discuss. We will convene another meeting in the middle of next week, and you will have a chance to get your issues on the table, then. Thank you for coming."

Around the table, stunned cabinet members gathered up their papers, then left quietly.

Only Tommy the Cork and Hull remained behind.

The President looked at Hull. "Chamberlain and Churchill are on board?"

"Yes, the Ambassador assured me. He gave me this." The Secretary handed the cable to Roosevelt. "Churchill is not a happy man."

***

The poker crowd was at the station. Sam and Marty showed up. Phil Hollister had called and said he would be listening with Bob at his house in Georgetown.

"My fellow Americans, we all know that Europe is near a precipice. Each day, it moves closer to the edge and below the flaming cauldron of war. As the leaders of countries shout challenges to the others, and deliver ultimatums and make threats, they may seem to many but aggressive souls challenging the others to a fist fight or a wrestling match. But we know they are not, because they are leaders with great machines that kill, and those that are threatened are not only the leaders, perhaps not the leaders at all, but ordinary men who will die because of what their leaders do.

The Great War in Europe killed 17 million people, and 20 million wounded. Seven million civilians, men, women and children were killed or died from disease or starvation. Five hundred thousand of our own lost. Twenty years later, there are new weapons, vast armadas of planes, ships and tanks that would kill far more and civilian casualties would far exceed those on the battlefields.

We must not let that happen again....."

The fireside chat lasted for thirty minutes. When the President finished, no one spoke at the radio station. Seth had instructed one of his technicians to play music the rest of the evening, soft orchestral music, no martial songs. Sam broke the silence.

"There a church up the street, Faith Baptist Church. Anyone want to join me?"

Sam Weinstein, "I pass."

Seth looked at his friend. "I didn't know you were a Baptist, Sam."

"I'm not."

"Any church will do, huh?"

"That's right. And I don't know how to pray, either."

Sam Weinstein:"OK, if I join you."

They walked out together. They could see the church from the steps of the station. People were going in, a line running from the door onto the sidewalk.

Seth spoke. "There are no scheduled services for tonight." The poker crowd walked toward the church together.

Wilhelm Franz Canaris was a small man, his features delicate, one not apt to be noticed in a crowd if not for his probing and watchful eyes. They were the eyes of a hero of the Great War, as submarine commander whose vessel claimed eighteen kills, the eyes of a spymaster, who persuaded Hitler to come to Franco's aid in Spain yet persuaded Franco not to allow the German army to march through Spain to take Gibraltar, a man who had never joined the Nazi Party and detested Adolph Hitler yet had risen to the top of the Abwehr, German intelligence. To Canaris, the path was clear, he knew what had to be done.

It was also clear to the men present in the home of Admiral Wilhelm Canaris in the spring of 1939 that Hitler was determined to go through with his plan to invade Poland. To the military leaders, this would start a war with England, America and Russia which

Germany could not win. From his appointment as Chancellor in 1933 until his mastery in his meeting with Chamberlain, the officers stood behind Hitler. It was his reckless move into Czechoslovakia beyond Sudentenland that moved them to act. Emboldened by the unwillingness of Britain and France to stand with Benes when Hitler threatened the Czech's, Hitler was ready to gamble again that they would sacrifice the Poles, as well. This time, the conspirators decided, Germany could not be lost to a throw of the dice where ones cover all six surfaces.

Present at the meeting that evening were Franz Halder, Chief of the General Staff, Ludwig Beck, former Chief of Staff and Graf von Helldorf, Berlin Police Chief. Canaris as Chief of Abwehr, German Intelligence was the leader of the group.

When Hitler's plans became firm, the first contacts had secretly been made with British Intelligence, M-16. From that first top secret contact came a proposal by the German military to remove Hitler subject to agreement by the British to secure an American and British commitment to support the new German Government. There followed a rapid flow of information in which the conspirators sought assurances from the allied powers to support a plebiscite on Danzig and the Polish Corridor. The response through M-16 was a proposal for Germany to withdraw from Czechoslovakia beyond the Sudetenland.

The news from the United States that Roosevelt proposed to act as a mediator heartened the group of conspirators. They were puzzled at the American President's change of heart but buoyed by the hope that it would control Churchill and that Germany would be heard when discussing the future of Europe.

***

The conspirators were meeting tonight to review the Canaris plan to remove Hitler. The Fuehrer was scheduled to be in Potsdam two days hence to review a newly formed paratroop division. General

Halder would be accompanying the Fuehrer in the General's car. Before reaching the parade ground, the car would be diverted, replaced another with look-alike passengers to continue toward the parade ground, then disappearing near the end of the route to be taken by Hitler and the General. From a private airfield, Hitler would be flown to a secret location where he would be placed under guard. Kept incommunicado, his location would not be disclosed until the new government was in place. Among those who met that evening, only Canaris knew that location.

Once the putsch was acknowledged inside Germany, Britain, France, and the United States would announce their recognition of the new government.

It was Helldorf who convinced the others that the German people would support the putsch provided the path to a representative government would follow. Much had been made in the foreign press about the adulation of Der Fuehrer by the German people. Helldorf noted that such adulation was often contrived by Goebbels and the memories of the German people were not so short that they could forget what happened after the Great War. Key to the transition would be the arrest of the leaders of the NAZI party and shutting down their propaganda machine. If this could be done quickly, the transition should be easily accomplished and the German people would support it.

The day broke slowly under a steel gray sky as the command car approached the main gates of the Chancellery. Bismarck once lived there, now the temporary home of Adolph Hitler awaiting the completion of a grander Reich's Chancellery.

"Waiting in the command car, General Franz Halder peered toward the great gate where Hitler was to appear. *Now, we will make it happen*, he spoke to himself. His heart was racing as the moment approached when the Germany's course would shift away from the precipice. The first step was his.

In the distance, he saw him striding toward him, moving quickly. Halder quickly stepped from the car to await his leader. As Hitler approached the car, one of the guards at the gate rushed to open the door for him. The General was not surprised that their leader was alone. No one questioned the man's nerve or confidence.

"Heil, Hitler."

"Good morning, General. It will a good day for Germany, don't you think."

Halder guessed he was talking about the new paratroop division to be part of the invasion forces.

"Yes, mein Fuehrer." He was calm as he looked at the man beside him. "It will be a day to remember."

The car was moving now. As they drove down Willhelmstrasse, Halder could hear the roar of the motorcycles as they placed themselves to the front and rear of the car. All of the cycle drivers were men hand-picked by him personally.

Word had reached Berliners that their leader would be travelling to the parade grounds just four kilometers away. The sidewalks were filled with admirers and the curious, waiting to catch a glimpse of the man who had raised Germany from the ashes.

"We have made them proud to be a German, General."

"You should be proud of what you have done, mein Fuehrer." In the last weeks, Halder had thought of how Germany had been transformed, that what Hitler said was true. He had raised Germany to where it was today. Other countries were struggling to bring themselves out of the economic depression, yet Germany had raced past them. Only a Hitler could have made Germany what it is today. Why, then was it necessary to do what must be done? Sadly, it was because the man who made Germany proud was about to destroy it. He remembered the last days of the Great War and the days that were to follow—yes the humiliation but more so the starvation and suffering and the sense of hopelessness that filled the hearts of the nation. Amidst the ruins, speculators flourished and radicals sought to use Germany's misery to create their own distorted utopias. We cannot go through that again.

Ahead, Halder saw the lone soldier pointing to a side street. As the leading cyclists approached him, he saw them lean their vehicle to the right then turn quickly onto the side street and accelerate ahead.

The passengers could hear the squeal of the wheels of the command car as it fell in behind. From the side street a second caravan, identical in appearance raced onto Wilhelmstrasse and continued toward the parade ground.

Halder turned toward the passenger beside him. "I am sorry, Mein Fuehrer, but you are under arrest."

For a moment Hitler said nothing. Then he spoke. "Was, General?" His eyes never left Halder.

"Warum?"

***

The President spent the morning reading congratulatory messages from all over the world, crediting his policy of engagement for removing Hitler. He thought of Lasting Peace and how pie-in-the-sky it had all seemed. And he thought of Margaret. The third term? Well, there is a life beyond the presidency, I'm sure.

He thought about the immigration of Jews, now underway. Well, nothing is changed there. Supporting the British on Palestine? Best to keep our word. He watched Mose coming toward him. He could smell the coffee. Mose appeared at the door. It was a beautiful Spring morning, the breeze gentle and warm. Life was good.

Part XXII

There was warm breeze this evening and the two men were in no hurry as they walked toward the hotel."

The Central Committee of the Jihad was located in Damascus, away from British guns. For reasons hard to fathom the French allowed the Committee to operate. The Committee's purpose was to provide arms and other supplies to the rebels fighting the British. It did so sporadically and with difficulty since Tegart had built the razor wire fence at the border. However effective it might be, Abu Kamal considered them just short of worthless, to the world they were the best single representatives of the revolt in Palestine.

It therefore caused a great stir in Britain, America and Palestine when the Committee announced that the rebels would lay down their arms in a gesture of goodwill in the hope that the White Paper would be approved by the British Parliament, and upon passage, the rebels represented by Amin al-Dajani, a Palestinian now living in Beirut, would work with the British to assure a peaceful transfer of power from the British to the new Palestinian Government. The Committee transmitted their decision to the British Colonial Secretary. The correspondence further expressed their hope that the Jewish Agency would join in the transition effort.

The major newspapers in all the major capitals of the world covered the announcement and the correspondence from Izzat Darwazi of the Committee to the British Colonial Secretary, Sir Malcolm MacDonald. The byline for the dispatch was by George Bissett and Andre Monet.

In the report containing the correspondence was mention of the role played by Ismael Latif, and a brief history of Latif, including his earlier flight from Palestine.

George and Andre were enjoying their stay in Damascus. They had sent the dispatch through Agence France-Presse and decided that they had earned a few days of peace and freedom from fear that was with them every minute in Palestine. Ismael had escorted them to Damascus and arranged for interviews with the leaders of the Committee including Izzat Darwazi, an urbane gentleman who had been a teacher and now chairman of the Central Committee of the Jihad.

It was Ismael's purpose to convince the Committee to issue the letter to Sir Malcolm MacDonald. The two were amazed that the letter was written and submitted within a week of their arrival in Damascus.

They had finished their work and were enjoying dinner in a small French restaurant. The city's lights were on and the warmth of the restaurant, the Syrian red wine, and the French food made for a joyous evening.

"Six months seems a lifetime. I will never forget those first days when I arrived at Abu Kamal's camp. I was frightened and excited at the same time. I pinched myself to see if it was real. Surely, I will waken in my little place in Montmartre and find I was only imagining what was happening."

George laughed. "I was scared and excited, too, just like you."

"Really? You seemed so sure of yourself."

"Well, I did have the advantage of being from the Levant and Ismael was with me from the time we left Argentina. But I'm not a warrior, and until you came along and I got a camera, I didn't know how I could help."

"The revolt looks like it could end. Will you be staying here or going back to Argentina?"

"I have family in Beirut and that is an option. But Argentina is my home. What about you?"

"I miss Paris. My family is there and a girl. She may have forgotten me."

"I think it is time to return to Palestine. The revolt is not over and there will be trouble with the Jews."

"Well, let us stay one more day. Spring is really beautiful here."

"Agreed. One more day."

When they left the restaurant, the streets were almost deserted. Only a couple remained at one of the tables. Standing outside the restaurant, they could see their hotel. There was warm breeze this evening and the two men were in no hurry as they walked toward the hotel.

***

Inside the restaurant the waiter who had served their table watched as the men walked toward their hotel. He thought how courteous they were toward him and the large tip they left. Perhaps they will return tomorrow.

The sharp popping sound startled him, as he watched the two men drop to the cobblestone street. Two men dashed from the alley they had passed and fired more shots into the now still bodies. Then they were gone.

The stricken waiter dashed into the street shouting for someone to call the gendarmes. Within minutes, a uniformed gendarme appeared and drawing his weapon, advanced cautiously toward the two fallen men.

Bending down, seeing the blood still pouring into the street from head wounds, he shook his head. He looked at the stricken waiter who had shouted for help.

"Someone will come soon. They will be taken care of. Did you know them?"

+++

A light rain fell in Damascus on the day of the funeral mass for the three fallen men at the ancient Virgin Mary Cathedral. Three caskets fill the center aisle near the altar. One is empty but contains articles precious to the old priest who died in Nazareth; a well-worn Bible, a Quran that was a gift from the Sheik al-Dajani, a rosary and a picture of him and his sister Marguerite. The other two caskets contain the remains of George Bissett and Andre Monet. Father Michael's large family is there. The closest of the family members, Marguerite with her husband sit nearest the Michael's casket. The Father's good friend Professor Charles Malcolm of American University in Beirut and George's relatives from Lebanon are there. Andre Monet has no family present, but like Father Michael and George Bissett, Andre Monet is mourned by the thousands who had walked silently and solemnly past the three caskets the day before and now come to pay their final respects, the great organ playing softly from the loft.

The eulogies that day are delivered by Ismael Latif for George Bissett and Andre and Amin al-Dajani, the young man who grew up under the tutelage of Father Michael to speak about Father Michael.

As sad as the moment is, Professor Malcolm wished the world could witness a funeral where three Christians are eulogized by two Muslims and that nothing could be more honest and true. He wishes the world could have known the priest who taught a young Muslim boy who grew to be a brilliant lawyer who loved justice.

He wished the Roosevelt's, the Churchill's and the Hitler's could be there to hear a Muslim warrior read what Hamad Osta had written and sent round the world titled the Ghosts of George Bissett and Andre Monet.

Commander Razzik was called the Ghost of Sheik Qassam. All of Palestine knows of Sheik Qassam who fought for the poor who had often been forced off the land. He was killed early in the revolt but his memory will live forever. The title of our Commander was given to him admiringly by the British, for when they thought they had him surrounded, he would disappear mysteriously, like a ghost. But the title is also a reminder of Sheik Qassam for his spirit never died. Andre Monet and George Bissett are like the ghosts of the great truth tellers in our past, and our memories will be of two very brave young men who told the world what is really happening in Palestine. When I first met the two of them, they were hiding from the British after their first dispatch on the atrocities committed in Nablus. George had come to Palestine with Ismael Latif, not knowing how he would help, but knowing he must. George had an uncle, also named George Bissett, who was a courageous editor of a paper in Jaffa and was assassinated in 1920. Andre was a journalist. He told me he first came to further his career, to become famous. But then he said Nablus changed all that and that telling the world the truth was more important than anything else he could do.

In many ways they were like Commander Razzik, always escaping despite the attempts by their furious enemies to find them. They knew what would happen to them if they were found, that they would disappear from the face of the earth and treated as if they never existed. In the short time I knew them, though, they never seemed to be concerned as much for their safety as reporting the next big story to the world. When the religious gathered in Jerusalem to call for peace, the two of them dressed as clergy sat in the audience on the grounds of the Government House! Their last story was of the horror that killed so many in Nazareth and took the life of such a wonderful man as Father Michael. They were in the crowd there, too.

Why do we honor these men so greatly? There is a saying that if a tree falls in the forest and nobody hears it, did it really happen. No one was there to hear it fall, to tell others what happened. And that is what Nablus and Haifa would have been, tragedies known only to the Palestinians, most likely blamed on Arabs. But these two men let the world know the truth and the world listened and, God willing, we will have our freedom and a nation.

So the ghosts of George Bissett and Andre Monet will always be with us, and they will always be remembered, surely in Palestine. It is my hope that what they did will inspire others in Palestine, for they remind us of the power of the pen.

The Professor shielded as his eyes adjusted to the bright sun that now filled the sky and lit the funeral procession as it left the dimly lit church. He stood to the side, waiting til the end when he would follow it to the cemetery.

"I loved him, Professor. He taught us all so much."

Malcolm turned to see that Amin had joined him "Hello, Amin. That was a wonderful eulogy. He reminds us of what life here on earth can be. He will not be forgotten. Without such men peace and justice are not possible because they teach us their essence: the love of God and our fellow man.

"And those two young men, too, have done so much for Palestine, because they have re-written history. History is about what happened, what was and who was there. But it is also about who the chroniclers are, for it is through their eyes that the information is passed to us. If it weren't for those two, the revolt would be described as a struggle between Arab gangs and British and Jewish settlers. Without them, those brave, angry, aggrieved and oppressed men and women never would be seen as noble or heroic in the eyes of the world. Their cause would be drowned out by the incessant reminder of the Zionists claims.

"And they did something else, they made the world see Arabs as they were, little different in their aspirations for freedom and liberty than the Jews, with the same rights to the land as the Jews. And they, too, will not be forgotten."

Professor Malcolm fell in behind the funeral procession. "Like our dear friend Michael," speaking softly to his friend, "they give us a reason to hope."

"There is a chance, Professor."

"I think so, too, Amin. There is a chance."

***

Shurtok expected Meyersohn to be at his door first thing. The two Frenchmen were in the news again. This time it was Agence France-Presse writing a scathing article about their murder and blaming the Irgun. But there was more. Under the title The Ghosts of George and Andre, a young Palestinian, Hamad Osta, wrote their obituary which was sent around the world by Agence France-Presse.

"How did you get in here without being announced."

"Your secretary had her back turned. I thought I would drop by to see if you had any good news." Meyersohn tossed the paper on Shurtok's desk. It was Le Figaro. "You read French? Meyersohn knew the answer. "I know, better than Hebrew."

"Palestine is haunted, Abe. First it's the Ghost of Qassam now it's the Ghosts of the two Frenchmen."

"This young man Osta is very good. We can thank the Lutheran School for that, too." He looked at Shurtok. "I would tell Raziel to leave Osta alone. The Irgun is not only burying Arabs, it is burying Jews."

"Very funny."

"It's not funny, Moshe. It's not even bittersweet. It stinks."

"How about a small glass of Smirnoff's."

"You Russians can have that stuff." Meyersohn saw the anger flash in Shurtok's eyes. Too bad, he thought. He's a real schlemiel, a bungler. The whole lot of them.

***

May 23, 1939. It would be hard to miss the angry stares as he left the Parliament. Crowds shouting murderer, Jew hater, and Hitler. Soon the crowd began to press in and Bobbies appeared wielding their truncheons to clear a path for him.

He was not surprised as he had read some of the hate mail since it first became known what was happening, that the British Government was placing before Parliament a White Paper which calls for a path to independence and an end to the policies of that followed the Balfour Declaration.

But it was done, by a vote of 268 to 179 CMD 6019 was British policy. It was over. The burning issue that had divided MP's with all the parties split within themselves. Now, in the midst of talks of war in Europe, it was settled.

There was hope for Palestine, Malcolm MacDonald thought because the President of the United States had offered his personal services in the cause of peace and in doing so, supported the British policy in the White Paper. Like the defeat of the Zionists in Britain, they had suffered a more damaging rebuke by the President of the United States, who opened the doors of his country to Jews while

345

calling for an end to emigration to Palestine. For once, he thought the United States was on our side when it came to the Jews.

He looked about him. The tulips were still in bloom, the leaves of the trees and the grass at his feet a spring green, the sun making its appearance and a warm breeze gently touched his face as he walked toward his Whitehall office. A little lady walking a small white dog smiled at him as he passed by.

"Thank you, Madam."

"You are most welcome, sir." She gave him a curious glance,

He felt better already.

***

Everyone he talked to really didn't believe the British would do that to them. For twenty years, they stood by the Jews and stood against the Arabs who protested the continuing immigration. Ben-Gurion and Weizmann were sure of themselves, sure that they would have their own country and somehow the Arabs would just fade away, helped on their way by the British and the Jews. But it happened. The White Paper and now Roosevelt is supporting the British. What should he say in his next editorial? Decisions came quickly to Abe. The Ha'aretz editorial would contain a simple measure. We're just going to have to get along with our neighbors. He was already thinking about offering Hamad Osta a job. He hoped he would accept.

There was anger and despair at the loss of the two foreigners that became their champions and now were dead at the hands of the Irgun. But men like Ismael Latif and Mohammad's men moved among the rebels throughout Palestine, urging them to honor the cease fire, and offer their help to those who would make Palestine an independent nation. The Ghost of Sheik Qassam, Commander Razzik, preferred to remain in camp, still suspicious of the British

Word was sent down the chain of command from Montgomery that Ismail Latif, if spotted, was to be left alone and that local commanders should pass the same message to the Jewish militia.

In the Agency, officials began to refer to Bissett and Monet as journalists, and publicly denounced their murders and the murderers.

There were still reports of violence. In retaliation for the action by the British Parliament, the Irgun firebombed British manned police outposts. When the British arrested suspects, the Irgun committed further acts of terrorism in response.

High Commissioner Sir Harold MacMichael was asked to put the policies of the White Paper into effect, starting by convening a meeting with Ben-Gurion and Jabotinsky asking for help in the hard work ahead. Sir Harold knew he would be a hated man among the Yishuv. It was not unexpected nor was he unprepared. He had served in Tanganyika and the Sudan before coming to Palestine. The key to an orderly transition, he knew, was thousands of miles away in New York and Washington. The news from there was encouraging. Nor was he concerned any longer with the bullying from London by Christian and Jewish Zionists, for now he was armed with the King's law and he intended to enforce it.

Sir Harold placed a call to the President of the American University inquiring about one of his faculty members and a practicing lawyer. When President Franklin was told the reason for the call, he enthusiastically endorsed Amin al-Dajani.

Amin had at first been hesitant, since he was fully occupied in Beirut but he knew it was his duty, and he, as much as anyone knew the task ahead. How he should approach the assignment, he was not sure. One thing came immediately to mind. He needed to talk to Charles. Charles had been a friend since he was a student at the Syrian Protestant College. He still had fond memories of the time when American University was the Syrian Protestant College. So many of his classmates had become important people throughout the Middle East. He must renew the acquaintance of many of them.

Almost twenty years ago, he remembered vividly being called into the Professor's office and the firm lecture given to him about civility in dealing with one's adversaries. In so many things he had accomplished since then, the words and thoughts of that lecture were with him.

Melancholy overwhelmed him when he thought of the second person he would talk to for he had spoken of him at the Virgin Mary Cathedral in Damascus. He remembered in all its detail the moment when the two of them had decided to search for the Will that they hoped would negate the sale of Arab land to the Jewish National Fund. The Father called it their quest. He smiled when he remembered his last conversation with Ismael when he recalled the meeting with Father Michael. He had told the three who met with him that the crusade for peace would be their quest.

+++

When the President made the decision to take up the cause of peace, Lasting Peace was not the only reason for his decision. While he saw the power of the movement, still he needed something to convince him that his efforts to secure peace in Europe had a chance to succeed.

The something was the news from England detailing the German Army's plan to remove Hitler. The vetting of the actors in Germany who were going to carry out the coup convinced Hull of its feasibility. Speaking for the President of the United States Hull had provided Britain and the conspirators the necessary assurances to move. Wrapped in the package were assurances from the President through Hull that he would support plebiscites in the Sudetenland and certain areas of Poland that were part of Germany before the Great War. All laws passed to persecute the Jews were to be suspended and Jews given the chance to stay or emigrate.

Convinced by Lasting Peace and the British, the President agreed the White Paper would be honored. After conferring with key Congressional leaders, they agreed to support for legislation to allow German Jews to come to America. It was left to Hull to deal with the ambitious head of Poland, Colonel Beck, reminding him he could expect no backing from Britain if he chose to oppose the plebiscite there.

***

Pat waited for the two to slide into their booth and then yelled: "Don't tell me that all this business happened without you two." He was holding a copy of the Washington Post pointing the huge headline toward them: HITLER GONE. WORLD THANKS US PRESIDENT.

Phil was grinning as the few customers in the grill turned toward the two Senators. "Our hands are clean, Pat. You can thank the President." He raised his own copy of the Post, pointing the headline at Pat.

"I guess you two had something to do with this thing about lettin' all those people come to America." Pat had a serious look on his face.

A customer sitting by himself scowled at the two Senators and shouted:" And not letting the Jews into their country."

The smiles had gone from the faces of the two Senators, who knew there was a price to pay for what they had done.

It was Bruce who responded. "Guilty on both counts", nodding to Pat and the man who spoke. "Pat, we think it was a price to be paid for peace, and by the way, I think it will pay dividends for all of us. Peace is the dividend, today and generations from now."

Pat began wiping the bar. He looked around the room, challenging everyone even before he spoke. "If you say so, Senator. I never met a better man in all my years here. We're really gonna miss you" Heads were nodding around the room "And to the young guy next to you, it's your booth, too."

Both men stood. Phil spoke. "No funeral til I'm dead, Patrick. See you tomorrow."

Bob followed. "Thanks for the booth, Patrick. We'll both be around for a while."

The walked outside. Today the sky was clear and their day had already begun.

Part XIII

It was a magnificent spring day, gentle wind from the river, billowing snow white clouds high above them, low humidity and spirited crowds out enjoying a rare New York day.

John had chosen the small Greek restaurant for lunch. The flowers were in full bloom all around Jerusalem and the grass still green. From where they sat, they could see the Golden Dome of the Mosque, the blue domes of the Church of the Holy Sepulcher and the gleaming gold domes of the St. Mary Magdalene. Below them was the Wailing Wall, once one of the walls of the great Jewish Temple. The nations of the three major religions had all ruled the land around them and it was still being contested.

He remembered Sarah's words. "It belongs to everyone and I think that is what the British will do. A nation of Palestine will have in its midst an international island which will be open to everyone. That has been the plan since the Ottoman Empire fell. The Ottoman's did not see rule precisely the same way, but they respected the rights of the three religions. They understood what it can never be."

John looked at Sarah. Since he had known Sarah he felt as he did today. He was in love with the beautiful widow and had been since the first day. But today, he would ask her to marry him. When he thought of asking before, he was always afraid she would refuse. Then he had thought, he could not risk their friendship and someday I will ask. But their time together working for peace in Palestine, and now the chance for peace greater than it had been since before the Great War, and everything changing around them; it was time. He knew that what he had done with Sarah was important to everyone in Palestine and he felt good about himself. So good that when they were drinking their coffee the words came.

"Sarah, will you marry me."

Sarah was not surprised. John was a lovely man. She liked everything about him. She put her hand on his, looking at him with a tenderness that made his heart melt.

"John, I cannot marry you. I am sorry. Long ago, when John died, I decided I would never marry. I knew that such commitments are seldom permanent, because the love of a man like you is a wonderful thing. But John, my commitment has not changed and it never will."

"Perhaps more time." He knew that sounded foolish but could think of nothing to say.

"I hope you will always be someone I can consider my very best friend. I hope you will find someone yet we will always be as close as we are today."

John said nothing but they sat in silence until the both realized it was time to go.

Sarah looked at John, "When will I see you again?"

"Sir Harold has asked the two of us for tea tomorrow. I'll meet you there."

"Goodbye, John."

John watched her until she turned down a side street and was gone. He had feelings that surprised him. He should be crushed. Instead he felt good. He would still have Sarah as a friend. He would still have his flock, which had grown when a local farmer, his wife and seven children decided they would like to join his church. Were they Muslims, he asked the husband. Yes, he replied. John smiled at the thought of them. It would be a challenge, but life is full of them.

***

It was a magnificent spring day, gentle wind from the river, billowing snow white clouds high above them, low humidity and spirited crowds out enjoying a rare New York day. Josephine, the cleaning lady for one of the apartments behind them, joined the two of them sometimes. Morty and Arach brought their own lunches but always kept their eyes on Josephine's lunch. She would just shake her head, saying something like "You men are all the same" and share something sweet from her lunch. Before she arrived, they had been there all morning kibitzing and playing chess, passing judgment on just about everything. Actually Morty did the passing, and Arach nodded, thinking his agreement would get Morty to move.

Before Josephine could sit down and place her lunch on the bench, Morty attacked. "Well, Josephine, I guess you heard what your President is doing."

"Mr. Morty, hold your horses. It's been a busy morning and I was dead tired before work started."

They both looked at her. "What happened?"

"My daughter's little boy Jackson, I told you all about him, got some kind of infection in his chest. I had to take him to the hospital because Levinia had to take care of the other kids. But I'm tired of tellin' people about Jackson.

How are you today, Mr. Arach?."

"Take this, Josephine." Arach knew the cleaning lady had some large medical bills she had mentioned last time they had lunch. He handed her an envelope with five one hundred dollars bills.

353

"What's in the envelope?"

"I want you to have it. I can't use all I have."

What's it for?

"For all those chocolate cookies."

Josephine had a look of concern as she looked closely at Arach. "You OK?"

"Couldn't be better. Morty asked if you knew what President Roosevelt had done. Well, God willing, he will save the lives of hundreds of thousands of Jews and many, many million lives by stopping a war before it starts."

Josephine loved her lunches with these two. They were like some kind of radio show. To keep it going, she turned to Morty, who was scowling and pouting at the same time. "So what is wrong with that, Mr. Morty?"

Morty shouted loud enough that strollers stopped to see what was the matter. "He's keeping the Jews out of Palestine."

She looked at Arach and winked. "Some people are just hard to please, Mr. Morty."

***

It was Thursday night, poker night. Seth had one of those tables with folding legs to take care of the extra players. Philip Hollister had brought his wife to town and Bob Bruce had done the same. Maggy was in town. Then there was the two Sam's, Seth and Marty. Seth tried to talk Maggy out of playing but she insisted. When Myra Hollister and Mary Bruce heard that Maggy was in the game, they wanted to come, just to watch Maggy. They settled for a shopping trip.

Seth made his terrible ham sandwiches over the protests of Maggy, saying he always made the sandwiches. The game was spirited, Seth had added an extra bottle of bourbon and a carafe of cheap red wine and the players were unusually reckless, doing more than the usual amount of bluffing and raising as much a five cents on more occasions that the old crowd could remember.

It was almost midnight when Seth noticed his old friend Sam Watkins drooping eyelids and the noise at the table was quickly subsiding.

Seth looked around the table; "Last hand?" The assent was unanimous.

"I wonder how Arach is doing?"

Sam Watkins looked up, yawning. "He's probably in bed where I should be."

Phil Hollister spoke. "I talked to him today, told him that everyone would be playing poker at Seth's tonight. He said to say hello. Also told me he was going to visit his daughter next month. I asked him if he thought he might be going back to stay. Said he was thinking about it."

"I guess Fred is holding his own at the Grill. "Maggy, when I talked to him yesterday he said to tell you hello and give him a call when you're in Washington."

Everyone was gone. Only Sam stayed behind. They looked at each other, smiles on their faces. Sam yawned and started for the door. "Next Thursday-- my house?"

Seth nodded. "Get some sleep." As Sam walked slowly down the path to his car, Seth called to him, 'but wait til you get home."

Sam lifted his arm as if acknowledging Seth's lame attempt at humor and without looking back opened the door of his Studebaker and slid behind the steering wheel. They all held their breath until the car kicked over and Sam was on his way home. They watched until it was out of sight.

***

The street looked the same. But watching the passersby, he could see that it was no longer a neighborhood where Jews and Arabs lived together. Tasneem and Fatima had both married and moved away. Mother was living with Tasneem. When he knocked on the door, he did not know what he expected to find out and even why he knocked.

The door opened, but only wide enough for an elderly lady to peer out at him; the eyes suspicious.

Ismael could only say; "My family lived here. I was born here and grew up here."

"What do you want? Have you come to take away our house now that the English did this to us."

"What did they do?"

"They are telling all Jews to leave. The country belongs to the Arabs now, like you."

He could see she was an old lady and god knows what she went through to get to Palestine. He thought, now you know how we felt, old lady. But he could only say, "The British will not make you leave, madam."

Still the hard stare. "What do you want?"

Behind him, he heard her voice. "Ismael?"

As Sarah ran toward him, the old lady shook her head, then slammed the door. "They moved into the house last year. There are three families living there; all from Germany. "What did she say to you?"

"She asked if I was coming to take her house." He shrugged. "I told her the British would not do that. I don't think she believed me."

It was Saturday, a holy day for Jews. There were few people on the street. It was still early in the morning, the street was in shadow.

"I came by to see you, Sarah. I don't know why but I knocked on the door of our house and when the old lady opened the door, I didn't know what to say to her except to tell her I grew up in that house. I told you what she said."

Sarah was looking at Ismael, remembering. "Do you remember what we did when school was out?"

"The three of us would ride all the way to Bethlehem and have a picnic in the cemetery of the Episcopal Church. We could see to the other side of the Jordan."

"Father Purcell married us there."

"I know."

"Well, it's a beautiful day."

"I saw a stable on the way in. I'm sure they have a couple of horses for hire."

They had ridden together until early afternoon, dismounting at the cemetery and standing together. Sarah moved close to Ismael, putting her arm around his waist. He looked at her and he pulled her to his side.

"I miss him. He loved you, Ismael."

"I know." As Ismael helped Sarah to mount, he looked up at her. "I will be leaving soon."

"This is your home, Ismael."

"I must see George's family. I need to tell them what happened and what he did here."

"Will you return?"

"Yes."

They rode back, neither saying anything. Sarah's question was on his mind. Would he return? He told her he would, but where was home?

Finis

Epilogue

October 2014

This was his last day in Palestine. To the Jews, it was Israel, their home. To the other citizens, most Arabs who ancestors had lived on the land throughout its history, they called it Palestine.

For all our faults, he thought, the now vanished British Empire imposed a peace on the land that has lasted for over six decades with no storm clouds on the horizon. That peace was forged at a time when his great grandfather Captain John Nevers and his wife Sarah lived in Palestine, and it was Sarah who did so much to create that peace. Sadly, Captain Nevers had not lived to see the birth of Palestine, but he would have approved of the new nation.

Thinking of Sarah made him think of the diary. One of the great family treasures of the Nevers family was the diary kept by Sarah. After she died the diary had been found among her possessions.

My father was the first keeper of the diary. Each Christmas Eve for the last thirty years the family would gather at our home in Cambridge and one of the children would be given the honor of reading a passage.

When was it? I was ten. Our family lived in the family home with grandfather. Uncles, aunts and cousins were there. My favorite Uncle Trevor and Aunt Milly sent their regrets from Canada, promising they would surely be there the following year.

The families had gathered several days before Christmas, giving them time enough to enjoy the others' company. Christmas Eve would be the day when for the first time one of the children would read from the diary of Sarah Poletsky Nevers.

We were all in the drawing room looking out over the hedges and gardens to the steel gray river beyond. There was a low sky, promising more rain. Inside, the field stone hearth was piled high with hardwoods, the flames burning red and gold; warming the great room.

The room was filled with laughter; several conversations going on at once. In walked my father with the diary in his hand. Everyone turned, knowing what he carried. To my surprise and shock, he handed it to me with pages marked to read. All heads turned toward me, and my face grew hot at the thought of what I was asked to do.

"Read it to yourself, John. Then, you can read it to the rest of us." Starting to read calmed me and by the time I had finished reading the marked entries I was anxious to read aloud. I stood before the fireplace so all could see me. I began. The date of the passage was the third of June, 1939."

'John had chosen the small Greek restaurant for lunch. The flowers were in full bloom all around Jerusalem and the grass still green. From where we sat, we could see the Golden Dome of the Mosque, the blue domes of the Church of the Holy Sepulcher and the gleaming gold domes of the St. Mary Magdalene. Below us was the Wailing Wall, once one of the walls of the great Temple. The nations of the three major religions had ruled this Holy Land at different times in its history.

'I said to John: 'All of this belongs not to any religion but to the world. People of all faiths will be welcome here."

'I looked at John, expecting some response but not the one he offered.'

'"Sarah, will you marry me?"

'As I write this, I find I cannot help but laugh at his response to my serious attempt at statecraft by making a marriage proposal. But at the time, I knew that to John McDermott nothing was more important and to dismiss it lightly would have crushed him.

'I told him I could not. He asked if I was in love with Ismael, and I explained I had always loved Ismael as a sister loves a dear brother. But John McDermott, the wonderful minister and friend could never replace the John who captured my heart twenty years before.

'In a way I think John was relieved that the reason I could not marry him was because of John Nevers, my dead husband. A living Ismael would have been a far greater blow. When I saw John later that week at the Smythe's he seemed as warm and friendly as ever, and I cannot help but wonder that he was relieved that I said no. I must admit I was a little disappointed that he seemed so little affected by my rejection."

When I finished, there was silence. I know my father felt the last entry funny but he did not show it but told me later. He said Sarah had a "dry" sense of humor.

Then one of my cousins spoke. He was from New Zealand and a year younger than me. "Who was Ismael?"

It was father who replied with a big grin on his face. "Well, that's for another time, Ian. Granny Sarah has a lot to say about Ismael Latif."

www.ingramcontent.com/pod-product-compliance
Lightning Source LLC
Chambersburg PA
CBHW051447260626
47162CB00001B/294